The Sweet Kiss

of

Friendship

The Sweet Kiss
of
Friendship

LAURA HODGES

authorHOUSE®

AuthorHouse™
1663 Liberty Drive
Bloomington, IN 47403
www.authorhouse.com
Phone: 1-800-839-8640

First published by AuthorHouse   09/13/2011

ISBN: 978-1-4634-4808-0 (sc)
ISBN: 978-1-4634-4807-3 (ebk)

Library of Congress Control Number: 2011914613

Printed in the United States of America

Chapter 1

The first day of school was today. There were several new people that came to some of our classes. There is this really cute new guy. I'm not sure what his name is but Jessica and I totally want to find out more about him. Jessica thinks he likes me because he smiled at me in English class. He sits in front of me and Jessica. I hope he likes me . . .

Present Day: September 8, 2009

I woke up at the sound of my alarm. The next would be the first day of school. It was going to be an exciting year: the last year of high school. It marked my last first day at a high school. I yawned, stretched, and got up to quickly have a shower and some breakfast. I stared at my reflection in the mirror as I started to get dressed. I was an average height; five foot five and had mousy brown hair and eyes. My figure was neither chubby nor skinny, but somewhere in between. Sighing, I went downstairs to start watching television and wondered if it would be too early to phone Jessica. I grinned as I looked at the time. It was only nine, far too early for Jessica to be up. Jessica had been my best friend since we were young. She was pretty different than me, being a bit eccentric, but we managed to be good friends. She had dark hair with red

1

highlights and deep brown eyes. She had a strong figure, and often looked confident. She was an interesting person, never too shy to say what she thought and sometimes so bold she came off as obnoxious. We were not all that similar, but the best of friends anyway. We met because both our moms were single and went to some single woman thing to meet other people and our moms hit it off instantly. Ever since, she was my best friend. Well, best female friend anyway.

I wondered if Adrian, my boyfriend, would phone. He was kind of dull, and I was not exactly sure why I was going out with him. If I was perfectly honest with myself, I had dated him for some summer entertainment. However, we didn't really do much besides go somewhere to make-out.

I knew Adrian had been trying to break up with me for the past three days but didn't know what to say to me. I should be nice and just do it for him, but Jess and I had made a bet about how long it would take. I had predicted it would happen on the first or second day of school, whereas Jessica believed he would have done it already. He had a history of unsuccessful attempts to duck out of relationships fairly quickly.

Turning off the television, I decided to phone Jenny. Jenny and I have been friends since high school started and Jenny, Jessica, Nicole and I hung out often. Jenny and Nicole were best friends and Jessica and I were best friends; it was perfect.

"Hello?" somebody said on the first ring.

"Hey Jen. How are you?" I asked.

"Hey Beck. I'm good. Why are you up so early?"

"I wanted to wake up earlier today so I wouldn't be so exhausted tomorrow. Want to go shopping?"

"Sure. Pick you up in an hour."

"Okay bye." I hung up.

An hour later, just like she said she would, she showed up. I had phoned Jessica at quarter to ten and she had groggily snapped at me that she was sleeping. I had laughed and let her go back to sleep telling her she was going to be dead tomorrow. She had jokingly asked if it would be okay to skip the first day of school.

I looked out the window as I waited for Jenny. I saw a couple of the more popular guys from school. Like probably every other high school in the country, there was a core "popular" group that all hung out together, dated each other, and partied together. They rarely let in anyone who was not of the same financial, athletic, or beauty status they upheld. However, I noticed that there seemed to be someone new hanging around with them. I frowned. He seemed somewhat familiar but I couldn't recognize him because his back was to me.

A few hours later Jenny and I were walking around the mall when we saw the same group of popular guys.

"Hey, look, there seems to be somebody else with our favourite high school jocks. I wonder if he just moved here," Jenny said thoughtfully.

"Yeah. I saw him earlier with them. They were walking past my house when I was waiting for you to pick me up." I stared at the new guy's back while he laughed at something. He sounded awfully familiar. Then I realized who he reminded me of.

"Jenny, doesn't he remind you of Jeremy?" I asked.

"Yeah." We watched them for a second and then I heard a familiar voice call out, "Hey, Becky! I haven't seen you in ages." It was Liam with his friend Darien. Jenny had a big crush on Darien. He was fairly popular with the girls. Darien had black hair which was always sleek and reminded me of a

3

dandruff shampoo add and gorgeous blue eyes. His smile was heart warming, but I rather liked blonds myself.

They came over to where Jenny and I were standing by the fountain. Jenny flashed Darien a shy smile and he gave her a faint smile back. I saw her blush.

I had met Liam last year at the start of senior high, just after Jeremy had left. He had gone to the same kindergarten as me and later on gone to a different elementary school. I had been drawn to him. He was incredibly perky and energetic, but obnoxious on occasions. He had a blond mane of hair that would sometimes hang in his incredibly bright green eyes. Somehow his obnoxiousness made him repel most girls, though.

"Hey, Becky," Darien said.

"Hey."

"So what are you guys doing here?" Liam asked.

"Girls, not guys, girls," I said.

"Women, actually," I heard Darien murmur. The three of us stared at him. I gave a faint smile.

"We're shopping. What are you two doing here?" Jenny asked.

"Looking for chicks. Hey, you know, we've found one," Liam said to me.

"Oh, yeah? Where?" I asked, guessing he was going to have a stupid answer.

"The water fountain statue there. Pretty hot, if I do say so myself." I rolled my eyes and pushed him away while he and Darien laughed. I imagined it was these jokes that kept the other girls in our class from swooning over him.

"Want to go grab coffee?" Liam asked me, his eyes twinkling. I glanced at Jenny to see if she wanted to. Chances are Darien would join us, but she had come to the mall in old stained jeans and a too big tank top. She shook her head at me.

"Not right now, I still have some things I have to do before tomorrow." I grinned at him.

"Well, we should get going. See you guys at school tomorrow," Jenny said as we waved and walked over to the door. I eyed the guy who looked like Jeremy as we were leaving, but I couldn't see much of him without being obvious. A lonely sensation filled my gut.

When we were driving home, we talked about the Jeremy look alike. Jenny said she thought he looked like Jeremy but obviously it wasn't. Otherwise, he would have told me he was in town.

"You think you'll have a hint of feeling for him because of who he looks like?" Jenny asked with a sly grin.

"Yeah right. I wouldn't do that. Well, maybe I would but hopefully I have a bit more sense than that." She rolled her eyes at me as I exited her car with a wave.

Diary Entry: September 15, 2004

I found out the new guy's name. It's Jeremy Jonhston. Jessica yelled hi to him today in English. I was really embarrassed because she asked him if he knew what my name was. He said yeah and she said "good because Becky is a very nice person to know!" He just blushed and said okay. I was ready to kill her.

Present Day: September 9, 2009

The next morning I showered and changed quickly. This was my last year before university and I had to make it count. Not like anything happened on the first day of school though. However, I couldn't help but feel excited about my last year before university. Probably not for the same reasons

5

as everyone else, but I had been dreaming about next year for, well, a year.

I hurriedly ate my bagel and orange juice, kissed my mom on the cheek and left, grabbing my money to buy something to eat for lunch with the rest of the gang.

I arrived at school ten minutes before the first class. The first two classes went by in a flash, Nicole was in both and Jenny was in the second one. We sat together and gossiped about our summer with our friends who we hadn't seen in awhile. It was Math class that seemed far too eventful.

Jenny, Liam, Nicole, and Jessica were in my Math class with me. We sat at the back. Liam sat beside me, Jess sat in front of me and Jenny sat beside Jessica. Nicole came in late and sat in front of Jenny. When the teacher was doing attendance, Liam and I talked. It was when they got to the J's that I practically fell on the floor from surprise.

"Jeremiah Johnston?"

"Here."

I stared at Jessica. We stared at the boy's back that had put his hand up. Jenny turned to me and whispered, "That's the guy we saw at the mall yesterday." He was back. Jeremy was back and he hadn't told me.

Diary Entry: October 4, 2004

Robert, Jeremy's best friend, told Jessica to tell me that Jeremy has a crush on me. I was embarrassed and didn't believe Jessica. Even if he does, I'm only thirteen; I don't think my mom will let me go on a date. Who knows though, maybe Jeremy does like me. He seems shy and doesn't talk much. The only class we have together is English. Maybe I should try talking to him . . .

Present Day: September 9, 2009

"Hey, Beck, are you listening or did you leave the land of the living?" Liam asked as he waved his hand in front of my face. I blinked and looked at him.

"What?" I felt like I had been punched in the stomach. Why hadn't he called? Why hadn't he written? Why hadn't he told me?

"Are you okay? You look kind of upset?" Liam asked softly. After a moment of staring at him I realized he probably didn't know who Jeremiah Johnston was. I had told him about my best friend who had left, but I didn't think Liam paid enough attention to realize what was going on. Plus, I didn't really talk about Jeremy, or what had really happened before he left.

"I'm fine. I just, uh, never mind. Um, what were you talking about before?" I listened while he talked about his great adventure over the summer. I was thinking about how maybe it wasn't Jeremy at all. Maybe just someone with the same name who looked really similar . . .

Jess threw a note on my desk. I picked it up and tried to read her scribbled writing.

> *Let's go talk to him after class. Maybe he didn't know*
> *if you were still here or forgot your phone number or*
> *something. We should all go, so he can feel intimidated.*
> *Ha, ha. You know I have always loved to bug him.*

The teacher finished attendance and I passed Jessica a note saying we could go over to his desk. I copied down the calculus notes while thinking. Jeremy is my first love. So far, only love.

Diary Entry: April 29, 2005

So I decided not to like Jeremy after liking him for five months and getting nowhere. I decided there are plenty of other fish in the sea (I hate that expression). Of course, none of those other fish seem to notice me, but, oh, well. Who needs a boyfriend anyway? But I'll always think he's cute.

Present Day: September 9, 2009

After class, with Liam still chattering away, I told him I'd meet him at the usual hang out for lunch. Jenny, Nicole, Jessica and I walked over to Jeremy's desk.

"Hey, Jeremy," I said. He looked up at me and continued putting his books away. The popular jocks stood around waiting for him and eyeing me suspiciously. Jess gave one of them a flirtatious grin and they backed away faintly. I almost snorted.

"When did you get back?" I asked.

"Does it matter?" he snapped coldly and walked off. The others followed him, smirking at me. I stared at the back of his head, feeling vaguely confused.

"Did I dream that?" I asked them slowly.

"No, Hon," Jenny said, rubbing my back.

"We're still in grade twelve, right? I didn't forget a year and we're secretly in college?" I was being ridiculous, but I felt a bit shocked.

"We could pretend?" Nicole said lightly.

"I don't believe it. How could he actually talk to you like that? I mean, you guys were like the best of friends. You were closer to him than you were to me. To tell you the truth, I was jealous of both of you. Jealous he hung out with you all the time and jealous of the fact that you had a guy hanging all over you. Can I go kill him?" Jessica tried to look innocent and I was about to say sure when Jenny nudged me.

"No. You cannot go kill him. I'm not sure why, but you can't. He probably didn't mean it. He probably just wanted to seem too good for us in front of those idiots. I mean, when we first knew him, he wasn't that popular. Maybe he thinks this is his chance to be popular." Jenny, always reasonable, said hopefully.

"By treating me as if I was nothing!? Yeah, right. Well, whatever, I don't care," I said bravely. None of them looked convinced. I myself wasn't convinced.

I had told them what had happened, about the last day he was here before he moved. I had also told them, Jenny, Nicole, and Jessica, what I had wanted to tell Jeremy but had been too chicken to admit. I had regretted not telling him ever since. Now, I wondered if I should be glad I didn't or maybe wish that I had. Maybe if I had told him . . .

"Don't worry Becky. Maybe he'll mature or something and call you up tonight. He probably just wanted to seem snotty in front of his new friends ok?" Nicole said softly. I nodded faintly and followed them out the room.

Diary Entry: September 7, 2005

Today was the first day of school. Again. Next year will finally be junior high where I can meet some new people! Maybe some new guys? Anyway I got stuck sitting with Jeremy in Socials and Science. Oh, yeah, he's in my Math and French class too. It sucks because I don't like him anymore. Oh, well. Maybe I'll get used to sitting with him.

Present Day: September 9, 2009

I sighed as the four of us grabbed our usual table at our regular coffee shop.

"Becky, don't look now, but they're sitting at the table over there," Jenny hissed, pointing.

"Can I go kill him now?" Jess pleaded. We all gave her a sharp look.

I saw Adrian coming up. He was looking around the coffee shop and I tried to duck. No such luck; he saw me and came over to the table.

"Hey Becky. Um, can I talk to you?"

"Oh, right now?" I stood up and stole a glance at Jessica who had pulled out her day planner and was counting days.

"Dammit Adrian couldn't you have done it yesterday? Where did my purse go . . .?" Her voice trailed off as she rummaged through her purse.

I got up and followed Adrian a couple of feet from the table. I tried to keep a serious expression and debated if I should attempt a sad look when we finished talking.

"I was thinking . . . do you think I'm right for you?"

"Oh Adrian, you're really nice. Why, do you not think I'm right for you?" I gave a coy look while I watched Jessica out of the corner of my eye count out ten one dollar bills.

"Well, I was thinking, with the new year and all, maybe you would be better off?"

"Better off with the new year? What do you mean?" I flashed a wide smile and winked at Jess.

"No no I mean better off without me." He fidgeted nervously and stared at his feet.

"I understand Adrian. It's okay, if you just want to be a friend that is fine with me."

"Oh okay great."

"Just don't go around saying it's because I didn't put out like you did with Emily Spooner."

Adrian laughed nervously. "Oh what? I'm not sure what you mean. Anyway, take care Beck!" He waved at Jenny, Nicole, and Jess and left.

"Never liked him. Why didn't you break-up with him sooner?" Nicole asked as Jessica handed me ten dollars.

"Boredom. There is absolutely nothing to do over the summer."

"Did you even like him that much?" Nicole asked slightly suspiciously. I shrugged.

Liam walked in and came over to our table.

"Hey, guys. Ordered yet?" Liam asked us.

"No. I wasn't waiting for you so I could order you around," I teased. We got up and went over to the cashier. It was busy since most people from school were here. The popular jocks Jeremy was with earlier were sitting together near the till. I turned awkwardly so they wouldn't see me.

"So what do you think of Sandy Gill? I saw her smiling at you today in geography. Maybe she digs you. She is pretty hot, you know."

"Yeah. She passed me a note saying she wanted to know where I came from. I thought maybe I should ask her out." Both Liam and I whirled around. I turned around because it was Jeremy saying he might ask out Sandy and Liam turned because Sandy is his twin sister.

For Liam, his hair and eyes and lanky figure are a bit of a curse. But on a girl, it's the total opposite. Sandy is his twin sister and she turned out gorgeous with the same hair and eyes that he was born with. She is tall and thin and guys are immediately drawn to her. Liam, on the other hand, doesn't have a clue what to say to most girls and repels them with his awkwardness and lankiness. Even so, he and his sister are extremely close.

"The new guy hit on my sister," he hissed to me, glaring at Jeremy.

"Um, Liam, are you sure she wasn't the one hitting on him?"

"Well, okay, so she was probably hitting on him but still . . ." He shrugged and looked at me helplessly. He was very protective of his sister.

"What's his name?"

"Jeremy Johnston. The guy who left last summer . . . the one that was my best friend."

"Oh." He looked over at Jeremy and then at me. He paused then asked, "Did something happen?" as he glanced at the door where his sister was coming in.

"I honestly don't know. He treated me like dirt when I tried to talk to him after Math class. Maybe something did happen."

"Hey Sandy. Over here!" One of the jocks called. Liam tensed up. She walked over and gave her warm smile that seemed to dazzle the other guys into thinking there were no other woman on the planet.

Because Liam and Sandy were twins, they seemed to have a language all their own. Liam gave me a confident look and nudged me. I already knew he had decided he would "take care of things." Never mind there wasn't much to take care of.

"Don't worry," Liam hissed at me. "Hey, Sandra," he said as he raised his eyebrows. She raised her eyebrows back. He nodded. She smiled.

"Hey, Liam. Everything okay?"

"Sure. But ah, I have a feeling recent ideas of yours may cause someone I know some anguish." He tilted his head towards Jeremy and then at me. I decided maybe his secret twin language wasn't quite as difficult for others to understand as he thought.

Sandy smiled at us and touched her nose. Again, they were so discreet. I turned towards the cashier to order a tea and wished I could be somewhere else.

"Well, Jer, I hope you like it here. I'm sure you'll have no problem finding someone to show you around. Maybe you could ask Becky." I felt my face flare.

"Um Sandy maybe we should—" I started to whisper to her when Jeremy interrupted.

"Hey Baby, I thought we were going to do some exploring together," he said slyly, looking her up and down. I coughed awkwardly into my arm to hide my surprise and annoyance. Liam tensed up but Sandy just smiled.

"I meant explore the city, not me. And if I were you, I would not say something like that to me again. If you do, I will have Kevin, our school's lovely football captain, break your neck." She smiled at him sweetly, high fived Liam, and said, "Now if you'll excuse me, I'm going to see how the quarterback is." She walked out with her head held high, Liam smirking, and Jeremy staring in astonishment. The other jocks sitting there were laughing and cajoling each other. Jeremy turned his stare towards me and Liam. I immediately ducked my head away again.

Liam and I hastily collected my tea and some sugar packets and hurried back to our table.

Diary Entry: September 17, 2005

I can't believe how damn annoying Jeremy is! I swear, I could kill him! My mom says I'm exaggerating but what does she know? He keeps insulting me and teasing me. Jessica says that when guys do that, they like the girl. Yeah, right! Not in this case! I hate him, and told him so. All he did was laugh. What an arrogant pig!

Present Day: September 9, 2009

As soon as we sat down Jess demanded to know what had happened. She advised the three of them had been watching with great excitement.

"You know, it's good to have a sister in high places. Now he won't be in school for a while!" Liam said cheerfully. Liam had a tendency to exaggerate the outcomes of his sister's threats. From my understanding, nobody was yet to be injured outside of a school football match. Currently, Kevin was less threatening than Jessica on one of her bad days.

"Why?" Jenny asked.

"Because," he exasperated like everyone should already know, "the football captain is going to kill him." I sighed, partially for the hyperbole and partially because Liam didn't see why the threat of death might not be the result I wanted. Since I hadn't told Liam the whole truth, he was probably going to wonder why I didn't want Jeremy dead.

"You can't hurt him!" Nicole said.

"Did I say I was going to? No. Not me, the football team captain. You should really pay more attention Nicole. Maybe you'd get better grades." I heard a thump under the table and he suddenly yelped. Nicole gave a satisfied smile.

"Nobody should hurt him. Or threaten him for that matter. So what if he doesn't seem to like Becky anymore, that doesn't mean we have the right to want his head on our wall," Jenny said.

"If he doesn't like Becky anymore, maybe, but if he's rubbing it in her face, can't we at least declare war?" Jessica asked. Liam nodded in agreement.

"Look, there is probably some sort of weird logic to this all, but until we know what it is, I don't want anyone hurting or threatening anyone else!" I said stubbornly.

"Beck, I don't think there is such a thing as weird logic," Liam joked. I kicked him under the table and he laughed. "Okay, I won't kill him or get anybody else to, but if he gives you real trouble, Becky, I don't care what you say, he's mine!" He grinned and we all groaned as he slammed his hand on the table. "Now can I declare war?"

Chapter 2

Diary Entry: September 22, 2005

I don't believe it! How could she do this to me! My mother is friends with Jeremy's mother! She invited the whole family over for dinner this Saturday. It is bad enough I have to sit with him in school, but to have to sit with him at the dinner table too? That's just too much. I'll just go to Jessica's house instead. There is no way I'm eating my dinner with that pig around insulting me!

Present Day: September 9, 2009

On the first day of school, there are never any classes in the afternoon, so the five of us went to the mall and walked around for a while. After that Liam drove me and Jess home.

I arrived home and had dinner with mom. We watched a bit of television and then I went to my room saying I had a bit of homework to do. I quickly reviewed my calculus questions before I pulled out an old shoe box.

After Jeremy left, we had both promised to write every day. Once it came to October after he left, though, he wrote a letter saying he was too busy to write everyday and asked if it would be easier if we just wrote every once in a while. I had been extremely hurt by this but had written that with school work, it was too difficult to write every day. He would write about every three or four weeks and after receiving his letter, I would wait two weeks and send one of my own. The thing was, I still wrote him every day, I just didn't send all of the letters. At first, I had written everyday like normal. Then, I had realized that the letters were becoming too much and I was wasting too much paper. So I wrote him a letter every week. Each letter said everything that had happened to me. It replaced my diary I had been writing in for so many years before. I started rereading the most significant letter of those I never sent:

> *Dear Jeremy:*
>
> *How have you been? I've been good. I'm kind of upset that you only want to write every once in a blue moon. Is something wrong? Since I know I'm not going to send this to you, I'll tell you this. When you told me you loved me, I loved you too. In love. I miss you and wish you could move back.*
>
> *Becky*

It had only been a short letter, a letter I had written just after I received his last daily letter. I realized tears were filling my eyes. I pushed my hair back from my face. What happened to him? On the last day he was here he told me that he was in love with me. I had been crying. I had known that I felt exactly the same way, but I didn't tell him. I was too scared to. Now, I regretted it deeply. I had realized that I would never be able to tell him in a letter or on the phone, and had thought that maybe that was my only chance to tell him. I had a chance now, but I wasn't going to take it. Not with the way he was treating me. I stared at the letter. I gently put it back in the box and brought out my other shoe box. This one held all letters Jeremy had written to me. I picked up the most recent one.

Hey, Becky. How are you? I'm good. Nervous about starting school again, but I don't know why. You? Senior year. I still want to be a Socials teacher. Hey, you could be one and we could teach together. Ha, ha. Are you still going to be an accountant?

Carrie says hi. She has lots of new crushes that she developed over the summer. She's convinced she'll manage to date them all without anyone knowing. You know, you probably wouldn't recognize her. She cut her hair and is now 5'6. I'm not in the least bit worried about her growing taller than me. What are the chances she'll reach 6'1?

Got any new boyfriends I should know about? Maybe I should come visit and scare them all away. And what about that Liam guy you hang out with? He sounds like an idiot to me. Is his twin sister hot? Just kidding. Write me back, and don't forget to mention the boyfriends (but spare the juicy details).

Jeremy

I had received that letter last Friday. He probably was already here when I got it. Feeling confused, I wondered why he didn't tell me he was coming back. He had mentioned coming to scare away the guys, but hadn't said when. Did he think I was going to interpret that as a signal he would be returning?

I also couldn't help wonder why he bothered to write such a casual letter that clearly displayed jealousy if he was going to ignore me upon arrival. It would have made more sense to stop writing or have written that he wanted to be left alone. I picked up a pen and debated writing a letter to him as if nothing had changed. Of course, I had no address to send it to as the return address on his most recent letter was still his Virginia address.

Maybe his move was only temporary and he didn't want to face what he said if he was only going to be leaving again?

I tilted my head up and began wishing he would phone and explain himself.

The phone rang. I jumped, startled. I picked up the phone and nervously whispered, "Hello".

"Hey, Becky what's with the voice?" It was a male voice, but not Jeremy's. It was Liam. I sighed in relief and in disappointment.

"Sorry I'm just feeling a bit freaked out I guess."

"After seeing that Jeremy person? I don't blame you. Anyway, I called to ask you if you want to come with me and mock the new Brad Pitt movie. Bring people along. It'll get your mind off of Jeremiah." We had a thing about mocking Brad Pitt and always went to see Brad Pitt movies.

"Sure. I'll bring along Jenny and see if either Jessica or Nicole is currently dateless. You should bring along Darien. When did you want to go to the movie and where?"

"Friday at the only theatre in town. Meet us at seven-thirty."

"Okay. See you." I hung up and felt a bit better.

Mom came in to say goodnight. She leaned over and read the letter.

"Hey, Beck. Missing Jeremy?" I turned and shrugged.

"No. Why would I miss him?" I asked sardonically. *Especially when he's living here*, I thought.

"Are you all right? You look a little upset. Is it because he's not here?" Mom asked quietly.

"I wish I did miss him. It doesn't matter. I'm fine. I'll just go to bed now." I turned off my desk light and indicated my bed. Mom hugged me and kissed my cheek. She softly whispered good night and closed my door. I changed into my pyjamas and curled up under the covers of my bed. As I lay there, I replayed the day's events in my mind. I was so mad! I didn't know what was going on, but I knew it had something to do with when he went to Virginia. Why would he act like he hated me? Like I didn't I matter?

With angry thoughts churning through me I gradually drifted off to sleep.

> *I was standing in a classroom. The classroom was filled with youthful school items like pyramid projects and maps of the continents. Jeremy was there, smiling and talking to me. We were our present age, but I realized it was a classroom from years ago. I smiled and felt relief trickle through me.*
>
> *The bell rang, signalling the end of class. We walked, hand in hand, through the doors. I arrived in another classroom, one from today. I turned around and Jeremy was gone. I hurried out to see if I could see him but the halls were too full of students. I started running and began to cry. I thought I could see him in the distance, walking farther and farther away, while I struggled to push through all the students, my legs feeling heavy. I felt like I couldn't move and was stumbling. Liam appeared and caught me and was yelling something but I was still trying to move forward. His voice started to come into focus and he was holding my shoulders.*
>
> *"Wake-up Becky, wake-up!"*

I opened my eyes as Liam's voice distorted and became my mother's. I stared at her, startled. My face was wet and I was gasping slightly.

"Are you okay?" Mom asked.

"I'm fine, I'm fine. I just had a bad dream. I'm fine, Mom."

"You were calling out Jeremy's name. Was the dream about him?"

"Yeah. Kind of. I'll be fine." She looked at me with concern.

"Maybe I should take you to visit Jeremy and his family in Virginia. Would you like that?"

I smiled. "Thanks for the offer, Mom, but it's okay." She looked at me uncertainly. She glanced at the clock beside my bed.

"Want to have a cup of tea or something? I'm fully awake now."

"No thanks Mom, I would rather just go back to sleep. School tomorrow and all." She nodded, pushed the hair away from my face, and left the room.

I lay awake for an hour after that, finally drifting off to sleep around four o'clock.

Diary Entry: September 25, 2005

I couldn't believe it! I couldn't go to Jessica's to avoid the dinner thing because Jessica was going to Seattle that weekend. But surprisingly enough, Jeremy was nice. He teased me, but in a nice way. His family is really nice and, while I would never admit it to Jess, I actually had some fun. Some. I probably would have had more fun with Jessica. Just the same, maybe Jeremy isn't so bad after all.

Present Day: September 10, 2009

The next morning I awoke with a dull headache. I rolled out of bed and had a shower. I walked slowly to the kitchen wondering if it would seem like I'm scared of Jeremy if I didn't go to school today.

"Hey, Becky, I have some interesting news," Mom said as I poured myself some juice and toasted my bagel.

"What?"

"Well, you know how you were thinking of old Jeremy yesterday." My eyes widened as I filled with hope. Had he phoned my Mom's line? Of course! He didn't know my cell number. Maybe he did try to reach me?

"Yeah?" I asked excitedly.

"Well, they're back! Andrea phoned me this morning and invited us for coffee on Friday. She moved quite close to where we live. She has all sorts of things she wants to talk to us about. Isn't that wonderful?!" I felt my heart sink. He hadn't tried to reach me. His mom had phoned my mom. I was suddenly glad that I had made plans with Liam on Friday.

"Friday, as in tomorrow?" She nodded. "I have plans with Liam at seven-thirty. Mom, remember last night when I told you I wish I missed him? Well, I already knew he was back. I've tried talking to him, but he ignored me. He snapped at me and was kind of cruel. I was upset because he came back, but couldn't seem to care less about me." I looked at her disappointed face. My bagel sprung up and I began to butter it. I wanted to crawl under a rock and stay there. I knew I shouldn't feel so miserable about a guy, but it was Jeremy!

"Oh. If you don't want to go, I guess you don't have to. I was going to head to Andrea's around 6:30 but feel free to skip out." She paused, slightly awkwardly, for a moment. "I'm sorry that Jeremy doesn't seem to care anymore. Maybe I should talk to Andrea about that."

"I'll come before I go meet Liam and the others. I would rather you didn't mention anything to Andrea. Listen, I got to go. I'll be late for school." I grabbed my books, stuffed the rest of my bagel in my mouth and hurried off to school. I thought about having to go to Jeremy's house. His mother (Andrea) was great. She loved him and his sister very much. She was one of those mothers who teased her son to death, mostly about girls. When I first met her, she tried teasing him about me. It didn't work too well so she tried getting names from me. Poor Jeremy was haunted to death if he even spoke to a girl at school.

I arrived at school and hurried off to class. I found out that Jeremy was in Spanish with me. Fortunately, I sat across the room with Jenny and Jess. Nicole and Liam were in some of my other classes.

I managed to get through the day and was glad to find out that so far, Jeremy was only in Calculus and Spanish. I was dreading Math class at the end of the day.

"Hello, class," Mr. Rambouski, the Math teacher said to us. "Please write down these questions in your notebook and leave room to write answers. Please, don't write the answers now. Wait until I read out the name of your partner first." We all started writing the questions down and I passed Jenny a note about the movie tomorrow. She said sure. I wrote Liam a note saying Jenny, Jessica and I would all come. He wrote one back saying Darien could come. I told Jenny who gave a bad attempt to hide her excitement from Liam.

"Okay, I'll read out the names of your partner. The point of this partner thing is to help each other with the questions. You will explain how you got your answers and help out your partner if he or she requires any assistance." He started reading the names of the partners. Bored, I doodled on my notebook while I waiting for my name to be called. Jessica and Liam got stuck with each other. Jenny and Nicole were lucky and were paired together.

"And now the final pair. Fortunately, this year, we have an even amount of people so there are no leftovers." I sat up realizing that neither Jeremy nor I had been called. Jessica looked at me and mouthed Jeremy's name. I nodded.

"Jeremiah and Becky." I groaned. Liam gave me a concerned look. He put his hand up in the air.

"Liam?"

"Can we switch partners?"

"Well, who do you want to work with?"

"Becky."

"Why?" I could see Jeremy watching curiously. I was suddenly glad I had Liam here to help.

"Because she is more at my intelligence level than Jessica is and I want to be challenged." Jessica threw a piece of paper at him and he smile while few people smirked.

"The whole point of having a partner is so you can help that partner and learn with the partner, not so you can breeze through everything. If Jessica is not at your intelligence level, then your goal should be to help her understand everything as well as you do, not to try to convince me to let you trade. Any other more important questions?" He looked around the room but we all sat there, a couple of people smirking at Liam.

"Thanks for trying," I whispered to him. He smiled.

"Okay. Find a place where you and your partner can sit together. I want you to work on these questions together." The class got up and Jessica sat in the desk beside Liam and pulled it over to him. I had a feeling Jeremy was just going to sit there and wait for me to come to him. I felt slight disbelief. Was this going to turn out to be a blessing or a curse? Feeling nervous, I got up and walked over to his desk.

"Are you going to sit on your royal hind at this desk or would you like to come over and sit in Jessica's desk?" I asked coldly. I figured if he wanted to be a bum, I might as well treat him like one.

"Whichever." He avoided my gaze.

"Well there's no room for me here so I would rather go sit over there." I indicated my books and desk on the opposite side of the room. Jeremy shrugged. He picked up his notebook and followed me over to my desk. He turned around Jessica's desk so it was facing mine and sat there staring at the questions, not looking at me.

"Why were you so rude to me yesterday?" I couldn't help asking.

"Why were you so rude to me just now?"

"Because you were rude to me yesterday." I could feel Liam's and Jessica's eyes watching me.

"Why do you care?"

"You know why I care." What a jerk. "Let's just do the questions. I won't talk to you, you don't talk to me."

"Fine." We remained silent while doing the questions. I tried not to look at him. I finished and sat there, annoyed and impatient. I wanted the exercise to be over with so I could talk to Jessica about Jeremy.

While I ignored Jeremy and he ignored me, Liam threw me a note.

> *Ha! You're stuck with Jeremiah. I hate that name. He seems sooo stuck up. I'm bored. I finished all the questions. How 'bout you?*

I smiled.

Hey Liam. I'm finished. You're right, Jeremy does seem stuck up. He didn't use to be. What should I do about him? Jess looks like she needs help with the questions. By the way, I need to tell you something about Mr. Stuck up. Won't tell you in a note. How about after the B.P. movie?

I threw the note and watched him read it. Jeremy cleared his throat and I glanced at him. Wordlessly, he handed me the questions he had done and I handed him mine. I started correcting them.

"Rebecca?" I glanced up at Jeremy, startled. It felt very peculiar to hear my name, particularly the full version, from him.

"Uh, yeah?"

"Um, Andrea would like to know if you're coming by this evening."

"Andrea?"

"Yeah, you know, my mom."

"I realize who Andrea is I just didn't realize you call her Andrea now. And yes, we'll be there at 6:30."

"Both of you?"

"Why, would you rather I fell into the earth?" He didn't say anything, just continued writing the questions. I felt bad for being so cold, but I was angry. I remember being so angry at him when I first got to know him. I hadn't liked him because I thought he was annoying. He had insulted me and bugged me until I was ready to kill him, then he would laugh. But at the moment, I'd give anything to go back to those times.

Diary Entry: September 27, 2005

Today, Jeremy was nice at school. We actually talked! He said that his mother wants me and my mother to go to his house next weekend. I might actually have fun. Ha! Jessica says I should like him again, but why would you want a boyfriend when you have a great friend right there?

Present Day: September 10, 2009

Liam threw me another note.

> *Okay, so what do you need to tell me? After the Brad Pitt movie is fine with me. You were right, Jessica did need help. This is boring. What are you doing after school? Liam*

I read the note and smiled. I handed Jeremy back his wrong answers. I only had one wrong. I quickly redid it and watched Mr. Rambouski put more questions on the board. I frowned and copied them down. I hated homework.

"Okay, class, these questions are your homework. You may work on them with your partner. Liam, that means Jessica, not Becky. I want these done on Monday, the next time we have class. You may start copying them down now. When you are finished, you may leave for the day." I sighed and continued writing the questions. Jeremy turned Jessica's desk around so he could see the questions.

After Liam and I finished, we stood around waiting for Jessica. As soon as she was done the three of us bolted from the classroom. I wanted to get out of there as fast as I could. I needed to calm down. I was feeling so confused and overwhelmed and didn't think I could handle being around

Jeremy at the moment. Sadly, a part of me wished he would go back to Virginia. So much for my fantasies of what it would be like to be reunited.

Diary Entry: October 2, 2005

Jeremy and I had so much fun! His little sister is nice. I'm looking after her next Friday with Jeremy. I figured, hey, why not? We hang out together now in school. Jess tries to talk to him but he told me Jessica scares him. I can see why. She asked him if he would go out with anyone who asked him and all he said was anyone but you. I laughed. Jessica has a grudge against him. Maybe they secretly like each other?

Present Day: September 11, 2009

Classes that day sailed by quickly. I was nervous about going to Jeremy's house after dinner. I told Jessica and Liam about it. Liam volunteered to pick me up, but I said no because if I had to walk, I would have an excuse to leave sooner.

That evening, after dinner, my mother and I walked over. Their house was much smaller than their old one. It was fairly close to our house, the walk only took a couple of minutes. I nervously rang the door bell and secretly hoped we had the wrong address. The door opened and I could see Jeremy's face. Bugger. Andrea came smiling up and invited us in. We walked into a small, but cozy house. There were still boxes shoved into corners but clearly Andrea had made a good effort to make the house feel like a home.

"Becky, I haven't seen you in ages! How are you? Jeremy doesn't talk much about, well, anything. I read all the letters you sent him and I think Liam sounds pretty nice. Then again, who needs men in their life?" I was startled by Andrea's comment, but smiled anyway.

"I'm good. Liam's nice. You'd like him. He has your kind of humour." Andrea laughed. She loved playing jokes on Jeremy and Carrie, his sister.

"Good. You've grown. Or maybe I just haven't seen you in a while. How tall are you now? Five foot six?"

"I'm around five five I think." I stole a look at Jeremy who still hadn't said anything.

"Carrie's that tall. I'm envious because she's bound to grow taller than me, like her father. By the way, Carrie and Tom say hi." I wondered where Carrie and Tom were. I was dying to figure out what had happened to everyone while they were in Virginia. Jeremy looked uncomfortable. He had his hands shoved in his pocket and was standing in one spot staring at the ground.

"Well, come on, sit down. I'll go bring some tea. Jeremy, show them where the living room is." Andrea bounded off to what I assumed to be the kitchen while Jeremy started walking down the hall to our left. Mom and I looked at him curiously and followed. He plopped down on a bean bag chair and pointed to a couch and a love seat. I sat on the unfamiliar love seat, wondering if they had sold their other furniture during the move back here. I frowned and looked at my watch. I tried to determine how long it would take to walk to the movie theatre from the house. If I had been thinking, I would have left my jacket at home so I would have needed to go back and get it.

Andrea came back carrying a large tray of tea. "Well, Jeremy says hello, even if he seems silent. You guys still take the same stuff in your tea?" We nodded and she started pouring the tea. I glanced at Jeremy while Andrea and my mom started filling each other in on the past year. They laughed about something and I heard mom mention her most recent boyfriend, Bob. I didn't really like him that much but I figure that most guys I date she doesn't like very much. As long as she didn't go marry him or anything.

"So, Jeremy, have you finished the calculus questions yet?" I asked to make small talk. I tried my best to sound polite. I felt like I was twelve again, stuck in his house because my mom had dragged me.

"You don't have to make small talk, you know," was all he said. I sighed.

We basically sat there silently for what must have been twenty minutes before my cell phone finally turned to seven p.m. I jumped up, relieved to finally not have to reminisce of better times while trying to appear as if I didn't care that Jeremy was ignoring me.

"Uh, Mom, I should go if I'm going to meet Liam and the others." I said. She looked at her watch and Andrea looked disappointed.

"Becky you haven't had the tour yet!" Andrea exclaimed. She gave Jeremy a pointed look.

"Oh that's okay Andrea maybe another time. I don't want to be late."

"Of course Honey, I should have asked Jeremy to show you around earlier." Andrea continued to attempt to message him with her eyes.

"Is Liam going to drive you home?" My mom asked. I nodded and stood up.

"You know, Becky, Jeremy's going to meet some friends soon. If you want, he can drive you?"

"Um, it's okay, I can walk." I stole a glance at him to see his face unreadable.

"Come on Beck, I'll drive you." I turned to actually look at him, startled.

"No I think I'm fine I got to burn off that popcorn I'm going to get!" I tried to sound cheery but my mom and Andrea were waving at me to go with Jeremy. He had grabbed his jacket and had his back to me.

"Go!" My mom mouthed. I made a face.

"Off you go with Jeremy then Becky!" Andrea stood up and threw Jeremy her car keys. If it was just my mom, I would have whined my way out of having to sit in a car with him, but there was no way I could stand up to Andrea. She was a force to be reckoned with and if she wanted him to drive me, that was the way it would be. In fact, that was probably why he hadn't protested.

"Uh, okay." I grabbed my purse and jacket. We left the house and I waited while he locked the house door and unlocked the car door. We got in and he started the car. It felt weird to have him drive me somewhere; before he left he had only just earned his licence and was not yet permitted to borrow the car.

"Where are you going?" he asked me.

"The movie theatre."

"There is still only one in town, right?"

"Yeah." I tried to think of something to say, but I found I was too confused and sad. I had a feeling I was also a little too hurt to take anything he might say at face value. I watched him drive. His looks were the same as they always were. He had deep sea green eyes and dark brown hair that looked black in the dark. He had a friendly but shy look about him, the kind where he wants to be your friend but is too scared to say anything. That probably attracted many girls to him, but he never seemed to notice. He had a lean face and wide set mouth which sometimes gave him the impression of a frown, but he was usually smiling. At least, when I remembered him, he was usually smiling. At the moment he was frowning with concentration.

31

"Jeremy?"

"What." I already knew this was a bad idea but the words were out of my mouth before I could take it back.

"What happened in Virginia? Did something happen? Did I do something? What is it?"

"Nothing happened," he snapped.

"Well, you told me something before you left and now, you seemed to have changed your mind."

"I don't want to talk about it."

"Yeah but . . . it's important. Can we talk about it later?" I felt a small twinge of hope. Maybe he just needed a bit of time and tomorrow he would be ready to hang out and talk . . .

"I just need some space right now."

"You need space so you treat me like dirt?"

"I'm not treating you like dirt, I'm driving you the movie theatre aren't I?"

"If you want some space you could just say so. Instead, you're acting like I have leprosy or something."

"I just don't want you crowding me."

"And what about what you said before you left?"

"What do you want to hear? Yeah I wish I had never said how I felt but looks like that wish is a year too late."

"What?" I whispered. "You wish . . . I, oh God, Jeremy, just pull over."

"What?"

"Pull over!" He pulled the car over to the curb and I undid my seatbelt and opened the car door. He had a surprised and worried look for a second which quickly vanished and was replaced by his cold look.

"What are you doing?"

"Getting out. I can walk the rest of the way." I began to get out but he grabbed my arm.

"Becky, don't. It's okay, I can drive you. Get back in." He actually thought he could con me into getting back in! Like everything is okay!

"Oh, I didn't want to crowd you," I snapped.

"Rebecca, come on. It doesn't matter. That's all in the past now, right? What I said, what you didn't say . . . it doesn't matter now. Just get back in. You'll be late if I don't drive you."

"I don't care." I had already pulled out my cell and was texting Jessica with shaking hands. I started walking. Jeremy drove very slowly alongside.

"I'll be far too early for meeting my friends if I don't go out of my way to the movie theatre." His head kept turning from the road and back to me. I finished my text to Jessica and started on one for Liam.

"I see so you were really only "going out of your way" so you wouldn't be early? Because that, what, breaks some sort of popular cool code?"

"Just get back in the car."

I turned to face him. "You know what? I'll get back in the car if you take back what you just said. Let's face it, if you don't give a rat's ass about me you wouldn't worry about upsetting me, so admit you care and I'll get back in." He had stopped again and leaned forward. I stepped closer to the car, the door still open from when I had gotten out. He looked up at me and for a moment I felt relief as he leaned forward more. He grabbed the handle of the door and the relief turned to disappointment.

"See you around," he said harshly as he slammed the door shut and drove off.

I took several deep breaths, trying not to tear up. I swallowed a couple of hiccups as I stood where he left me for around ten minutes, ignoring the beep of my phone reminding me that Jessica had texted me and I had an unfinished text to Liam.

After I decided I had finally regained my composure and the tears could wait, I started walking towards the theatre. I opened my phone to read my text from Jessica:

> *We should kidnap Jeremy, drive 2 Forks, leave him in the woods and tell him Twilight is real.*

I smirked. Jeremy was (or at least had been) terrified of vampires. We had thoroughly enjoyed this irrational fear and had told him he looked like Dracula and insisted on watching vampire movies.

Our small town just outside of Bellingham was close enough to Forks, but it seemed like a dumb idea just the same.

I texted Jessica back:

> *I think I'll move to Romania instead. Definitely no chance I'll see him there.*

We continued to text each other until I reached the movie theatre.

I was early, but Liam and Darien were already there. Darien was looking at the advertisements for new movies and Liam was standing around watching people buy tickets. I came stomping up.

"Wow, hey Becky, was the save the whales program cancelled again?" Liam smiled, but the joke did not hide the trace of concern flash across his face.

"Oh, ha, ha." I sat down on a street bench and Liam sat beside me.

"I'm guessing that the visit to see the Johnston family didn't go so well," he said softly. I glared at him. Despite my brief cool down period, I still felt too upset to really deal with anything else. I wanted to go home and curl up in bed far more than I wanted to watch some movie.

"It's okay Beck. Everything always works out. Besides, things will seem much clearer when he's in the hospital bed with a broken face."

"Liam, don't bother with the empty threats. They don't make me feel any better. And if they're not empty, they don't solve anything."

Jess and Jenny came up at that moment and Jenny went over to give Darien a shy smile. Jessica, also stomping angrily, came up to the bench we were perched at.

"That idiot. Don't worry Becky, you'll feel much better after he's lost his looks when I rearrange his face." She gave a firm nod and grim smile. Liam turned to me, grinning.

"Liam pretty much said they exact same thing. I told him plan broken face is a no go."

"I would like to clarify I never said anything about his looks."

"Sure you didn't." Jessica winked at me. I gave an inkling of a smile.

"Well . . . on that note . . . time to get our tickets?" We stood up and headed towards the ticket booth where Jenny and Darien were purchasing their tickets.

"Beck, let me get your ticket, least I could do to cheer you up," Liam offered.

"Oh that's okay, thanks though. I don't think a movie ticket will make me feel any better right now." Jessica nudged me and she and Jenny exchanged a look.

"What?" I mouthed to her. She shook her head. I shrugged, not sure what she was meaning.

We entered the theatre, bought a couple of snacks, and took our seats. We were fairly quiet and shamefully I spent a fair amount of the movie texting Nicole.

After the movie rolled its credits and the five of us said good-bye, Darien and I went in Liam's car while Jessica went in Jenny's. Liam dropped off Darien and then we went out to get some coffee. We ordered our coffee to go and went back into his car. I assumed Liam had wanted to sit in his car instead of the coffee shop in case I teared up. We remained silent for several minutes, while I contemplated what to say and he watched me out of the corner of his eye.

"So," I finally said.

"You don't have to tell me, Beck."

"I know." I paused and put the coffee on the dash board. "Okay, so when Jeremy told me he was leaving I realized that I, I . . . that I loved him. Not love like I love, I don't know, Jessica, but like I would . . . a boyfriend." Liam, oddly, looked both happy and disappointed.

"So you happened to develop feelings for a man friend."

"Yeah, only I never told him. Anyway, there's more. On the last day, he told me he was in love with me, only I didn't say it back. But, he did kiss me good-bye. Like, you know, kiss kiss, not a peck on the cheek. Then, when he moved away, he wrote me a letter saying that it wasn't such a hot idea to write to each other every day. We had been for the past few weeks, but he didn't want to anymore. I'm not sure why. I was a little hurt, but I didn't think too much of it then. Anyway, today, I went to the house right?" Liam nodded. "And when I left his mom asked him to drive me, which he did. Which, by the way, was confusing. Then we were talking in the car and he said something about me crowding him and then he said he wished he had never told me he loved me before he left and then . . ." My voice trailed off as I bit back tears. For a distraction, I pulled out my phone, which had been going off constantly with Jessica's phone calls, and turned it on silent. "So then I got out of the car and we yelled a bit and I tried to get him to admit that he cared and he slammed the door and drove off." I tried to hide the hiccup in my voice but Liam clearly heard it. He awkwardly tried to put his arm around me but settled for patting my back.

"You know, if he doesn't love you, then he doesn't deserve your love back."

"I know."

"Do you still . . . love him?" I shrugged. Nicole had asked me the same thing in her text messages.

"I'm too upset right now to really know."

Liam nodded and started to rub his hand around on my back.

"You know, Becky, I'll always . . . you know . . . be there for you . . . and stuff . . . you know . . ." I looked at him and smiled. I'm not sure he had ever looked more awkward.

"I know. Should I say I know twice more to answer all three "you knows"?"

"Funny.

"Thanks though, I appreciate the thought." I smiled at him and he smiled back. He gave me a final pat on the back and turned to start the car.

I gave Liam a long glance as he turned his head to pull out of the parking lot. Despite his brass humour, he had a good heart and was very good to me. He always looked out for me. His green eyes turned to me and I felt a slight heave in my stomach. I suddenly wondered if Jessica was nudging me earlier about Liam offering to buy my movie ticket. Was his concern possibly more than just friendly protection? And, if so, how did I feel about that? Shaking my head, I decided to push those thoughts aside. I had far more to worry about at the moment.

Chapter 3

I thanked Liam for the ride home and promised him I wouldn't mope over Jeremy all evening. I walked up to the house and opened the door calling hello. I heard two laughs and Andrea and my mother appeared from the kitchen.

"Hi Becky. How was your evening?" Mom asked.

"Okay," I said, shrugging.

"Do you happen to know where my little brat of a son went off to?" Andrea asked.

"Nope," I said. "And I don't particularly want to know either," I muttered softly to myself. I smiled sweetly while Andrea said good-bye and left.

"You and Andrea came back here?" I asked my mom as I followed her back into the kitchen.

"Yes, I wanted to show her the new deck out back and a picture of Bob." I nodded nonchalantly as I grabbed some juice.

"So, what happened between you and Jeremy?" Mom asked as she sat down. I glared at her for a minute and then relaxed my gaze. It wasn't her fault I was mad. She was just curious.

"I'd rather not talk about it. He was very . . . well he wasn't nice."

"What did he do?"

"He said . . . well he said he wished he'd never told me that he loved me." I sat down and sighed at my juice glass.

"You know that is absurd right? He is saying it to push you away?"

"Why? Why is he pushing me away?"

"Honey . . ." she paused for a long moment and patted my hand. "Becky, I need to tell you something. It might make you understand why Jeremy has been so different. Andrea told me why he's so upset right now, and I think you should probably know. He discovered his father was cheating on Andrea. He . . . is pretty upset with his father and has been quite rebellious ever since." Despite Carrie and Tom's absence, I was quite surprised.

"Is that why he and Carrie weren't at the house? Andrea got a divorce?" She nodded.

"Tom was sleeping with a nurse who received a job offer in Virginia. Tom wanted to follow her so he uplifted the family to Virginia. He had lied about the big job offer and promotion; he sought for the job himself and it was not the position or pay he had promised Andrea when they were here. Andrea didn't have any reason to suspect anything though, but it came to light that Jeremy had accidentally seen his father with the other woman. Andrea kicked Tom out of the house and filed for divorce. In the meantime, Jeremy took it all very badly and hasn't quite been the sweet kid he use to be. He failed some classes, skipped on school frequently, and Andrea almost never knew where he was. She eventually took him to a counsellor and together they decided it would be best for both Andrea and Jeremy if they moved back here."

"Seriously?"

"Yes. So far, moving seems to have helped a bit. As far as Andrea knows he has been pretty clean but she's fairly certain he's still drinking. He's still moody but he hasn't been as rebellious or as difficult. The hard part is, Tom is marrying the other woman and has been pursuing Jeremy to be his best man. Jeremy doesn't even want to speak to him. Being here is giving both of them some time to clear their heads and deal with their feelings. Unfortunately, I think you are a situation Jeremy doesn't have the mental maturity to handle right now and it is far easier for him to push you away than to acknowledge any feelings for you. Plus, if you were close, he would have to tell you what happened and he might not be ready to do that yet."

"So it isn't because he doesn't care about me? He still loves me?"

"Probably. Also, he probably has some fear about hurting you or getting you involved in his problems. While he was gone, you were a form of escape, he could write to you and you knew nothing and had no involvement. It is unlikely you would accept not knowing or discussing anything with him if he let you get close again."

"Is Andrea okay?"

"She is now. She was upset at first, but now she says she's fine and would rather concentrate on Jeremy."

"Okay, well that does make me feel a bit better." My eyes widened. "I didn't mean because of what they went through I just mean—"

"I know what you meant Becky. Anyway, don't mention any of this to Jeremy, would you?"

"No, Mom. Don't worry. I'm going to go to bed, I need to sleep some of this anxiety off." I left the room to get ready for bed. I felt better knowing Jeremy didn't have anything against me. I did feel kind of hurt that he didn't want to tell me and that he did all those things. I realized he must have been really hurt to have been affected that much. I wondered what I should do. Should I try to win him over or just leave him in peace? If I left him in peace, that might mean he might fall in love with someone else right before my very eyes. But if

I tried to win him over, it might complicate things too much for him. It might be selfish to try to badger my way into his life if he wasn't ready. Plus, I'm not really sure how Liam fixed into everything. That situation may be more complicated than I had originally thought.

Lying down and turning off the light, I decided I need a couple of weeks break from making any decisions or worrying about what was going on. Jeremy needed space, and I needed to digest all the information at hand. There would be time down the road to decide how I felt and determine how Jeremy felt. And, I had to acknowledge, how potentially Liam felt.

Diary Entry: July 15, 2006

I have totally neglected my diary because of my new boyfriend, Jeff. He is my first real boyfriend. (After all, who counts holdings hands and playing board games with Kyle in grade four?) Jeremy thinks this whole "boyfriend" thing is funny, but I told him he was just jealous because he couldn't get a girlfriend. He couldn't even get a date! Anyway, I am finally documenting this relationship down because Jeff ended it. He's dating another girl! From a different school! How could he? My first real boyfriend—does anyone get over that loss? Clearly, even if my heart recovers from this event my social life will not. Thank God it is the summer. Jeremy said everyone will have forgotten by the time school starts but I think he's just saying that to make me feel better. After all, he has no idea what to say to me now I'm all heartbroken and stuff.

Flashback

"Jeremy, Jeff broke up with me. Something about how he likes some other girl now. He's been seeing her for the past couple of days behind my back. And you know what the worst part is? He broke up with me because he thought she would be mad if she found out he hadn't really broken up with me like he said he had." Jeremy stared at me with shock.

"Are you serious?"

"Yeah," I mumbled as Jeremy took me in his arms.

"Beck, if he's going to be that way, then he isn't worth talking to. Don't bother with him again."

I sniffled. "I know, but it still hurts." He sighed while I began to cry. He was more used to me crying over soppy old movies rather than something real like this.

"Becky, it doesn't matter. Forget about him. Do something with me today."

"Like what?" I snapped wearily.

"I don't know. Um, do you want to go watch those sappy movies you love to watch with me?"

"But you hate them!" I said with surprise. He shrugged.

"I'll live. Hey, you sat through several Bruce Willis movies with me. And that vampire movie I still regret renting."

"I know. By the way the only reason I agreed to that vampire movie is because I wanted to record you phoning me in the middle of the night saying you thought you heard a vampire outside your room."

"Ha! As if I have ever done that."

"You have! Carrie will remember you woke her up. Ask her if you don't believe me."

"She'd only agree with you to mock me."

"Yeah, Jer, whatever." I smiled faintly at his annoyed expression.

"Hey, at least you're half cheered up now." I smiled. He was right, I did feel a little better. After all, who needed Jeff? He wasn't nearly as fun to hang out with as Jeremy.

We walked over to the video place and rented a couple of comedy movies and a classic romance movie. After paying for our grand total of four movies, we did a grocery store trip to buy enough junk food that would normally last us a week. We walked back to his house and curled up on the couch eating. I wasn't exactly in the best of moods and Jeremy wasn't really sure what to say to help.

Three hours later, Andrea and Carrie came home. Carrie started snorting at Jeremy for watching anything with romance and they started bickering loudly. She turned off the television and we both yelled at her. She was in a good mood because the cute guy in her class told her he thought she was hot. She was bouncing around gleefully mocking Jeremy because no girl had ever told him he was cute. I laughed and said he was cute, he reminded me of a cute cow. Carrie laughed even harder. He just started muttering to himself. The entire ordeal of the sibling bickering made me relax far more than the movie had. Wanting a bit more comfort, I slinked up to Jeremy when Carrie disappeared to her room. He pulled a blanket up beside me and laid his arm over me.

Several hours later someone was shaking me.

"Hey, Becky wake-up. You don't want to be lying on the same couch as my brother when you're asleep." I jerked up and looked at Carrie.

43

"*What?*"

"*You guys fell asleep. It's three in the morning. I could hear Jeremy snoring and came to see why it was so loud. I wondered if he was like, choking or something in his sleep and was going to end his suffering by pushing him on the floor so he could panic with worry that his pitiful life was going to end. I discovered he was curled up with you on the couch. Not a pretty picture.*" I looked over at Jeremy, who really was snoring quite loudly.

"*I slept through his snoring?*"

"*Yeah. Amazing, isn't it. Hey, Jer, there's an ant crawling up your face.*" Carrie threw a pillow at him and he groaned and turned over. Because he was on the couch, when he rolled over, he fell off the couch. I laughed with Carrie as his mother came in. Andrea yawned and looked at the three of us. Jeremy was sitting up and rubbing his eyes.

"*What is going on?*" Andrea asked.

"*Mom, Jeremy's snoring was keeping me up. Couldn't he just sleep outside with the rest of the dogs in the neighbourhood?*" Andrea gave her a sharp look and Carrie shrugged and muttered that he would be fine out there. Jeremy got up and started walking with his eyes closed. He stumbled towards me and Carrie. Carrie smirked and pushed him on the couch. He rolled over and started snoring again.

"*Um, does my mom know where I am?*" I asked Andrea.

"*Yes. I told her that when you two realized what time it was, you could either sleep on the couch or Tom would drive you home. Come on Jeremy.*" She shook Jeremy awake and led him over to his own bedroom. Carrie yawned and wandered back over to her room.

*Andrea came back and set up the blankets on the couch
and tucked me in. I smiled happily, feeling safe in the
Johnston's warm house, I drifted back to sleep.*

Present Day: September 12, 2009

The vivid memory of waking up on the couch with Jeremy
was reassuring, but I still missed him. I rolled over and looked
at the clock. Two in the morning. I was not going to be happy
tomorrow.

A few hours later my mother's humming woke me up. I
was a light sleeper and most sounds woke me. I groggily walked
towards the kitchen where she was buttering toast. Andrea was
sitting across from her chatting away. I poured myself a glass of
orange juice and glared at both of them.

"Hello sleepy head. Have you come to join the rest of us
living ones?" Andrea asked. I groaned. She smiled. "Jeremy has
always woken up early. He woke-up at seven-thirty today."

"How is Jeremy?" I asked.

"He's okay. Don't take anything cruel he says personally,
Beck. He's just in a bad mood since we moved back. He still
cares you know. He just doesn't know how to express it."

"I, uh, told her pretty much everything you told me,
Andrea. I hope you don't mind," Mom said.

"I figured you would. Just neither of you mention to Jeremy
that you know, okay?" We both nodded and she smiled a thanks.
"Becky, this must be really difficult for you. For now, though, just
give him some space. As much as you can, just until he seems to
be somewhat normal." I nodded groggily. I was tired. I ate some
toast and made my way upstairs to get dressed. I thought about
what Andrea said. She was right. He probably needed some space.
I decided to give him a month or so before I would try talking to
him again. I just hoped by then he was his old self.

Chapter 4

"Okay, Beck, we have to make this work." I stared at me and Liam's clay model of a cow.

"Um, I think it resembles a cow. Looks like you!" I said cheerfully. He gave me a dirty look. We were sitting in art class trying to make a cow. We were supposed to sculpt an animal, so I had suggested a cow. Unfortunately, cows are harder to sculpt then I thought. What we had now was a big blob with sticks out of its bottom representing legs and a couple of blobs on top meant to be horns. It did not look like a cow.

"Maybe we should do something else," Liam suggested.

"Like what?"

"How should I know?"

"Oh, Liam, I have an idea. You stand over there and I'll sculpt you."

"I thought we were supposed to be sculpting animals, not people."

"I know. I was going to sculpt a pig. You looked like the perfect specimen." I grinned as he grabbed some clay and dumped it on my shirt. I yelped and threw some on his hair. We started having a clay war when our teacher, Mrs. Morgan, walked by.

"Oh, I see you two have been working hard," she said sarcastically. We laughed, slightly embarrassed.

46

"Sorry Mrs. Morgan. We were just trying to decide if I looked like a pig. I think we should sculpt Becky into a cow." Liam grinned as a glared at him.

"Me? Into a cow? Oh, you are so dead." I snapped. He grinned.

"I would recommend you pick something neither of you think the other resembles and kill each other when you're finished," Mrs. Morgan teased. We said okay and agreed to attempt to sculpt rabbit instead.

Things with Liam had been slightly weirder since Jeremy had returned. Jeremy and I never spoke, but Liam seemed constantly on edge whenever he was anywhere near us. Also, he kept asking pointed questions about what Jeremy said before he moved away and why I did not admit to reciprocating his feelings. I secretly felt like he had a notebook he was documenting these various conversations in.

Jessica was also constantly asking about both Jeremy and Liam. She kept asking how much I had told Liam and what I was going to "do about him." I kept vaguely saying I wasn't sure what she meant. At one point, only last week, she had said I should go up and kiss him and see what happens. I had declined the idea, much to her disappointment.

Half an hour after starting our rabbit sculpture we had completed her. Or, rather, I believed the rabbit was a she but Liam seemed to think all rabbits needed to be named Peter and therefore had to be a he. I was going to agree with him as soon as I had given a decent argument; I did not want to determine such a deformed sculpture to be female.

After class, we were walking down the hall to my locker when I saw Jeremy. I had recently decided he had enjoyed enough time without me "crowding him" and I was free to speak to him if I chose. However, I was still too chicken to so much as look directly at him let alone utter any word his way.

47

"Are you going to do anything today?" Liam asked, referring to Jeremy.

"No."

"Becky," he whined, "you have to. If I'm going to glare harshly and grunt empty threats at him, I need him to have behaved like an ass first! Which he isn't going to do as long as you only longingly stare at his back. You have to say something first."

"I don't longingly stare at his back!" I objected.

"Yeah sure you don't. Math class you pay full attention Mr. Rambouski, never Johnston's back there. And I've never seen you narrow your eyes if he happens to smile at a girl. No, no, if I didn't know better I would think you didn't even know he existed!"

Liam turned his back to me and opened my locker.

"How did you get my combination?" I asked.

"You'll never know," he teased. I got the books I needed and closed my locker.

"Anyway, I can't say anything to Jeremy without some sort of reason. I need an excuse."

Liam threw his hands up in the air. "What? Why? What kind of girl nonsense is that?"

"Girl nonsense? Oh because you just happen to walk up to girls all the time with nothing to talk to them about and strike up a lively conversation, do you?"

"Becky you don't need to have an excuse to talk to someone. I phone you up all the time to ask what day it is. Who really cares?"

"That's different. We're friends."

"You were friends with him. Why can't you just go up and say, "hi, how are you? By the way, what day is it today?" I do that all the time to girls."

"No wonder you're dateless." I laughed as he glared at me. I muttered sorry as Jeremy walked past. We both stared at his

back. I realized Liam would try to catch me staring at his back and we both quickly turned to each other at the same.

"Were you just staring—"

"Nope."

"Ah anyway, if you go say something, I'll go with you. There's nothing to be afraid of, he's just some dumb dude who, by the way, won't last long with the popular jock idiots."

"Why do you say that?"

"As far as I know, he hasn't hooked up with any of the promiscuous girls that hang around their parties and he doesn't play any sports. He'll be back to regular status like the rest of us in no time. I give it until Halloween."

"Halloween?" I purposefully decided not to ask about how Liam knew whether or not Jeremy was hooking up with anyone at parties.

"He hasn't been invited to any of the jock parties yet. And he's not going to be. Oh, and how long are you going to bounce on your toes while you wait for me to reveal how I knew he wasn't getting it on with the ladies?"

"Until now. How do you know all this?"

"Sandy."

"She's been keeping tabs on Jeremy?"

"She keeps me posted. He's been going to the jock parties so far but he hasn't been quite as party-like as the rest of them. He hasn't shown any interest in the girls, he doesn't drink as much as they do, he's not at any school games, and he doesn't come from a family known for waddles of extra cash. Nobody has bothered to tell him where they all are for Halloween and he hasn't asked. Even if he did make it, I doubt he would be the life of the party. I mean, I go to some of these parties but that certainly doesn't let me sit with the jocks during an assembly."

"True enough," I said thoughtfully.

"Who will he hang out with then?"

"Ah, see, this is why it would be a good time to re-introduce yourself. With me at hand of course. Just because Sandy said he's pretty uninterested in behaving like a jock doesn't mean he won't behave like an ass."

"You don't need to protect me from him, you know."

"Of course I do!"

"I can handle Jeremy on my own; I don't need you to get involved. It's not like you're my boyfriend or something." I winced as soon as I said it.

"Right, as if I didn't realize that one. Thank God you pointed it out; I might have embarrassed myself by making you a sappy Valentine or asking you to prom. I'll make a note here: Becky does not need my help and we are not dating, no go on the heart shaped red construction paper this February." He angrily made a writing motion into his hand.

"Sorry Liam I didn't mean—"

"No I got what you meant. Now that Jeremy's around, he can be your pseudo boyfriend again. And as your current pseudo boyfriend, I probably won't fit into that scenario too well."

"No Liam I want you around I meant this is something I need to handle myself!"

"I was just trying to look out for you; I would do the same thing for my sister. And FYI: I don't need anyone to advise me on my relationship status with her. I got the memo when we shared a uterus together."

"I'm sorry Liam I didn't mean it like that—" I hiccupped, trying to hold back tears. "I feel like everyone is trying to tell me what to do and how to do it and when and everyone wants to protect me from him but he's already done the damage, there's nothing to protect me from now, and I just want to handle this myself, not with you or Jessica leaning over my shoulder like over protective parents worrying about a bully." I hiccupped again. "And I don't want to replace you with him. Do you really feel like . . . like my pseudo . . .?" I shook my head. I couldn't finish the question.

"Look I got to go to class, if you want to talk about this more can you phone me later?" Liam still looked angry but his gaze had soften slightly.

"Fine." I bent my head away from him but he grabbed my arm.

"Will you be okay getting to class?" he asked. Nicole came striding down the hall at this moment. She took one look at my face and ripped Liam's hand off of my arm. She gave him a menacing glare and Liam recoiled. (She reserved them but when they came out they were far scarier than anything Jessica mustered up.)

"I'll take her to class," Nicole hissed and pushed me forward. Liam looked slightly unnerved and Nicole and I marched away from him. As soon as we turned the corner we raced to the bathroom.

"Oh Honey what did he say? He's such an idiot sometimes and he doesn't know when he's being mean and he's probably confusing you rather than helping you." She had taken on a motherly tone and hugged me fiercely. I began to hiccup again and repeated what happened while she gave me sympathetic looks.

"I should not have said that thing about him not being boyfriend," I said sadly.

"He had it coming. He behaves like he is when it suits him without ever bothering to make a move to be your boyfriend."

"But am I leading him on or something? Does he want to be . . . does he think of me like that?" Nicole shrugged.

"To be honest it is really hard to tell. Sometimes it seems that way but sometimes it doesn't. And it's not like he hasn't asked out other girls or anything. This isn't like what happened with Jeremy; this isn't Liam pining for you while you obliviously drape all over him." I gaped at Nicole.

"I didn't drape all over—"

"Yes you did. But you didn't realize. And Jeremy was perfectly happy with the way it was. He didn't want to risk changing your relationship by telling you he wanted something else, and he seemed content with that. And he was never angry with you for not behaving differently. Liam is upset that you're pining for Jeremy. He's probably jealous, but that doesn't mean he wants to be your boyfriend. Like I said, he has pursued other girls. And it's not like he has tried to form a closer relationship with you. He randomly implies it, but you've never shared a story with me about him almost kissing you, or licking brownie batter off your finger. Which, by the way, was a hot story. Anyway, point is, yes you have let him be your pseudo boyfriend but he is the one acting like your pseudo boyfriend without trying to change it. And for the record, I do not think you act like a pseudo girlfriend to him. He should butt out of this Jeremy business and you had every right to tell him so."

I nodded. Nicole was right.

"Thanks Nicole. That makes me feel a bit better."

"No problem. I do think you need to talk to Jeremy soon though. Either that or give up on him. If it goes on too long it will become too hard and too awkward and nothing will happen. Ultimately it is up to you, I just think it'll be easier to do it sooner rather than later."

I nodded again. Nicole pulled out her phone.

"Class is fifteen minutes in, want to skip and grab a coffee?"

"Yes and you can tell me about your anniversary date with Rick." Smiling, we left the bathroom. As we swung the school entrance doors open, I decided I would do something about

Jeremy, and soon. Nicole was right, it was only going to get harder, not easier.

Flashback

It was a nice surprise when the Johnstons invited me and my mother for a vacation. They had a cabin up in Canada and went there every year. The cabin was located on Lake Buntzen, close to Vancouver (where they came from) and the cabin next door was available for rent. We rented it for a week.

There was a V.C.R in our cabin and after we unpacked, Jeremy wanted to rent a horror movie.

"Come on, Beck. I love horror movies. Please. I promise I won't get scared." I sighed. Jeremy loved horror movies but I didn't like them. It wasn't that I got nightmares (because I haven't had a nightmare from a horror movie once) it was just that Jeremy got so freaked out.

"You aren't going to phone me at three o'clock in the morning and tell me to lock all the doors and put the hospital on hold because you think you heard a scratching sound?" He sometimes overreacted and would phone in the middle of the night saying he heard something or saw something. It was really annoying.

"I won't phone you in the middle of the night. I promise." He gave me a pleasing look. This was true: there were no phones around for him to phone me with.

"Oh, fine. But, before the week is up, we have to rent a movie of my choice."

He grinned. "Sure, Becky." He grabbed my hand and pulled me towards the door. Wearily, I followed him.

Half an hour later we were eating Kraft Dinner and sitting in front of one of the Halloween movies. There were too many of them. I was beginning to wonder how many lives Michael Myers had. I was fine as we watched the movie, but I had a feeling that later Jeremy would freak. He didn't like serial killer movies because he claimed the events could really unfold in the same fashion, unlike zombie movies.

Several hours later I was dreaming that pink dogs called Omnicks from Mars had come to Earth and wanted to be our friend. I had laughed at them, but then they started scratching at the floor. I wasn't sure why. Now they seemed to be knocking on it and calling my name. I suddenly woke-up realizing that the scratching and knocking sounds were coming from my window. I stifled a scream and fearfully looked out the window. I relaxed as I saw Jeremy.

"Becky, let me in. I swear I heard Michael Myers in my room. I'm not kidding this time." I opened the window and he carefully climbed in. He quickly shut the window and closed the curtains. I groaned.

"Jeremy, I can't believe you came here at this time of night. You did not hear Michael Myers. He's fictional. And if he wasn't, he would seriously be dead by now."

"I know. I'm just scared. Sorry. And hey, at least I didn't phone you at three in the morning."

"No, you decided to scare me half to death by making sounds at my window and whispering my name while I'm sleeping. I think this is worse!"

"Well, if he comes for you, I'll be here and if he comes for me, he'll probably kill Carrie off instead. See, everyone is better off." I glared at him and rolled over.

"I'm going to sleep. You can stay here and do whatever, sleep on the couch or go back to your own cabin."

"I'll stay here and keep watch." I stared at the wall while trying to go to sleep. After what felt like half an hour of Jeremy just sitting there watching the door, I sat up.

"Jeremy, I can't sleep with you sitting here like a watch dog. Go to sleep if you're going to stay here."

"I can't sleep. I'm too scared." I groaned and leaned against him.

"This is pathetic. That is the last time I'm watching a horror movie with you," I said.

"You know I'll just go watch horror movies with Robert and then phone you anyway to warn you about whatever danger the movie foretold. And then you get freaked out because it's fresh in your mind. So you might as well watch them with me."

"The only reason I get scared is so you think I'm going to be cautious and careful. When you think that, you relax and let me go back to bed."

"Sure Beck." He yawned.

"We're pathetic," I said.

"Umm, why?"

"Well, I'm sitting here wishing I could go to sleep and regretting the fact I watched one of your stupid horror movies and you're sitting here scared to death hugging me because your convinced the murderer is going to walk in and kill us at any moment. We're pathetic."

"You're right: we should have game plan in case something happens. Do you have any axes lying around?"

"*You're ridiculous.*" *I sighed and glanced at him. His hair looked black in the darkness and was hanging in his eyes which were glowing in the moonlight. I jumped back, startled.*

"*What?*" *he asked.*

"*Nothing.*" *I had never noticed them do that before and I found it weird. Not really his eyes, more how I felt about them.*

"*Hey, Jeremiah?*

"*What.*" *I laughed at his expressionless, annoyed tone.*

"*Don't be so blunt sounding. You don't sound happy.*"

"*I'm not exactly at my best right now.*" *I ruffled his hair and he gently pushed me away.*

"*Let's go watch T.V. There's bound to be some cartoons on or something,*" *I suggested.*

"*Okay. But no horror movies. As much as I love them, I can't stand to be scared any more than I already am,*" *he said. We got up and slowly walked out of my room with Jeremy anxiously looking around for any potential danger. My mother's door opened and we both screeched and clung to each other. She came out with a peculiar look on her face and her hair all tussled. Jeremy and I let go of each other and relaxed slightly.*

"*I don't think you two should watch horror movies. Jeremy, what on earth are you doing here?*" *Mom asked as she squinted at him in the dark.*

"*Umm, sorry if we woke you. I was scared and Carrie kicks in her sleep. Dad didn't wake-up and Mom just told me to go back to bed. So I came here knowing Becky would let me stay injure-free.*"

"You're injure-free now, but tomorrow when I'm at my perkiest you won't be injure-free," I growled at him. He smiled.

"Okay. Well I assume you're going to go watch television?" We nodded a confirmation. "Fine. Jeremy, you can sleep on the couch if you get tired." Jeremy nodded again. We walked over to the couch and curled up together. We flipped through the channels and Jeremy demanded that we watch the news. I wasn't really interested in the quality of news they had in the middle of the night, but agreed anyway.

Half an hour later Jeremy had started snoring loudly. I looked over at him and smiled. He'd make a terrible person to live with. I should probably mention that to him tomorrow. Feeling a surge of affection, I leaned over and kissed his cheek and pulled the covers around him.

Several hours later I woke-up to someone screaming. Startled, I bolted out of bed. At first, I couldn't figure out where I was. Then I remembered I was at the cabin next to Jeremy's. I wondered where the scream came from, by who, and why. Trying to stay calm, I slowly retraced my steps and remembered Jeremy coming through the window during the night. Deciding it was female scream, I worried about my mother and raced out of my bedroom. Andrea burst in the front door just as I left my room.

"Jeremy's gone! I can't find him!" she shirked. My mother, calmly sipping from a mug, pointed to the couch where a loud snore emerged from underneath a pillow. Andrea, looking slightly confused, walked over to the mound of blankets on the couch that was Jeremy. He had the pillow over his head, the blankets over him and

*was snoring loudly. She sighed and hit him on the back.
There was a muffled groan and he rolled over. Andrea
looked annoyed. I covered my mouth and giggled. Carrie
came in at that moment humming.*

*"Hey, Beck, great news, Jeremy is missing!" she
grinned and sat down on the couch without looking at
it first. Jeremy yelped and pushed her off. She screamed
and started hitting him with pillows. He got up to hide
behind me while she screamed at him that she could
become paralyzed and she could sue him. Jeremy scowled
and walked over to his cabin. Carrie stormed after him
with threats of suing. Andrea scowled and went after
them. And me? I went back to bed.*

Present Day: October 23, 2009

Since it was close to Halloween, I was trying to figure out
what to do for Halloween this year when Carrie phoned. I
hadn't heard from her in over a year and was slightly surprised
she was phoning me.

"Hey, Becky. How are you? I have a great new crush. He
lives next door and is absolutely so cute! Beck, I seriously think
I'm in love." I laughed.

"Hey, Carrie. I'm good. What's this guy's name?"

"Ricardo. I think he's Spanish," she said wisely. I
groaned.

"So, Carrie, how did you get my number?" I asked.

"Oh, Jeremy had it. I got it from him. Anyway, I thought I
should tell you I'm having a Halloween party on, guess which
day, Halloween! Aren't I original? Want to come? You can meet
Ricardo."

"Sure. Um, just two questions. How did Jeremy get my
number and is he going to be there?"

Carrie snorted. "Yeah, the pain in the ass boy is going to be there. Don't ask me how he got your number. I assumed you gave it to him. So can you come meet Ricardo? He has beautifully tanned skin and he writes poetry in his spare time."

"Does he really?"

"Yes I mean have you ever met a Spanish guy that doesn't have tanned skin?"

"No I meant does he really write poetry?"

"Oh! No clue but in my imagination he does. I saw him sitting outside writing in a book."

"And that wasn't his homework?"

"Well . . . it probably was but seriously, writing poetry is way more romantic than finishing homework." I rolled my eyes. Carrie was sometimes a little boy crazed, but she was fun. Besides, going to this party could be a good chance to try to talk to Jeremy. As I daydreamed about how to talk to Jeremy, Carrie started to yell out my name and curse phone connections.

"What? Sorry Carrie I'm here I was just thinking. What time?"

"Seven, but it would be great if you could come a bit earlier and help me set up. Plus, I'd love to catch up a bit, I haven't seen you in like forever. Do you maybe want to come by around four?"

"Sure thing, Carrie. I'll be there around four."

All I needed to do now was make a plan. That and make a costume. Come to think of it, the costume part might be harder than the planning part.

Chapter 5

I nervously rang the doorbell of Jeremy's house. It was finally Halloween. Carrie had told me I could change into my costume at the house. I looked in the bag with my Cinderella costume in it. Carrie opened the door and screamed. I stared at her, startled. I then tried to look around to see what was so frightening.

"Where's Ricardo? He should be here by now. Oh, Becky, what if he isn't going to come?" Carrie was moaning softly and angling past me to look at the house next door. I stepped in the house and out of her way of her desired view.

"Hey Carrie. Excited about Ricardo coming?" I asked. She nodded eagerly. I heard music start and then stop. Jeremy swore and I peeked into the room. He was sitting there trying to do something with a stereo. I wouldn't trust him with my stereo, but I guess Andrea didn't think of that.

"Jeremy, are you done yet?" Carrie whined. He winced and glared at her.

"What the Hell do you think? I'm sitting on my ass having to fix this thing which refuses to work while you whine about your stupid boyfriend who hasn't shown up yet and Becky stares at me like I'm a damn idiot! Do you think I'm done?!" he exploded. Carrie glared at him.

"Ricardo is not stupid!" she yelled back at him. I couldn't help but snort into my own hand. Being around Jeremy and Carrie often made me relieved I was an only child but other times made me wish for a sibling. They were always annoying each other, but it always seemed to bounce off and sometimes it looked more fun than anything else. Jeremy groaned as Carrie stood there with her hands on her hips, glaring at him. I wondered if Carrie was being particularly difficult with him due to her anticipation of the Spanish beautifully tanned Ricardo.

"Carrie, calm down. I thought you said your party started at seven, right? It's only four fifteen, I'm sure he'll make it by seven. Besides, maybe he's writing you a poem."

Her eyes widened. "You think?"

"Uhhh . . ."

"Oh that's totally what he's doing right now! Thanks Becky you're so right." I winced, wondering if I had made things worse.

"Right well anyway, did you want me to help you with anything?"

"Yeah. Help Jer fix the stereo. I don't think he's capable of doing it himself." I stared at her. Jeremy stared at her.

"I don't need Becky's help," he snapped.

"Well, I just thought you might want to talk to your girlfriend and all. Sorry." I had a huge urge to cough into my hand while muttering "awkward."

"Uh, Carrie, he's not my boyfriend." I said gently. Seemed like a better approach than the awkward cough.

"Oh, well the other guy must be pretty cute then. You should have invited him to the party. Oh, wait, Jeremy would have been horrified. Oh, well, all the more reason to invite him." She grinned suddenly, then frowned at my face.

"I don't have a boyfriend. There is and never was another guy." Carrie turned and looked at Jeremy. She looked confused for a second as she looked from me to him. Finally, after analyzing our faces, she turned her gaze over to Jeremy, glaring.

"You!" She said accusingly. He stepped back with his hands in the air.

"I didn't do anything."

"I bet you didn't do anything. That would certainly explain why nothing is going on between you two." She turned towards me. "Did he even tell you he was coming? Or did you have to find out through our mom?"

"I uh . . ." I looked at his slightly pleading face and then Carrie's angry one. To hell with it. "I found out at school."

"Jeremy!" She turned towards him again and he took another step back. "You are utterly ridiculous! Do you even understand why mom packed up and moved back here? You got your wish, you're away from dad, stop being an asshole! What are you, afraid you'll cheat on Becky? Or do you think you're making it easier on everyone by keeping her away from you?"

"You don't know—"

"Don't know what? What don't I know? He was my dad too! What's your excuse then? Lets here what you have to say for why you decided to cut Becky out of your life!" We both looked at him expectantly.

"Screw this I'm out of here I don't have to tell you anything." He grabbed his jacket and headed out, slamming the door behind him. I winced. Carrie muttered a couple of ominous threats under her breath.

"Sorry Becky," she said after a long silence.

"For what? You didn't do anything."

"For . . . I'm not sure I guess inviting you over without asking if it was okay for you to see Jeremy. Or I guess I'm sorry

I freaked out at him a bit in front of you." She gave a long, heavy sigh. "A lot has happened in the past little while That's why he's behaved like a . . . well not like he use to."

"It's okay Carrie."

"Anyway, if you like, I can fill you in a bit. I mean Jeremy would probably prefer I didn't, but I think you have a right to know. Especially if he's been a cow towards you."

"Best to just leave it. I don't want to make it worse for him. I think I know all I need to anyway. How about we forget about it for now and put up some decorations?" She brightened slightly.

"Okay. And I can tell you about Ricardo?"

"All about him and his lovely poetry."

Several hours later I was squeezing past some snogging teenagers to head outside. My phone was going off but I knew I wouldn't hear anything as long as I was inside.

The party had been okay, but most of the people were around Carrie's age group. She was fifteen and likewise most of her guests were around fourteen to sixteen. I didn't mind hanging around the younger crowd, but I didn't actually know anybody except Carrie and Andrea. (Andrea was chaperoning.)

"Hey," I said as I answered my phone. The display had told me it was Liam. I was wondering what he was doing calling me at eleven. We hadn't yet fully discussed the awkward and angry conversation about him not being my boyfriend yet. I figured he wasn't calling to invite me to a party this late, nor was he calling to discuss anything either, he would be out partying with Sandy.

"Oh good, I got a hold of you." The background noise was not what I expected. I could hear an intercom and the low murmur of distant chatter. It was not exactly party noise.

"Yes you did."

"Listen Becky, I uh, well Sandy and I went to a party."

"Yes I assumed as much."

"Right well anyway," there was a muffling sound and I heard him say something about it being awkward and why was he bothering anyway.

"Liam?"

"Yeah sorry. So somewhere around nine I guess Jeremy showed up. He was a bit drunk when he showed up and had more liquor with him. Nobody particularly cared, even though nobody had invited him. Anyway, he started getting a little . . . I don't know too drunk I guess and Jack told him it was time for him to go home. It was only just past ten and he wasn't in great shape." Jack was one of Sandy's friends and was basically our school champion: captain of various sports teams, straight A student, volunteer, and all around good guy. Jack was probably concerned mostly for Jeremy drinking too much more than anything else.

"Was he all right?" I asked.

"Well, he didn't want to leave and Jack was trying to convince him to let someone drive him home and he stumbled or something, I'm not even sure what he was trying to do, and he fell and his hit head on a table."

"What?"

"Yeah so Sandy and I drove him to the hospital. He's just been admitted. I thought I should wait until he was admitted before calling you in case he got mad at me."

"Is he okay?"

"I think so. His head was bleeding and he was kind of going in and out of consciousness in the car, but we didn't know if that was the hit on the head or the booze. The doctors didn't seem overly concerned."

I heard Sandy in the background say something about how they doctors told them it was just another drunken fall.

"Did you want me to come get you?" Liam asked. I glanced through a window of the house. Andrea was on the phone and she looked distressed. She had her finger plugged in one ear and the receiver smashed up against the other side of her face.

"I think I'll be able to get down there, but thanks."

"Okay well Sandy and I will stick around until you show."

"Thanks Liam." I hung up and went inside. I ran straight to Carrie's room where I changed out of my costume and into my jeans and t-shirt. Bolting out, I almost banged into Carrie.

"Jeremy is—"

"I know," I interrupted her. "Where's your mom?"

"She's phoning your mom now. She's having her come here while she goes down to the hospital."

"Okay thanks Carrie." I turned to go but she grabbed my arm.

"Becky, can you tell him I'm sorry?"

"What?"

"I didn't mean to upset him, things have been rough for him, I shouldn't have yelled. Can you tell him I'm sorry?"

"Carrie I don't think it's your fault, but I'll tell him you're sorry."

"Thanks." I gave her a quick hug and pushed my way through the costumed crowd towards Andrea.

"Thanks Pam, I'll phone you from the hospital," she was saying. She hung up and turned to me. She looked at my jeans and t-shirt. "Coming?" she asked. I nodded. She bee-lined towards the door and we jumped in her car.

"Who said what to piss him off?" she asked as soon as we had pulled out of the driveway.

Startled, I started to stammer but she waved her hand at me and sighed.

"Never mind. Anything he does is his own fault."

"I didn't mean to make things worse," I said, feeling slightly defensive.

"I know you didn't. You probably want to make things better."

"Do you want me to stay away from him?" I suddenly felt a sick lurch in my stomach. I didn't know how I would handle Andrea asking me to stay away from her son.

"If I wanted that I wouldn't have brought you with me. He's over-reacting to something. He hasn't pulled a drunken rebellion in a couple of months; I should have known it was coming."

"Carrie and I may have said something, I think he was upset with me showing up at the house."

"Doesn't matter. Like I said, anything he does is his own fault. He chooses to get drunk and fall over because he didn't have the co-ordination to move properly. Don't think this is your fault and don't let him say it is either."

We reached the hospital and pulled into the parking lot. Andrea angrily stuck some money in the machine and tapped her foot as she waited for her parking ticket. She thrust it on the dashboard and we hurried inside.

The waiting area was surprisingly sparse considering it was Halloween. Sandy and Liam were waiting by the entrance and stood up as we came in.

"Did you bring him in?" Andrea asked. They nodded in twin unison.

"Well, thank you. I hope he didn't puke in your car or anything."

"Actually he—" Liam began but Sandy nudged him and he closed his mouth. Andrea turned towards the reception.

"Thanks guys," I said softly.

"No problem, Becky. Neither of us had been drinking so it seemed best if we took him. Just so you know, he's a bit agitated," Sandy advised me.

"Okay well thanks for the heads up." Now that I was there, I didn't want to be. I didn't want to go see him in the hospital room, and I didn't want him to know I cared enough to come down to the hospital.

Liam and Sandy were watching me with an identical look of mild concern on their faces. They were both in Halloween costumes and I pictured them suddenly as little children walking down streets together, hands entwined, as they trick-or-treated.

"I guess I should go follow Andrea," I said, indicating her with my thumb.

"Yeah we should get going," Sandy said. She glanced at Liam and stepped back a couple of feet.

"Thanks Liam," I said feebly. I was feeling awkward and wished I had gotten around to talking about our fight before tonight. I turned to follow Andrea but he grabbed me around the waist.

"Hey, just let me know if you need anything or want a ride home or something, okay?" I nodded. "Promise?" I nodded again. "Promise for sure and not like when you said you would phone me to talk about that stuff we said?" I sighed.

"Promise for sure."

"Okay." He slid his arm away and followed Sandy out the door. I walked over to Andrea who was waiting with a nurse. We followed the nurse down the hall and were lead into a small room with a bed. Jeremy was lying in bed, snoring.

"You can wake him up if you like, or you can let him sleep for a bit," the nurse told Andrea. Andrea thanked her and the nurse left. Andrea and I stood on either side of his bed, looking down at him.

"They gave him stitches. He has a mild concussion. They said his skull isn't fractured and he should be fine within a couple of days. He doesn't need to be kept awake or anything like that. But he needs to be monitored for the first 24 hours." She looked directly at me and I winced. She was going to have me stay with them and help monitor him.

"So we'll let him sleep for a bit while your mom winds down the party and then we'll head back."

I nodded. We pulled up some chairs and Andrea pulled out her phone. I glanced around the room for something to keep me occupied. I spied a magazine and idly flipped through it.

Forty minutes later I was bored out of my skull and desperate for a distraction. I was also extremely suspicious of the lack of snoring coming from Jeremy. Andrea closed her magazine and looked at me carefully.

"I'll go grab us some coffees," she said.

"Sure," I said as quietly as I could. I had not actually said anything since we had arrived and I hoped he didn't know I was here. Assuming he was faking being asleep and was really trying to figure out how to explain this to his mother.

She stood up and eyed Jeremy suspiciously before leaving the room. I nonchalantly continued to flip through a magazine I had already gone through twice.

"What are you doing here?" I jumped slightly and turned towards Jeremy. His eyes were closed; he was not yet looking at me. I decided to remain silent in case he did not yet know it was me. Which seemed like a dumb thought, but nonetheless I didn't want to acknowledge my own presence.

"Becky?"

"Oh me?" Clearly I had not been as stealthy as I had hoped.

"There's nobody else in the room." His voice was slightly slurred but he sounded fairly normal other than that.

"How do you know?" I asked. He opened one eye and looked at me, then around the room. He closed his eye again.

"Well, anyway, I only came to see that you're okay. You seem fine to me now so I think I'll just be on me way." I stood up and grabbed my jacket but he shook his head.

"You should stay."

"Why?" For someone who had put serious effort into keeping me away the statement seemed slightly abnormal.

"Andrea will be back in a couple of minutes and she's going to be mad. Less likely I'll receive the full brunt until you're gone."

"Oh I see, I'm quite useful then, aren't I?" Angrily I shoved my arms through my jacket sleeves.

"Liam drove me here you know." I paused.

"I know."

"He doesn't like me but he drove me here anyway." For whatever reason, I felt a tug of curiousness as to why he was bringing Liam up. I sat back down.

"You probably didn't deserve his kindness."

"Probably. But he didn't do it for me, he did it for you." I gapped at him, not sure what to say. His eyes were still closed. I wasn't sure what to say: no he didn't do it for me? Yes he did do it for me?

"Well who cares why it was just nice that he and Sandy were able to drive you here." I decided to add the fact that Sandy came too.

"He did it because he wants you." My face flamed up and once more, I gapped at him.

"You don't know that."

"Yes I do. I see the way he looks at you." Whatever Jeremy intended me to take from the statement, I felt a faint warm glow in knowing he cared enough to observe.

"Are you with him?" Again, Jeremy could be prying for information out of concern. And perhaps jealousy.

"No." I touched my cheek, wishing I could stop blushing. At least with Jeremy keeping his eyes closed he couldn't see the colour of my face.

"Why not?" I fidgeted nervously. I didn't have an answer to this question and after talking to both Liam and Nicole, I wondered the same thing. Was it because I wasn't attracted to him? I didn't think that was the issue.

"Perhaps it is because I still carry a torch for you. Which, if so, won't be an issue for me for much longer as you have done a great job trying to extinguish it."

"I'm not—" He fell silent as we heard Andrea's voice outside the room. I couldn't hear what she was saying but she came in balancing her phone between her ear and shoulder while she carried two coffees. She handed me one and sat down.

"Okay sounds good. I'll phone you tomorrow." She hung up, leaned back, and started sipping her coffee.

"Uh Andrea you know—"

"Oh I know he is awake. But he's already ruined my evening; he's not ruining my coffee. We'll go when I finish." She took another sip of her coffee and smiled.

"Oh okay, sure." I took a sip of my coffee and winced. Hospital coffee was not exactly high quality. Plus, I wasn't exactly a coffee drinker.

"Sugar?" Andrea handed me a packet of sugar and I gratefully took it.

We sipped our coffee in silence. Jeremy remained very still with his eyes closed. The entire situation felt very weird.

After ten minutes Andrea stood up, looking very assertive and ready for a battle.

"Okay Becky, time to go," she said.

"Oh right." I picked up my jacket that I had shrugged off during the conversation with Jeremy regarding Liam. "I'll just walk home then?"

"What's that? Oh no Sweetie, you're helping me monitor Jeremy here. I propose we will do it in shifts. And we have to wake him every hour and if he doesn't wake easily we take him back here." She turned to glare at him sharply. He continued to stay still with his eyes closed.

"If you don't snore I know you're not sleeping," she muttered darkly to him. He gave a loud, fake snore and she rolled her eyes.

"Up you get!" He opened his eyes and glared at her.

"We might as well stay here." Talking to her, his voice sounded more slurred than when he had spoken to me. He continued to attempt to glare at her but then rubbed his eyes and squinted funny.

"Drink this." She handed him a water bottle and he gratefully took it and downed the entire thing in one breath.

"All in one go?" I asked them both.

"Look at Becky here, I bet she's never been drunk!" They both looked at me expectantly.

"Um well, I don't think I have been." Jeremy rolled his eyes, then groaned and rubbed them.

"Then you've never been drunk," Andrea advised me. She turned back to Jeremy to rip the covers off of him. Unfortunately, Jeremy was only wearing a hospital gown.

"Oh yikes," I muttered as I quickly turned to face the wall. I couldn't see anything, but felt embarrassed just the same.

"Where are your clothes?" Andrea asked loudly.

"What? My clothes? Oh did someone undress me?"

71

"You don't remember? Oh this is perfect."

"Oh wait, I puked. And then . . . someone gave me this and put my clothes in a bag and they went . . . they went there." I still wasn't looking at him and couldn't see where he was pointing but Andrea moved past me and opened a cupboard. A foul smell erupted out as soon as she opened the door and we both withdrew.

"Gross," I said as I covered my mouth.

"Seriously Jeremy?" Andrea took out two bags and handed him one. "I'll be back in a moment." She left with the other bag.

"Extinguishing more and more with every passing moment," I muttered.

"My shirt!" I heard him say with faint glee.

Andrea came in holding a pair of wet jeans.

"Here. You can change when we get home. Don't even think about complaining that they're wet."

"I think I'll go wait outside." Andrea didn't say anything to protest so I slinked out the door. I felt awful. The situation was highly embarrassing and even though Andrea was handling it well, I felt very sorry for her. I also severely regretted coming to the hospital.

After a moment Andrea came out.

"Can you help me get him up?" she asked.

"He's not able to himself?"

"I'm sure he is but as we're here because he couldn't manage to move with enough co-ordination to keep himself upright I was thinking it would be best if we helped him up and to the car."

"Oh well . . ." the idea of being that close to Jeremy made me nervous. It wasn't that I was scared he would do something, it was just we hadn't touched since he had left and having been so close and touchy before, I wasn't sure I could pretend everything was okay. "I don't want to touch him." There really was no other way to put it.

"Because he left his dinner on his jeans? I agree but right now there are more important things to consider."

"No, not because he puked on himself. I don't want to be that close to him because . . . because I haven't in a long time and he's been so . . ." I shook my head. I suddenly felt like I might cry.

"Oh," was all Andrea said. Surprisingly, she leaned forward and hugged me. I hugged her back and swallowed the large lump in my throat.

"Okay well maybe you should go home," Andrea said gently as she pulled away.

"Go home? But you need help monitoring him and what not."

"No I don't. He's my problem. I've been selfish expecting you to sit around and wake him up every hour so I can have a nap. I forgot about your feelings in this. This can't be easy for you; better I phone Pam to pick you up."

"No Andrea, I'll come, its fine. I just . . . I need to keep my distance and feel I'm maintaining some control, that's all. I want to help you. Once upon a time he would have done this for me."

"I still think—"

"I'd rather come. Besides, this is definitely helping me get over him." She sighed.

"Well I'll say this, though it won't help you get over him: if it was you who was drunk and had hit your head, even now, he would be here. He wouldn't want you to know, but he would definitely be here."

"You're right, that doesn't help me get over him." She smiled and we went back inside. Jeremy was sitting on the edge of the bed, his head rolled down, snoring gently. He was fully clothed, shoes and all.

"We were only outside a couple of minutes. I'm shocked he didn't eaves drop!" Andrea went up to him and pushed him back a bit from the edge of the bed.

"Up!" He startled and blinked several times.

"Oh right," he muttered. He wearily stood and Andrea gripped his waist. Anxiously, I held open the door.

"What about a wheelchair?" I offered feebly. They both gave me a look implying neither wanted him wheeled out of here.

We managed to make our way to the car. Jeremy shuffled his way into the back and Andrea and I took our seats up front. Jeremy promptly fell asleep.

"So I think it is best if you take first watch and I'll have a nap, and then in a couple of hours you can go home and I'll take over for the rest of the evening. Or morning I suppose," Andrea said.

"Sure."

"Will you be okay to stay over for that long? It's almost one now."

"I'll just have to phone my mom and tell her where I am."

"Oh she actually just left my house, she knows you're with me."

"Right, I forgot she went over to look after Carrie's party."

"Anyway, she said she wasn't worried and would come pick you up if you like at any time. I phoned her from the hospital, telling her to go home. That's who I was talking to when I came back with the coffees."

"Ah." Andrea pulled up to the house. She woke Jeremy up and they slowly made their way inside. I followed from a short distance.

Inside, Andrea took him to his room saying something about his clothes. She came out a moment later and grabbed a pillow and a blanket.

"Here," she said, handing them to me. "In case you want to have a nap; I don't expect you to stay awake the entire time, as long as you can get up and wake him every hour or so."

"Thanks," I said and took them to the couch.

"Try to convince him to drink some water when you're waking him. I'm going to set my alarm for three hours. Is that okay with you? You can get me up earlier if you like."

"It'll be fine."

"Okay. Thanks Becky. I really appreciate this." She gave me a small smile and went to her room. I sat down on the couch and set my phone to go off in an hour.

A moment later, I heard some shuffling and Jeremy came in. He wordless sat down and closed his eyes.

"What are you doing in here? You're not going to sleep in your room?"

"You want to come into my room and wake me?" he asked. I thought about it for a moment.

"No. When did you decide to consider me in all this?"

"When Liam decided to take me to the hospital."

"Maybe it was Sandy's idea."

"Either way." His head tilted to the side and he rubbed his neck. With his head tilted, I could see where they shaved off a bit of his hair and stitched him up. I felt a rush of sadness hit me.

"Why did you go get so drunk? Liam said you showed up at the party drunk and it was still fairly early. Where were you drinking before then?"

"Doesn't matter."

"Well it was a dumb idea." We were silent for a long moment. I pulled out the blanket Andrea had given to me and bunched it around myself. I hoped he would fall asleep.

"I'm sorry," he said out of nowhere.

"What?"

"You heard me." I peered at him. His eyes were open but he wasn't looking at me. He grabbed a water bottle he had brought in with him and drank from it.

"For what? What are you sorry for?"

"My plan not panning out as I hoped."

"What does that mean?"

"It means I meant to make you angry and obviously I just hurt you instead. I just wanted you to leave me alone and that is not how this is working out." I felt hurt that he seemed to still want me to leave him alone.

"Well, like I said at the hospital, torch extinguishing. I think I'll be leaving you alone after this. Anyway, how do you know I'm hurt and not angry?"

"If you were angry you would have given me a piece of your mind, then Jessica would have done the same, and that would have been the end of it. You wouldn't have told Carrie you would come to the house today without telling her what I had said and she would have kicked me out before you showed up. And then I probably wouldn't have had the same amount of booze."

"Ah I see so this is all my fault then?"

"No, it's mine, that's why I said I'm sorry." We had another silent moment.

"Liam wouldn't have driven you to the hospital if I was angry instead of hurt," I finally said. I wasn't even sure why I was saying it.

"No he would be busy trying to get somewhere with you."

"Excuse me you don't—"

"Leave it," he interrupted me. I closed my mouth and glared at him. I crossed my arms and looked away. I heard my phone go off and inwardly sighed. It had not been an hour; I was getting a text message. I already knew who it was from. I ignored it.

"Want to watch T.V.?" Jeremy asked.

"You don't want to get some sleep?"

"Are you going to sleep?" I could see his point: there was no way I could fall asleep at the moment.

"Fine," I muttered. He rummaged underneath a cushion and pulled out a remote. He turned on the television and flicked through the channels. He continued to drink his water as we watched a cartoon.

"I'm out," he eventually said as he finished the last of his water. He shuffled and I felt like he was going to go get his water.

"I'll get you some," I said as I stood up.

"No, I'll do it, you stay here," he responded.

"No, you're all unbalanced and what not, I'll get the water, you stay here."

"Yeah right." He started to stand and swayed. He grabbed my arm to steady himself and we both flinched. He recoiled and I jerked my arm away. We stared at each other for a moment and I fought the urge to rub my arm. It felt hot and I knew my face was flushing.

"Sorry," he muttered. He unsteadily sat back down and I went to the kitchen. I poured both of us water and came back. As I sat back down, my phone rang. I tried to keep a straight face as I reached into my purse for it. It was Liam.

"Excuse me," I mumbled as I went into the hall.

"Hey," I said as I opened my phone.

"Hey," Liam said on the other end.

"What's up?"

"I was just phoning to see how you were."

"I'm okay."

"Yeah?"

"Yeah."

"How's Jeremy?" I didn't think he was really concerned but it was nice of him to ask.

"Okay. We've left the hospital."

"Where are you? Have you gone home yet?"

"Ummm . . ." I didn't really want to tell Liam where I was. "No, I'm at his house."

"Do you want me to come pick you up?"

"I'm fine. I'm here to monitor him. His mother is napping; I'm going home after that."

"You want me to come hang out with you until then?"

"No, it's okay." I didn't think Jeremy would like Liam coming by. Liam also probably thought Jeremy was asleep and I was twiddling my thumbs by myself.

"Okay. Well listen, I'm sorry about some of the things I said the other day. You're right, it's not my business and you can take care of yourself. I've probably pushed some boundaries a bit."

"I'm sorry too, I shouldn't have said what I said. I didn't mean . . . you know."

"I know. Well . . . I'm going to go to bed if you don't need anything then. Have a good night."

"You too. Bye." I hung up and heard a shuffle sound, a bang, and the sound of Jeremy swear. I came back in the living room to see him nursing his toe.

"What were you doing?" I asked. He was leaning against the wall and was attempting to hold his foot up.

"Going to the bathroom," he said.

"You're lying."

"What's going on with Liam? Why is he phoning you so late?

"He was concerned. He asked how you were."

"Whatever. You talked for longer than that. What else did he say? What did you say "you too" to?"

"You shouldn't eavesdrop. It's not your business."

"You're right, it's not, you know what is? When you didn't say "you too" to me!"

"What? Jeremy, that would have been "me too" you idiot. And since this seems so important to you, he said "have a good night" and I said "you too." End of story. Sit down and stop acting like a child before you wake up your mom and sister." Jeremy hobbled back to the couch and sat down.

"I really do have to go the bathroom," he said.

"Go then." I also sat down and ignored him as he got up, swaying again, and using the couch and walls for support, made his way to the bathroom. He came back within a couple of minutes.

"Are you jealous?" I asked after a moment.

"Of?"

"Of Liam."

"No." He paused. "Maybe, like you, I have an extinguishing torch." He looked me in the eye. Feeling hurt, I turned away.

"There's something I should say," I said after a long moment.

"Do I want to hear it?"

"Probably. You've brought up this incident a couple of times now." I wasn't really ready to tell him how I felt, but I thought I could at least tell him how I did feel two years ago.

"What is it?" I kept my head angled away from him and fidgeted nervously.

"Two years ago, you said something, right? We both remember?"

"I don't want to talk about that."

"Really, you do, because you just brought it up two minutes ago. So I don't care if you claim you don't want to talk about it." I took a deep breath. "When you said, what you said, I should have said "me too" but instead I was scared and I didn't . . . get around to it."

"You didn't "get around to it"? You forgot or something?"

"I didn't forget, I was nervous and it just didn't come out before you left and I wanted you to know that just because I didn't say the same thing as you doesn't mean I didn't feel the same way as you."

"So you did feel the same?"

"Yes." I was still avoiding looking at him.

"Do you still feel the same way?" He shuffled closer to me.

"I don't want to talk about how I feel now, I've said what I wanted to say."

"Hey, I didn't want to talk about what I said then, but you talked about it anyway."

I turned to look at him. "Tell you what," I said, thinking of a compromise. "I'll tell you if you tell me."

"Nope."

"Then you can forget it." I curled up on my side and pushed the pillow under my head. "I'm going to sleep," I said. I felt emotionally drained and didn't think I could take anymore. I pulled the blankets around me. I felt Jeremy lean over to peer at me.

"What?" I asked.

"You're not tearing up, are you?" he asked.

"No."

"Just checking. Night then." He scooted over to the other end of the couch and I closed my eyes, hoping sleep would mend my mental anguish.

Chapter 6

Diary Entry: August 20, 2006

So Jeremy was my best friend along with Jessica. However, life, right now, was kind of boring. There wasn't much to do. I had had a boyfriend and didn't really want one for a while. I had been on vacation quite recently with Jeremy's family and didn't want to go on another. The reality of small towns is sometimes there isn't any entertainment. Sure, we're near Seattle, but how often can you go shopping? So what did I do? I hung out with Jeremy, when he asked me the weirdest of all questions.

Flashback

I was beginning to get tired. There was absolutely nothing on television. Jeremy sighed.

"Hey, Rebecca?" he asked.

"What?" I asked sleepily.

"What do you think being in love is like?" I sat up to look at him. He had his earnest expression on his face. That usually meant that he was going to get all serious on me.

"How should I know? I don't think I've ever been in love. Maybe you should ask your mother or father. Why do you want to know anyway? You think you're in love or something?" I teased. He sighed.

"I don't know. Maybe." I was surprised. He hadn't mention liking anyone recently, and because it was summer the only girls he had really hung out with were me and my friends.

"Okay, either you are suddenly going through male hormones and you have it big for the latest swimsuit model of your sports magazines, or you suddenly realized you should give Jessica all that love she has been asking for in these past few years."

He shook his head. "No. I'm not in love with a person I don't even know or Jessica. You can relax."

"Well, Jess is going to be highly disappointed it isn't her, you know. But if it isn't her that you think you could be in love with, then who?" I turned to look at him and his green eyes bore into mine.

"You don't know who it could possibly be?" he asked. He was looking at me kind of funny. I shook my head. I tried thinking of someone he could like.

"Maybe it is better you don't know, Rebecca." He twirled my hair on his finger and gave me an amused smile. I frowned. Who could it possibly be?

"Well, I'm not sure what being in love is like, but from what I read in stories and what I hear in movies, it supposed to make you feel on top of the world or something. Like you want to be with that person every second of the day. Every time you are with them, your heart beats faster, your palms sweat, your stomach churns, and you feel sick with exhilaration but deliriously happy at the same time. You feel like nothing could go wrong, your lover or whatever will always take care of you." I looked at his confused face. "So, do you think you're in love?" He smiled.

"Are my palms sweaty, do I feel like I'm gone to hurl and do I think some girl is going to take care of me the rest of my life? Well, maybe I just have the flu and believe that Mom will always love me enough to pay my bills." He shrugged and I laughed and nudged him with my foot.

"That was no reason to kick me, Rebecca."

"You were making fun of me," I accused.

"I was not!"

"You were too. You were making fun of what I think people feel like when they're in love. You probably planned the whole thing so you could mock me. Well, that's the last time I answer any of your questions." I started to get up but he grabbed my arm. He pulled me back down and smiled.

"Becky, I didn't mean to make fun of you. I wouldn't do that to you." He was leaning down and pushed the hair out of my eyes. I suddenly felt my palms sweat and my stomach churn. He could probably hear my heart because it was beating so loud! He was leaning close. Was I in love, nervous, or did I (hopefully) just have the flu?

"Rebecca?" He leaned down even closer and slid his arm around my waist.

"Yes?"

"Can I—" His mother suddenly opened the door at that moment with a cheerful hello. Jeremy sat up and nervously ran his hand through his hair. I sat up too, and tried to make my smile look cheerful. I couldn't believe that had just happened. We had never been that close to kissing before. I sighed and they both looked at me. I gave a weak smile and Jeremy got up to help his mother with the groceries. I got up and straightened out the blankets on the couch, then helped with the groceries. After that

I went home. I never told anyone what happened and Jeremy and I never mentioned it again.

Present Day: November 1, 2009

I woke-up to a beep from my phone. I groggily sat up and turned to see Jeremy mucking around with it, trying to stop the beeping.

"What are you doing?" I asked sleepily. While I felt like I could only have been asleep for twenty minutes, I noticed he was watching what looked like a movie and enjoying a pot of what I assumed was some sort of boxed macaroni and cheese.

"Trying to turn off your phone. I re-set the alarm in case I also fell asleep and meant to change it but forgot. Mac and cheese?" He offered me the pot and his fork.

"No thanks," I mumbled. "How long was I asleep?"

"A couple of hours." He sounded much more cheerful and there was no slur left in his voice. I noticed a half-full water jug, a tea pot embraced in a tea cozy, several Halloween candy bar wrappers, and an opened box of cookies sitting on the table.

"What's going on?"

"Ah, see, when I sober up I *love* food so I made myself some snacks. I also have some left over pizza if you'd like that instead."

"Pizza? You ordered pizza?"

"No, the frozen kind. Who delivers pizza in the middle of the night in this town anyway?"

"Well, whatever, I'm good without food for now. What are you watching?"

"Some bad romantic comedy my mom and Carrie watched the other day. I couldn't find any of my DVD's. It's not that bad; you would probably like it." I stared at him suspiciously.

His behaviour was quite different than it had been earlier. His voice had a different, more jovial tone to it, and his aura was slightly less angry and a bit more positive.

"I'm noticing you're . . . well when you sober up you seem to be in a pretty good mood." From what I understood, usually people were moody after they sobered up from too many drinks. Perhaps he was the exception.

"I have had some time to think. I've formulated a new plan that I think will turn out a bit better for me. And, probably, everyone else."

"In the time I've been asleep you've formulated a new plan? What kind of plan?"

"Nothing for you to worry about. You should go back to sleep, you're probably tired."

"I'm awake now," I muttered dully. I sat up and drank some water.

"Oh, here, I made you some tea." He leaned over and grabbed a mug from the end table beside him and lifted the tea cozy to pour me some tea.

"You made me tea?"

"Yeah, you like tea when you get up in the morning." I also liked juice, but decided it wasn't the time to point such things out.

"I like milk in it," I mumbled.

"I put milk in the mug in advance." He handed me the mug and sure enough, the liquid was a rich caramel colour.

"Thanks," I said, now staring at my tea suspiciously instead of him. "But, I have to ask, why did you make me tea?"

"I already said, you like tea in the morning. Well, actually, you like tea more often than that but you get the idea." He leaned back and resumed eating his pasta.

"Okay, new question: since when are you trying to be nice to me?"

"Since a couple of hours ago."

"It came with the new plan formation?" Jeremy nodded. I sipped my tea. I wasn't really sure how to handle his new mood. I also wasn't really sure how long it would last for. Snuggling into the couch, I decided the best bet was to just enjoy the movie he was watching.

After about twenty minutes my phone went off again. Jeremy flipped it open and turned off the alarm.

"What was that?" I asked, secretly wishing I could stuff my phone back in my purse. Who knew when Liam would text me and ruin things.

"Andrea will be getting up soon. She will be wanting to drive you home or something."

"You mean your mom."

"Yeah, Andrea, that's what I said."

"Why do you mostly call her Andrea now?"

"I don't know." He shrugged. "I guess she stopped being only my mother and started being someone who has her own life and her own issues. She's not just my mom, she's also Andrea Johnston."

I wanted to pry and see if he would elaborate what had happened as to why she became a person other than his mother, but I knew he wouldn't yet. Besides, I already knew; I could be as patient as he needed.

"Anyway, when she gets up you can leave if you want but I think you should just sleep here for a bit and go home when it is light out." I didn't say anything. I was debating between the two options in my mind.

"Morning," Andrea said as she entered the room with a yawn.

"Hi," we both replied as we turned to look at her. Her hair was tussled and her face was red. She had looked better.

"I guess it is time to drive you home, Becky," she said.

"Maybe I should just have a nap here and go home later," I said. Jeremy turned towards me and gave a faint smile.

"Are you sure?" Andrea squinted at me.

"Yeah. You're probably too tired to drive right now and I don't feel like walking. Do you have somewhere I could sleep?"

Andrea looked from me to Jeremy and to me again. She gave Jeremy a second, slightly suspicious look and then shrugged.

"Suit yourself. You can sleep in my room. I'll grab you a sleeping bag." She started to move but Jeremy stood up. I noticed he did not waiver or grab onto anything.

"I'll do it."

"Listen drunky, you sit there. You're going to get an ear full when I come back." She pointed her finger sternly at him and then the couch. He sat back down. Andrea ushered me towards the hall where she opened a closet and pulled out a sleeping bag. I followed her to her room where she lay the sleeping bag out.

"I'm too tired to change sheets or any of that business; you can just use the sleeping bag on top right?"

"Sure, thanks Andrea."

"No problem. Now, before I go out there and ream him out, who is he sucking up to, you or me?"

"Probably both."

"No, seriously, which one is getting the bigger brown nosing? Wait, I know: did he make tea or coffee?"

"I'm not sure if he made any coffee . . ." My voice trailed off. I didn't want to say that he had made me tea.

"Ah so he made you tea then! It's you! Well that's probably more ideal." She smiled.

"More ideal? Also, how did you know he made me tea?"

"There was a mug on the table. If you had made your own tea you would have said so. If he didn't make me coffee it means he made you tea. Anyway, don't worry about it for now. Go to sleep, relax, forget about the unpleasantries that happened this evening and forget whatever you two yelled about briefly before I fell asleep. I'll see you when you get up." She gave me a motherly hug and closed the door on her way out.

Diary Entry: August 30, 2006

School is starting again soon. I'll be turning fifteen soon (enough) and my mom says I can have real dates! Not the kind like with Jeffrey before, where really he just came over and watched a movie with me and my mom. Maybe I'll even (finally) get my first kiss! Jessica and I talked about it and she said I should have it with Jeremy! As if! I asked her if she needed to go to the loony bin but she made some argument that he would be nice and then my first kiss would be done with so I wouldn't be clumsy when I kiss someone else later. While this is a good point, seems awkward to kiss Jeremy, plus how would I bring that idea up? Better to just wait and see if someone this year will ask me out and I can have my first real date . . .

Present Day: November 1, 2009

I woke-up feeling groggy and confused. I smashed my hand around the bed, hoping to find my phone next to me. No such luck. Sitting up, a clock next to Andrea's bed told me it was just about noon.

I got up and rolled up the sleeping bag. I didn't know where to leave it, so I left it sitting on the bed. Wishing I had a hair brush and a toothbrush, I ran my fingers through my hair and prepared to leave the bedroom.

I found Andrea in the kitchen, eating a sandwich and reading the paper. The only sound I could hear was the hum of the dishwasher. No sign of Carrie or Jeremy.

"Hey," I said as I slid down into the seat across from her.

"Oh hey Becky," she said, looking up from her paper. "Want a cup of coffee or anything?" She motioned her head towards the counter where a coffee pot sat.

"No thanks," I mumbled. I looked around the room, wondering where Jeremy was.

"He's sleeping," Andrea said as if she could read my mind.

"Who?"

"Jeremy. I have to wake him in about twenty minutes. I think he's fine. He doesn't seem too concussed and he probably was more drunk than anything else. He's sober now and seems fine."

"Right." I wasn't really sure what to say. "Did you talk to him about . . . I guess about what he did?"

"Of course. He's getting off pretty easy this time. I was going to have him mow the lawn at your mom's but November isn't really the season for him to play gardener, so instead he's cleaning the bathroom every week for the next month."

"He's going to be cleaning my bathroom?" I wasn't sure if I felt amused or embarrassed at the idea of him scrubbing our toilet.

"Your's and mine. It'll be good for him to do something nice for you and your mom. Besides, he probably wants to redeem himself a bit towards you." Andrea got up and put her plate in the sink. She went to the fridge and started taking out sandwich ingredients. "Sandwich? Ham and veggies?" She held up a deli package and a jar of mayonnaise.

"You're a good mom," I blurted out. I hadn't meant to be so blunt but I couldn't help admire how together she seemed.

"Because I offered to make you a sandwich? Thanks Beck." She smiled at me. She was joking.

"You know what I mean. And yes, I'd love a sandwich." She started preparing a sandwich for me.

"You're a good friend, Becky," she said as she lathered the bread with mustard. "Not everyone would be willing to sit in the hospital with me, and few would be willing to come over and monitor him. Especially after he's been distant and kept everything from you." She put a plate with a sandwich in front of me and sat back down. "He's lucky you care enough to deal with his problems." I nodded and bit into the sandwich. We stayed silent for a couple of minutes as I ate and Andrea rifled through her paper.

"Okay, well, I'm going to go check on him. If you like, I can drive you home after."

"Sure," I said, feeling nervous. I didn't know if Jeremy would get up or not. I wasn't sure what would happen after this evening with him. I felt like there was a change, but I didn't know if we would become closer or still stay at a distance.

Andrea got up and disappeared into the hall. I read a couple of articles in her paper while I waited. Eventually they both walked in.

"Morning," Jeremy mumbled as he sat down. I decided not to be cheeky and mention it was now the afternoon. He leaned his head down on his arm.

"Hung over?" I asked. I had never been hung over myself, but from what I gathered it was very unpleasant.

"Just tired," he muttered. Andrea put a glass of water in front of him.

"Well, will you be okay here for a bit?" she asked.

He moved up his unburdened arm to wave at her. "Sure."

"Okay. Becky, would you like me to drive you home now?" Jeremy sat up.

"I can walk, it's okay Andrea."

"Don't be silly, it's only—"

"I'll walk her home." Jeremy was looking slightly more wide-eyed and he gulped down his water. He stood up, indicating he was ready for the task.

"Will you now?" Andrea squinted at him suspiciously.

"Yeah, you stay home and relax, Mom, you're probably tired."

"Calling me Mom instead of Andrea are you? Sucking up I see? Well, I suppose I better enjoy it. If Becky wants you to walk her home that is fine, but I expect you to come straight back. No disappearing on a long soul filled walk to avoid me."

"Of course, Mom." He gave her an awkward pat on the back. They both turned to me expectantly.

"I guess I'll walk with Jeremy?" I said uncertainly. They nodded. Clearly my questioning answer was sufficient for them both.

"You ready?" Jeremy asked. I nodded. I put my empty plate in the sink and followed him with a wave to Andrea. He picked up the bag containing my Halloween costume and handed me my coat.

We walked out into the brisk, November air. The sky gave a gloomy gray to the neighborhood. I hoped the chilly air and ominous clouds indicated we would have some snow soon.

Jeremy came up to stand behind me, still shrugging his jacket on.

"I guess we'll just go straight to your place then," he said. I nodded and we silently started walking towards my house.

We remained silent for the entire walk. I didn't really know what to say to him. I wasn't sure how he would behave after last night and didn't want to push my luck by asking questions. I wanted to know more about his new plan for himself.

We arrived at the pathway to my house. I turned towards him, feeling far too awkward. Neither of us said anything for a moment.

"Well, thanks for walking me home," I said. I couldn't think of anything more exciting or clever to say.

"Sure. It's the least I could do considering you had to sacrifice such an exciting Halloween evening to sit next to me in the hospital."

"Do I detect sarcasm? Are you implying I'm boring?"

He grinned. "I'm not meaning to insult you. I was implying you're naïve. It's weird for me to come back and you're so similar to how you were before and I'm . . . I'm not." We fell silent again. "Anyway, I wanted to say something."

"Okay," I said nervously.

"Last night you said you were going to leave me alone after this. Well, I was thinking, maybe you could not leave me alone?"

"I'm not entirely sure what you mean. I'm supposed to not leave you alone?"

"You just want me to spell it out to be difficult don't you?"

"I have no idea what you're talking about." I smiled faintly.

"Ah I probably deserve that. What I mean is, maybe you could not avoid me? And maybe you could . . . give me some hints about that extinguishing torch you mentioned?"

"Hints?"

"Okay bad metaphor. Maybe you could help me, or I should probably say let me, repair some of the damage I've caused."

"Hmm . . . damage to what?"

"Seriously? You seriously want me to spell it out more?"

"Yes." I smiled coyly.

"Fine. I mean because I have been less than awesome am I able to try to make it up to you?"

"I'll think about it."

"You're being coy. Just say yes so I can go home before Andrea thinks I've joined a gang and moved to Los Angeles." He smiled and I felt a rush of affection. He looked softened and warm, like I remembered him.

"Yes. I'm curious to see how you'll make it up to me."

"You're not the only one." We stood there, smiling slightly sillily at each other. "I guess I should go," he said.

"Probably." We both stepped forward but then both leaned back, unsure what to do.

"It's too awkward to hug or something right now, so I'm just going to go." Jeremy started stepping backwards and jerked his thumb behind him. I nodded and turned to the house.

Diary Entry: October 15, 2006

Well, I haven't been asked out by anyone so far this year. Jessica has been doing the asking herself with guys. I'm not sure how that is turning out for her.

There is a guy I kind of like in my Science class. His name is Craig. I'm too shy to say anything to him, plus Jeremy is already my lab partner. I haven't told Jeremy as I'm not sure how he would react. Therefore, it seems unlikely I'll get the courage to talk to Craig as long as I have Jeremy cutting the sheep's eyeball for me. Oh well, at least this way I don't have to do any dissections!

Present Day: November 2, 2009

The next day I avoided Liam and Jessica. I had told Jessica a couple of things, but didn't really want to tell her the whole story. I also thought Liam might not be too pleased that I stayed at Jeremy's place. I finally had to go to Math class where I knew I would end up being coerced into telling them more. No way was I telling them the whole truth. I walked over to my locker on my way to Math class trying to figure out how much to tell Liam and Jessica. When I reached my locker, Liam was there getting his books out of my locker.

"Hey. I hope you don't mind that I've been using your locker since I know the combo," he said.

"It's okay. I don't mind." I dumped some books in my locker while he stood there watching. I turned to him, waiting for him to ask.

"So how did it go at Jeremy's?"

"I'll tell you in Math class." He shrugged.

"I'll meet you there, then." He walked off while I collected my books.

"Rebecca?" I whirled around to see a nervous looking Jeremy with a shoe box.

"Um, yeah?"

"Uh, I just came to say, uh, never mind." He started to walk off but I had a hunch the box was important.

"Jeremiah?" He turned around, chewing his lip.

"Yeah?"

"What's in the box?" He walked forward and handed the box to me.

"Here. I wanted to give this to you." I opened the box to see a bunch of letters. "I wrote you some letters I didn't send off. I wrote how I felt and what happened. I thought maybe this would be a good start to make things up to you?" I was astonished.

"Jeremy, you don't have—"

"No, Beck, just read them. I owe you that." He walked off with me staring at him, dumbfounded. I shoved the box in my locker and closed it. I ran into Math class just as the bell was ringing. Mr. Rambouski gave me a stern look and Liam grinned. I sat down and looked at Jeremy who was at the other end of the room. He was talking to Chris, one of the popular rebellious guys. I wished Robert still went to our school; before Jeremy and Robert hung out almost as often as I did with Jeremy.

I started writing my note to Liam while the teacher went through the review. Most of the partners Mr. Rambouski had assigned in September had problems with each other. Now, we were given the freedom to choose whoever you wanted as long as all the work was done. I had been extremely grateful for that because Mr. Rambouski was going to change the seating arrangement so you were next to your partner. While now it might not have been so difficult to be forced to sit next to Jeremy, it would have fairly awkward before and I wouldn't be able to pass notes with Jessica or Liam.

I threw Liam the note and watched him read it. He made a face at it. He handed the note to Jessica who quickly read it. Liam was scribbling down something on a piece of paper for me. He threw it on my desk and I picked it up.

> *So, Becky, you are some what getting along with Jeremiah. Huh. You two talked and he's going to be nice now? I'm not sure if I believe that. But then again, I barely know our friend Jeremiah. (do you think he minds the fact I call him Jeremih instead of Jeremy?) Anyway, I think I'll go talk to Jeremiah about this whole thing. I still don't like him.*

I sighed. I had thought Liam would get the idea I didn't need him to interfere. I had specifically left out all the stuff about torches and admitting I had been in love with him but too scared to say so.

I started writing him another note.

> *Liam, I don't think you should talk to Jeremy. I know you still don't like him, but you have to let things rest. Oh, and by the way, I don't think he knows you call him Jeremiah.*

Jessica then threw me a note. Mr. Rambouski still hadn't noticed that we were passing notes.

> *Beck, spill. You have to tell me what really happened. Liam may believe this abbreviated version, but I don't. I know there's way more details you're withholding. You're not holding back because something sexy happened, are you?*

I rolled my eyes. I decided I might as well tell Jess everything. I looked at the board to see that Mr. Rambouski was still copying notes. He told us to get together with our partners and work on some of the questions together. I moved my desk over to Liam's and we finished the questions. We were both fast at this type, although most of the class was struggling. Liam was basically good in all subjects. My main subject was Math.

"So it's all right if I talk to Jeremiah?" he asked.

"No." Liam sighed and tapped his pencil on his desk. "Liam?" I asked cautiously.

"Yeah?"

"What do you think of the idea of Jeremy getting therapy? Do you think it would help him?" He shrugged.

"Maybe. He probably should get therapy. Why, are you thinking of suggesting it to him?"

"I don't know. It was just a thought."

"Probably his mother either got him help already or tried to get him help. On that note, you remember he is her problem and not your's, right?"

"Sure sure."

"Which means you didn't need to spend Halloween in a hospital or at his house instead of partying."

"I know."

"And you don't need to spend all your free time worrying about him when you could be worrying about me."

"I need to worry about you, do I?" I asked him with a grin.

"Definitely. Who knows what I might do next. In fact, I had this devilish plan to rob a bank and head down to Vegas. I'll then gamble my money and multiply it and buy Vegas, where I will promptly re-name it 'Las Liam.'"

"You got a fake idea to get into the casino?"

"I'm still working on that. But as soon as I do, watch out, bank robbery and Vegas here I come!" I rolled my eyes at him and pushed him away.

For the remainder of class we were lectured on pre-calculus. Jessica kept giving me firm looks and pointing at her nose. I mostly ignored it. Liam smirked every time she touched or pointed to her nose.

When class got out I gave Liam a quick and sharp elbow as he watched Jeremy put books in his backpack.

"Leave him alone, would you?

"I want my thank-you for taking him to the hospital!" Liam objected.

"I thank-you. Will that do?"

"Not quite but it might if you—" he cut himself off as he caught me watching Jeremy leave the room. Jessica nudged him. I looked over to see her shake her head at him.

"Right well yes, Beck, I'll accept your thank-you in place of his. I'll see you ladies later." He picked up his bag and headed out without us.

"Is he mad or something?" I asked Jessica.

"Oh yeah, he's crazy all right. Anyway, tell me more! And what happened after Liam texted you, did Jeremy freak? Get jealous? Are they going to fight over you?" Her eyes filled with excitement and she practically bounced up and down.

"What, physically? Yeah right. Besides, Sandy would fight in place of Liam. How did you know he texted me anyway?"

"He told me."

"When were you talking to Liam?"

"I saw him in the hallway on my way to class this morning. So what did Jeremy say after Liam texted you?"

"I didn't tell him it was from Liam. However, when Liam phoned me . . . that was a different story." We reached my locker and I opened it, forgetting about the box Jeremy had given me.

"What's that?" Jess asked.

"It's part of what really happened. Here, hold." I handed her the shoe box and grabbed my books. She opened the box and looked inside but I closed the box and slammed my locker shut. We walked off with Jessica trying to open the box again.

We headed to her locker while I told her some of what really happened.

"So clearly he's threatened by Liam. And he seems to have decided to stop acting like a moron. But what on Earth does this shoe box have to do with anything?"

I raised my eyebrows at her. "Don't you have any gossip you want to share with me?" I asked. Her eyes widened and again she started attempting to maintain her bounce.

"Did you hear? I'm sooooo excited Will asked me out what should I wear? Small black skirt with my silky green shirt or go casual with my skinny jeans and expensive royal blue turtle neck?"

"Where are you going?" I had thought she was far too excited for just news about Jeremy.

"The movies."

"I don't know, maybe a bit more casual? What about the silky green top with the jeans? Did this happen on Halloween?"

"Hmm I suppose I could wear the green top with my jeans, slightly fancy but not too fancy . . . oh and yes, he asked me out on Halloween."

We left the school with our heads huddled together, talking as quietly as we could about our individual Halloween's. We avoided any groups of people in the hopes they couldn't hear our excited whispers. Can't have the entire school knowing Jess is excited about her date.

We arrived at my house and I opened the door to see Mom on the telephone with who I presumed was Andrea.

"Oh, yeah, that sounds great," she said. I waved to Mom who smiled and Jessica and I went to my room.

"So, should we read the letters?" Jessica asked as I put the shoe box down on the bed.

"I don't know, Jess. He probably wrote some pretty personal stuff in them. He meant for me to read them, not you."

"Oh, yeah. Well, what do you want to do?" I shrugged. We talked for a while, did some homework and read magazines. She left a few hours later and I went to talk to Mom.

"So," I said as she hung up the phone. "Jeremy gave me some letters he never sent to me."

She raised one eyebrow, a trick I have been trying to teach myself for several years.

"Really?"

"Really. I haven't read them yet. For all I know the letters are full of gibberish."

"Did he say what the letters were about?"

"Not really, but I assume the letters all had to do with when he was in Virginia."

"A fair assumption. If I were you, I wouldn't share them with Jessica though. They're probably fairly private. And giving you the letters is a way for him to tell you what happened to him without actually having to verbally say it to you. Be considerate of these letters."

"I know. Anyway, I'm hungry."

"Good, because I ordered pizza."

The pizza came shortly thereafter and we quickly ate it. I was eager to start reading the letters. After we finished, I went to my room to open the shoe box.

The first couple of unsent letters seemed more like rough drafts of letters he had actually sent me. They were mostly about things he had told me about: the new house, the new neighbourhood, Carrie's new crush. However, the forth unsent letter was fairly intense.

Rebecca:

> *Hey. I'm not really sure where to begin. I doubt I'll ever send this to you, so I guess it doesn't even matter how I start. I told you that I didn't write every day. This will probably be a little confusing for you. I know, seems out of character of me. The real deal is, I don't want to*

tell you what has been really going on. Why? I'm not sure. I guess I don't want to bother you with it. Anyway, things haven't gone too well. One day, a few months ago, I came home sick. (This is obviously when I still lived in Washington State.) I walked into my house to hear . . . well I didn't know what I was hearing. I was confused and walked toward the room where the sound was coming from. It was my parents' room. I knew it wasn't my mom, I had phoned her from school and knew she was at work.

For whatever reason, I walked into the room. I wish I hadn't. My dad was in bed, and he wasn't alone. I didn't know what to do. He didn't see me, so I left the house as fast as I could. I grabbed the spare key to your place and stayed there until two-thirty. I got home about twenty minutes before my mom. I didn't tell her.

I stared at the letter. I realized that must be heartbreaking for him. My own father had passed away when I was quite young, so neither of my parents could betray the other. But he must have felt betrayed by his father. If I had known, I don't think I would have been able to be in the same room as Tom, and he wasn't even my father. I pushed the letter away, wondering if I could skip a couple of paragraphs. Picking it back up, I decided I should finish it.

So nobody, including my father, knew I saw him and the other woman. Beck, I didn't want to tell anyone because I thought maybe I imagined it. I was sick that day; I had a high fever. I thought that maybe if I didn't tell anyone, it would go away. You know? You told me everything in your life. I'm sorry I kept a secret from you. But, eventually, I couldn't keep the secret from my mother.

After we moved, I thought for sure I had imagined it. Why would Dad move away from the girl if he didn't really love my mother? I found out I was wrong. The girl, Christina, had gotten a terrific job offer over here in Virginia. My dad arranged to get a job over here as well. I found out when Carrie and I went to visit him at his work and I saw her leave his office. I asked questions and found out she had, in fact, also just transferred to the hospital from Washington State. The whole reason I had to leave you, Rebecca, is because my father was sleeping with another woman. It's bad enough that he's cheating on my mother, but to make the rest of us move away from our home? I hated him! I had to tell my mother the truth. I told my father I saw him. He didn't deny it, but he asked I keep it from Carrie and my mom. He said he would tell them in time, when they were ready. As if they will ever be ready! So I told them.

Probably the hardest thing I have ever had to do is tell my mom what I saw. But I did it. I hate my father for what he did to me and my family, for moving us all for his own selfish purpose. I don't know if I'll ever forgive him.

Jeremy

I gulped a faint lump that had crept up into my throat. I wished I could take back what he had had to go through. If they had stayed here, perhaps he could have told me first and I could have been there with him when he told his mom. Maybe I could have made things easier for him. Maybe . . .

One of the sad things was I had always thought highly of Jeremy's father. He had always been, as far as I knew, a decent man. Maybe it was because he saved lives for a living that I had regarded him so well, but it was still a blow to read how he hurt his own family. At that moment, I also hated him.

I wanted to phone Jeremy, but besides not having his cell number (assuming he had a cell phone) I thought it would be best to keep reading first. I read through a couple more letters, mostly outlining fights with his parents. He started to write about trying drinking and the parties he went to. His attitude in the letters shifted significantly as he began partying; he sounded more angry and, I felt sad for thinking, selfish. He wrote about how he didn't care that his mom would cry when she would find bottles in his room.

I then came across a letter I wasn't entirely sure he meant to include.

> So . . . recently I've been partying with this girl, Kim. I don't really know much about her, and to be honest, haven't really cared. She's a break away from the madness of home, and we spend our time drunkenly groping each other.
>
> Anyway, Tom announced he was going to marry his girlfriend, Christina. I was . . . well pissed doesn't quite describe it. So I found Kim and we got plastered at a party at some house, I don't quite remember where, and we slept together. I didn't really mean for it to happen, it just did. It's not like I was trying to save myself or something, but I know this is something you won't shrug off and I know I would be stunned if I found out you had done the same.
>
> A part of me is panicking: I barely even like her and who knows where she has been before me. I'm fuzzy

103

on how safe I was and I can't imagine what would happen if I impregnated her. I have enough crap to go through without thinking about a baby. Not like I can even imagine how I would raise one, especially without wanting to be anywhere near Tom.

As soon as I find out if Kim is up the pole or not, I'm out. I don't know where I'm headed right now, but waking up the next day I realized I wish I had done things differently. She's not going to be good for me and I have to get my life in better order before my mom ships me off to boarding school or something.

At least boarding school would be better than being a father.

If I ever give you this letter, or ever tell you, I hope it doesn't change your view of me. I hope you can still see me as the guy who barely even had a date and worried more about vampire attacks then pregnancy.

Jeremy

I read on, ignoring the clock next to me reminding me that I was staying up far too late. I couldn't think of pausing to go to the bathroom, let alone stop reading to go to bed.

More letters described trips to a therapist with his mom. The therapist advised her he needed a change in location, a fresh start. While the therapist did not say anything about moving away from Tom, Andrea decided the best thing for both of them would be to move back here.

Dear Rebecca:

I'm moving back. I wrote a letter to you today. I put in it about coming back to scare off your boyfriends. I seriously doubt you will figure out that I'm moving back from that. I wish I could talk to you, but I'm not going to say anything. I can't tell you what's going on, Beck. You would hate me if you knew what had happened. I don't want you to hate me. You'll probably be upset because I won't talk to you. But you'll live. You have the Liam guy you wrote about in some of your letters. Just keep him from hurting me, will you? Oh, and I'm not actually going to scare off your boyfriends if you have any. Maybe just glare from a distance and wish bad thoughts upon them.

Tom wants me to be part of the wedding. Yeah right. I'm so glad to be leaving him behind. I'm hoping if I'm in Washington State I can stay away from him and his wedding.

Anyway, by the time you get the letter I sent off, I'll be there. In time for school to start. I guess I'll see you soon.

Jeremy

I felt mildly surprised he knew he was coming back and made a conscious decision to keep it from me. A small part of me had thought perhaps Andrea had sprung it on him after he had written the most recent letter I received. Of course, it had been optimistic thinking to hope he hadn't told me because he hadn't known himself.

I packed the letters back into the box and got into bed. I felt like crying and I knew it was because he had slept with someone else. It's not like we were together; we didn't even live in the same city and had made no commitment to each other. Just the same, I felt betrayed. I also felt like an idiot. I had been denying to myself the entire time he had been gone that I wasn't holding myself back for him, but reading what he had done, I knew I had been holding back. It wasn't just physically holding back, I hadn't been attached to any guy romantically since Jeremy had left. My closest male attachment was to Liam, and only recently had I began to suspect there may be something beyond friendship happening.

The two guys I had briefly dated had always tried to take a "next step" with me. The reality is, with all of them, I simply came up with an excuse for the situation and broke-up with them thereafter. Every time a boyfriend would try to even grope more than my breast, I claimed female problems and exited. It wasn't just sex: I wanted all of the steps to be with Jeremy and I would think it every time the situation came about.

I curled up in my bed, trying to breathe slowly to keep myself from crying. It wasn't his fault I had held back. Besides, I had had no intention of sleeping with any of them and by cutting them off at my chest I never had to explain they weren't going to get there. But I could have given more emotionally.

I remember knowing Adrian, my most recent boyfriend, was only asking me out because he had a reputation for trying to crack the more prude girls at our school. He hadn't said it, but I had known. And I had thought, whatever, it'll be fun to date him for awhile, make-out at a couple of parties, and then leave him to complain in the locker room about me. I didn't care that he probably had no real interest in my personality, and I certainly hadn't had an interest in his.

I sighed. I was making myself feel more and more like a tease and an idiot. Determined to fall asleep, I listed vampire movie titles out loud to distract myself until eventually I stopped muttering and drifted to dream land.

Chapter 7

When I arrived at school, I was determined to talk to Jeremy. I wasn't sure what to say about him sleeping with what's-her-face, but I needed to bring it up.

Unfortunately, I had a test in the morning and I had barely studied for it. The test was right before lunch, so I spent every moment I could before looking through my notes.

At lunch, after my test, I found Jeremy. He was sitting on the steps of the school with a math book. I envied him, feeling confident enough to sit by himself with a book. I never sat around the school by myself; if I didn't know where any of my friends were I wandered around until I found someone to study or sit with.

"Hi," I said as I sat down beside him. He looked up, smiled and closed his book.

"Hi."

"You studying or something?" I asked. He nodded. "I can come back later, if you want."

"No, it's fine." I began to chew my lower lip nervously. I found it slightly peculiar he didn't look at all faltered or anxious.

"So, I read the letters last night."

"All of them?" he asked in surprise. I nodded.

"Um, there was one in particular that I wasn't really sure if you meant for me to read right now. Well, I don't know, maybe you did I mean you gave it to me to read what else would you want me to do with it . . ." I was muttering and not sure what to do. His brow furrowed as he thought.

"You know what, you don't even seem to realize what I'm talking about so really, lets forget I said anything, obviously it's not important to you so I think I'll just . . ." I started to get up as he looked confused.

"Wait . . ." He pulled his backpack onto his lap and started rummaging around in it. He pulled out a folded piece of paper. I rolled on my feet, wanting to leave. I had a horrible anxious feeling in my stomach and thought it would be a good time to find Jessica and sit near a bathroom.

He opened the paper and started reading. His eyes widened in shock and he turned to me, his mouth gapping.

"Shit I think I . . . did you read something about . . . I didn't mean for you to find out like . . . I . . ." his voice drifted off again. I sat back down.

"So you . . ." I couldn't actually say the words so I stopped talking. I turned my head away slightly.

"Shit," he muttered again as he put his head in his hands. We sat there silently for a couple of minutes.

"I was going to tell you later. I thought I pulled that letter out of the bunch, but I pulled out the one after," he said.

"Okay. Are there any other letters you pulled out? Any other secrets I might want to know about? Or maybe not?"

"No, that was the only one. I pulled that one out because I thought . . . well you made several references to an extinguishing torch on the weekend and I figured that might make it worse. Besides, I probably sounded a bit bitter or nasty about it, if I told you myself I could sugar coat it a little." He fell silent and I didn't bother to respond. I still wasn't looking at him.

"Listen I'm sorry I know if you had—"

"Can we talk about it later?" I turned to look at him. He had leaned closer to me and I could see he was inching his hand to mine. He sighed.

"Yeah. I guess now isn't really the best time. Maybe we could—"

"Hey." I jumped, startled. Jeremy stopped talking, cut off by the greeting. I turned to see Liam standing behind us.

"Hey, Liam, what's up?" I asked, trying to sound casual.

"I was wondering where you were. Jessica said you were off finding someone, so I assumed you were finding Jeremiah."

"Jeremiah?" Jeremy said in confusion. Nobody but me called him Jeremiah. Even then, it was rare I called him by his full name, mostly he was just Jeremy.

"Yeah. That's your name, isn't it?"

"I guess so. Nobody calls me Jeremiah but Rebecca."

"Just like nobody calls her Rebecca except for you. Isn't that cute?" I winced, not enjoying his sarcasm.

"Why were you looking for me?" I asked Liam. He shrugged.

"I wondered how your test went."

"It was okay." Liam nodded. None of us said anything.

"Well, Becky, I'll see you later." Jeremy stood up and picked up his backpack and book. I stood up too.

"Oh okay, sure." I felt relieved one of them had decided to leave.

Jeremy leaned forward so his mouth barely brushed my ear.

"I'm sorry," he whispered, then leaned back. I pushed my lips together, trying not to show too much emotion. Liam watched through narrowed eyes.

Jeremy gave Liam a firm nod and started to turn away.

"Oh, Jeremy, wait," I said, thinking of something. He turned back.

"Um, isn't there something you would like to say?" I provided awkwardly. He looked confused. I made a drinking motion and he stared at me funny.

"Oh! I see. Right. So hey Liam, thanks for taking me to the hospital and all." Liam gave a curt nod in return. Jeremy smiled at me and left.

"So . . . what's up?" I couldn't really think of what to say to Liam. He had been kind of weird the day before and I wasn't really in the mood to fight with him.

"I don't know. Just thought I would see how you were. Maybe get my books from your locker. He isn't using your locker, is he?"

"Who, Jeremy?" Liam nodded. "No, he has not used my locker and I did not give him the combination. If you were taking your books from my locker there's no need: Jeremy doesn't have access to steal them or anything." Despite my thoughts about not wanting to argue, I felt annoyance rush through me and knew I had started to raise my voice.

"I meant take my chemistry books out before class started. I did not mean permanently."

"Oh." I felt a little like an idiot, but Liam had been acting moody since the pseudo boyfriend argument.

"Hey, are we okay?" I asked, not really sure how else to bring it up.

"Yeah, of course."

"Okay, well are you okay? You've seemed a bit disgruntled lately."

"You know what? I don't really like him that much. I'm not too excited about the prospect of him coming to our movie nights or meeting us at a coffee shop after school or joining us for the occasional video game marathon."

"And you think that what, because he spoke to me the other day before class and you found me talking to him just now that I'll bring him along to everything?"

"Whatever. Lets just go to your locker." I opened my mouth to argue with him, but decided against it and followed him to my locker. We both took books out of my locker silently. I was contemplating asking Liam if he wanted to hang out on the weekend, but I wasn't sure if I was asking because I wanted to hang out with him and his grumpiness or if I was asking in the hopes it would make him feel better. Besides, he would probably first ask if Jeremy was coming before agreeing to anything.

"I'll see you later?" I asked sceptically as I closed my locker. Liam nodded and turned towards his chemistry class. I sighed, shifting the weight of my books while I thought about him, then turned to go to my history class.

Later that night I was ignoring my history paper while I thought about Liam. I knew Jessica had been trying to imply for the past little while that Liam liked me, but I wasn't really sure how true it was. It was very hard to know if Liam's reaction was jealousy because he liked me or jealousy because he was not the centre of attention. Often, when I hung out with him, he had been the person I talked to most and showed the most interest in. Not because he was more liked or closer to me than the others, but because I found him funny. Or, at least, I use to. We use to sit in class and pass notes poking fun of something (often, poking fun of each other) or making ridiculous diabolical plans that would never be fulfilled. Sometimes he would have me in stitches over something nobody else seemed to think was funny, but I found hilarious. I doted on him for it. While I did tease him constantly, I often prided on his wit and make a point of showing how much I enjoyed his company. There really was no reason for me to sit next to, and pair up with, Liam in math class over Jessica.

I knew that whatever Jessica thought was going on with Liam, it could be pure jealousy that perhaps it would be someone else who would become the focus of my attention. I doubted it was really the idea of Jeremy coming to movies and the like with us, but that it would be Jeremy I would whisper to in the theatre, make private jokes with and basically dote on. The reality is I probably would switch my attention to Jeremy if he started coming to things. It wasn't like he made me cry with laughter, so much as I had often felt so close to him. There had been times we had done tasks out of habit in unison and coordination. We did things seamlessly and easily together, and I was always drawn to be nearest to him. I felt drawn to Liam out of amusement, but drawn to Jeremy out of understanding and closeness.

My phone rang, startlingly me out of my thoughts. I glanced at the number. I didn't recognize it.

"Hello?"

"Hey," Jeremy's voice said on the other end.

"Oh, hi. You have my number?"

"Yes, that would be why I managed to correctly dial it."

"Ah, yes that makes sense." I felt my face flush slightly. For some reason, I felt a small thrill go through me because he was calling.

"What are you up to?"

"My history paper. Speaking of which, when did the war end?"

"Becky, do you know how many wars there were?"

"No."

"Ah. Well how about I come over and help you?"

"When?"

"Now."

"Oh." I wasn't really sure what else to say. It was only eight, which meant plenty of time for him to come over and help me before I wanted to go to bed.

"Well you know, my project isn't due for another week so I can probably—"

"Great then we'll have time to talk about other things. I'll see you soon." He hung up before I had the chance to finish. I started at my phone with surprise and annoyance. Who did he think he was just inviting himself over?

"Mom," I called, running out from my room. I found her in her room, watching television in bed.

"What's up?"

"Jeremy's coming over for a bit. He won't stay late though," I assured her. She raised her eyebrows.

"I guess that's fine," she said as the phone rang. She turned to grab it and I raced back to my room. I picked up my books and notes on my paper and took them to the living room. I raced around for the next ten minutes, brushing my hair and teeth, tidying some things in the living room, and then trying to calm myself down. I was nervous.

The doorbell rang and I breathed out very slowly. I was still in the process of changing; I had traded my sweat pants for jeans but was still braless under my class of 2010 sweatshirt.

"You going to get that?" My mom called as the doorbell rang again.

"Yes," I called back. I abandoned my closest and went to the door.

I could see him peering in. I opened the door.

"Hi," I said, hoping he couldn't notice my lack of support.

"Oh, hey, I actually thought you might not answer." I rolled my eyes and stepped aside to let him in. "Where's your mom?" he asked.

113

"She's watching television in her room." He nodded. I debated excusing myself to change, but then decided I didn't want to think I was changing for him. I could fake needing to use the bathroom and put a bra on?

"Living room?" he asked. I nodded.

We sat down in the living room. He (I believed purposefully) waited for me to sit and then sat right next to me. He clearly ignored the other couch, or even the other side of the couch I had sat on. Grumbling to myself, I wiggled around and adjusted to a cross legged position angled towards him. This way, it was much harder for him to inch closer with my knee in the way.

"So can we talk?" he asked. I ignored his question and passed him my notes for my paper. Despite my two month long desire to speak to him, I found I would rather just not talk about the letter he had given me. Well, particularly the one letter.

"Can you look over my notes for me? Make sure they seem accurate?" He sighed, not looking too thrilled, but took my notes and started looking them over. Silently, he read through my notes, making occasional marks, while I wrote out my outline for my paper. I was also still thinking about my bra/bathroom idea.

"Here," he said after about fifteen minutes, passing me back my notes. "So, you read all the letters? In one night?"

"Yes. I wanted to understand what had happened."

"Well, I have the letter I took out if you want to read it as well." I shrugged. Jeremy attempted to shift a bit closer, trying to avoid my knee. "So I really am sorry I—"

"That must have been hard for you," I interrupted. I wasn't sure I was ready to talk about him sleeping with someone yet. Besides, didn't he have more to apologize for than that? Of course, he could have been finishing with "said to you that stuff back in the car in September."

"What?"

"Seeing your dad with another woman. That must have been hard. I mean, seeing him in the heat of the moment would be traumatizing enough, but with another woman . . . well that just sucks." Perhaps it was callous of me to just say it, but that was what I really wanted to talk about.

Jeremy leaned back, moving farther away from my knee. I carefully moved my open history book onto my chest as I also leaned back. Who needs a bra?

"Yes, it was hard."

"Why didn't you tell me?"

"What I saw? Or everything thereafter?"

"Both."

"I don't know." He looked away to stare at his hands. "I guess I felt like . . . well I think I even said in one of my letters that I didn't want you to view me differently and obviously knowing everything changes how you think of me."

"Yes, I believe you did write that in a letter." I grimaced as I remembered he wrote it in the letter where he admitted to losing his virginity.

"Yeah well . . . you think of me differently now and I had idealized home or I guess I should say home here, and you, and I wanted to leave both untainted. I imagined being able to come back and forget everything and I would go back to being who I was before. Without the problems and mood swings and stuff."

"Well, you kind of botched that plan by avoiding me and then behaving like a dick. If you had been all jovial and excited things may have been very different."

Jeremy smiled. "But that would also be unrealistic of me. I would have had to have told you about everything at some point, and you would have wondered why my mom and I came by ourselves. Besides, you would have wanted to know about me sleeping with someone before we discussed you know . . . us." So there was now an "us" to discuss?

"Yeah," I mumbled, now being the one to look down at my hands. Jeremy scooted forward again, banging his thigh into my knee.

"I know you're upset about it," he said softly. I shrugged. "I know how I would feel if it was reversed."

"You don't know how I feel," I said sharply.

"You're right, I don't, and I never said I did."

"Were you careful?" I asked slightly accusingly. I turned towards him, staring him straight in the eye. He looked startled.

"Probably not," he admitted.

"Probably not?"

"I don't remember. But I went to a clinic."

"Really?"

"Yeah, really. I'll find the form for you if you want. All clean."

"I only need it if I'm going to be at risk so don't worry, I won't be needing it any time soon, if at all," I said darkly. "And no babies?"

"No I secretly brought triplets with me, didn't you notice?"

"Dude I don't know how long ago this was, maybe she's about to pump one out, how am I suppose to know?" I gave him another glare for his sarcasm.

"Any babies she has will no relation to me. Though I don't have a form to prove that one."

"Again, not like I have a reason to need any of these "forms" from you."

"Right. No worries." He fell silent. "So will you tell me how you feel about it?" he asked.

"About what?"

"What do you mean 'about what?' About me sleeping with someone!"

"You want to know how I feel?" I asked. If he really wanted to know, I would tell him.

Jeremy nodded. I sat up straight, trying to be level with him.

"Okay. I feel stupid."

"Stupid? Why?"

"Because I held back. I was holding onto the idea of you and I did jack all with anyone the entire time you were gone." Angrily, I pushed the book aside. It had fallen onto my lap when I had sat up.

"Really?" Jeremy seemed pleased. He was grinning slightly. "Why?"

"Because every time someone tried to reach a point beyond where you got with me, I thought of you. I wanted all of it to be with you so I held out. Held out everything."

"Even . . ." he stared at my breasts.

"Hey! Eyes here. And no, I didn't hold that out, you already got there so that was fine. But nobody got farther than you."

"Wow seriously?" He was looking delighted and smiling smugly.

"Don't look so smug. I probably have the iciest reputation in school because I wanted to share things with you and discover that you went ahead and did everything with someone else." I frowned.

"Sorry," he said. He still kept glancing down to my chest. Remembering my bra, I felt my face flame and crossed my arms over my chest.

"Sorry," he said again, trying to put on a straight face. "I was smiling because I don't know what I wouldn't have given for that two years ago and somehow I got it anyway."

"You're an—"

"But you're right," he said, cutting me off. "I didn't bother to keep it in my pants and, well, you definitely kept your pants on if nobody got farther than me. Before we continue, why aren't you wearing a bra?" He raised his eyebrows at me.

"Well you said you were coming over and I only had time to put my jeans on before you arrived."

"Right so you thought it would be better to stick to your firm "pants on" policy considering I've already fondled the upper area?" I bit my lip to avoid laughing. I couldn't help it.

"I was wearing pants just different ones!" I protested meekly.

"Sure you were. Care to explain why you were wearing different pants before I arrived?" He was leaning forward again, and had shuffled as close to my knee as he could get.

"I spilled mustard on the other ones," I said, still trying not to laugh.

"Uh huh." He gently pushed my knee out so he could lean in closer.

"Really," I said softly. He was now close enough he could bend forward to kiss me.

"You were enjoying mustard while you worked on your paper?" he was smiling widely and touched the side of my face with his finger.

"Mustard sandwich," I provided feebly. Jeremy curled his hand at the back of my neck and tilted his head towards mine.

All of a sudden, I felt a surge of panic. I didn't know if I was ready for him to kiss me, and for whatever reason, I couldn't stop thinking of Liam. I knew I did not want to have to tell Liam about this. I wasn't ready to deal with how I felt about Jeremy or how Liam fit into anything.

I quickly ducked my head down and tried to slither away slightly. Jeremy withdrew. I put my head in my hands, feeling embarrassed. After a moment, Jeremy placed his hand on my back. When I didn't say anything to protest, he rubbed it up and down.

"I'm sorry," I mumbled after awhile. "I guess I really am a tease or prude or whatever."

"No you're not. I'm sorry. I shouldn't have tried so soon. You weren't ready; I knew that from the way you were sitting. I just thought if I had the right moment it would be okay."

"Yeah well . . ." I fell silent, not really sure what else to say.

"Anyway, lets go back to what we were talking about before I asked about your bra. So nothing happened physically with any dudes, but what about mentally? I mean, did you . . . I don't know decide to fall in love with anyone?"

I peeked out from behind my hands to see him watching my closely.

"Obviously not you thick head. Why would I refuse everything beyond half-way to second base because I want to experience it with you if I'm in love with someone else?"

"Right, right, just checking. But you dated, right?"

"Yes. I actually stopped dating someone the first day of school."

"Oh yeah, Adrian." I lifted my head from my hands.

"You knew about that?"

"Yeah. Why did you date him anyway?" I shrugged.

"I don't know. Seemed like a fun idea at the time. Nothing much to do over summer; I figured I might as well have someone to call up for Saturday night making out."

"But doesn't he have a reputation for trying to devirginize girls or something?"

"He sure does! Which is probably why he asked me out. I wasn't worried, I knew he wasn't going to get anywhere. But how did you know all this?"

"I'm in his gym class. So I literally heard the locker room talk. I actually already knew before this evening that at the very least he hadn't gotten farther than me. He talked to the guys about it at the start of school."

"Did he say we broke-up because he couldn't seduce me or something?"

"No." Jeremy hesitated slightly.

"What?"

"Well . . . I know why he asked you out and why he approached you to break-up on the first day of school."

"Really? He said all of this in the locker room? You weren't even here when he asked me out, it was on the last day of school."

"I know."

"So how do you know? And why did he ask me out and break-up with me?"

"You really want to know?" Jeremy asked. I nodded. "Okay, well he made a bet that he could seduce you over the summer."

"What? A bet with who?!" Jeremy winced and looked away.

"I don't think I should tell you."

"Well it wasn't you because you weren't here, so I think you should." He sighed.

"If I tell you, do you promise not to let anyone know it was me who told you?"

"Yeah fine," I said.

"Liam."

"What?! Liam?"

"Yeah and Liam collected the ten bucks from Adrian on the first gym class. Liam asked him for how far he had gotten and was quite smug about it. To be honest, if it hadn't been Liam who made the bet, Adrian probably would have lied and told everyone in the room he banged you. Probably would have put me in a worst mood for a couple of weeks, so let's consider it a good thing it was Liam who made that bet."

"Would Adrian have even asked me out if they hadn't made a bet?"

"I don't know, I wasn't here. Are you upset that he may have only asked you out because of a bet?"

I thought about it for a moment. I wasn't really upset about the bet, more that Liam had made the bet. After all, Jessica and I had bet on when Adrian would try to break up with me.

"No. I wasn't exactly attached to him. Why are you trying to defend Liam anyway?"

"I don't know. It was a good bet." Jeremy smiled slightly and I smacked his arm.

"Why would Liam make the bet anyway?"

Jeremy shrugged. "Besides the easy money?" I nodded. "Well, and this may sound weird, it's a way to find out what you do with boyfriends."

"Why would he care? And if so, why wouldn't he just ask?"

"Asking you how far you get with your boyfriends would be pretty awkward and slightly inappropriate. Only girls can ask girls those questions."

"Sure but I just told you," I said."

"I didn't ask though, you volunteered. And, which may explain why Liam wanted to know, you're telling me because you know I have an interest in you physically and where you've been physically. Perhaps Liam has an interest in you physically?"

"You're asking if Liam has the hots for me?" Jeremy shrugged. He had already said Liam wanted me before, but now he was acting nonchalant about it.

"Do you think he has the hots for you?" I contemplated for a moment. Liam did not display jealousy like Jeremy had, and he had asked out girls since I had become friends with him, but he had been very different since Jeremy had arrived and I had confessed our history.

"Honestly, I'm not sure. Sometimes I think he does, sometimes I think he's just weird. Most of the time, I don't think it's an interest in dating me, so much as enjoying my attention. I'm not really sure how to explain it, but generally it's hard for him to receive positive female attention, and I provide him with plenty of positive attention. I mean, when I dated Adrian nothing changed between myself and Liam because I had little interest in Adrian and continued to lap attention to Liam." I smiled, feeling satisfied with my answer.

"And why, exactly, do you give so much attention to Liam?"

I was about to say "the same reason I gave you so much attention" but realized Jeremy may point out that later turned into a romantic interest.

"He's funny. And he appreciates my company."

"I appreciate your company."

"Indeed you do, which is why he may be feeling left out. While you were gone, he was the only male around to appreciate my company. Now you're here and my attention is divided. Even before we started talking, I spent a fair amount of time worrying about you and how I was going to try to talk to you. When I have spent time with him, I've been distracted. I think he assumes he'll be cut out of my life once you're back in it." I thought back to the argument we had where he referred to himself as my pseudo boyfriend.

"I'm not going to ask you to stop hanging out with him," Jeremy said.

"Sure, but you probably don't want to hang out with him. If I spend as much time with you as I did when you were here before, I won't have much spare time left for Liam when you consider my other friends, school, preparing for graduation . . . it's not like the three of us are going to go to the movies together." Jeremy nodded thoughtfully.

"So speaking of graduation, what's going to happen when we graduate?" he asked.

"What do you mean? We go to college."

"Yeah, I realize you were planning on going to college, I just meant . . . where were you planning on going?"

"I don't know yet, I thought you wanted to wait a bit before deciding." Suddenly I realized what he meant. We had agreed before he moved away that we would go to college together, and in the summer had written letters about choosing colleges. Jeremy had said he wanted to wait until the school year started before deciding.

"Do you mean are we still going to go together?" I asked him.

"Yes. Did you want to?" I thought about it. I did. I had had nice daydreams of us going to college together, living on campus together, exploring a new city and a new life together. Of course, that had all been before he came back with a darker side.

"I think so," I finally said. He looked relieved.

"Where did you want to go?" he asked me.

"No clue, you decide."

"Me?" he questioned.

"Yes you. You make all the big decisions."

"What? I don't make all the big decisions!" he objected.

"Sure, boss." I gave him a faint grin.

"Well, whatever, what schools did you have in mind?"

"Not sure. Are your grades okay right now? I imagine they must have slipped at some point and the schools I mentioned to you in the letters might not want us."

"You mean they might not want me," he corrected.

"You, me, whatever." Jeremy sighed.

"My grades aren't too bad. That's actually why I said before I wanted to wait before deciding. They're not as great as they use to be, and I have a drunk and disorderly ticket that might be on record."

"Really?" I asked, feeling kind of annoyed. Jeremy shrugged.

"Anyway, I don't want to hold you back. I don't want you to go to a crappier school because of me."

It was my turn to shrug. "How much do you really think the school I attend will affect my future paycheque? It's not like we're talking about going to Harvard or something. Besides, we could switch schools if your grades get better."

"I guess. Still I . . ."

"Don't worry about it. But could you make a list of schools please so I can get started on our forms and stuff?"

"Why don't you pick the schools and I'll do the forms?" he asked.

"Because you have tiny scratchy handwriting and refuse to computerize documents and you, like I said, make the big decisions. When we're accepted into schools we'll decide on where together," I said firmly.

"Sure, boss," he said with a smile. "Where will we live?" he asked. I winced, feeling slightly awkward.

"Residence?"

"Are they co-ed?" I hadn't really thought about living in a co-ed dorm.

"I think it'll depend on the school," I said.

"We could . . . share a place . . ." I opened my mouth and then closed it. We sat there, fairly awkwardly, for several minutes.

"Do you really think that's a good idea? We only recently started talking again. It's a big step," I finally said.

"It wouldn't be for another ten months. I imagine by then we'll be ready for it."

"Okay, possible, but do you mean share a place . . . like a one bedroom or a two bedroom?" It occurred to me we were not even dating yet, and an admittance of love a year ago was not enough for me to share a bedroom let alone a bed.

"I don't know, I suppose it'll depend on price and availability, either way both would be bigger than a dorm room and . . . oh, wait, I see what you mean." Jeremy raised his eyebrows. "I meant like . . . um . . . I did mean sharing a bedroom, but maybe I shouldn't assume."

"And what were you assuming?" I felt myself blush slightly.

"Not that we would be sleeping together in a sex way, if that's what you're worried about."

"Good because—" Jeremy waved his hand to cut me off.

"You can stay virginal as long as you like, I wasn't thinking about that. I meant I shouldn't assume we would be together in a way that would warrant sharing a bed, whether or not we're having sex in it. I mean like sharing a place without you having some other dude worry about why his girlfriend is sharing her living quarters with me." Jeremy gave a sly grin.

"I'm forced to date you, nobody else wants to go near me with you marking me as your territory!"

"Damn straight," he muttered. "Well, I'm glad we decided we'll start dating at some point, you out of necessity and me out of . . . oh I guess I shouldn't say desire I just said I wouldn't have sex with you."

"That's not what you said, you said you would wait, which is very sweet." I smiled at him fondly.

"Ah, well, I already did it and it's not as big of a deal as I thought it would be. Besides, plenty of other in between stuff." He shrugged and I wrinkled my nose.

"Jeremy, that was less sweet."

Jeremy grinned and leaned forward, grabbing both of my arms.

"If it is with me, you can wait as long as you want. I would rather wait for you than do it with anyone else." I blushed as he grinned at me.

"That was more sweet, thanks," I said softly. "But, anyway, I haven't yet agreed to date you, I just said you attempt to force my hand. I'm still deliberating on the decision to date you, assuming you even ask me out."

"Right, right, I know. I'll get there. We'll get there." He smiled at me and released my arms.

"How about we decide on living situations after we are accepted and decided on a school?" I suggested.

"Sure," he said.

We talked for a little longer before Jeremy said he should get home. Before he left, he gently held my hand and leaned in to kiss my cheek. I knew he was trying to suck up to me, but I couldn't help but feel a giddy twist in my stomach.

Chapter 8

I managed to go through Wednesday without any complications. I avoided Liam as much as I could, not knowing how to tell him I knew he had placed a bet on my virginity. I was feeling pretty annoyed about the whole thing, and knew eventually I would have to tell him I had found out and tell him I was upset.

I did, however, tell Jessica everything that had happened, including ducking away from Jeremy's kiss.

"You need to figure out what's going in with Liam," she advised. I made a face. School had finished for the day and we were at Jessica's place. Her wardrobe was spread across her bed and her final outfit for Friday's date had been chosen.

"That's just plain awkward. How about I ignore the issue instead?" I proposed.

"Right and not kiss Jeremy ever again because you feel concerned about Liam?" she countered.

"I didn't not kiss Jeremy just because of Liam; I also ducked away because I'm not sure how I feel about Jeremy yet."

"Really?" Jessica asked doubtfully.

"Sure. I mean he has an edge to him he didn't have before and he said some mean things when he was trying to keep me away."

"Yeah I think you want him badly but are holding back a bit because you feel confused. I think not only do you want Jeremy, you want him to work for it just a little." She held her fingers up with just a small space in between and looked at me through it."

"No," I disagreed, feeling slightly taken aback.

"Of course you do! And who wouldn't after he tried to hurt you so that you would be pissed off with him. Worst plan ever, by the way. It's fair enough to hold out on him a bit, he's been gone for a year and comes back a jackass. Well, maybe like a jackass coating over his usual self."

"Do you think he started behaving nicer because I told him I had been in love with him too?" I asked.

Jessica shrugged. "Probably. To be fair to him he may have been a bit bitter that he told you and you didn't return the favour. He may have also avoided you just to avoid dealing with that complication. And no offense, Becky, but he would have the right to be a bit bitter. It's not like he stayed here to have a chance to deal with the equivalent of a rejection."

"I guess," I said.

"Which brings me back to my point: I think you should sort out Liam so you and Jeremy can go fool around in some bushes. And then, after, we can double date!" She smiled in delight as I rolled my eyes.

"I'm not sure about your bushes idea, and don't you want to date Will without someone else there so you can put your moves on him?"

"I mean later, after I've put the moves on him. And you're right, you're probably not a bushes kind of girl. So what are you going to say to Liam?"

"I don't know. Maybe: "Liam I've noticed you've been a little hostile since Jeremy has made an appearance and am wondering why you made a bet with Adrian about how far he could get with me and why you seem so perturbed by Jeremy?" What do you think?"

"How much do you really care about the bet with Adrian? I mean, we made a bet as to when he would break-up with you."

"If the bet didn't end with the start of the school year you would have won," I pointed out.

"Right! Better bring up that bet then, tell Liam he owes me ten bucks. But seriously, do you care?"

"Not about the actual bet. I mean, it was a dumb bet and I didn't care much for Adrian anyway. I'm just concerned that Liam is trying to make money off of my prude status."

"Well, at least he tried to then buy your movie ticket with that money the same week," Jessica said.

"As if that makes up for it. I would have rather he told me about the bet."

"For sure. So, mention the bet, and then what will you say about Jeremy? Are you going to tell Liam you like Jeremy?"

I sighed. "No. I don't want to know how he would react to that."

"He may ask you."

"If he asks me I'll be honest, but I'm not going to volunteer it. Besides, it's not like I've told him about crushes or anything."

"Becky that's because you haven't had any. Except for that movie star, the blond one, what's his name . . ."

"Nathan Sweeney?"

"Yeah him. Anyway, bottom line is you haven't had an interest in anyone since Jeremy left."

"Except Nathan Sweeney," I pointed out.

"You know what I mean. Maybe you should just tell Liam "look, I like Jeremy, and I think it's bothering you, what's your problem?" He'll either say nothing and back off or tell you his problem and you guys can discuss it or something."

"Maybe you're right," I said.

"Of course I'm right! Now, time to style my hair. I need to figure out which style will go best with Friday's outfit."

We spent the rest of Wednesday afternoon choosing Jessica's hair and make-up styles for her upcoming date. After, I went home to continue work on my history paper.

The next day, I went to math class to see if I could arrange a time to talk to Liam. I sat there, staring at the door, waiting for him to appear. He did, apparently at the same time as Jeremy, and they elbowed each other slightly roughly as they entered. Jeremy sneered at Liam and Liam glared in return. I rolled my eyes at their immaturity.

"Hey," I said as Liam took his seat. Jeremy took his on the other side of the room.

"Hi," Liam said, not looking at me.

"I was wondering if—"

"Hello, class." I was cut off by Mr. Rambouski. I sighed and Jessica turned to give me an encouraging smile. I decided to write Liam a note.

What's going on with you? I was hoping we could talk sometime. I passed him the note and while he still didn't look directly at me, he did take it. I watched him read it and write something down himself.

I don't want to explain to you here. When are you free?

I wrote another note back.

I'm hanging out with Nicole after school. I can hang out after dinner. Did you want to come over? This time, he looked at me when I passed him back the note. Some sort of sensation I didn't know how to explain flashed through me. Nervousness? Attraction?

How about you come to my house? Play a video game or something? Liam wrote.

Okay, I'll come by after dinner. I might bring some homework by, if that's okay with you. Anyway, I have to pay attention now because Mr. Rambouski is giving me dirty looks.

I threw the note on his desk and watched Mr. Rambouski explain why pre-calculus is so important for a college education.

I wondered if Jeremy would say anything to me after class. He left without coming over, so Nicole and I packed up our books and headed to my locker after saying goodbye to Jenny and Jessica.

We slowed as we approached my locker. Jeremy was leaning against it.

"Hi," I said as we reached him.

"Hey," he replied, moving off of my locker so I could open it. Nicole gave him a friendly smile.

"What's up?" I asked.

"I was just wondering what you were doing later. I made a list of schools."

"Already?" I asked in surprise. He shrugged. "Well, I'm hanging out with Nicole and then later . . . I'm going to Liam's . . ." I let my voice trail off.

"You can hang out with us if you want," Nicole kindly offered.

"No, that's okay. I'll just text you the list then Becky?" Jeremy asked.

"Sure. You already have the number, right?" I asked.

"I'm assuming you haven't changed the number since I phoned you the other day," he said with a teasing smile.

"How did you get that anyway?" I asked as I pulled out all the books I needed to take home.

"Adrian."

"Adrian?" Nicole asked, looking confused. "Why would Adrian give you her number?"

"I asked for it."

"Do I want to ask for more of an explanation than that?" I asked, looking at him suspiciously.

"Nope." He grinned at me, touched my hand briefly, and waved to us as he walked off. Nicole and I shrugged at each other and headed to her locker.

After Nicole and I hung out, I made dinner for myself and my Mom while I told her my day. After I had eaten, I called Liam and told him I would walk over. I grabbed my homework and headed out the door.

I arrived at Liam's house twenty minutes later.

"I could have picked you up," Liam said as he opened the door for me. I shrugged.

"You know I love walking. So, what are you doing?" I asked as I referred to his papers on the table.

"Homework. Did you want to set up your homework here?"

"Sure." I dumped my homework on the table and sat down on the couch. Liam chewed on his pencil and sat down beside me. I had the feeling he didn't really want to talk. For that matter, neither did I, but it was a necessity.

"So . . . want to do some homework or talk or play a video game?" he finally asked.

"I can talk and do my homework at the same time," I said. Liam shrugged. We wordlessly opened books and started writing. After a few minutes, I waited for Liam to say something. He didn't. I decided if we were going to talk, I would have to start the conversation.

"So, I here you made a bet with Adrian that he couldn't shag me?" I asked. Liam looked startled.

"What? Where did you hear that?" he asked. I shrugged. I hadn't decided what to say if he asked.

"Did you?"

Liam winced. "Yeah I bet he couldn't give it to you. So what?"

"So what? Why did you bet on me like that? And why didn't you tell me?"

"Because I knew you would be mad!"

"Then why bet on me in the first place? What, is my friendship only worth the ten dollars you bet? You would risk me being mad at you for ten dollars?"

Liam sighed.

"Adrian was mouthing off, saying he could melt any girl, no matter how icy she was or thick her exterior. He was acting challenging towards me, saying he could do what I couldn't."

"What do you mean? You've never tried to have sex with me." I tried to think back to determine if he had. No, definitely not.

"Actually, we were originally talking about going out with someone. He was asking about you, and I said you had some sort of baggage and you had no interest. He said he bet that wasn't true and he could date you no problem. Because he was so boastful, I said that would be all he could do with you, so we upped the ante and he said he could not just date you, but go all the way."

"So when you said he was saying he could do what you couldn't, he meant go out with me?" I asked, suddenly understanding a bit better.

"Yes. I didn't mean for it to escalate into what the bet became, but once the offer was on the table, I couldn't back down. Besides, I didn't think you would get hurt or anything; I thought the biggest risk would be Adrian might spread a nasty rumour to cover his own reputation like he did with Emily Spooner."

"Okay, well, why were you two talking about being able to go out with me?" Liam sighed and leaned his head into his hands.

"Do you really want to know?" I thought back to Jeremy asking me that two days ago when we discussed the bet. My life might be less complicated if I hadn't known it was Liam who made the bet. Just the same, I wanted to know.

"Yes, I do."

"I said I hadn't asked you out because I thought you had feelings for someone else and I had no clue who that someone else was." I stared at him, not sure what to say.

"So if you hadn't thought that . . . you would have asked me out?" Liam nodded.

"Shit," I muttered. "Well, that would explain why you don't like Jeremy."

"I never said I was jealous."

"No, but this would certainly explain a few things."

"Look, calm down, do some homework for a moment, we'll talk about Jeremy in . . ." he glanced at his watch. "In ten minutes."

"What?"

"You get all hyped up and then we just yell at each other. I'm doing my homework and in ten minutes, we can talk about Jeremy." I glared at Liam and snatched my notebook off the table.

I couldn't really concentrate so ended up doodling until my phone beeped at me. I had a text from the number Jeremy had called me from on Tuesday. It was a list of schools he wanted us to consider. I gave Liam a quick glare again before coping down the school names.

Finally, Liam put down his text book. He glanced at my notebook and then watched me doodle. I had calmed down a bit, but I still felt highly emotional. I wasn't even sure why; it would be totally understandable if Liam was jealous with Jeremy arriving. Jeremy would have been the reason he hadn't made a move before and he would be the reason he would not be making a move now.

"Did you want to talk?" he asked.

"So if you're not jealous, what is it then?" I asked, trying not to sound too sharp.

"What's this list you're writing down?" Liam asked, ignoring my question.

"Schools I'm looking into for after grad. Why?"

"Where is Jeremy from? Was he born here?"

"No, he's Canadian. He moved here from Vancouver somewhere around five years ago. Again, why?"

"Do you know where Simon Fraser University is?" I glance down at my list. Liam was pointing to the university off of my list. I did not actually know where Simon Fraser University was.

"Yes," I said. No point in Liam knowing I had no clue.

"And am I really suppose to think you're looking into a Canadian school with no outside influence?"

The surprise on my face probably revealed I had not actually known where Simon Fraser University was.

"What is your point?" I asked.

"Jeremy influences you."

"You don't—"

"You spend all your time worrying about him and I worry about what he's doing to you. He's some jackass with rebellious issues who spends his time drinking and screwing girls."

"Oh, you mean girl singular, the one in Virginia? Don't make it sound worse than it is." Liam looked surprised. I suppose he had been saving that one up as a shocker for me.

"Just because he's eased up on bad habits in the past few days does not mean he won't continue them next week. And you're ready to jump on command to make him happy just so he'll show some interest in you again. Are you seriously thinking about leaving the country to follow that dipstick to a school with a lower drinking age? You have other friends and people who care about you, why bother with him? He told you he wished he'd never said he was in love you!"

"You don't understand Liam! He didn't mean what he said and I—"

"You what? Love him? You barely know him now. You've probably spent the past year building him up in your mind and you refuse to even think about how absorbed you are in his drama. He hurt you and you don't even seem to care. He has you wrapped around his finger and your rose coloured glasses don't even let you see it."

"I'm out of here." I angrily picked up my books and marched to the front door.

"Becky, listen to me—"

"Screw you Liam. You think you're so much better than him? You made a bet over my virginity, ten freaking dollars, and I'm suppose to believe you have my best interests at heart? You don't even respect me; for all I know this is just part of another bet. So here," I scrambled around in my bag and pulled out a ten dollar bill. I smashed it into his palm. "To cover your expenses for losing this one." I turned around and left, slamming his front door behind me.

Diary Entry: July 17, 2006

Ever since Jeffrey, whenever I had a date, Jeremy would try to somehow scare off the guy. I mostly left it alone, thinking any guys worthy of my attention wouldn't be intimidated by Jeremy. Jeremy is a pansy anyway! I don't really understand why he bothers, but up until recently it hasn't really mattered. Until I met Craig. Craig was a guy who had been in a few of my classes during school. The day before summer holidays began, he asked me out. I said sure. Jeremy went away to his cabin for two weeks, so I realised that I could potentially date someone for a couple of weeks before Jeremy tried to scare them off. And we had a great two weeks, watching movies, going for walks . . . I even had my first kiss! But then Jeremy came back and ruined everything.

Flashback

I angrily stomped my way home. I couldn't believe what Craig had just told me. He had said he couldn't see me anymore. And I knew why.

Craig had said he was going up to Seattle anyway, so it didn't really matter. However, it did to me. He said he didn't want a long lasting relationship, just some summer fun. I knew what had really happened. And as soon as I entered my kitchen to see Jeremy waiting for me, I knew I was right.

"Hey, Rebecca," he said, as if everything was normal. I ignored him. I walked over to the fridge and poured myself some milk. I read the note my mother had left on the fridge door. She wasn't going to be home until six o'clock. I drank my milk and put the glass in the sink. I began to leave the kitchen but Jeremy jumped up and grabbed my arm.

"Is something the matter?" he asked. I glared at him.

"You tell me," I said challengingly. He sighed.

"Are you mad about something?" he asked fairly innocently.

"No. I'm furious! You don't know, Jeremy, what it's like! You have never been in a relationship!" I exploded. "You don't understand! You had no right to try and end the relationship between me and Craig."

"I do know what it's like! I know the pain you felt when Jeffrey broke-up with you because he was worried that the girl he was cheating on you with would find out he hadn't broken up with you like he said you had! I know what you went through, I remember!"

"It's my life, not yours!"

"I was just trying to protect you. I don't want you to get hurt again."

"Jeremy, I need to experience this stuff. I need to get hurt every once in a while. You can't just distrust ever single guy I even look at. You have to let me spot the bad guys for myself! I'll never learn otherwise."

"Becky, I'm sorry. I just thought . . ." He just sighed and stood there helplessly. I started hiccupping as I tried not to cry.

"I liked him, I really did. He was so sweet and nice. I really thought he wouldn't be intimidated by you, that he would like me enough to ignore you. I guess I was wrong." I started crying as Jeremy pulled me close to him. His arms tightened around me. The soft, soothing, humming sound he was making against my forehead made me slowly relax. I stopped crying.

"Rebecca, I love you. I do," he said softly. I sniffled and wiped my nose on his sleeve, thinking I didn't really care if it was gross, it was his fault I was crying anyway. He kissed my eyelids and I felt slightly embarrassed. I wasn't sure why. He wiped my eyes with his thumb and continued to kiss my eyelids. I just stood there numbly. I was mad at him, but I knew he just wanted me to be happy. I just wished he wouldn't always interfere.

"I love you," he whispered again. He softly kissed my earlobe. For a moment, thinking about Craig, I didn't even notice. I felt slightly startled as I realized Jeremy had kissed my earlobe. Why would he do that?

"Jeremy?" I asked softly. He was rubbing the back of my neck.

"Yeah?" He leaned away from my neck to look at me.

"Do you think Craig would still go out with me if I told him you didn't mean what you said?" Jeremy's eyes clouded. He stepped back from me. He pursed his lips, and remained quiet for a long time.

"I don't know. Ask him if you want." He walked over to the kitchen table and sat down. I frowned. I decided that Craig wouldn't. It wasn't his style to do something like that. I looked over at Jeremy's annoyed face. I wasn't sure why he looked so angry. I walked over to him and hugged him. He kind of just sat there, limply.

"Jeremy?"

"What?"

"Would you trust yourself?"

"What? Becky, what are you talking about?"

"With my feelings. You know how you don't trust any guy, well, would you trust yourself?" He looked confused.

"Beck, I, I'm not sure. I mean yes, I would trust myself, but I'm not sure what you're getting at."

"Jeremy, you scare off the guys because you don't trust them with my feelings. Well, what I'm trying to say is that you have to trust someone." He frowned. He stood up and pulled me over to him. He looked vastly confused.

"I would trust myself because I'm the one that doesn't want you hurt. But I do see your point. Maybe, sometimes, I should back off. It's only because, because . . ." His voice trailed off as he started to stammer. "Beck, I'm, I'm, I'm in . . ." I waited for him to finish, but he didn't. Finally, he just muttered something I couldn't make out and left. I was confused. What was this all about? What was he trying to do or say?

The next day I talked to Craig. He made it easier for me to understand why Jeremy did what he did. He told me the guy just cared and would rather shield me from the rest of the world then risk having me fall in love. I understood. But I still didn't know what Jeremy was trying to say.

Present Day: November 5, 2009

I banged loudly on the front door of Jeremy's house. The tears had dried from my normally twenty minute walk. I looked at my watch to see ten minutes had gone by since I left Liam's. I was probably full of adrenaline.

"Hey, Beck," Jeremy said as he opened the door. I stormed in and threw my coat on the coach. He picked up my coat and hung it up in the closet while I plopped down on the couch. My face was stern and angry as Jeremy cautiously sat down beside me.

"Am I too absorbed in you?" I asked. He looked startled. "Absorbed? What do you mean?"

"Am I wrapped around your little finger?"

"I wouldn't think so. Becky, are you going to tell me what's wrong?"

"Do you boss me around?"

"I would think it's more the other way around. Beck!" I got up and walked in the kitchen. I was annoyed. Mom and Andrea were playing *Scrabble*. I sat down to watch. Jeremy came in the kitchen after me.

"Hey, Becky. Back from Liam's?" Mom asked. I heard Jeremy curse Liam under his breath. Andrea looked up to glare at him.

"Clearly I am," I muttered sarcastically.

"Okay. Earthquakes," Andrea said triumphantly.

"Andrea, you forgot the u. There is a u in earthquakes," Mom said. Andrea frowned.

"Earth, then. Becky did you want anything to drink?" Andrea asked.

"Do you have any juice?" I asked, just as Jeremy reached for their kettle. He put it back down.

"Sure, but I think the one in the fridge is empty. Jeremy, can you go get a carton from downstairs?"

"I'll get it, Andrea," I volunteered. Anything to get away from Jeremy, despite the fact I had come here to see him.

"Okay. The storage area is to your right. You should walk into a room. I think Jeremy tried to fix the light switch, so don't be surprised if it doesn't work."

"It works, Mom!" Jeremy exclaimed. Andrea shrugged and I walked down the stairs. I turned to my right at the bottom. I could hear their muffled voices upstairs. I opened the door and sneezed. I flicked at the light switch. I was rewarded by a dusty light bulb showing me piles of boxes. This wasn't it. Andrea had a tendency to give the wrong directions, so I decided to go in the door at the end of the room.

I opened the door and flicked the light switch. Nothing. This must be it since Jeremy was rarely successful in anything he attempted to fix. I blindly walked along the room and banged my leg on a table. I swore softly and continued to walk around. It was creepy in here. I thought I heard the squeak of a mouse, but figured that it was just my imagination. I walked forward and stepped on something warm, soft and furry. A rat! I let out a slight scream and tried to rush away, banging into something in the process. I yelped again and started rubbing my hip.

"Jeremy!" I called feebly, wondering if he could hear me. I continued to rub my hip, trying to soothe the sharp sting.

I sat down on the floor, not wanting to attempt to manoeuvre my way back in the dark. I started to think about the fight with Liam again, feeling slightly nauseous about shoving the ten dollars into his hand.

"Becky?" I heard Jeremy call out.

"I'm in some dark room, I can't really see. I ran into something."

"Where are you?" I could see his outline in the doorway.

"Here." I stood up, wincing at the pain in my hip. I heard him rummaging with something and then he turned on a flashlight. He shone it at me. He came forward and as soon as he was within reach, I leaned into him and burst into tears.

"What's going on?" he asked softly as he stroked my hair. I sniffled into his shoulder.

"I hurt my hip," I said hiccupping.

"Your hip will probably be okay. I mean, what's going on? Why are you so upset? You're not crying about your hip."

I hiccupped a couple more times before responding. "I got into a fight with Liam. It was about the bet and you and I feel awful about everything."

"Okay. What did Liam say about the bet?" I hiccupped again, thinking it was a great excuse for me to think. I wasn't sure I should really tell him Liam was discussing asking me out with Adrian.

"I don't know," I finally said.

"I'm not going to be upset if he said he likes you or anything. And I won't ask you not to be friends with him anymore."

"Okay." I repeated the discussion with Liam earlier.

"Are you mad?" I asked uncertainly, after I had finished.

"Why would I be mad? And at whom? He's entitled to his feelings; unless this means the two of you are becoming a couple and I'm instructed to stay clear, I have nothing to be mad about."

"So far so unlikely. There's more though. He said you're a bad influence on me and I'm wrapped around your finger. He also said I spend too much time worrying about you and ignoring my own needs and stuff."

"Do you think that's true?" Jeremy asked. I shrugged, then remembered we were in the dark and he may not have seen.

"I shrugged," I said weakly. I had stopped crying.

"I know, I felt it. Listen Becky, the bad influence thing is fine; clearly on paper I'm not the greatest. However, I don't think I've been influencing you to behave any differently."

"No, you haven't," I said, thinking even if he was drinking he had not encouraged me to. As well, seeing the results of it probably influenced me to stay away from drinking.

"Okay, well, here's the big question: do I make you happy?"

"Happy? Happy how? I mean, I wasn't too excited about things when I sat in that hospital room with your mom."

"Are you glad I'm here? Are you glad I moved back?" Jeremy pressed.

"Yes," I said instantly. I didn't even need to think about it.

143

"Are you sure?"

"Of course! I feel better with you around . . . I feel . . ." I wanted to say 'complete' but decided against it. "I feel secure," I said. Close enough.

"Things aren't too much of a rollercoaster?" Jeremy asked.

"Things are a rollercoaster with Liam! You keep me calm and stable. You're like my rock."

"I got to say, there's more excitement sitting on a rollercoaster than sitting on a rock," Jeremy said dryly.

"That is a weird metaphor. I'm not sitting . . . never mind, it just became weirder." I glared at him in the dark.

"I know, sorry," Jeremy said. I wondered if he was smiling.

"I'm with you, not sitting . . . you know what I mean. Besides, you can take a rock anywhere, but not a rollercoaster. For example, you can take a rock to a Canadian school." Jeremy laughed.

"I sense some annoyance?"

"Liam was all like "lower drinking age! Bad news for you, good for him!" He was very hyper about it. It was annoying."

"Right. Well, how about we talk about schools upstairs?"

"You don't like being alone in the dark with me?" I teased.

"I do, but my mom is going to be concerned any minute now."

"Fair enough. Um, listen, I think I stepped on a rat or something."

"Seriously?" Jeremy sounded doubtful.

"Yes, and it might be hurt. Can we look for it?"

"What makes you think you stepped on a rat?"

"I stepped on something furry?"

"Did you hear any kind of squeak after?

"Yes."

"Was that you or another squeak?"

"Well, I probably drowned out the sound of a rat squeak. Can we look please?" I pouted at him in the dark. Jeremy sighed and started shining the light on the floor.

"Was this it?" He held up a dusty teddy bear.

"Oh! Yes probably. But I thought it was warm."

"You're imagination. It's just Boo-boo, my old bear," Jeremy said.

"Awww, how cute! Why is he called Boo-boo?"

"Carrie tried to perform surgery on him." I smiled as Jeremy placed the bear on a pile of boxes. He held out his hand to me and I carefully stepped closer. We moved slowly through the room, avoiding the boxes and furniture. We came out of the room and Jeremy turned off his flashlight. He placed it on a shelf.

"Follow me," Jeremy said. We walked through the room and just before the stairs, Jeremy pulled me to the left and into a small storage area. He pulled on a chain attached to a light bulb.

"This is where the juice is," he said.

"Ahh, very nice," I said, smiling. He closed the door slightly to the storage area and turned the light off, leaving us in darkness.

"What are you doing?" I asked, confused. He put his hand on the side of my face, cradling my cheek. His other hand snaked around to my back and he gently pulled me closer. I felt warmth flow throughout my body as I tilted my head up towards him.

He traced my lips with his thumb and ever so softly, he brushed his lips against mine. I smiled as he pulled away, my lips tingling.

"Juice?" Jeremy asked as he turned on the light.

"What?" I asked, feeling too giddy to think about juice.

"You came down for juice?" He handed me a carton of juice and pushed the door of the storage area open again. I smiled a thank-you and we headed upstairs.

"So where have you two been?" Andrea asked.

"Becky got lost," Jeremy said as he poured me a glass of juice. We leaned against the counter and watched their scrabble.

"Okay. Mom, I don't know if you've noticed this, but argue is spelt with a U." Andrea looked at the word and added a U from her pile of tiles. I smiled. Mom stood up and announced that she won. Jeremy began to pull me towards the living room while Andrea started arguing that she had won.

"They'll be arguing for a while. Want to watch T.V.?" he asked.

"Sure." We sat down and Jeremy flicked on the television. We sat very close together, our legs and sides touching. After a couple of minutes, he put his arm around me. I looked over at him to smile.

"What?" he asked.

"Nothing." I leaned against him and turned back to the show. It was some sort of nature shark show.

"Hey, so you wrote down the schools?" Jeremy asked after awhile.

"Oh, right, I meant to bring that up again. So you want us to move to Canada?"

"I was just thinking, the school is close to the lake we use to stay at, we could go camping or rent a cabin there on long weekends and stuff. It'll only be a couple of hours drive back home. And the tuition will be cheaper, especially for me, over there."

"And Canada will let me live there problem?"

"What, the mounties? Of course! Do you not remember what it was like when we would go over the border to get to the lake? They ask if it's for a vacation or not and if we're carrying any illegal or dangerous goods, then wish us a good day. Anyway, if you're going to school I'm pretty sure it's easy to live in Canada. Besides, you wouldn't be a full time citizen; you would only be living there for eight months of the year."

"Well, okay, I suppose I won't cross it off the list."

"And just think, Rebecca, of curling up in a tent by the lake." Jeremy leaned in closer.

"We've done that," I reminded him.

"Yes but without anyone checking on us. Or an awkward conversation about breast touching. We'll be able to hear the waves . . ."

"There's no waves at a lake," I pointed out. Jeremy tried to lean in closer still. I grinned, knowing he was trying to sound romantic.

"Moonlight shining down on us, toasting marshmallows by the fire, reading our books by the water . . ." just as he reached the point of kissing me, Andrea came in muttering about words and spelling. We pulled away from each other. Jeremy sighed in annoyance.

"Oh, Jeremy, you don't look happy with me. Did we interrupt something?" Andrea asked.

"Of course not. Question is, can you spell it?"

"I T. I'm still more clever than you," she leaned down and kissed the top of his head and he muttered something under his breath.

"Time to go, Becky," my mom said.

"Okay." I stood up and looked at Jeremy expectantly.

"What?"

"Where did you put my jacket?" I asked, not remembering what he did with it when I had come storming in.

"It's in the closet." He got up and retrieved it for me. I smiled thanks and walked to the front door with my mom.

"Okay, well thanks for having us over, we'll see you later," my mom said cheerily.

"No problem!" Andrea said just as cheerily. They both waved and then turned to us expectantly.

"Can I talk to her a sec?" Jeremy asked Andrea. Both of our mom's exchanged looks.

"I'll wait for you outside, Becky," my mom said.

"I'm going to have a bath," Andrea announced. They both left, leaving us alone. Or mostly alone, we could hear Andrea humming as she turned the tap on.

"Are you okay?" Jeremy asked.

"I guess," I said.

"Do you want me to talk to Liam for you?"

"No. What would you say that would help the situation?" Jeremy shrugged. "Better to just leave it alone. I just need to chill for a bit before talking to him."

"If that's what you want to do. I just want to make sure you're not going to start hiccupping at school," Jeremy said.

"Why would I start hiccupping at school?" I asked, confused.

"I don't know, maybe because you start hiccupping when you're upset and about to cry?"

"Don't be silly. Anyway, I have to go, I'll see you at school tomorrow." I leaned in to kiss his cheek but he stopped me.

"What are you doing tomorrow after school?" he asked.

"Why? What are you thinking?"

"Maybe we could do something?"

I smiled. "I'm hanging out with Nicole and Jenny. Maybe Saturday?"

"You wanted to see what I was going to say before telling me you had plans," Jeremy said with a grin.

"Who me? Anyway, see you tomorrow." This time I was successful in kissing his cheek. I waved at him as I left, feeling much better.

Diary Entry: August 5, 2006

After the whole Craig thing, I was pretty mad at Jeremy. I didn't think he had the right to interfere. I keep wondering if I let him understand how upset I was. What if he does something like this again? Ultimately, though, Jeremy is my best friend, and Craig is just some guy. I'll get over Craig, but I don't know if I could get over losing Jeremy.

I'm feeling a little weird about how the scene played out when I confronted him about Craig. I keep thinking back to it. The affection he was giving me when I was upset was . . . different than normal. Like, what was going on with him? I hadn't thought of it much at the time, but now I'm wondering why he kissed my earlobe.

Jessica is quite suspicious of the behaviour and keeps muttering things about "feelings" and stuff. Then again, Jessica is also convinced her neighbour is avoiding her because he's in love with her and too shy to tell her, not because he caught us spying on him.

Anyway, I think I'm going to have to observe him carefully. He's been his usual self the past couple of weeks, and there haven't been any more earlobe incidents, but who knows with him.

Chapter 9

I woke up Friday morning feeling a bizarre combination of hurt and exhilaration. The kiss with Jeremy made me feel happy and filled my gut with excited butterflies. As I got ready for school, my mind kept replaying the kiss and I felt a thrill of anticipation for seeing him again.

On the other hand, the fight with Liam gave me a sick lurch every time the memory poked into my thoughts, interrupting my giddy feelings. I felt so hurt by the turn of events with him. I didn't understand why he had been so stupid as to make the bet, or worse yet, keep it from me. I knew the bet was something other than the money, but pride, knowledge, or whatever aside, I felt I deserved more.

With those thoughts plaguing me, I slowly drudged towards Math class at the end of the day. I felt so nervous Liam would try to say something to me and I would just burst into tears.

"Becky!" I turned around to see Jeremy trying to catch up to me.

"Hi," I said softly as he touched my hand. He gave me a warm smile. A flow of glee surged through me, making me feel a bit better about my upcoming fate.

"What are you doing?" he asked.

"Going to Math," I said, as if it was obvious.

150

"You don't want to skip?" We both turned and looked at the end of the hall where the math class door was open in a far more menacing way than usual.

"What if I miss something important?" I asked feebly.

"You're good in math; I think you'll be fine if you miss one class, Beck."

"Yeah but . . . I don't like skipping." Jeremy rolled his eyes at me.

"You're choice. If you want to skip we can go get coffee or something instead."

"Maybe Liam will skip though and then there would be no point in me skipping!" I suggested brightly.

"Is he as big of a goody two shoes as you?" Jeremy asked with a teasing tone. I thought about it for a moment. I couldn't recall Liam ever doing anything that was against school rules.

"Potentially bigger, I skipped one class this year, he probably hasn't skipped any."

"Then he'll probably go to class. We should skip."

"You use to be a goody two shoes!" I said to Jeremy slightly accusingly.

"Indeed. I also use to be a virgin and who had never thrown up vodka on my pants. Class?" He nodded his head towards the end of the hall. I chewed on my lip.

"I'm suppose to see Nicole and Jenny after class," I said.

"We can text them. Again, up to you, I shouldn't be a bad influence on you." He grinned. I made a face, crinkling up my nose.

"I will feel all bad and stuff if I skip," I said weakly.

"Hey guys, what are you doing?" At that moment, Nicole came up to us.

"Debating skipping class," Jeremy said.

"After that fight with Liam? Obviously we should skip class! I'll text Jenny in case she already went. Oh, want to go see a matinee movie? Cheaper in the afternoon."

"Oh what one? I'm in the mood for something girly," I said.

"I don't believe this, I ask if you want to skip and you're all like 'but I'm innocent and don't break rules and never upset my mom' and Nicole offers to skip with you and you want to go see a chick flick?" Jeremy rolled his eyes heavenward and muttered something under his breath.

"What? You're a bad influence, Nicole isn't. If I told my mom Nicole skipped with me because I was too upset to see Liam, she would nod sympathetically and say I shouldn't run away from my problems, but she understands. If I told my mom I skipped class with you, she would muttered about you being rebellious and phone your mom. I was being logical." I smirked at him slightly.

"Whatever. How about I go to class and message you to let you know if Liam's there. If he is, you and Nicole go see a movie, if not you come to class?" Nicole and I looked at each other. She nodded.

"Okay, thanks Jeremy."

"I'll talk to you later," he said as he walked down the hall. Nicole and I turned around to wait for his message in the bathroom. The bell rang, signalling class was supposed to start.

"Do you think he'll have gone to class?" Nicole asked me.

"Who, Liam? I don't know. I don't want to talk to him right now though."

"Well, you'll have to eventually. Plus, I think he owes you twenty bucks," Nicole said.

"Twenty?"

"Yeah. Ten bucks for the first bet, ten bucks you threw at him yesterday. Twenty bucks. See, we don't need Math." We grinned at each other.

My phone beeped and I read the text from Jeremy.

"No Liam," I said as I closed my phone.

"Did you want to go?"

"To class? I guess. We're hanging out with Jenny after anyway, so we might as well wait for her in class." Nicole shrugged and we made our way to the classroom. We gave an attempt to sneak in, but Mr. Rambouski still gave us the evil eye as we took our seats. Jeremy, I noticed, was sitting in Liam's seat, while Jessica wasn't even there.

At the end of class Nicole, Jenny, Jeremy and I stood up and looked at each other.

"Where's Jess?" I asked Jenny and Jeremy. Jeremy shrugged.

"Getting ready for her date," Jenny said with a faint smile.

"She had to skip a two o'clock class to get ready for her date? What time is the date at?" Jeremy asked us.

"We don't know," Nicole said.

"Really?"

"Yes, she thought if she told us what time we would follow her there," I told Jeremy.

"Would you?" The three of us looked at each other. Jenny shrugged and Nicole grinned.

"Probably," I admitted. "I'm bummed I wanted to tell her about last night!" I said to Jenny and Nicole. Jeremy raised his eyebrows.

"What part about last night," he said with a slight cockiness to his voice.

"The fight with Liam," I said pushing him as I rolled my eyes. Of course, I was more eager to share the kiss with Jeremy but I couldn't tell him that.

"I was so hoping that would be the most exciting news of the day," he said dryly.

"Why were you sitting in Liam's desk?" Nicole asked.

"I thought if he showed up late at least he'd be forced to sit somewhere else. He could have been planning to come late just to avoid having to say anything to anyone."

"Good call," I said, nodding at Jeremy.

"Well, anyway, want to go home now?" Jenny asked us. Nicole and I murmured agreement.

"Phone me later?" Jeremy asked me.

"Sure." He leaned in but didn't kiss me, just touched the small of my back with his hand, pulling his hand away slowly to my hand, which he quickly squeezed.

"See you guys later," he said as he turned to go. We waited for him to leave the classroom before saying anything.

"Well he's definitely better than he was," Jenny said, looking at the door he had just gone through thoughtfully.

"I'll say," Nicole said. "And Becky, have you noticed his PDA?"

"His PDA?"

"Public Display of Affection?"

"I know what it means, what about it?"

"Well, before, he was all over marking you as his territory or something without any actual affection, and now he tries to give you affection without seeming obvious or crossing any lines or what not. Totally different style."

"Very true. Do you think that's a good thing?" Both Jenny and Nicole nodded at me.

Behind us, Mr. Rambouski cleared his throat. We turned around.

"Can I help you girls with anything?" he asked us.

"Oh, no, we were just leaving," Jenny said, and we scurried out to rent a movie and indulge in some girl talk.

Diary Entry: August 13, 2006

So I have officially decided that the weird earlobe/kiss incident was just because Jeremy was feeling crazy that day. Probably because of the guilt he was feeling about me having to break up with Craig. He's been acting the same way he always has. Shy around girls, obnoxious around Jessica, friendly around everyone else. So I have come to a conclusion. He was nuts the day I was crying over Craig. I think the theory works. Jessica has a different one. She says that he was trying to put the moves on me because I was "vulnerable and available." As if! Jess can get carried away pretty easily, so I think she's still looking for romance from Jeremy's side whether or not it's really there. Still, there was the incident yesterday . . .

Flashback

I walked into Jeremy's house noting that yet again, he left the door unlocked. I sniffed the air. Was he cooking? No way. Probably Carrie was still here cooking something to impress a guy with.

"Hi!" I yelled out.

"Hey, Beck. Come on in the kitchen," Jeremy called. I walked in to the kitchen to see brownie clumpy batter splattered all over the counter tops.

"Jeremiah, what on earth are you doing?" I asked. He glanced up from the magazine he was reading and shrugged.

"I don't know. That's why I phoned you. See, I got a date and I decided to make brownies. I don't think I'm doing a very good job." I tried to hide the surprise on my face. He got a date? When had this happened? Why hadn't he told me? I felt a flicker of annoyance.

"Well, first of all, what's with the magazine? And what recipe are you using?" Jeremy handed me the magazine. It was an article on the four best ways for a guy to find his way into a girl's heart. I frowned at the magazine article, then at him. He was actually taking tips from a magazine to impress this chick? Who was she anyway and why did he all of a sudden care enough to bake for her? I didn't particularly feel inclined to help him out with his date.

"Jeremy, it says here that when making something for your future girl that you shouldn't call up another girl to help you," I pointed out.

"I know. I just figured I wouldn't tell her that you helped me make them. Here's the recipe I tried to use." Jeremy handed me a book and I wiped off the brownie batter. The recipe seemed normal. I sighed and handed him the book back. I felt another ripple of unpleasantness go through me.

"Who's the girl?" I asked. He smiled faintly. I felt my stomach turn around inside. I glared at his happy expression.

"Melanie, the one in our Socials class." Melanie was a tall thin girl with long brown hair and blue eyes. Most guys liked her, but she was shy and timid and was nervous around most guys. Jeremy was basically the same way with girls he liked, so they were perfect for each other. Somehow, I found myself angry with that thought. I didn't like the idea that they would be perfect for each other.

"Okay. Let's get started with the brownies," I said briskly. Jeremy snapped out of his day dream and blinked. He looked at me curiously for a minute as I cleaned up some of the mess he had made. I ignored him. I didn't want to deal with the strange emotions going through me.

"Hey," Jeremy said softly as he grabbed the cloth away from me. Our fingers touched and I held my breath to keep from showing the surprise on my face. His fingers felt different, warm and soft. I had never really noticed that before. I crossed my arms over my chest.

"Now that I've told you my exciting day, do you want to tell me yours?" he asked.

"My day was pretty boring," I murmured. Actually, it hadn't been. Jessica and I had gone shopping and some guys had come over and asked us out. I had mostly just laughed off the idea, but Jessica said sure. Jeremy glanced at me and shrugged. He could probably tell I was annoyed.

Half an hour later I was putting the brownies in the oven. Jeremy hadn't said a word. Neither had I. I had been thinking about the fact that I was jealous. I didn't really want to admit it, but I knew I was. I finally came to the conclusion that I was jealous because I only wanted him to pay attention to one girl in his life, his best friend. Selfish, but he pulled similar nonsense with Craig.

I glanced at Jeremy who was cleaning off the counter tops. I picked up a spoon with batter on it. I turned around and banged into Jeremy. The spoon hit him on the cheek.

"Hey!" he objected as a brown streak appeared. I snorted behind my hand. He picked up the bowl with the batter scrapings in them and wiped some batter on my cheek.

"Hey!" I took some batter from him and wiped it on his nose. Pretty soon, we were at war.

"Jeremy, you look hilarious!" I said as he tried to wipe the brown guck off his face a few minutes later.

"You don't look to hot yourself, there, Beck," he said as he grinned. I giggled as he tried to wipe the chocolate substance off his nose. I gingerly wiped the batter off his nose for him. He gently wiped some off my cheek, caressing it in the process. His eyes suddenly turned serious as he took my hand with the batter on it. I gasped as he took the finger I had used to wipe the batter off him with and slowly pulled it in his mouth. I was startled.

"Jeremy," I whispered, but he put his finger to my lips. He very delicately licked brownie batter off of my index finger. I swear it felt like it took him an hour to do it. He was going so slowly and gently. I stepped closer, feeling slightly mesmerized by the experience.

He finally finished and our fingers laced together. We stared at each other for a long moment. He bent his head down and softly kissed my chin. I couldn't help myself; I leaned up and brushed my lips on his chin.

Beyond the thrills of excitement rushing through, some part of my mind kept nagging me that he had a date tonight. For the first time since my younger school girl crush, I wanted to kiss him. His hand felt warm and soft in mine and for whatever reason, streaks of brown on his face aside, he had never looked more attractive. Just the same, I didn't want him to regret kissing me if it happened.

"You have a date tonight with Melanie," I whispered softly. I felt sad as soon as I said it, and almost wished I could take it back. Jeremy took a step back, staring at me uncertainly. He let go of my hand.

"Yeah," he said softly. "I'm going to go wash off my face. I'll be back in a minute." He left the room and I felt ashamed. Quickly, I washed my face off in the kitchen sink and scribbled a note to Jeremy saying I had to go home and I hoped his date went well. I left the house through the back door and ran home.

I couldn't believe what I had just done. I had wanted so badly to kiss him. I had never felt that strongly attracted to someone, not even when I had liked Craig. Feeling too confused to think I curled up in bed and pulled the covers over me, hoping I could push aside my sudden attraction.

A few hours later I woke to the ringing telephone.

"Hello?" I asked groggily.

"Hey, Beck? It's me Jeremy. Are you all right? Your voice sounds kind of hoarse." I groaned.

"I just woke-up from my nap." Suddenly, everything came rushing back at me. I felt a stab of some sort of jealousy. Would Melanie get to have the nice Jeremy kiss I had ruined earlier today? Was his date now over and he was going to tell me all about it? I glanced at the clock beside my bed. It was only eight thirty.

"Are you supposed to be on your date?" I asked.

"Well, yeah. But she went home after an hour. It wasn't going to work. There just wasn't a spark or whatever."

"Why not?"

"I don't know. She said something about me being distracted. I guess I was thinking about you." That took me a bit off guard.

"Me?"

"Yeah. Whatever, who knows what was going on with me. Anyway, uh, Beck, I wanted to make sure you were okay and all. You left the house in a hurry."

"Uh, yeah, I'm fine. I just didn't want to, uh, forget to phone Jess and I was supposed to phone her then. Or something like that." Even to me, that sounded really lame. I winced.

"Okay. Um, Beck?"

"Yeah?"

"I'm sorry for what happened when you were over here. You know. When we were in the kitchen and everything." There was a long pause. I bit my lip. I wanted to tell him I hadn't minded at all. If he were to try the same thing again, I wouldn't be angry or upset. More like pleased.

"I don't really care. I'm over it. Don't worry." I wasn't sure that came out the way I meant it to.

"It won't happen again," Jeremy muttered. I wasn't sure that was the answer I wanted to hear. Could I be falling for Jeremy? No! I smiled. It was just because I had felt lonely or something. That was all. I didn't really like him.

"Okay. Are we still going to watch the movie at my house tomorrow night?" I asked casually.

"Yeah. I'll phone you before I come over tomorrow. Um, well, bye, Rebecca," he said softly.

"Bye." I hung up and collapsed on the bed. What on earth was going on?

Present Day: November 7, 2009

The next morning I started working on my history paper. I only had a couple of days left to finish it and it was not exactly the polished piece I was hoping for.

Somewhere around two I heard the doorbell ring. As my mom was out, I left my room wearily. I had phoned Jeremy the night before as promised and we agreed to hang out around three.

"Oh," I said in surprise as he answered the door. "What are you doing here? I thought we weren't hanging out until three."

"Yeah, I have to clean your mom's bathroom." He stepped inside and I could see he had brought a bucket with some cleaning supplies. I laughed.

"I forgot about that! So you're spending an hour cleaning the bathroom and then we're hanging out?"

"Something like that." I closed the door and followed him to the bathroom.

"I feel so honoured to spend time with you thirty seconds after you clean a bathroom. You'll smell so fresh, like bleach!"

"I brought a change of clothes," he muttered as he set his bucket down on the bathroom floor. I rolled my eyes at him. "Where's your mom?"

"She's out running errands and the like. Why, should we take before and after pictures as proof for her?"

"You're funny. I was asking in case I wanted to sneak a hug or something."

"You have to sneak a hug? Like, with some sort of stealth ability you picked up back east?"

"Seriously, super funny. You should consider making a career out of." His voice dripped with sarcasm and I smirked at him. He pulled me close to him and hugged me.

I wrapped my arms around his neck, enjoying the warmth of his body.

"Okay, I have to clean this bathroom, I think it'll go faster if you don't watch," he said when he drew away.

"In other words, you want me to leave?" I gave him a teasing smile.

"Pretty much."

"Okay. Will you look over my history project when you're done?" I asked hopefully.

"Yes," he said with slight exasperation. "I said last night I would look over it for you today."

"Thanks Jer." I leaned over, kissed his cheek, and left to go back to my own room.

Around an hour later he came into my room. He had changed from his previous clothes of sweats and was now wearing dark jeans and a hoodie.

"All done?" I asked as I stood up from my desk.

"Yeah. I left the bucket in there, I hope you don't care." I shrugged.

"Forty minutes? You must have really scrubbed. I'm impressed." He shrugged.

"All part of the agreement with my mom. That, and I have to go to some therapy again."

"Therapy? She's making you go to therapy?"

"Well, in Virginia after some of my fun drinking adventures I had to go. The agreement when we came back was if there was no bad "episodes" I wouldn't have to go to a new therapist. However, as going to the hospital counted as a bad episode in her mind, I am now signed up for three sessions. They should be a blast. We can talk about my dad and affairs and marriage and dealing with problems . . . no better way to spend an hour."

"That sucks," I said. "Though, to be totally honest, it sounds like it's probably a good idea for you to have the opportunity to go. Even if you don't think it helps."

"Oh no, it helps. I don't want any more than three sessions; I'm not drinking again until college." Jeremy sat on the bed and smiled at me. I sat down next to him.

"Awesome, so I can deal with any issues then! Great plan."

"Don't worry, I'm not going to be a complete idiot and try to crash parties and fall over in an attempt to seem threatening."

"So I will only have to deal with the drunkenness, not the hospital. Terrific."

"What I should have said is I'm not going to be a complete idiot and drink like that." He shrugged. "I mean, so far as a coping mechanism it hasn't really been working out as well I originally hoped, so chances are any drinking will be for social reasons. That being said, let's face it: if you decide to have even one I'll want to watch you like a hawk which usually means staying sober. Anyway, enough about booze; we should talk about schools."

I sighed. I hadn't really thought much about the schools he had listed for me, other than to make fun of him a couple of days ago for the one in Canada.

"I guess we have to get started on that soon."

"You seem reluctant," Jeremy observed.

"It's not that, I just . . . I'm nervous about moving away for college."

"With me?"

"No. Well maybe a little, but that's not it. Leaving my mom and Jessica and . . . everything is going to be different."

"In the summer you seemed pretty eager to decide on a school."

"Only because I was anticipating on you procrastinating the decision. Also, I thought it would be much harder for us to co-ordinate picking a school as we would be doing it mostly over the phone or through emails. You know, if I could convince you to use your email."

"Okay, fair enough." We lapsed into silence for a moment. After awhile, I inched my hand closer to Jeremy's. He rubbed it in his own.

"We can always take a year off and work or something before going," Jeremy finally said.

"Maybe," I said uncertainly. "Even if we did that, probably Jess would still leave."

"Probably. Same with Nicole and Jenny."

"Well, we should go after we graduate, as planned. No year off. It's not like we have the money for some soul-searching trip to Europe to waste a year with. Might as well move forward with our lives right?"

"If that's what you want," Jeremy said with a smile. "And you're still okay to go together, right?" he pressed.

"Yeah. I mean, a small part of me worries that you'll freak out over an issue down the road and you'll turn on me or run away or something."

"Turn on you?"

"Yeah, and say something like you wish you'd never told me you loved me and then I would be left horrified, at some school in Canada where I don't know anybody. That would suck."

"Becky I think we should cross Simon Fraser off the list. Also, I feel pretty confident I'm not going to try to push you away again. You know I only said that to push you away, right?" I shrugged. We hadn't actually discussed the evening he drove me part way to the theatre shortly after he moved back.

"I did only say that to push you away."

"So you didn't mean it then?" I asked. He sighed.

"To be totally honest, a small part of me had meant it. I felt like such an idiot for saying it. After I said it, I wasn't sure what you were going to expect from me."

"Did you feel like an idiot because I didn't say it back?"

Jeremy turned so he was facing me. He took both my hands in his.

"Do you really want to know?" I nodded. "No, seriously, are you prepared for an answer you don't want? Think back to the bet Liam and Adrian had: would you feel better if you hadn't known it was Liam?"

"Maybe but isn't it better I know?"

"This is different, we're talking about my old feelings of regret, not how I feel now."

"I still would like to know."

"Okay. Yes, I felt like an idiot because you didn't say it back. And when I came back I was kind of bitter about it. I didn't want to talk about it, I had all these other issues, and I knew even if you didn't bring it up, I would think about it. If you brought it up, it would mean I would have to either reject you or re-acknowledge it, neither of which I was prepared to do, and if you didn't bring it up it would be because you honestly did not feel the same and it would be awkward to bring it up."

"Reject me? Why would you reject me?"

"I was not ready to date you. And if we had started dating when I arrived, I'm pretty sure you would have broken up with me shortly thereafter. You got to miss several weeks of issues with the school and my mom and Halloween was not the first time I was drunk since returning. Andrea just doesn't know about the other times because I didn't end up in the hospital."

"Have you—"

"No, nothing since. No joke, last night I watched a movie with Andrea. Pretty lame."

"Okay, well, that aside: is this why you ended up changing your attitude towards me?" I asked.

"I'm not following," Jeremy said, looking confused.

"After Halloween, you changed your attitude towards me. Is it because I told you when you said "I love you" I felt the same but hadn't said it?"

"No," Jeremy said.

"Really? Because that would explain the 180 you pulled in the time it took me to have a nap."

"I don't know, maybe it did. I was feeling tipsy and confused and when you said that I felt very relieved and then I felt like an asshole. I realized all I was doing was hurting you and clearly I did want you because I was so upset about Liam. Though I kept thinking it was highly unlikely anything would happen, he could probably grab your breast and you wouldn't assume he had feelings for you."

"Hey! That is so not true!"

"Right so when I lived here before you just thought it was normal for opposite sex best friends to fondle with no actual attraction?"

"I chalked up all your unexplainable behaviour to man hormones."

"What other unexplainable behaviours?"

"Um, you kissed my earlobe when Craig broke-up with me," I pointed out. Jeremy looked up towards the ceiling thoughtfully.

"You're right I did."

"And you licked brownie batter off my fingers before your date with Melanie!" I slapped him on the shoulder for being cheeky all that time ago.

"Yes I definitely remember that one. By the way, since you've brought that up, what was going on with you that day? You didn't exactly look like you were feeling upset about the finger licking goodness we had going on."

"I wasn't upset. I wanted you to kiss me."

"Then why did you remind me of my date with Melanie?"

"I didn't want you to regret kissing me if you did. I thought it would be better if you at least remembered you had a date with Melanie before you decided on what to do next. You're the type to feel guilty if you kissed me before your date."

"I probably would have just cancelled the date. My excitement was mostly for having a first date, not because it was with Melanie."

"Just the same, I thought you liked her," I smiled at him sheepishly.

"Ironically, things would be different if you hadn't said anything. Chances are even if you thought I kissed you due to "man hormones" as you so nicely put it, I doubt you would so easily put aside why you kissed me."

"Agreed. I have no idea what would have happened if we had actually kissed then. Though, I thought about it enough."

"Really?"

"Yeah. After you told me you were moving to Virginia, I would think about the brownie batter incident quite often and what would have happened should we have kissed. That's how I eventually realized perhaps I actually wanted you as more than a friend." I grinned at Jeremy as he leaned forward and kissed my nose.

"You still want me as more than a friend?" he asked softly.

"Oh well, since you've brought that up, I was thinking we shouldn't go to any more basements or dark rooms in case you get away with kissing me again," I said sarcastically.

"Don't tease me. Right now, we're still mostly friends, it's not like we've discussed what we are yet."

"Jeremy, you kissed me two days ago!"

"I also fondled your breast a year and a half ago, that didn't mean we were dating! I feel like you keep forgetting that."

"Fine, fair enough. Your point is taken. Yes, I still want you as more than a friend," I said.

"Good. I still want you as more than a friend." We stared at each other for a bit.

"Well where does that leave us?" I finally asked.

"I don't know. I was hoping we could leave it at that for now?" I shrugged.

"Well anyway, what did you want to do today?" I looked at my watch. "It's about three fifteen now."

"I was mostly thinking of just hanging out, you know, watching television or a movie or something. Maybe go for a walk, I hadn't thought about it too much." I decided he was thinking of renting a movie rather than going to one. So far it didn't seem like we were having a date, more like hanging out.

"Sure," I said, feeling slightly disappointed by the idea we weren't really having a date today.

"Is that okay with you?" he asked. I shrugged. I wasn't going to press the issue; if he wasn't ready then he wasn't ready. Either way, spending time with him was better than not spending time with him.

"Did you want me to look at your paper for you now?" he asked.

"Sure, that gives me a chance to change." I was still wearing my sweat pants and felt slightly casual next to him in his dark jeans. I hadn't put any make-up on, but didn't think I could manage that without him noticing at this point.

"Change into what?" he asked. I had a feeling he was setting me up for a joke.

"My jeans."

"Are these your pants you got mustard on last time?" he asked with a grin as he pulled out the edge of them.

"Ha ha. What do you want me to say, I changed into my jeans because you were coming over? I would also change into my jeans if Jessica was coming over." That was only partially true. I would change into them if I thought she would drag me out, if she was in a television and nail painting mood, I wouldn't bother.

"I couldn't help but notice I can see a bra strap next to your tank top strap there," Jeremy said, outlining it with his finger. I pushed him away with a smirk.

"Yes, I remembered to put on a bra this morning! How lovely of you to point it out."

"Well this way if you remove it now in order to draw my attention, it'll be obvious."

"You're awful. Go read my paper in the living room, I want to change. And no more cheeky comments." I pushed him out as I handed him my paper. I waited until I saw him go to the living room before closing my door to change.

Ten minutes later I came out in jeans and a nice royal blue sweater. I hadn't been sure how casual to dress and decided a sweater counted both as a casual item and as a fancy item. I had brushed out my hair, but hadn't bothered about make-up.

Jeremy was sitting on the couch with a notebook on one side of him, my text book on the other, and my paper in his lap. He looked very studious with all the school work around him. I smiled.

"How's it going?" I asked as I sat down next to him. Or rather, next to my text book.

"Good. I made some editing notes on your paper. Seems to be pretty decent." He moved the text book to the coffee table.

"Only decent?" I asked.

"Not A+ but still good." He smiled at me, his lip flickering up slightly. He was teasing me. "Anyway, school stuff." He handed me the notebook that had been on the other side. School brochures and applications spilled out. The notebook had random notes on information regarding residential on campus and off campus living.

"There's quite a bit of work here," I said, looking at him in surprise. I had expected I would be stuck doing most of our research and applications.

"I know. I didn't want you to feel obligated to do it all."

"Yes but maybe if you spent more time worrying about homework and less about schools . . ."

"I'm fine. Worry about your grades, not mine."

"I'm sorry," I said, startled. "I didn't mean to offend you."

Jeremy sighed. "You didn't. I just . . . I prefer worrying about you than you worrying about me."

"Ah. That explains your desire to take care of our post-secondary education." I pointed to his massive accumulation of brochures and applications.

"I'm more use to looking out for you than you looking out for me," he said softly.

"That's just a tad chauvinistic, don't you think?" I asked him.

"Sure, but Jess looks out for you more than you look out for her. You're very innocent; it makes people want to look out for you."

"I'm not innocent," I muttered. I probably was fairly innocent.

"It's not a bad thing, Beck. Besides, if I hadn't had a nice rebellious year, I would be probably just as innocent as you. At least you have had an actual relationship."

"With who, Adrian? That was like two months and there wasn't exactly heavy feelings attached. Besides, you've gone much farther than me in terms of a sexual relationship."

"That was part of my rebellious year. And I've never really dated someone, emotional attachment or not. The girl I did it with, Kim, I never asked out or had a real date with. At least you have."

"I've never been on a date with a girl," I said with a teasing smile. Jeremy rolled his eyes at me.

"You know what I meant."

"Are you saying all this to make me feel better for saying I'm innocent?"

"Yes. Anyway, seriously, can we look at schools?"

We spent the next hour going over brochures and information on various schools. Most of the ones we looked at were in Washington State, meaning we wouldn't be very far from home. I noticed Jeremy did not hand me the brochure for his Canadian school. I wondered if he felt bad about my jokes over moving to Canada. It wasn't like it was a bad idea, going to school so close to the lake.

My mom came home and announced Bob was coming for dinner. Jeremy and I packed up our stuff and headed outside as I gave him a look implying I had no urge to stay for dinner with my mom and Bob.

"Why don't you like him?" Jeremy asked as we stepped outside into the cold air. I shivered and pulled my zipper on my winter coat as high as it would go.

"I don't know. It's weird, them dating. I'm sure you understand."

"Did you see them boink?" he asked. I gave him a bad look.

"No."

"Different situation then. I mean, Carrie seems okay with Christina. She must, they live in the same house."

"Maybe it's just me then. Have you ever officially met Christina?" I asked.

"Not really. I mean, obviously I've seen her, but I've never spoken to her. Carrie says she isn't too bad. Carrie's a pretty forgiving person, though. I guess she'd have to be; how many guys has she fallen for that turn out not be Spanish song writers?" I smiled.

"I miss Carrie," I said.

"Me too," Jeremy said. I was surprised. Before, they had fought constantly and the brief time I had seen them together since he got back, they had argued and he had stormed off.

"Really?"

"Don't seem so shocked, she is my sister. She was pretty concerned with trying to iron out the family kinks when everything went haywire. She spent a fair amount of time talking to our mom and would often act as the messenger. All she wanted was for all of us to be able to be happy, and for Tom, if that meant being with Christina, she was okay with that."

"That's pretty mature of her."

"Every once in awhile she reminds us all she's far more mature than her boy crazed attitude lets on. She really wanted me to straighten myself out. After I would come home drunk, she would come into my room and we would watch television until I sobered up and then we would make large amounts of food together. Sometimes, if Andrea had been feeling particularly down, she would hide any evidence of my drinking and scold and lecture me herself instead. She use to actually mention you during those times; she would tell me you would be sad to see what I was doing and hurt than I hadn't admitted anything to you. To be honest, I think it was Carrie who put the idea in Andrea's mind that if she were to move away with me, we should move here. She thought I would come back and you would straighten me out immediately. Which is why she was so mad I had kept you at arm's length. You know, the fight we had on Halloween?"

"I remember," I said. "By the way, I think I forgot to tell you Carrie is sorry she upset you."

"Oh, doesn't matter, I knew. She made me a silly card out of construction paper. She drew a picture of a pizza on it. I was mostly relieved it didn't have any Spanish style poetry."

I laughed. "That's not silly, that's nice! She was trying to make you feel better."

"That or practice making construction paper valentine cards for the neighbour."

I tried not to visibly wince, remembering Liam sarcastically saying he wouldn't make me a valentine out of construction paper. I was still feeling pretty bad about the whole Liam thing. It didn't help knowing he had been contemplating asking me out last year. I also felt a tad guilty: would I have gone out with him had he asked? What would have happened should I have said yes and Jeremy came back?

"Becky?" Jeremy asked. I snapped out of my thoughts.

"Oh sorry, did you ask something?"

"I asked if you wanted to see if my mom made any dinner."

"Sure," I said.

"Did you maybe want to rent a movie or something first?"

I shrugged. I didn't really care either way. I was beginning to feel hungry, but renting a movie first seemed more practical.

"Let's do that then," Jeremy suggested.

We walked to the rental place without much chatter. I was mostly thinking about the fact Jeremy had not yet attempted to hold my hand or anything. I had purposely not worn gloves in case he did try. I had been contemplating taking his, but didn't quite have the boldness to make the move. However, I felt nervous he wasn't going to make much of a move on me at all this evening, and at the very least I hoped he would give me a kiss goodnight. A proper one too, not a kiss on the cheek or something.

We reached our town's local rental store and wandered around quietly. I saw a couple of people I knew from school, and wondered if they thought Jeremy and I were on a date. I couldn't help but blush from the idea and tried not to look directly at them in case they tried to talk to me.

"Here," Jeremy said, handing me his choice. He was smiling faintly.

"A horror movie?" I asked, trying not to give him a sceptical look. "Can't we save watching those until college or something? When you can actually sleep in the same bed as me if you get scared?"

"You haven't yet agreed to live with me when we go to college."

"Either way, at least then nobody is going to flip out if you sneak out to see me in the middle of the night because you're too scared to sleep."

"I'm not going to be too scared to sleep."

"Oh so there's no vampires in this one?" I quickly scanned the back. Zombies. How romantic.

"Scratch this one, maybe we should get something funny," he said. I handed him my choice, a romantic comedy. I smiled at him sweetly. He wrinkled his nose slightly.

"I kept thinking my days of watching bad romantic comedies were over," he muttered.

"You watched one last week when I was asleep!" I reminded him.

"I was also still slightly drunk. It seemed pretty amusing at the time. How about this?" He handed me a fairly sexually neutral looking drama. "It has Brad Pitt." I felt a small pang. I usually watched Brad Pitt movies with Liam. In fact, looking at the cover, I had probably seen that one with him.

"I think I've seen it," I muttered. "Ohhh, how about this one? It has a talking dog," I said in delight.

"Sounds super exciting. Too bad I'm not eight and can fully appreciate it," Jeremy said dryly.

"Fine. I bet Nicole will watch it with me." I put it back.

"Okay how about this?" Jeremy handed me a recently released action movie. It looked okay, did not have any talking dogs or Brad Pitt, and seemed to have a slightly believable plot.

"Sure. But first, can we check for any new Nathan Sweeney movies?" I pleaded.

"Who? Oh that blond idiot you like? Um, he hasn't been in anything recently," Jeremy said. I gave him a suspicious look.

"I'm sure they will release one in time to make a double feature with the talking dog movie you and Nicole will watch together." Jeremy grinned at me.

He paid for the rental and we left, still without holding hands. We walked the short distance to his house, where Andrea greeted us warmly.

"We didn't want to eat at my house," I said to her as she poured us each tall glasses of milk after we told her we wanted some dinner.

"Why?" Andrea asked.

"Becky doesn't like her mom's boyfriend," Jeremy said as he sat down at the table.

"That's not true!" I objected. I sat down next to him.

"Um, yes it is."

"Well, whatever." I couldn't think of a better argument.

"I hope you're happy with pasta," Andrea said as she put a bowl with parmesan cheese in front of us.

"Sounds good," I said to her. She hummed to herself as she pulled things out of the cupboard. "Did you want any help?" I asked. She shook her head.

Jeremy told Andrea about the schools we looked at while she made dinner.

After a fairly talkative dinner, Andrea cleared away the plates and gave us a large smile.

"I'm going to go watch a movie in my room," she said.

"What are you so smiley about?" Jeremy asked her.

"I'm just feeling pleased that you're home on a Saturday night and you're here with Becky. I love you lots." She leaned down and kissed his cheek. He rolled his eyes and she left.

"That was awkward," he muttered.

"No it wasn't." I smiled at him and squeezed his knee.

"Did you want to watch the movie now?" he asked. I nodded. We got up and moved to the living room, where Jeremy handed me a large blanket.

"Did you want popcorn?" he asked as I curled up with the blanket around myself.

"Up to you," I said feeling pretty content. He shrugged and put the movie in. He sat down next to me and I moved

The Sweet Kiss of Friendship

closer to him, hoping it would encourage him to put his arm around me. He did.

Fifteen minutes into the movie Jeremy paused the movie and turned to me. I sat up, startled.

"I'm trying to go slow," he said.

"What?" I asked, not sure what he was referring to.

"With you. I'm trying to really think about everything before I do something. I don't want to screw it up."

"Oh." I wasn't really sure what else to say.

"That's why I haven't made a move or tried to make this into a date or anything."

"Oh," I said again.

"I just thought I should tell you, in case you were wondering what was going on." I had been wondering what was going on, but didn't really want to admit that to him.

"Why did you kiss me then? On Thursday after I came over from Liam's?" I asked after a moment.

"I'll give you a hint: think back to my behaviour before I left." I sat there, contemplating for awhile.

"Because you wanted to kiss me then but could never manage it?" I finally suggested.

Jeremy smiled. "You're so . . ." He touched my cheek. "You're so very you. No, that's not it. Well, I shouldn't say that: I did want to kiss you but not because I couldn't manage to pull it off before."

"So you kissed me because you wanted to?" I asked, feeling confused. Somehow, I felt like there should be more to the answer than that.

"Yes," Jeremy concurred.

"And?" I pressed.

"And I didn't want anything to happen with Liam."

"So it was a manipulative kiss then?" I asked, understanding now what he meant by his behaviour before he left. He had

177

been fairly manipulative then, and attempted more than one scheme to keep my romantic encounters to a minimum.

"Sorry. I just . . . he had said he had been thinking about asking you out and I wasn't sure if you understood I still wanted you nor did I know if you still wanted me. I just thought if I kissed you, at least if Liam did ask you out you would know where I stood before you gave him an answer. Then I realized the next day I could have just told you how I felt and I should be more worried about how you felt rather than whether or not Liam was going to ask you out."

"Are you planning on kissing me again or was that just some method of keeping me date free while you contemplated how you want to proceed with me?" I realized I may have said this with a slightly icy tone. I did not like the idea that he was stringing me along. I also thought if this was the case, Liam may have been right about a couple of things. Still didn't change the bet Liam made, though.

Jeremy glanced at the hall, probably towards wherever Andrea was.

"Not this very moment. You're probably not in the most ideal mood for it. And Andrea is like ten feet away. By the way, just so you understand: I know how I want to proceed with you, I just want to give everything thought before I dive into it. I don't really have too much confidence in myself not to behave erratically should something happen I'm not prepared for. I just don't want to feel overwhelmed."

"Do I overwhelm you?" I asked.

"No." Jeremy hesitated. "I'm not really sure how to explain this. I started fooling around with that girl last year, right?" I nodded. "And at the time I was going through issues so I kind of just used her as an outlet."

"Okaaaay," I said.

"Well, I don't want you to be my outlet."

"Jeremy we already established I'm pretty much dumb when it comes to these kinds of conversations, can you help me out here?"

"I don't want to just fool around with you. So I want to be careful about what steps I take and how soon I take them. And you're not dumb; you just happen to think the best of people and sometimes miss the negative point of view because of it."

"I think I understand what you mean," I said. "And to clarify: you do want a relationship you just want to take some time in getting there?"

"Yes. I already said earlier today I still want you as more than a friend. I don't need alot of time getting there, but I don't want to rush."

"Okay," I said.

"Can I turn the movie back on?" Jeremy asked.

"Sure."

Jeremy picked up the remote but instead turned to stare at me for a long while.

"What?" I finally asked. He smiled.

"I do want to kiss you but . . ." he glanced towards the hall again. "Maybe later?" I nodded. He put his arm around me and put the movie back on. I snuggled up against him, feeling better.

When the movie ended, I stood up to stretch. Despite the high action and adrenaline style of the movie, I was feeling rather sleepy.

"I'm tired," I said to Jeremy as I yawned.

"Me too," he said, yawning in return. I briefly thought about how nice it would be if we lived together at college and after watching a movie, could fall asleep together. Instead, I had to make my way home.

"Did you want me to walk you home now?" Jeremy asked.

"Yeah," I mumbled. I walked over to the closet to retrieve my jacket. He disappeared down the hall and I could hear him talking to Andrea. He came back within a moment and took his own jacket from the closet.

"Did you have fun?" Jeremy asked me as we headed outside.

"Sure."

"I mean, I know it probably wasn't quite what you were hoping for this evening."

"You're being ridiculous. This was just as awesome as when we use to rent movies and watch them on your couch." I smiled at him.

"Are you being cheeky?" he asked. He reached out and took my hand. I bit my lip to hold back another smile, feeling happy he was holding my hand.

"I'm never cheeky," I responded.

We teased each other for the entire walk to my house. When we reached my door, I was giggling and attempting to avoid his tickles. Which, should he have reached me, probably would have been fairly ineffective over my winter coat.

"You win." I grabbed his hands to stop him from tickling me.

"What do I win?" he asked.

"The tickle war!"

"I mean, do I get a prize?"

"What would you like?" I asked coyly. I raised my eye brows at him, then winked.

"I'll give you a hint: what I want is right in front of me."

I made a show of looking around the porch. I picked up an umbrella from my mom's umbrella stand.

"Oh is it this lovely umbrella Jer? I believe it is a ravishing shade of lavender. It'll go very well with your current outfit." I handed him the umbrella with a grin. Jeremy smiled, took the umbrella, and placed it back in the stand.

"I think I'll just claim it for myself," he said softly. He cupped my cheek in one hand and circled his arm around my back with the other. We leaned towards each other, closing the distance between us. When our lips finally touched I reached out and put my hand on the back of his head to press against him more firmly. I did not want a sissy lip brush this time.

When we pulled apart he immediately started grinning at me.

"What?" I asked as I wiped the corner of my mouth.

"What was that?" he asked.

"What was what?"

"Your death grip on me." I snorted.

"I didn't have a death grip on you!" I retorted.

"Sure. Either way, I got your message."

"You're imagining things," I muttered. I pulled my keys out of my pocket and unlocked the door. I turned back to him.

"Well . . ." I said.

"I'll call you later?" he suggested.

"Okay." Jeremy turned to go, but paused and turned around a couple of feet away.

"Oh and Beck?" he said.

"Yes?"

"Maybe this wasn't quite like our old movie nights." I stuck my tongue out at him as he waved and turned back to leave. I entered my house and leaned against the door, grinning. In just a mere week we had gone from not speaking to kissing outside my front door. Progress had definitely been made.

Chapter 10

Diary Entry: September 9, 2007

It's the start of the school year. Basically, it's the same as last year. Everyone thinks Jeremy and I are dating or something. I think that's Jessica's doing. Jeremy is scared of her. Oh, well. It turns out several people found out about the Craig thing. I don't really care. Craig doesn't seem to care either. So now all I have to do is convince everyone I'm not dating Jeremy. Simple, right?

Present Day: November 8, 2009

The next morning, after sufficient time to joyously re-think the previous evening, I phoned Jess.

"Hello?" she said groggily.

"I miss you!" I said.

"Oh, Beck, I miss you!" Her voice brightened slightly.

"Can you come over?" I asked hopefully. It was ten in the morning, which was generally far too early for her to appear outside on a weekend.

"You come here, I'm still in bed."

"Okay, I'll be there in an hour."

"Good. And wear comfy clothes, it's a bed day."

After a long shower, I put my hair into a pony tail, threw on my comfiest sweats, and walked over.

Jessica and I spent the majority of the day lying on her bed and giggling over each of our previous evenings. It was only broken up by the occasional need to urinate and twice with phone calls, one from Jeremy and the other from Will. Both conversations involved Jess and I pressing our ears against the phone in a desperate attempt to both hear the entire conversation. While it worked with Will, after a couple of minutes Jeremy randomly said he thought Jessica's outfit the other day was surprisingly conservative of her. She had immediately started objecting and asking which outfit was too conservative. Clearly, she had missed he was setting her up to reveal listening in on our phone conversation.

After the day of lounging with Jess, I went home and finished the last of my homework before heading to bed. After turning off the light and relaxing for a moment, it hit me I would probably see Liam at school the next day. I had not spent any time deciding what I wanted to say to him or if I was even prepared to talk to him. All I knew was thinking about the bet with Adrian made me want to cry. Whatever Liam had thought he was achieving from the bet, all he got was ten dollars and my anger.

Diary Entry: September 30, 2007

So it isn't exactly easy convincing everyone that I'm not dating Jeremy. Especially since Jeremy refuses to deny going out with me. He gives this awful mysterious smile whenever anyone asks him. He just tells them it's none of their business. I got mad at him today during Science and I asked him why he refused to say he wasn't going out with me. All he said was "Why, does the concept upset you?" What's that supposed to mean? I asked him that and he just shook his head and grinned. Now what am I supposed to do?

Present Day: November 9, 2009

The next day I arrived at school and anxiously watched out for Liam at every corner.

"You look nuts," Jenny advised me as she gathered books from her locker. "Stop looking for him. What are you going to do if you see him anyway? Run away?"

"No," I said, slightly defensively.

"Well, then, don't look for him. Ignoring him will look far more natural if it doesn't appear that you've seen him. It's either that or jumping into my locker. Oh, there he is!"

"What?" I moved the locker door and tried to hide behind it.

"I'm joking. I wanted to see if you would jump into my locker." She closed her locker and shook her head at me.

"I don't know what to do," I said with a pout.

"Go hang out with Jeremy. Liam will avoid you if you're with him."

"I don't know where Jeremy is," I muttered.

The bell rang so without discussing where he might be, Jenny and I took off for class.

A couple of hours later, I found Jeremy sitting with Jess at our usual lunch spot. Nicole, Jenny, and I sat down with them.

"He thinks he's cool enough to eat lunch with us," Jessica said.

"Really?" I asked.

"Yes but I told him it is our time to discuss penises."

"This is true," Nicole said. It wasn't, but just the same we all gave Jeremy a knowing smile.

"Yeah, I have one, I can probably discuss them better than at least two of you."

"Two of us?" The four of us looked at each other.

"Which two does he assume are the lesser experienced ones?" Jenny asked.

"Well he knows I haven't done anything, so I'm one of them," I said.

"Oh, Jenny, I bet he assumes I'm the slutty one and you're the innocent one," Nicole said to Jenny. Jenny nodded.

"Actually I said at least two because I'm not sure about either of you. But I felt it was safe to assume at least one of you was on a similar experience level as Becky, otherwise she would have complained about being the only one."

"He assumes I'm slutty," Jess said.

"So does everyone else," Nicole said with a smile.

"Hi, Becky." We all turned to the voice behind us. Sandy was standing there, looking pretty as usual. While she often looked quite intimidating, today she was offering a friendly smile.

"And this is why I actually came to sit with you," Jeremy said.

"Hi, Sandy," I said cautiously. I tried to look around her to see if Liam was standing nearby. He wasn't.

"Can we talk for a moment?" she asked.

"No," Jess and Jeremy said at the same time. I turned to look at them.

"Anything you want to say to her, you can say to us," Jess said firmly.

"She'll just tell us anyway," Jeremy added.

"She doesn't need a babysitter, and the matter is private. Whatever she chooses to tell you is up to her, but until then I don't need either of you glaring at me just because I live in the same house as Liam. Now, Becky, I would like to talk for a moment if you have the time?" She had glared at Jess and Jeremy, but turned to me with a sweet smile.

"Yeah, okay," I muttered. She would find a way to talk to me one way or another, I might as well get it over with. I got up and followed her about ten feet away from the others. I saw Jess start to stand up but Nicole pushed her back down. I turned to face Sandy.

"I understand," she said. I gave her a confused look.

"Sorry?"

"I understand what this is like. For you."

"Oh." I wasn't entirely sure what she meant and why she thought she understood.

"What Liam did was shitty and dumb. He's an idiot and he doesn't understand how to talk himself into and out of situations."

"Okay," I said, still confused.

"Between you and me, and I guess potentially your two guardians there, there's a reason I don't really date." I was surprised. I somehow assumed Sandy was always dating. However, thinking about it, I realized that she flirted with whoever suited her. "Before Liam and I started here, I use to really like this guy, Mark. He was great. But I left junior high and came here and he goes to a senior high school outside of Bellingham. I still like him, but I never see him anymore and I never really told him how much I liked him. He started dating someone last year from his new school, and he has been ever since. So yeah, sometimes I lead guys on or make-out with them at a party, but I don't really date. I'm still pining for Mark. I'm still trying to get over it. I'm still regretting not saying something when I had the chance. So I get what's going on with Jeremy and I get that you spent last year pining for him. You were unavailable emotionally; even if Liam had asked you out you wouldn't have dated him. It's far easier to date dipsticks like Adrian who have the emotional capacity of pickle jar and much harder to date someone who's company you genuinely enjoy. But Liam doesn't understand that. All he knows is he waited around for a year to determine what was going on inside that pretty head of yours and ended up stuck in a dumb bet with Adrian in his attempt to figure out what's kept you from seeming attracted to the male species. The poetic justice of it all for him is Jeremy's arrival finally clues him in, only in turn preventing him from making a move. So I wanted you to know: I understand. But I want you to understand Liam is an idiot and he caught himself in a mess he didn't know how to back out of. He never meant for the bet to take place, and he certainly didn't think it would hurt you. He didn't know how to back out of the bet so he just kept it a secret. And while he isn't thrilled Jeremy is here, he wasn't in love with you or something, he was interested. It's not the end of the world that he's missed his opportunity, he just doesn't know how to behave. He also doesn't know how to explain himself."

"Which is why you're here," I said.

"No, he doesn't know I'm here. I didn't tell him I was going to talk to you and frankly I wasn't planning on telling him. I'm just hoping to shed some light for you. That's all."

"Okay. Well, thanks Sandy."

"No problem." She pulled some gum out of her mouth and threw it in a garbage can nearby.

"I won't tell anyone, Jeremy and Jessica included, about that guy and stuff," I said.

"I appreciate it. Now, I'm off before someone sees me talking to you. No offense or anything, but all my nerd time is reserved for Liam."

"Right. See you around." I gave her an awkward wave as she flounced off. I walked back over to the others, who all had curious expressions on their faces.

"What did she say? Liam is hot? Because, you know, I'm not so sure he's the best looking guy in school. No offense to him or anything," Jess said.

"No she wasn't trying to convince me to be attracted to Liam or anything. She just wanted to explain that's he can be dumb and did not know how to handle the situation with Adrian."

"We all knew he has his idiotic moments," Nicole said. I shrugged.

"Did it make you feel any better? The talk with Sandy?" Jenny asked.

"Yeah."

"Well then it served a good purpose. That's all that really matters," she said. Jessica rolled her eyes.

"Sandy puts far too much effort into helping Liam out with his social skills. If he had just gone to her in the first place, chances are she would have told him how to handle the bet fiasco and Becky would never have gotten upset with him in the first place. He needs to learn to ask for advice when he needs it and handle his problems when he screws up," Jess said.

"Jess, I actually agree with you. That was surprisingly wise," Jeremy said.

"Thanks Jer."

"Well, anyway, now that that's over, I'm off." Jeremy stood up.

"You knew Sandy was going to talk to me?" I asked him.

"No but I figured one of them would say something. Besides, I'm not welcome here; you guys want to talk about penises."

"Only Jess does," Nicole said with a grin.

"Whatever," Jess muttered.

"Anyway, I'll see you guys later." Jeremy waved at us as he turned to leave.

"He's so odd," Jessica said sourly.

"What are you upset about?" I asked.

"Who does he think he is only coming by to act protective or something? I can do that, we don't need him here!" Jess said. Nicole laughed.

"We all know you can protect us, he's just forgotten," Jenny said, patting Jessica on the back.

"Don't worry Jess, I'll set him straight and let him know you're my go to suit of armour," I said to her, trying not to laugh.

"You better," she muttered.

We spent the rest of lunch gossiping. Jenny and Nicole hadn't yet heard much about Jessica's date with Will.

The rest of the afternoon went by without any excitement. Liam came to Math class and took his usual seat, but he didn't speak to any of us. He barely even looked our way. The others watched him with curiosity, but I avoided looking at him.

Jeremy sat at his usual seat at the other end of the room and didn't bother to notice Liam before or after class. I figured he was probably trying to avoid making matters worse. I appreciated him not making a scene or being sneery towards him. It certainly wouldn't help the situation.

While I did contemplate trying to say something to Liam, I wasn't sure what I could possibly say that would solve anything. I wasn't about to apologize; while I felt a twinge of guilt for what I had said, it wasn't as if I had said something untrue or unfair. He didn't know the other side of Jeremy or how he treated me; he only saw the bad bits. Even then, he had never witnessed anything, just heard second hand information.

The bet Liam had made was undoubtedly a bad decision. I felt fully justified in waiting for him to apologize for it. There was nothing I would or needed to say to make that any better. It was up to him to decide what he wanted to do.

When I lay down in bed that night, I decided that I would just wait for him to make the first move. Even if it meant Liam never said anything to me ever again, I wasn't prepared to repair the damage without him putting in the first effort. So I would wait, even if it meant waiting forever. Ultimately, I realized, my pride was more important than my friendship with Liam, and while that may seem harsh, I believed I was holding onto my integrity. I would not allow him, or anyone else, to think it is okay to foolishly bet on me and potentially play with my feelings. It was up to Liam to make things right, not me.

Diary Entry: November 10, 2007

Jeremy, I have decided, is very confusing. I did not know how to handle him refusing to tell people we weren't dating. So I decided to put the rumours to rest myself. I asked Craig to go to the Halloween dance with me to confuse all the people under the assumption I'm just denying my relationship with Jeremy. Craig said he was glad to do the favour. Jeremy wasn't exactly thrilled that I went with Craig, but he didn't say anything to me about it. Also, I think he started telling people we were not an item, nor had we been. Probably because he didn't want everyone to think I had dumped him.

Anyway, at the very least, I asked him the other day if he would be nice to anyone I have an interest in and not try to scare them off. He had muttered a bunch, but concurred. However, I doubt there will be many guys around to date. Nobody seems to know what's going on with me. Ultimately, though, I guess it doesn't really matter. I would rather have Jeremy around as my best friend than anyone as a boyfriend.

Present Day: November 13, 2009

The rest of the week went by without any incidents. Liam did not speak to me or any of my friends, and I did not speak to him.

Jeremy and I were still in some sort of limbo. We had not kissed since the previous Saturday and he had made no attempts to make a date. We had hung out, but with the exception of going over to his place to watch television on Thursday night, we had been hanging out with other people around.

On the 11th we had the day off school and Jess and I had met up with him and Robert. I hadn't seen Robert in well over a year. It had been a fairly casual day; we went to a matinee movie before Robert and Jeremy left to catch up on some sort of martial arts video game. Or maybe it had been car crashing.

"So still nothing?" Jess was asking me as we walked to Math class on Friday afternoon.

"No, no kiss goodnight, and his mom drove me home."

"Seriously? I assumed he didn't kiss you on Wednesday because Robert and I were there, but nothing last night either? He is taking his time!" I shrugged. We had cuddled on the couch but no kissing.

"Maybe he didn't kiss me because Andrea was there? She drove me home, not him. Maybe if he had driven me home we would have had a moment for a kiss?"

"I don't know. Perhaps something his head shrinker said," Jessica suggested.

"Head shrinker?"

"You know, therapist. You told me he had to see a psychologist right?" As per Jeremy's agreement with Andrea, he had gone for a session this week.

"Yes I'm just not sure if you would call one a head shrinker. Anyway, you could be right, the therapist may have suggested he take things slowly. He didn't want to share their lovely hour long talk, so I have no idea what the person said to him."

"He probably didn't want to tell you because he only wanted to talk about his fear of vampires or something useless like that."

"Well, I'm not asking him," I said.

"I will if you like!" Jess offered.

"No thanks," I said quickly. We reached our class and peeked inside. No Liam. We entered and took our seats.

"If you want more smooches from him, you should stop spending time with me after school and start spending time with him," Jess hissed at me.

"You mean more time with him? I saw him twice this week!"

"And what are you doing this evening? Spending another Friday night with Nicole and Jenny? It's date night!"

"Hey, I'm a great date!" Nicole leaned in to get in on the conversation. "Besides, he didn't want to watch the talking dog movie."

"Oh, it's going to be so cute!" I said to Nicole. She nodded. Jessica rolled her eyes.

The bell rang and Liam sauntered in. I had a feeling he had been waiting outside the door until the bell rang. This way, there was no chance I would speak to him before Mr. Rambouski started class.

As soon as class ended he was out the door without so much as even a look my way. We all gave his back a firm glare.

"Hey," Jeremy said as he came over to where we were packing away our books.

"Hi," I said. The others gave him friendly smiles and nods.

"Did you want to do something tomorrow?" he asked me.

"Sure," I said. I kept my thought of "yes I'd love another non-date!" to myself.

"Cool I'll call you tomorrow morning. See you guys, enjoy your talking dog movie."

"Not me, I'm going on a date!" Jess yelled at his back as he left.

"I have one tomorrow," Nicole said defensively.

"I don't," Jenny said with a small pout.

"You're too mature for the guys in our school, they don't appreciate your kindness," Jess said to her warmly. Jess was rarely warm, but Jenny seemed to bring it out of people.

Jenny shrugged. It wasn't just that the guys didn't appreciate her niceness, she was far too shy to ever offer up hints of attraction. If Liam was around, Nicole and I would encourage more time with Darien, but as it was it seemed unlikely we would be able to use Liam as a conduit for a blossoming romance between Jenny and Darien.

"Well, ladies, I will see you all later. I have to get ready for my Friday night date!" Jessica grinned at us excitedly and flounced off. We grumbled about Jess and her date boasting before heading off to rent out talking dog movie. I don't know who Jessica was kidding: talking dogs were far cuter than any guy.

Diary Entry: January 22, 2008

So after the Christmas dance I'm pretty sure everyone is up to speed with my relationship status. I went and Jeremy didn't. Any remaining rumours circulating were axed when I showed up to the dance with Jenny and no date.

That aside, I've been worrying about Jeremy a bit. He's been a little peculiar this week. He was sick the end of last week and ever since has been very quiet. He keeps avoiding his house and says he doesn't want to see his parents. If I ask him why, he shrugs and mumbles stuff about feeling uncomfortable. I'm concerned, but I don't really know what to do. I think I'll just watch his behaviour and see if it gets worse or not.

Present Day: November 14, 2009

I woke up feeling groggy and confused. Something had woken me. I smashed my hand around my nightstand in the dark for my phone. It showed no missed calls or text messages; something else had woken me up.

I peered into the dark as I heard a funny sound outside my window. I slowly got out of my bed, feeling nervous. I grabbed a large pair of scissors and dialled 9-1-1 on my phone without hitting call. I edged towards my bedroom window as I heard some shuffling and something mumbled. I was definitely not imagining someone outside my window.

I yanked the curtain back quickly, hoping to surprise whoever was out there. Sure enough I startled Jeremy who jumped in surprise and dropped his phone.

"You scared me!" I hissed at him as I opened the window. He picked up his phone.

"I didn't think you'd woken up; I was about to phone you."

"What are you doing here? It's like one in the morning!"

"I know that," he snapped. He climbed through the window and glared at me.

"What are you glaring at me for? You're the one who woke me up in the middle of the night," I said, slightly angry.

"Sorry," he mumbled. I closed my phone and put the scissors down as Jeremy put his backpack on the floor. I noticed not only did he still have his school bag with him, he was in the same clothes from earlier today. It seemed unlikely he had gone home after school.

"What's going on?" I asked him. I shivered as the cold air started to seep into my room.

"Nothing," he muttered. He sat on the edge of my bed and I sat down next to him. His phone beeped at him but he ignored it. I decided to stay silent.

"You're shivering," Jeremy observed after a bit, looking over at my bare arms. I felt slightly embarrassed as I remembered I was in my pyjamas: light pink fleece pants with a matching pink t-shirt with a cupcake in the centre and the word "Yummy!" below it. The t-shirt was only a thin fabric and for the second time in the past couple of weeks I was very aware I was not wearing a bra around him.

Jeremy got up and closed the open window. He sat back down next to me, only this time put his arms around me and started to rub my arms with his hands.

"What are you doing here?" I asked him again.

"I couldn't be at home."

"Why?" Jeremy didn't say anything. His phone beeped again.

"Who's texting you?" I asked.

"Andrea." Well, at least that meant she knew he wasn't home. We lapsed into silence.

"Can I stay here?" Jeremy asked after awhile. Immediately I wondered if he meant my room and I started to blush and feel nervous.

"Here?" I squeaked. "Overnight?"

"I just need a place to crash. I wasn't able to stay at Robert's and I didn't know where else to go."

I wanted to ask why he didn't go home, but I felt it was unlikely he would tell me. At least not at this moment.

"Well, I'm not sure if I'm ready to have sleepovers and stuff." I wanted to let him stay, but I felt very nervous and fidgety over sharing a bed.

"I meant the couch," he said bluntly.

"Oh." I wasn't sure if I felt more embarrassed at the idea of sharing a bed and how not ready I was for that, or at the assumption I had made. "Yeah, you can stay on the couch." I didn't think my mom would care. At least not too much.

"Thanks." We lapsed into another silence which was occasionally broken from his phone beeping. After several beeps, he pulled out his phone and dialled.

"Hi," he said, standing up. "Yes, I'm here." I assumed, and hoped, he was talking to Andrea. "I don't know," he said. He handed me his phone. I took it, startled.

"Um . . . hello?"

"Becky? Jeremy wants to stay there, is that okay with you?" Andrea asked.

"Yes."

"Okay. Don't let him take advantage of the situation okay?"

"Sure," I replied, feeling mildly confused.

"I guess it's just nice timing for him considering I gave him that photocopy yesterday," Andrea said.

"What?"

"Nothing. Anyway, what about your mom? Will she be okay with this?"

"I think so."

"Good enough for now. I'll phone her early tomorrow and explain things. Listen, Hon, you get some sleep, don't worry about Jer. Can you pass me back to him?" I handed Jeremy the phone. He talked to her for a moment before hanging up. I didn't ask what it was all about, I simply got up and went to the hall closet to get him a pillow and blanket. He followed me to the closet.

After handing him the pillow and blanket he stared at me.

"What?" I asked him quietly, hoping not to wake my mom.

"Do you want to watch T.V. for a bit? I don't think I can sleep right now," he said almost as quietly. I shrugged. We went to the living room where I plopped down on the couch as he searched for the remote. He found it, sat next to me, and flicked the T.V. on.

After he found a cartoon channel he took his blanket and wrapped it around my shoulders. I didn't say anything, feeling confused.

"I'm sorry," he mumbled. I turned to look at him. "For coming by in the middle of the night and not telling you why."

"It's okay," I said. There were probably worse places he could be.

"I don't really want to talk about it right now though. Maybe later."

"I know."

Jeremy smiled suddenly.

"What?" I asked him.

"I'm proud of myself."

197

"For?"

"I was upset and I told my mom what was going on and I came here instead of going to a random party or drinking or something."

"Well then, this is worth losing beauty sleep over," I said, returning his smile. He took my hand and squeezed it gently. I leaned my head against his shoulder and started to relax as I watched animated creatures inflict harmless violence upon each other in an attempt to be funny. After awhile I started to feel sleepy. My eyes were drooping and I had occasionally become aware of some drool. I sat up, wiping my mouth.

"Did you want to go back to bed? I'm fine here," Jeremy said. I did want to go back to bed, but I was worried he would sneak off and I wouldn't find out what was going on. Then again, he had the decency to tell his mother where he was.

"I'm okay," I fibbed.

"You should at least stretch out to sleep. It'll be more comfortable."

"I don't need to sleep," I said unconvincingly.

"Right. Listen, I'll still be here in the morning, I'm not going to go find myself a two a.m. drug deal because you're not babysitting me."

"You did drugs?" I squeaked.

"I was making a joke. Go to bed." He leaned over to kiss my forehead and pull me up from the couch.

"You didn't answer my question," I said accusingly. Every once in awhile I forgot to be daft and picked up on these things.

"Oh my God you're right! Anyway, I'll see you in the morning. Night Rebecca." He gave me a light shove away from the couch and smiled at me.

"You're explaining yourself tomorrow," I said firmly, eyes narrowed.

"Have a nice sleep." He sat back down and started to flip through channels. I glared at the back of his head for a moment. Then, feeling a surge of gladness he had come here rather than do something dumb, I walked over, kissed the top of his head, and left for my room.

Diary Entry: February 17, 2008

Jeremy seems okay now. I figure it was just some sort of strange stage he went through. Perhaps it was just something to do with school?

Anyway, Craig got a girlfriend. Guess who? Melanie. What a shocker that was. I don't think Jeremy cares in the slightest his first date is now dating my ex. He says he's quite pleased Craig found someone. My guess is he was more anxious about the possibilities of me and Craig than himself and Melanie. Whatever, it's time Jeremy found himself a girlfriend before some dumb jock decides he's gay or something. If he doesn't announce feelings for a girl at some point I'm pretty sure everyone is going to wonder . . .

Chapter 11

Present Day: November 14, 2009

When I woke up my first thought was of the previous evening. Was Jeremy still here? I tried to listen as best as I could from where I lay in my bed, but I couldn't hear anything to indicate if he was still here or not. Getting up, I then had to decide if I wanted to get dressed before I left my room, or just come out in my pyjamas. Jeremy had seen me first thing in the morning plenty of times, from trips up to the lake in Canada to falling asleep on his couch at his old house. Somehow this seemed different.

I decided getting dressed would be pointless considering I would still have to shower, so I brushed out my hair before putting on my robe.

As soon as I opened my bedroom door I could hear him in the kitchen talking. I assumed he was talking to my mother. I wandered in slowly. I felt slightly weird that he was here and that I didn't know why.

"Morning," my mom said as I appeared.

"Hey Beck," Jeremy said.

"Hi," I said to them both. I sat down in my usual spot at the table. Both were drinking tea and my mom had an empty plate with crumbs on it. Jeremy was eating cereal.

"Did you sleep well?" Jeremy asked. I shrugged. "Did you want some tea? There's a pot on the counter." I got up to where he pointed and poured myself some tea.

"Well, I think I'll go shower." My mom stood up and took her plate to the dishwasher before leaving.

"So . . . did she say anything about you being here?" I asked Jeremy.

"No. Andrea phoned her this morning pretty early, so she knew I was here before she even saw me. She actually came to find me and confirm with my mom that I was still here."

"Ah." I sipped my tea, not certain if I was yet able to wisely ask him what had happened.

"So you're probably wondering what's going on," Jeremy said to me with a smile.

"Who me? Oh, well . . . just a little . . ."

"Tom's here." Jeremy said it without a hint or irony or emotion.

"Your dad?" I asked stupidly.

"Yes."

"Where?" I felt even more stupid for asking where. Clearly, Jeremy meant in town, I wasn't entirely sure where else he would mean.

"In town. I don't know where in town, but in town."

"I'm assuming this is unexpected."

"Yeah. I left the school yesterday by the north exit and saw him waiting by his car. He didn't see me amongst the crowd so I left by the gym exit and went to Robert's. I phoned my mom and she thought I was being paranoid until she phoned Carrie who said he had left for a medical conference for an unknown period of time. Robert went by the house to see if he was hanging out there and he was, but he must have left before Andrea came home from work because she didn't see him. However, he came by this morning looking for me and

Andrea yelled at him and made threats to call her lawyer or something. Which probably wouldn't do much. Either way, I'm pretty pissed the jackass is stalking me."

"I don't know if stalking is the right—" Jeremy gave me a bad look. "Yes, stalking you, how unfortunate." I sighed. "So that's why you were all moody yesterday? You were upset that he was hanging outside the school?"

"Yes, stalking me."

"Right, stalking," I corrected myself, trying not to roll my eyes at his drama.

"I don't want him around! I don't want to talk to him! The whole reason we moved here was so I could get away and sort myself out!"

"Of course," I said soothingly.

"He doesn't respect any of my decisions. This is just a prime example of him thinking he can barge in and muck around with our lives as he sees fit. Move me to Virginia, cheat on my mom, marry that whore." I winced at Jeremy's choice in word. "I'm not seeing him."

"You have every right to avoid him," I confirmed. "But, just how do you plan on avoiding him?"

"Your mom said I could stay here for a couple of days while Andrea sorts out some sort of parental right or something like that. I get to sleep on the couch."

"He's not going to look for you here?"

"Last Carrie has heard we weren't speaking so he probably wouldn't think to look for me here if she's been passing along gossip as we can all assume. I haven't told Carrie anything since Halloween in case she was over excited and decided to come out for some sort of double date with that Greek guy from next door."

"Greek guy? I thought she liked a Spanish guy," I said, confused.

"He's Greek, And his name is Richard, not Ricardo. She just assumed he was a Spanish song writer. She likes Ricky Glasy-something right now."

"Enrique Iglesias?"

"Sure. Anyway, unless Andrea has told her otherwise, you went home after seeing me at the hospital."

"Did you lie to Carrie?" I asked somewhat accusingly.

"I wouldn't say lie . . . I left out stuff. I said you did come to the hospital and you were mad at me and said after this you didn't want to be around me anymore. Or whatever it was you said about avoiding me. I didn't say we talked about it beyond that or that we . . . you know kissed or anything like that."

"Okay and you didn't tell her this in case we had to go on a double date with the neighbour next time she was visiting?" Jeremy squirmed slightly, looking uncomfortable.

"No."

"Then . . . ." I let my voice trail off as I looked at him expectantly.

"In case I jinxed it by telling anyone."

"Seriously?"

"Whatever Beck, you use to freak out over cracks in the sidewalk over that "step on a crack break my mother's back" rhyme."

"Use to, when I was like thirteen."

"Or sixteen," Jeremy muttered.

"So you feel confident Tom won't come around here looking for you?" I asked, wanting to get back to the real topic of interest.

"He might, but I'm not about to answer the door so it'll be easy enough to fool him."

"And my mom said it was okay for you to stay here?"

"Yes but she has some "ground rules" she would like to go over with us." He said it with quotation marks.

"Oh," I said, wrinkling my nose.

"Yes and I know why. Which reminds me, I have something to give you."

"Oh really?" I asked, delighted.

"It's not a present if that's what you're thinking," Jeremy said with a smirk.

"I wasn't," I said, trying to keep a straight face. "What is it?"

"I'll wait until your mom leaves."

"She's in the shower."

"No she's not, the water isn't running anymore. I'll wait until she doesn't interrupt. It's kind of weird. You'll understand later." I shrugged. He was right, the water wasn't running anymore. Jeremy finished his cereal and put the bowl in the dishwasher before coming to sit back down.

"What about clothes?" I asked him, noticing he was wearing the same clothes as the day before.

"Your mom and my mom are meeting up and Andrea is going to give them to Pam then."

"Ah. They are quite diabolical those two," I said.

"Hmmm." Jeremy nodded.

My mom came in fully dressed and holding her shoes.

"Okay, I'm going out to meet Andrea, but while you two are both sitting here, I would like to go over some ground rules. Oh! I guess first I should ask you Becky if you're okay with Jeremy staying here. I suppose I should have asked you first."

"I don't mind," I said with a shrug.

"Great," my mom said. "So anyway, Jeremy you sleep on the couch. You're not allowed in Becky's room after I go to bed and before I get up in the morning. Becky, you are to be in your own room between midnight and seven, not hanging out in the living room."

"Midnight? I have a curfew at midnight?"

"Other than sleepovers with Jess, how often do you stay up past midnight?"

"Not very often but—"

"It's only while Jeremy is here. Besides, it's a guideline rule: you can still go to the bathroom or get up and make tea or something, I just don't want you and him doing whatever you feel like while I am trying to sleep."

"Pam I'm not about to disrespect you in your own house so don't worry I—"

"But if I go to my room at ten and you're still up he's allowed to come in?" I cut Jeremy off mid-sentence. He sighed.

"Sure. With the door open. As long as you are both in their, the door is to remain open. Now, I admit, you will still have plenty of opportunities for hanky panky, I'm going out right now and cannot ensure nothing happens but just don't let me worry about it while I'm at home!" She pointed a stern finger at me. I pouted.

"I won't have sex with her while I'm here," Jeremy said fairly bluntly. We both turned to him in surprise. He shrugged. "Just saying."

"Jeremy," I hissed out of the corner of my mouth.

"What? That's what she's worried about, and that's not happening now," he said to me. He turned back to my mom. "And Pam, just so you know, she has the prudest reputation in school."

"Jeremy!"

"What? You do. Besides, I told your mom, not some random dude you're trying to impress."

My mom raised her eyebrows. "Well, thanks for the all the information Jeremy. I suppose I feel a bit better about taking off for awhile. I'll see you both later." She gave us a bizarre look before heading out.

"What the hell Jeremy?" I turned to glare at him.

"Give me a second." He got up and disappeared into the living room. He came back with two pieces of paper. He handed them both to me.

"What's this?" I asked. They both looked like medical forms. I started to read.

"That's what I mentioned I had to give you earlier. That is why your mom was nervous and making rules. She knew I had these to give to you."

The forms looked identical, but were both dated differently. I reviewed the earlier one. It gave some basic physiological information on Jeremy, such as his gender and age. Then there was a list of words, some familiar and some unfamiliar. All had a note of either negative or low risk next to them.

"Are these all diseases?" I asked. All the familiar words were. Actually, they were all sexually transmitted diseases.

"Yes."

I looked at the second one, which showed all negative results. It was dated only a couple of months ago, in September.

"Why do you have two?" I asked.

"Because not all STD's test positively immediately."

"Why are you giving these to me? I didn't ask for them, and you just told my mother we're not having sex while you stay here. And if this is why she was all worried and making rules, how does she know about this?"

"Okay, well, I hope you don't mind but yeah I made the decision we have to wait until I go home before you lose your flower or whatever the sugar coating term is."

"I think it's seeding the flower?" I suggested.

"Blooming the flower?"

"Poking the flower?" I smirked. Jeremy did as well.

"Poking makes the most sense. Anyway! I'm sure you're okay with that decision because you're far off from . . . flowering . . ."

"It's our decision to make together," I huffed. It's true I wasn't about to have sex with him anytime soon, but he still could have spoken to me about it before announcing it to my mom.

"Very true but the reality is it takes two to agree but only one to disagree. I disagree for while I'm here, enough said on that." I shrugged. He had a point.

"But sex aside, there's still in between stuff," he said.

"I know."

"And you need to know for pretty much everything in between we haven't already done."

"Everything?"

"Do you need me to explain why?" He looked slightly amused.

"No," I mumbled. I would ask Jessica later why I would need to know for manual stuff.

"If someone cut their hand there's an open wound that can pass things to and from," he said, still looking amused.

"I knew that," I mumbled. "That still doesn't explain why you're giving me the forms now. I don't actually need them right now; we haven't done anything yet and by the sounds of it, won't be for awhile."

"I figured it would be pretty awkward to try to take off your pants and then pause to review the forms with you."

"Oh," I said, blushing. "But are you assuming . . ." I let my voice trail off.

"No. I just thought I should do it before I assume so it doesn't seem like I'm assuming."

"Okay." I handed him back the forms.

"You keep them," Jeremy said.

"Don't you need them? Just because we're kind of similar to dating doesn't mean you'll never do something with someone else again."

"Those are copies." Jeremy rolled his eyes at me.

"Did you like, make copies at school or something?" I gaped at the pages; thinking of how they could have altered his social status in school for the remainder of the year had someone discovered what he was copying.

"No, my mom did them for me at her work."

"Andrea made you these copies? So she knows about this?"

"Who do you think took me to the clinic, Carrie? Of course she knows! This was probably the last straw to help her decide to leave Virginia!"

"You told your mom!" I now gaped at Jeremy, surprised he had done such a thing.

"I didn't tell her why I wanted to go to the clinic, and all she asked was if it was needles. I said no so she said fine and made an appointment."

"I guess this explains her random comment about timing and photocopies last night," I mused.

"And how your mom knows. I'm assuming Andrea told her this morning as a fair warning before giving the okay to let me stay."

"Well, I gotta say, this is all . . . mature of you." I spread my hands over the forms and looked him in the eye.

Jeremy shrugged. "I wanted to get the test for peace of mind. I'm giving it to you to give you peace of mind."

"And that's very responsible. Not all seventeen year olds would be so responsible and mature about sex."

"Yeah, well, not all seventeen years old are hoping the prudest girl in school will be less prude with them." He smirked at me.

"Funny. You know, you should tell Adrian, maybe he would have had better luck if he'd given me test results for SDT's. I mean, you're right, not all seventeen year olds are trying to de-prude me, but you're not the first to attempt it."

"Right so I'll make a bet, get to second base, and then give Adrian tips and collect my winnings."

"As long as the winnings are spent on me."

"Yeah I think I'll skip the bet part. I'm pretty sure the real reason Adrian didn't get anywhere isn't because he didn't have this same lovely form to present to you, but because he is callous enough to make a bet on your virginity. Any guy making bets on a girl's virginity doesn't truly care about her."

I winced. I knew Jeremy was meaning Adrian, but it stung a bit to think that Liam never cared about me.

"What?" Jeremy asked, looking at me funny.

"Nothing," I said. I must have looked upset or something. Perhaps the wince gave me away.

"You winced. What are you upset that I implied Adrian didn't care about you? I'm sure he did to some degree or . . . oh, you were thinking about Liam." Jeremy sighed. "Liam was just being dumb."

"You're defending him?"

"No, I just don't want you feeling upset about him. Look, I did some stupid things when I was confused about you."

"That was different," I mumbled.

"Was it?"

"You never made a bet about my virginity. If I had fallen for Adrian . . ."

"Liam probably would have interfered had he thought you were going to get hurt. Or, at the very least, if he couldn't think of a way to interfere I'm sure he would have figured a way for his sister or someone else to."

"Whatever." I crossed my arms over my chest. Jeremy leaned back and remained silent as he watched me closely.

"I'm going to toast a bagel," I said after awhile. I stood up to get the toaster and bagels out. Jeremy watched me until I finally sat down again, buttered and toasted bagel in front of me.

"Did you want to do something later?" he asked, taking my hand.

"Like what?" I wasn't sure I was up for another almost date. As much as I enjoyed our time the previous weekend and on Thursday, I was kind of hoping for something a bit more defining than watching something from the comfort of the living room.

"Maybe go for a walk? And some coffee?"

"Hmmm." Coffee was slightly more date-like. "Like make some coffee and bring it in travel mugs on our walk?" I was purposely forcing him to be specific.

"No, like go out for a coffee."

"You're not worried about your father stalking you?"

"It seems unlikely he'll look for me in a coffee shop."

"Okay, well, what about Jess?" I asked, still trying to press the idea of how date-like this would be.

"What about Jess? Is she also stalking me? She's doing a horrible job."

"No, did you want to invite her?"

"Why would I invite her? Especially if she is stalking me."

"What if she doesn't have anything to do and phones me up to see what I'm doing? Should I invite her?" Jessica would not be asking me what I was doing with the intention of getting an invite; Jess had been the one to announce less time with her in order to get more "smooches."

"If Jess phones I would rather you didn't invite her."

"Why?" I was being ridiculous, but he was somewhat skirting the issue. Probably for fun more than anything else.

"Because I would rather we went out for coffee just you and me."

"You would rather you and I go out for coffee alone?" I repeated.

"Yes."

"Why? We'll be spending most of the day alone. And with you staying here, I'll imagine we'll have plenty of time together alone. I can even make coffee during this time together." I smiled playfully.

"You want me to specifically ask, don't you."

"Ask what?" I asked innocently.

"You know, I've only asked someone out before once, it's not easy."

"I don't know what you're talking about. Wait, you've had sex but your only date was with Melanie three years ago?"

"Who else would I have asked out?"

"Um, that chick you slept with?" I suggested.

"I told you, we didn't date, we just fooled around."

"How suave of you. And now you're trying to date the prudest girl in school? Seems a little like you're going for the opposite extreme."

"Who said I'm trying to date the prudest girl in school?" Jeremy asked, raising his eyebrow.

"I guess nobody! After all, as far as I can tell you haven't actually asked."

"Well I am trying to date the prudest girl in school. Assuming that is you. So, did you want to go out for coffee later?"

"Yes," I said softly. Jeremy leaned over and kissed the top of my forehead. "But first I'd like to shower." I smiled.

"And put a bra on?"

211

"No more bra jokes! I'm going to have to sleep in my bra while you're here."

"That definitely makes you the prudest girl in school."

"You're an ass. I'll be back in a bit." I stood up and stuck my tongue out at him,

"Enjoy your shower," Jeremy said with a smile. I left him to go shower and change. I started smiling to myself as soon as I was in my room. Finally, he had asked me out!

Diary Entry: February 28, 2008

Everyone seems to be coupling off. Other than Craig being happy with Melanie, there's Jessica with her new boyfriend. His name is Mike. Nicole is going out with some guy named Ryan and Jenny just started going out with a guy named Dan. So I'm the only one who isn't going out with anyone. It makes me feel kind of stupid, but oh, well. (Actually, I guess Jeremy isn't going out with anyone but I never really think of him as ever going out with anyone.)

Something's wrong with Jeremy. He told me his parents have been discussing something major. He's scared they're getting a divorce or something. The thing is he told me maybe that would be for the best. I don't know why. So far, he hasn't found out exactly what is going on, but he's promised to tell me when he finds out. I hope everything is okay. I would hate to have Jeremy go through pain . . .

Present Day: November 14, 2009

After a couple of hours of homework, Jeremy and I were working on our college applications when my mom came up to us. She had been home from wherever she'd been with

Andrea and had given Jeremy a bag of clothes. He had since showered and changed and smelled very fresh sitting next to me. I was finding it slightly intoxicating.

"I'm making pork chops for dinner," my mom said.

"Okay," I said, reviewing Jeremy's application for a school in California we were applying to.

"That sounds nice," Jeremy said, reviewing my application for the same school. Neither of us bothered to look up at her.

"And Bob's coming."

"Bob?" I looked up and tried not to visibly wince. Jeremy nudged me.

"Great, I'll have the opportunity to meet him!" Jeremy said with what sounded like fake enthusiasm.

"You're keen to meet Bob?" my mom asked him, looking slightly confused.

"Uh, sure, he sounds . . . interesting . . ." Jeremy looked at me for help. I ignored his plea for assistance.

"Well that's very nice of you Jeremy. And that's also great you two are working on your college applications."

"Yup," I said, hoping she would leave to go make Bob's pork chops.

"Dinner is at six."

"Right, we'll be ready at six," Jeremy said with a big smile. She left to go to the kitchen to prepare or whatever.

"You're such a suck-up," I muttered.

"I want to see if this guy is actually annoying or you're just being judgemental. I gotta say I'm leaning towards the later. Besides, your mom is letting me stay here."

"I guess."

I handed him back his application and picked up another package we had for a school in Oregon. I was getting a bit tired of filling out applications, but with Jeremy here it was a

---

Laura Hodges

good time to get the task over with. It needed to be done one way or another.

After another hour of applications and school discussions, Jeremy and I went to the kitchen to help my mom set up for dinner. She talked away of some sort of shoe shopping adventure she and Andrea had experienced earlier in the day. Jeremy and I mostly just spent the time smiling at each other while we washed vegetables and used every available opportunity to touch each other's hands.

"Oh!" My mom said as the doorbell rang at two minutes to six. "Bob's here."

Jeremy wiped his hands on his jeans and took my hand. I sighed and followed him and my mom to the door.

"Hello," Bob said to us as he stepped through. He was a middle aged man, perhaps a couple of years older than my mom, with dark hair speckled with wisps of gray. He generally had a friendly look about him and smiled often.

"Bob, this is Jeremy," my mom said, smiling and outstretching her arm towards Jeremy. Jeremy let go of my hand to shake Bob's. I managed not to make a face at either of them.

"So good to meet you Jeremy! I've heard quite a bit about you." I hadn't told him much about Jeremy, but chances are my mom had.

"Thanks, you too." Jeremy was looking like a massive suck up with a big smile and the hearty hand shake. It was taking a large amount of effort not to roll my eyes.

"Hey, Becky, nice to see you," Bob said in a fairly warm tone. Really, he was the suck-up.

"You too," I said. He was over often enough, but clearly having Jeremy here made the difference as my mom started to fuss as if he hadn't been by the house in a long time, rather than two days ago.

214

"Pam, it's okay I'll put my own jacket away," he was murmuring as she tried to take it from him.

"Okay, well everything is ready for dinner!" my mom said brightly.

We sat at the table and proceeded to have small talk for a good hour while we had dinner. Mostly the small talk centred around how delicious everything was and how cold it had been recently. The usual safe and boring conversations.

"So what are you two doing this evening?" Bob asked us near the end of the meal.

"Um . . . having coffee . . ." I felt slightly awkward, not wanting to make it appear as a date with Jeremy sitting there.

"Oh that's nice, where are you having coffee?"

"I'll probably take her to "Joe's Cafe," that local place by the movie rental," Jeremy said. I started to flush.

"Like a date?" my mom asked, looking excited. Despite her previous reservations about Jeremy staying here, clearly she was enthusiastic over the idea of us going on a date.

"Umm . . ." I started to mutter.

"Yes, like a date. I know it's not much of a real first date but . . ." Jeremy shrugged. "It would probably be nicer if I took you to dinner or something a bit more cheesey like a horse and carriage ride," Jeremy said, this time to me.

"Why? I don't care, as long as it's just you and me." This time, Jeremy blushed ever so slightly. He rarely blushed, and when he did you could only really see it on his neck, but I could see it now.

"That's . . . very nice of you to say," he said. We stared at each other for a moment before I remembered we were sitting at the table with my mom and Bob. I turned to look at them, feeling slightly embarrassed.

"Well that sounds very sweet. I hope you have fun," my mom said.

"Yes," Jeremy and I murmured. We exchanged a mutual look of giddiness combined with faint embarrassment.

The movie my mom and Bob were going to didn't start until later, so Jeremy and I decided to head out as they started pulling out coffee fixings and washing dishes.

Before leaving the house Jeremy peered through several windows, looking for something. Or, rather, someone. Tom wasn't there, so after a couple of minutes of this, we put on our coats and headed outside.

I wasn't sure if Tom would bother "stalking" Jeremy here; he had been at Andrea's house again today, but as far as I knew that was the only place he had taken the time to stake-out.

Outside, Jeremy took my hand and smiled at me. I smiled back, feeling slightly giddy. We walked without saying anything for quite awhile.

"Bob seems okay," Jeremy said after ten minutes of comfortable silence.

I shrugged.

"Seems pretty nice. How long have they been dating again? I know you wrote to me about it, but I don't remember when that was."

"Valentine's."

"Right." Jeremy paused. "You still think of him as a "new boyfriend" not a long term thing, don't you?" I did actually. I often thought of him as her new boyfriend.

"Well, it hasn't even been a year."

"Nine months is still a fair amount of time. I'm pretty sure you don't think of Nicole's boyfriend as new, and didn't they just celebrate a six month anniversary?"

"We're younger. Six months is a long time at seventeen; six months is less time to someone who is in her forties."

"I'm just saying, perhaps he'll stick around. After all, you'll be gone next year and it would be nice for your mom to have someone to spend time with other than my mom," Jeremy pointed out.

"I guess." We lapsed into silence. I was thinking about my mom and Bob.

"Do you think they'll live together after we leave for school?" I asked suddenly.

Jeremy thought for a moment before answering. "No. At least not in the first year. Your mom is a cautious person and she will want you to come back during the summer term."

"Good call."

We reached the coffee shop by the video rental place. Jeremy opened the door for me and I blushed slightly as I stepped in.

It was very warm and very busy. There weren't many things to do in town, so most weekend evenings people from our school partied, went to the one theatre in town, or hung out at coffee shops. In particular, the "in" thing to do (if not partying) was to go to or rent a movie and then sit down with your ridiculous non-fat extra hot sugar-free cinnamon spiced caramel latte. Or whatever drink you chose.

We stood in line and I started to think about what I was going to get. I didn't drink coffee; not so much for the taste (those cinnamon spiced things didn't really taste like coffee to me) but because I couldn't be bothered with some over the top custom drink. I would rather just have tea.

I looked at Jeremy and somehow I knew he was thinking about whether or not I would get tea or branch out.

"What are you having?" I asked slyly.

"Hot chocolate." He smiled faintly, looking like he was trying to avoid smirking. "You?"

"I was thinking of tea," I admitted. "But, maybe I'll get hot chocolate. Tea's pretty boring." I looked up thoughtfully. That would mean we would be getting the same thing, which would be silly. Or was I silly for thinking that would be silly?

"Two hot chocolates," Jeremy said as we reached the counter. He pulled out his wallet and I felt a surge of weirdness. I couldn't even explain it. It's not like he had never bought me a beverage before. But before, it had always been different.

"You just . . ." I said as he turned back to me.

"I what?"

"I hadn't confirmed . . . you . . ." I wasn't sure what to say. He had just ordered for me. Realistically, I wasn't actually annoyed he had ordered for me.

"Did you want something else?" Jeremy asked.

"No."

"Had you decided on what you wanted?"

"No."

"Were you going to?"

I thought about it. I probably would have just asked him what I should get.

"No."

"Are you annoyed I ordered for you?"

"No."

"Okay." We headed to the counter for drink pick-ups.

"Look." Jeremy nudged me. I looked at where he was pointing. Pouring far too much sugar into a drink was Adrian. It looked like he was on a date. Next to him was Rhea Matthews, a girl Jeremy and I had gone to school with for years.

"I see, yes, Adrian, how exciting." I already knew Jeremy was going to be obnoxious if I didn't keep him away from Adrian. I could hear it in his voice when he had said "look."

"Is that Rhea from school? The one we had grade eight math with?"

"Grade seven science, and yes."

"It was math, with Ms. Owens."

"We weren't in math together in grade eight, and in grade seven we had Mr. Carvo. Grade nine we had Ms. Owens."

"Oh," Jeremy said. We picked up our drinks and I saw Rhea leave for the bathroom.

"Let's go," I said quickly as Adrian turned towards us, carrying both his drink and Rhea's.

"Hey Adrian!" Jeremy called.

"Jeremy if you—"

"Oh, hey Jeremy," Adrian said as he moved closer to us. Jeremy gave him a firm slap on the shoulder with a big smile, jostling Adrian's drink. I inwardly groaned.

Adrian looked at me and did an obvious double take.

"Oh . . . hey Becky . . ."

"Hi," I said with a broad smile.

"I didn't know you two were . . ." Adrian let his voice trail off. The moment would have probably been awkward if it was anyone but Jeremy I was on a date with. However, Jeremy gave an obnoxious smirk. I leaned back to pinch the back of his leg.

"Yes, dating," Jeremy confirmed, ignoring the pinch. I probably didn't pinch him hard enough.

"Right, I guess that's why you asked for her number." Adrian looked at me nervously. "I hope it's okay with you that I gave it to him, Becky," he said. He was such a pansy.

I bit back my "obviously I wouldn't have agreed to go out with him if not" comment and settled for smiling and saying "totally okay."

"Yeah, speaking of which, Adrian, there was a bet I wanted to place with you," Jeremy said with a slightly evil smile. Adrian looked horrified and gaped at me, eyes wide.

"Jeremy if you—" Yet again, he cut me off.

"Do you really think the Blackhawks will beat the out the Canucks this year?"

Blackhawks? What?

"Oh!" Adrian looked relieved and gave an awkward laugh to cover it. I glared at Jeremy who was grinning.

"For sure man, they have Sopel."

"What's a sopel?" I hissed at Jeremy.

"Well, what do you say to a wager? Ten bucks? That seems like the appropriate amount for a bet, don't you think Becky?" Jeremy turned to me, eyebrows raised. Adrian began to look nervous again.

"Make it twenty. I want half of your winnings," I said. I couldn't help myself. "I'm worth ten bucks, don't you think Adrian?" We both turned to him.

"Ahhh . . . sure . . . yes, twenty dollars then . . ." Adrian stammered slightly. He kept looking at my face, as if to read if I knew what he had done.

Rhea came out of the bathroom and walked over to us.

"Oh, hey Rhea, great so glad you're back. Do you know Becky and Jeremy? They're dating. Good to see you guys, we have to go, night!" Adrian started to move towards the door. Rhea waved at us, looking slightly confused.

"Nice to see you Rhea!" Jeremy called. "Good luck with him!" He gave her a thumbs up and I smacked his arm.

"You're awful! I'm going to kill you!"

"That was awesome! Did you see his face?" Jeremy asked.

"You're horrible!" Jeremy grinned and took my hand. I let him lead me to the door outside.

"Come on, Beck, you have to admit he deserved that. At the very least he won't be making any bets about Rhea now."

"I guess. Still, I can't believe you! You're such a jackass."

"I thought he was going to shit his pants. I think he really thought for a moment I was going to bet him something about you."

"He's not the only one," I said accusingly.

"Oh come on, you know I wouldn't do that to you."

"Yes but for a moment I was like "oh my God, what is he doing?" I knew you were going to be obnoxious, but that?" I sighed and shook my head at him. Sighing and head shaking aside, I was smiling. "Such a jackass," I repeated softly. Jeremy was grinning at me and moving closer. He let go of my hand and put his arm around my back, pulling me closer to him. I wondered where I should hold my cup. Close to my chest? To the side? Lowered to the side or higher up?

Jeremy leaned forward and kissed me softly.

"Lets go rent a movie and then walk for a bit," he suggested.

"Okay." He kissed me again and then took my hand. We headed into the movie rental store.

I had to admit, as nerve wracking as that situation was, I felt awesome and somehow satisfied after seeing Adrian's nervous face. So far, the date was going pretty well.

Diary Entry: June 30, 2008

So Jeremy finally told me what his parents had been discussing. I had not seen this coming. It's probably the most unbearable news I could possibly get from him. He just told me yesterday. This news changes my world. And his.

Flashback

"Okay, Jeremy, what is it?" I asked him. Jeremy had called me over to tell me something. He was looking slightly nervous and I had a feeling he didn't want to tell me whatever he was about to say. I was curious, but I

221

knew that I shouldn't pressure him into telling me what was bothering him. He would just keep it to himself.

"Okay, Becky, this is big. Really big. Now, you have to promise not to optimistic about this," he said. That surprised me.

"You don't want me to be optimistic?" I asked in confusion. Jeremy nodded. I gave a shrug.

"Sure. I can assume the worst." Jeremy gave me a bad look. I smiled. He was being very serious and I needed to be perky to keep myself from fearing the worst.

"Okay. My dad got a really good job offer. He's going to take it," Jeremy began.

"You don't want me to be optimistic about that?" I asked, confused. But by the look on his face and I knew he wasn't finished and that whatever the rest of it was, it was bad. That was when it hit me.

"Where is the job?" I asked numbly. Jeremy sighed. He bowed his head and closed his eyes. He didn't want to tell me.

"It's in Virginia. West Virginia." I closed my eyes in an effort to control my emotions. He was moving. My best friend in the world was moving.

"Okay," I whispered, my eyes still closed. I wanted to cry, but I thought that Jeremy needed some strength right now. I could be strong. I hiccupped.

"Come here, Beck," he whispered. I scooted over to where he was sitting on the couch. He pulled me close to him and held me.

"When?" I asked, realising he could be leaving at any moment.

"The end of August. Listen, Beck, we have all summer to do stuff and I promise you that I'll be back. We'll still go to university or college together, so I'll at least be back by

*then. Don't worry." He was rubbing my back in a soothing
motion. I tried to swallow another hiccup. I blinked back
the water that had accumulated in my eyes and looked up
at him. He looked vulnerable. Hugging him tightly, I told
him what he needed to hear: "I love you."*

Present Day: November 14, 2009

"So what's a sopel?" I asked Jeremy as we left with our
movie rentals. Foolishly, I had let him convince me to rent
a horror movie. However, it was in exchange for a romantic
comedy and I had told him we couldn't watch the horror
movie until tomorrow morning.

"A soap ball?"

"No, sopel. You said to Adrian something about having
a sopel. What were you betting anyway? Canucks are hockey,
right?"

"Yes, and Sopel is a player."

"Ah so I get ten bucks if Sopel wins?"

"No you get ten bucks if the Canucks win the Stanley
Cup." Jeremy smiled at my ignorance.

"Do I have to give you ten bucks if they lose?" I wrinkled
my nose.

"I'll cover your betting costs." Jeremy started to lead me
towards a different area of town, away from the main centre.
After awhile, I realized we were going to one of the parks. I
gave him a confused look.

"What are we doing?" I asked.

"Going for a walk."

"Going where for a walk?"

"You'll see." We walked in silence, holding hands and
drinking our hot chocolate. I had a feeling I kept giving him
ridiculous smiles.

"Here, we'll go along this path," Jeremy said, pulling me towards some bushes. I had a brief flashback to Jess discussing make-out in some bushes. I fought the urge to snort and pull out my phone to text her.

However, there was a path, and after a moment I realized it was the path to an area Jeremy and I had played at when we were much younger. Before we had started junior high we had played kiddie games at one of the parks in town.

Sure enough, after a couple of minutes we came to a clearing where some sort of pothole had formed from the stream that ran through the park. I imagined it was man-made, but it was very pretty just the same, seeing the stream flow down the rocks and into a small pool.

"I remember this place," I said to Jeremy, smiling.

"We would swim here sometimes in the summer."

We had. It was far too small for us to swim in beyond the height of five feet, but at age twelve we would swim and get freezies after and think it was the best thing ever.

"And sometimes if Robert and Carrie were with us we would play fort," I added, thinking back to the various hiding locations we would use as scouting points for our forts. "How come we stopped?" The obvious answer is because we grew older. The pothole was too small to swim in (plus probably not very sanitary) and we became too "cool" to play games like fort.

"We started junior high and you and Jess started to hang out with Nicole and Jenny. You guys ditched our youth for more boy obsessions. You think Jeffrey would have taken you to the movies with Jess and whoever she brought if he knew you spent your free time building fake castles here?"

"I guess. You started playing more video games with Robert."

"Very true." We swung our hands and stared at the scene thoughtfully. I wondered how different it would have been for me at the age of twelve to play here and know five years later Jeremy would bring me here as a date instead of a battle companion.

Jeremy moved closer to me and I tried to hide my smile. I probably had been smiling at him too much like a ridiculous idiot.

"Remember when we were here and I shoved dirt and grass down your shirt and you and Jessica ignored me for the remainder of the week?" he asked. I did. We had screeched at him and left in a huff while he laughed.

"Yes." He stepped so that he was facing me. I put my empty cup on a rock nearby. Jeremy did the same.

"I promise not to do that again," he said with a slight smile. He moved closer and put his arm around my waist.

"Good because it would be pretty difficult to ignore you for a week while you're staying at my house." I smiled and tilted my head up, waiting for him to eventually lean in to kiss me.

"Uh huh." He was now just staring at me. He touched the side of my cheek. I started to blush. I always blushed.

I put one hand up on his shoulder so if I wanted to stand on my tiptoes I could lean on him for support. He was only around half a foot taller than me, but just the same. Besides, I might literally swoon. When he eventually got around to kissing me.

Jeremy (finally) angled his head down towards mine and started to kiss me. I ran my hands through his hair as he gripped the back, pulling me as close to him as possible, while his other hand tenderly held the back of my neck. I moved my hand that was on his shoulder down to curl around him.

We continued to kiss, firmly pressed up against each other, breathing heavily through our noses. This was unlike before. Before, even my "death grip" kiss had been light compared to this. Besides all the emotion I was feeling, it was a full open mouth kiss with our tongues darting around.

We had kissed like this once before, the last time I saw him before he left for Virginia, but then we had been inexperienced and upset. Plus, I think I might have hiccupped into his mouth.

After probably several solid minutes of making out we pulled apart. I was breathing heavily and knew my face was flushed. Jeremy was also slightly flushed, but probably from the cold.

"Okay," was all I said, because for some reason I felt like I should say something. "That was different."

"I've French kissed you before," Jeremy said, sounding slightly out of breathe.

"Not quite like that."

"I guess not." We stared at each other again and I wondered if we would do so until our breathing normalized before repeating the activity.

"Are you cold?" he asked, touching my hands and face.

"No," I said. How could I be cold after that?

"It is cold out though, maybe we should head back to the house?"

"If you like." I didn't care, my mom would probably be gone by the time we got there.

"We should, more comfortable. I think your mom and Bob should be gone by the time we get there," Jeremy said.

"I was just thinking that!"

"That making out is more comfortable on a couch?"

"No, that they would be gone. Never mind." I picked up our empty cups and stacked them together so I could still hold

Jeremy's hand. Hand in hand, we left our old memories to go make some new ones.

Diary Entry: July 3, 2008

I was heartbroken after Jeremy told me he was moving. I had sat there with him for the longest time (or what felt like the longest time) and tried not to cry. He was moving. I didn't say anything optimistic; I had nothing happy to say at all. My mom said something about a silver lining will appear but what silver lining? Like, maybe there won't be any mysterious rumours that I'm dating him? As if that compares to him leaving!

All I can think of is Jeremy. And not thinking of him quite as I use to. I mean, every once in awhile he would be in some sort of day dream, but now his appearance in my day dreams is totally different than they use to be. Last night I couldn't sleep and I think I'm coming to the conclusion I might like him more than just as a friend . . .

Flashback

I lay in bed, wondering how long I would stay awake for. I couldn't sleep. For the past three nights I would lie in bed and day dream. Not my usual day dreams either, but the kind that left me crying and feeling confused.

All these day dreams were of Jeremy. Primarily, I would think back to making the brownies before his date with Melanie. I would think back to the afternoon and spend a good chunk of time reminiscing over him licking the batter of my fingers. That would be the moment I would curl myself into the fetal position, close my eyes, and let my thoughts drift to a "what if" place. What if I

227

hadn't reminded him of his date? What if we had kissed? What if we had kept kissing?

After I envisioned a lovely (if not confusing) fantasy of making out with maybe a little more, I would day dream of the cabin Jeremy's family had in Canada. We would go together and I would fantasize some scenario where we would go for a picnic and the romance or cheese sandwiches or something would lead to making out. Or maybe he would save me from sort of mildly endangering situation and I could kiss him out of gratitude and adrenaline. If he saved me, nobody would think it was a bit peculiar for me to kiss him. Of course, I preferred the idea that I could save him from something, but hadn't worked out a scenario, other than me developing ridiculous super powers, what this situation would be that I would save him.

All the day dreams resulted in the same making out ending. This particular evening, I had finished going through about six scenarios, had had a good cry about how unlikely they all were, and now was lying in bed thinking about it. Why was I day dreaming of kissing Jeremy? Was it because he was leaving?

"What if it's more than that?" I whispered to myself out loud. The concept was something I had begun to contemplate. Perhaps I was fantasizing of kisses because I wanted a relationship with him that actually involved kisses. Perhaps I wanted to be more than friends. Perhaps I loved him as more than a friend.

It had occurred to me we may not be the most normal set of best friends. As far as I knew, nobody else cuddled with their opposite sex friends on a couch while watching movies. Likewise, none had ever shared any of the extent of affection Jeremy and I had. Jessica had been saying for some time it was rather suspicious that we hugged as frequently as we did, cuddled at all, and actually said "I love you" in any way what so ever. She pointed out I don't exactly verbalize how much I love her, but I have to Jeremy. Which is very true. So I was feeling rather confused as to what was going on. Clearly, I was awake at night day dreaming of being in Jeremy's arms for a reason. And, I had to admit to myself, whatever the reason was it was probably not because he was leaving; him leaving was probably bringing the reason to light.

I got up and started pacing around my room. I wanted to phone Jess, but it was far too late and I didn't know if I was actually ready to admit out loud to her that I might have romantic feelings for Jeremy. Besides, he was leaving in a couple of months; it wasn't like we would have time to explore a relationship. Assuming he even felt the same way.

I was fairly certain he at least had moments of attraction or something along the same lines. The brownie incident proved that. But what I didn't know if it was just a hormone moment or a genuine attraction to me. How am I to know if these individual moments add up to feelings beyond friendship or teenage guy desires? Kissing my earlobe after Craig broke-up with me does not exactly constitute an invitation to start dating.

Still pacing, I opened my diary to write, but found it too difficult to write much. I sighed, put it away after a couple of sentences about realizing things, and decided to make a plan for myself.

Jeremy was leaving at the end of August. I did not think I could handle starting an actual relationship with him that I knew would be ending in less than two months. Besides, the risk of him rejecting me would not *be worth a possible summer fling. He meant too much to me, as a friend or as a boyfriend.*

So I would wait. Watch him, look for clues, and wait. I could tell him at the end of August that I had feelings for him. That way, if he doesn't feel the same, he would be off shortly thereafter anyway. It wouldn't make a difference. Of course, if he did feel the same, I may regret not saying it sooner. But the risk was too great, so I would wait.

Feeling a bit better, and less confused, I lay back to day dream. This time, I felt less plagued by the nagging thoughts of "why are you hoping he'll kiss you?" and let myself relax. I couldn't keep him from leaving, but maybe I could at least offer him a reason to come back.

Present Day: November 14, 2009

A couple of hours later we were lying on the couch finishing watching a movie. Or, really, we were making out while the movie was on. We had arrived back at the house and my mom and Bob had left for their movie. We had put on the romantic comedy one, and about ten minutes in had started making out. I hadn't bothered to look at the television since. Now, the end credits had begun to roll.

I pulled away and cleared my throat. Jeremy wiped the side of his mouth. Despite having made out for close to two hours, he hadn't made a move for anything more than kissing. We had already reached the point of my shirt removed over a year ago, so I didn't mind doing that again, but he had made no attempts to even touch my breasts, let alone remove my shirt.

"What do you want to do now?" I asked.

"What do you mean?" he asked. His eyes had glazed over ever so slightly and he felt very warm.

"The movie finished."

"Oh!" He sat up to look at the screen. We had originally been lying on the couch together with me facing the television and him spooning me from behind, but I had rolled over fairly quickly and I had probably blocked his view of the screen since. I couldn't see it, but I could hear the music indicating the movie had ended.

"Turn it on again?" he suggested. He picked up the remote. I also sat up.

"Sure." I wondered how long we would watch it this time.

Jeremy skipped to the point at which we had stopped watching and turned it on again. As soon as he put the remote down he cupped my face in his hand and we started kissing again. I smirked, which made him pull back slightly.

"What?" he asked.

"I had wondered how long we would watch this before we starting making out again."

"Did you want to watch it?" I did, but I didn't care enough to watch it now.

"Not right now. Maybe when my mom's back." We lay back down to continue making out.

Sometime later, maybe twenty minutes or so, we both heard the jingle of keys in the door. We both sat up and started wiping our mouths and I ran my hands through my hair, not sure what kind of state it was in.

"Hi guys," my mom said as she walked in.

"Hey," we said in unison.

"What have you been up to?" she asked, picking up the DVD case.

"We just turned this on about thirty minutes ago," Jeremy said.

"How is it?" she asked. He looked at me.

"Uh . . . usual romantic comedy. You know, like, I already know how it's going to end." I gave a smile and a nod.

"Do you mind if I watch it with you?" she asked, taking off her coat.

"Umm sure," Jeremy said. We scooted over so she could sit down next to me.

"What's happened so far?" she asked. I wondered if she was doing this on purpose.

"Well . . . we were introduced to the main character, this chick here, and the guy she's so obviously going to end up with, who isn't here right now, that's her current boyfriend but he's a dick." I pointed to him on the screen. I was hoping I was right; I was using what I had read on the back in the video store to assume things.

"How long have they been together? It wouldn't be very nice if they had been together a long time and were committed and then she decides to leave him for the other guy." I saw Jeremy wince.

"Mom!"

"What? Oh, Jeremy . . . hey you know what? Who wants some tea? I'll go make some." She disappeared into the kitchen in a hurry.

"Is that really the plot of this movie?" Jeremy asked. I hadn't really thought about it much when I had read the back, but it was occurring to me now perhaps it wasn't the best choice.

"Umm . . . I was making stuff up," I said. I snatched the DVD case from the table and started reading. "At least my mom left," I said lightly while I read. "Ahh . . . it's not her current boyfriend, it's her ex-boyfriend, and he's trying to get in her pants again but it's made her friend decide he's in love with her so he's also trying to get in her pants now. Only he's more romantic probably."

"Right so it's like you and Liam then?"

"What? How is it like Liam?"

"I show up and behave like a dick and Liam decides he better confess he was planning on asking you out. How is it not like this movie?"

I wondered if there were any romance movies that didn't have a plot Jeremy would find a relation to. I made a face at him.

"You're not my ex. And Liam was a bigger dick."

"Has or is?" Jeremy smirked at his own joke and I rolled my eyes.

"Anyway, saying I wish I could take back admitting love might be worse than making a bet with Adrian," Jeremy said thoughtfully.

"Why do you constantly try to make Liam sound better? Do you feel guilty or something?"

Jeremy shrugged. "Sometimes. I remember being pretty upset when you dated Craig. I know how he feels."

"Yeah, but we were younger and you mostly hadn't made a move because you didn't know how and didn't know what it would do to our friendship."

"You're assuming that."

"So that's not why you didn't make a move?" I asked suspiciously.

"No that pretty much sums it up. It seemed way easier to spread around a rumour that we had made out than to actually ask you out."

"I knew it!" I slapped his shoulder. "I remember when everyone thought we were dating and since Jess hadn't spread any rumours around, I was pretty confused."

"I thought you just said you knew it?"

"Well, later, it occurred to me that since you weren't denying anything you were at fault to some degree." I sighed.

"Sorry. Anyway, point is, age aside I was pretty dumb because I didn't know what to do and Liam's just as dumb, he just doesn't remember to consider the side effects of his behaviour as well as I did."

"Whatever."

My mom came back with two cups of tea that she put down in front of us.

"You know," she started, "I was thinking perhaps I would just go to bed. I can see this movie later. Besides, I'm getting up early for yoga."

"Fair enough," Jeremy said, picking up his tea.

"I'll just enjoy my tea in my room. But I'll be checking on both of you later," she added sternly. We nodded solemnly. She went to the kitchen and after a couple of minutes we heard her bedroom door close.

We watched the movie in silence for a bit as we drank our tea.

"Are you thinking what I'm thinking?" Jeremy asked after awhile.

"Probably not. I'm thinking it might be best not to make-out right now as she's home," I said.

"That's what I was thinking."

"Oh then yes." I smiled at him. He leaned over and kissed my cheek. We shifted until we were more comfortable, his arm around me and my legs curled up next to me. We watched the remainder of the movie like this, cuddling together and feeling happy.

Diary Entry: July 12, 2008

Realising that I was potentially in love with Jeremy was starting to feel like a problem. Why? Besides not being able to fully express myself, I spend far too much time analyzing everything! No joke, I just started a second diary outlining moments between us to examine for hints of romance. Things would be a lot easier if I just knew how he felt . . .

Not only that, I haven't told anyone else yet. I would love more than anything to tell Jess, but I'm nervous she would blurt it out and embarrass me. In fact, I'm almost positive that's exactly what she would do. She would tell me Jeremy would want to know and make up some nice opinions about how he would want to fool around in some bushes or something ridiculous like that. (By the way, I'm wondering if she has recently fooled around in a bush, this is like her new favourite saying and she keeps mentioning how great it is to "fool around in some bushes.") I would go ahead and just tell someone like Jenny who would help me analyze all my notes except Jessica would probably be upset if she found out I confided in Jenny and not her. So, I'll just keep making my notes and looking for clues and hope I can figure this out by the end of August.

Present Day: November 15, 2009

The next morning I woke up to my phone ringing. I groaned and picked it up.

"Hello?" I asked sleepily. I squinted at my clock and noticed it was only 8:15 in the morning. Nobody usually called me that early.

"Becky?" A male voice asked on the other end. The voice was vaguely familiar, but I couldn't place it. Also, it sounded a bit more like a man's voice than a teenager's. A school teacher perhaps?

I sat up. "Yes?"

"Hi, this is Tom Johnston." Well, that would explain the familiar voice.

"Oh!"

"I know it's been a long time since I've seen you, but I wanted to talk to you about something." I felt slightly panicked. Should I go get Jeremy? Tell him who was on the phone? No, there was no need to upset him. Besides, there was a chance Tom didn't even know Jeremy was here. After all, he hadn't phoned the main line, but my cell. He was clearly phoning for me.

"Umm . . . what did you want to talk about?" I asked nervously.

"Jeremy. I know perhaps you haven't had quite the relationship you had with him before, but I was hoping to talk to you anyway."

"Well yes, we're not quite on the same terms as when he lived here before," I said. That was true. Now we were dating or something.

"But would you be willing to talk to me anyway? I just want to know . . . do you know if he's still drinking? Is he skipping classes?" I was surprised. Somehow, that was not what I was expecting.

"Why aren't you asking Andrea this?"

"Well, she might know about the drinking and maybe the school would let her know if he was skipping, but whether or not you're talking to him you'll know the school rumours."

"Fair enough." I didn't answer, still contemplating what I should tell him.

"So what do you know? Has he been . . . is he being okay?"

"I guess. He drank on Halloween but I don't think he's been partying as much since." I knew he hadn't been partying, but felt I should add the think so as not to appear to know too much.

I heard Tom sigh in relief. "What about school?"

"He hasn't been skipping the classes I have with him, Math and Spanish. I don't know about his other classes." Again, I did, but no point advising that. "He doesn't have any reputation for problems right now."

"Do you know if . . ." Tom paused. "Do you know if he's been promiscuous?"

"Ahhh . . ." I felt very awkward answering that. It also occurred to me that if I wasn't really speaking to Jeremy, I shouldn't feel too bad giving away information.

"Why are you asking all of this?" I asked, suddenly realizing I also wouldn't necessarily know what was going on if Jeremy and I weren't speaking.

"Well, I don't know how much you know, but things have been rough for him and I just want to make sure he's okay. He won't talk to me so the best I can do is try to keep track of him. I'm sorry, I shouldn't have asked about his promiscuity, that's not totally appropriate to ask you. I just want to make sure Andrea moving him back was the best thing for him."

"Okay," I said dumbly.

"I was wondering if maybe I could talk to you in person? I promise, I'm not trying to make things awkward for you, but I want to apologize for whatever he's done and just find out a bit of how he's doing. I know you might not be the most informed with his current mental state but you do go to school with him and do know the rumours. I would really appreciate it."

I thought for a moment. On the one hand, I didn't like what Tom had done to his family, and I felt it would be slightly traitorous of me to meet him, but on the other he sounded genuinely concerned for Jeremy and perhaps if he had some information he would be willing to go back to Virginia. At least for the time being. Besides, it would be interesting to hear what he had to say.

"Sure, I guess."

"Can you meet me today?" I thought about it. Unless Jeremy went out somewhere, it would mean I would have to directly lie to him about where I was going.

"Today isn't good. What about on my lunch break tomorrow?"

"He already thinks I'm following him. I guess he must have seen me when I went to talk to one of the school counsellors last week." Well, that would explain why he was hanging out by the school.

"Maybe the coffee shop by the school? I can only stay for a bit, but lunch starts at 12:05, I can meet you there around 12:10?"

"Okay, sounds good. Thanks Becky, I really appreciate it."

"Sure," I said, feeling a small pang of guilt. Jeremy would not want me to go meet his father.

"See you tomorrow." Tom hung up and I put my phone back down.

I got up and put on my housecoat. I walked into the kitchen to see Jeremy frying some eggs.

"Morning," I said as he leaned over to kiss me. "Where's my mom?"

"She just left for yoga about five minutes ago. You're up early," he observed. I shrugged. I poured myself some juice and sat at the table.

"Did you want an egg?" Jeremy asked as he slid his eggs onto a plate.

"No thanks." I sipped my juice as he sat down and started to eat.

A moment later, the doorbell rang. We exchanged a look.

"Are you expecting anyone?" he asked me. I shook my head.

"Your mom?" I asked hopefully.

"I phoned her when I got up, she didn't say anything and your mom isn't home." The doorbell rang again. I stood up.

"What if it's Tom?" Jeremy asked, lowering his voice as he said it.

"I doubt it, but if you're nervous, stay here." I walked to the front door. Jeremy stayed in the kitchen.

It was Liam. I could see his face as soon as I got close enough to the door. I started to walk slower.

"Hi," I said when I finally opened the door. He was holding flowers. He thrust them to me, looking nervous.

"Sorry." I looked up from the flowers to him, startled.

"Umm . . . okay." I didn't take the flowers he was still outstretching towards me. I wasn't sure I wanted to.

"These are for you. Because I shouldn't have done what I did." He bopped the flowers up and down. I tried not to wince. This was potentially the worst apology ever. He clearly didn't know what to say. I took them and put them aside on the hall table. Normally, I would have asked him if he wanted to come in, but Jeremy was in the kitchen. The fact that he hadn't come out yet indicated to me he didn't know who I was talking to. Either that or he was trying to stay out of the way in case Liam over-reacted.

"Thanks?" I said uncertainly.

"Listen, I kind of see now what a shitty thing that was. Sandy pointed out what if Adrian had managed to . . . bed you? And then dumped you? That would have been pretty harsh and I would have been partially at fault. I mean, fortunately that didn't happen and you didn't do much with him . . ." Liam's voice trailed off and he looked around.

"Is your mom home?" he asked, his voice lowered. "Maybe I should have been quieter I don't know how much you tell her." He again looked around and put one foot in the door.

"No, she's not home."

"Oh, I thought I heard something." Probably Jeremy.

"Anyway, I was going to add even if you didn't do anything together but you got attached to him that would suck. So . . ." he started to look towards where the kitchen was. "Is someone there?" This time, I also heard Jeremy. He had rustled a paper or something.

Liam stepped inside. "I think I should check it out."

"No, Liam, it's fine." I didn't want to outright deny the presence of someone in the house, but I didn't want him and Jeremy to start arguing or something. However, Liam ignored me and walked past me towards the kitchen. He stopped in the doorway as he stared at Jeremy who looked up from his paper. Liam turned from Jeremy to me and looked at my robe suspiciously.

"Why is he here?" Liam asked, looking annoyed. "It's not even nine in the morning and your mom isn't here, why is he?" Jeremy stood up.

"Liam it's a long story but—"

"How ironic. I came here to apologize because Adrian thought he could get in your pants within two months and I discover this asshole manages that within two weeks."

"Liam no, he's just—" I hiccupped.

"He's just what?" He shot at me.

"It's not your business," Jeremy said, finally speaking. Liam turned to look at him. "You're assuming things, she slept in her own bed by herself last night."

"So you thought you would just sneak over after her mom left?"

"Liam I haven't—" I hiccupped again, cutting myself off.

"What difference does it make? Listen, I get that you think you're better than me, or better for her, or whatever, but since I've been around all you've done is upset her, and now, even with your weak attempt at an apology you're causing trouble by assuming things and distressing her." Jeremy's voice was cold and firm. I hiccupped again. Liam and Jeremy stared at each other for a long moment while I hiccupped a couple of times.

"Screw you," Liam eventually said.

"If you have an issue with me, fine, but you can sort that out with me, leave her out of it." Jeremy pointed at me.

"He's just taking advantage of you," Liam said sourly to me.

"He's not!" I started to cry, not knowing how to handle Liam. I felt so confused.

"You're so gullible you don't even see it."

"All you can see is how jealous you are!" I shot back. I couldn't believe I had actually said it to him. "You just assume things, about me, about him, you don't know! Liam, if you would just calm down, give me a chance to show you he's not so bad, we could go back to being friends, please, I miss you." I gave him a pleading look, but his face didn't soften. I had stopped crying but was still hiccupping. Jeremy remained silent, watching both of us carefully.

"I can't," Liam said after a long while.

"What? But you came here to apologize and now . . ."

"That's before I thought you were sleeping with him. I'm outta here." He stomped out the door and I started crying again.

"Stay here," Jeremy said quietly as he hurried past me out where Liam had gone. I sat down on the floor sniffling. After maybe five minutes Jeremy came back. He sat down next to me but didn't say anything.

"What did you say to him?" I finally asked.

"That we hadn't slept together. I wanted to tell him he was being childish and selfish, but I didn't think that would go over so well, so I told him to knock it off and any beef he has he can take up with me. I think he thought I was going to hit him."

"Were you?"

"No. That wouldn't have done much. If he wanted to fight, I would, but I'm not going to suggest it or start it." Jeremy stretched out his legs.

"Would you really? Fight him?" Jeremy shrugged.

"He needs to get his feelings out one way or another, it's not the most useful way but if it would shut him up at least you'd feel better. You know, after you'd forgiven me for fighting him."

"I guess." We were silent for a moment. I was thinking about how dramatic Liam was being.

"You were pretty upset," Jeremy finally said softly. I looked at him.

"I don't want him to be hurt and I don't want to just cut him out of my life because you're here. That seems ridiculous."

"Yeah but all he's done is upset you. I know I did when I first got here, but he's getting a bit ludicrous. I tried to avoid you so I wouldn't make it worse when I was being an ass, but he can't keep his mouth shut long enough to contemplate how he's affecting you."

"I thought you felt bad for him and had been defending him."

"Yeah, well, that was before he decided to flip out at you because I happen to be here at eight forty in the morning. He's jumping to conclusions and making you feel bad about it. If he knew you well he would probably know that chances are I'm not here because I've snuck over or because we're doing it while your mom is out." Jeremy sighed.

"I don't know Liam was worth his drama before, but now I'm not so sure." I folded my knees towards me and leaned my head on them. Jeremy touched the back of my head lightly.

"I'm just worried that . . ." he let his voice trail off. I lifted my head to turn to look at him again.

"Worried about what?"

"You're not upset because a part of you has feelings for him, are you?"

"No."

"Are you sure?"

"Jeremy how can you ask that?"

"You didn't cry when I told you about the bet but you cried because he accused you of sleeping with me. One is far worse than the other and it's not the one you cried about."

"I was mad, not sad about the bet."

"And you're sad about what happened here?"

"Yes. For whatever reason he's holding firm on his dislike of you and I'm not sure he can let it go. I don't even know why. To be honest, I didn't even consider if he had feelings for me until you came back. He never made a move and now he's acting like it's the worst thing ever that I date you. If he doesn't let this go I won't be able to be friends with him and that's sad. Really sad. To lose a friend just because he doesn't like you . . . well that sucks." I put my head back on my knees. Jeremy stroked my hair.

"Sorry," he finally said.

"For what?" I mumbled. It wasn't his fault Liam didn't like him. Liam had somehow decided it as soon as it looked like Jeremy might be in my life.

"That I can't fix this for you."

I shrugged. "Not your fault."

Jeremy stood up and outstretched his hand for me. I didn't take it.

243

"Come on, I'll make you some breakfast," he suggested. I looked up at him suspiciously. I definitely doubted his cooking abilities.

"Make me what?" I asked.

"Uhh . . . pancakes?"

"Do you even know how?"

"No." I rolled my eyes.

"I don't want pancakes."

"Okay, how about toast?" He bent down so he could reach my arm with his outstretched hand and started to gently pull.

"French toast?" I asked, knowing he would have no idea how to make French toast.

"Sure. What else is there besides the toast part?" he asked. "Milk?" I hadn't actually made French toast before. Ever.

"There must be something else besides milk. It would be soggy not crisp or creamy."

"Cream?" he suggested.

"Yogurt?"

"Pudding?"

"Sour cream?'

"Cinnamon sugar?"

"I'll have toast and cinnamon sugar," I said, finally smiling. I let him take my hand and he pulled me up.

"If I fry it will that make it French?" he asked.

"I don't know. Do it however you want." Jeremy smiled and kissed me softly.

"Sure."

I sat down to watch him make some sort of fried toast with cinnamon concoction he clearly was making up as he went. Feeling better, I decided to put this Liam crap out of my head for the time being. Besides wanting to fully enjoy Jeremy's company, if I was going to worry it should be about seeing his father tomorrow. After all, Jeremy would probably be fairly upset if he knew . . .

Chapter 12

So Jeremy's family is going to be selling their cabin in Canada, which totally sucks. I love that place. However, they're going at the end of August and they're taking me! I don't know if my mom's going too, or if it's just me and his family. It should be fun. Anyway, I'm going off to a movie with him so I'll just find out if my mom's coming then.

This could be a good opportunity. Staying with him and his family for four days . . . well anything could happen and perhaps I could finally tell him how I feel. Not only will it be a good setting for it, but as we're going to the cabin shortly before he leaves it means if he doesn't feel the same it won't make much of a difference at that point anyway. Plus, I can kind of play up some key moments to analyze. Like, flirting is way easier if you go swimming. I think. We'll see.

Present Day: November 15, 2009

Several hours later we were sitting at the table with both of our moms. Andrea had come over for dinner and was now telling an energetic tale of some sort of customer who hadn't liked his vacation. Or something like that. I was only partially paying attention; Jeremy and I were playing footsies under the table. Well, probably not normal footsies as we were both trying to capture each other's feet and hold them for at least five seconds. Every once in awhile my mom would look over at us as he would hold up fingers in a countdown while I squirmed.

After Jeremy had made me an interesting breakfast, we had watched his horror movie. As soon as it had been over, I had showered and left to go see Nicole. I had felt a bit bad for leaving him with not much to do at the house, but he was suppose to clean the bathrooms and I was desperate to gossip about everything that had happened. Jess had been busy with Will and neither of us had been able to get a hold of Jenny, so it had just been the two of us. It had been nice to repeat and discuss the crazy ups and downs that had occurred over the past two days. It had actually been even nicer to come back to kiss Jeremy hello and watch some cartoons with him. Or whatever had been on while we'd been making out.

"Well, anyone want some coffee?" my mom asked everyone as Andrea wrapped up her story.

"Oh, Pam, I'd love some but let me make it." Andrea got up and Jeremy and I exchanged a look. I was hoping he was as desperate to leave the table as I was.

"We have school stuff to do," he said as he stood up. "But thanks for dinner."

"School stuff? I thought you did it all yesterday," my mom said suspiciously.

"Studying, not homework," I added as I also stood up.

"Studying for what?" Both moms looked at us with scrutiny.

"Becky has to study for history and I'm going to help," Jeremy offered.

"After you just had to hand in that big project?" my mom asked. "That doesn't seem fair."

"It's just a quiz, really, I just want to review." I gave a large smile, hoping that would suffice.

"Okay well have fun," Andrea sat as she got up to make some coffee. We left them to go to my room. Once there, Jeremy took out a text book.

"What are you doing?" I asked, concerned he was actually wanting to study.

"Well your mom said we can't close the door." He put the book between the door frames and closed the door as much as the book would allow. "See? Still open but we won't be visible."

"Nice." I sat down on the bed and grinned at him. He came over to me and cupped my face in his hands.

"You're awesome," he said softly. I blushed.

"Thanks. You too." He leaned down and started to kiss me. Within moments we were back to full making out, now lying on the bed and pressed against each other.

"How long do you think they'll have coffee before they come check on us?" I asked breathlessly as I pulled away for a moment.

"Twenty minutes? Half an hour? Better not waste it." He grinned before leaning back in to continue kissing.

Sometime later, we could hear the scraps of chairs on the kitchen floor and hurriedly got up. We both brushed out our clothing in case it was wrinkled and Jeremy handed me a notebook as he widened the door and opened the text book previously preventing it from being shut. Within moments I could hear footsteps coming towards my room.

"Jer?" Andrea asked as she stuck her head in. We looked up from our books.

"Are you off?" he asked.

"Yeah but I would like to talk to you for a second."

"Oh, I'll go . . . do something." I got up and left for the kitchen.

"Was the door open?" my mom asked suspiciously when I came in. I rolled my eyes.

"Yes."

"Did you get any studying done?" I was no good at lying but I wasn't about to admit we had left the table to fool around.

"Just a quick review. So . . . how's Bob?" I was hoping to change the subject.

"Good as usual. I was going to sleep at his place next week if you didn't mind but I don't know if Jeremy will have left yet . . ." her voice trailed off and she looked in the direction my room was in. There were several walls between her and my room, but she was looking as if she could see or hear what was going on in there.

"What difference does that make? If he was staying at Andrea's and we really wanted to sneak around, he could still stay in my room and you wouldn't know." My mom raised her eyebrows. I realized perhaps that was not the best thing to point out.

"Very true, but at least he has promised not to have sex with you while he's staying here; he hasn't promised to continue that once he goes back home."

"Ah don't worry about that." I waved my arm at the thought. "Not happening for a long time."

"If you say so. But I still don't want to discover that he has stayed in your room."

"What about when we leave for college? Chances are if we live together he will be every night."

"You are going to live together when you leave for college?" She raised her eyebrows again. "Since when?"

I shrugged. Had we even decided on that for sure? Maybe we had said we would decide later . . .

"That's not for sure. We just talked about it. Nicer and potentially cheaper than staying in dorms. At least if I share with Jeremy I won't have some random roommate I have never met who could be part of a cult or something."

"Well, when you decide I would like to talk about it with you, but I suppose no matter what you'll be out of my house and it won't be my decision anymore who is in your room and when." She stood up and started to load the dishwasher.

I shrugged, not sure what to say to that. I helped her load the dishwasher while I thought about what it would be like to actually live with Jeremy. I mean, he was here now but only temporarily and we were at my mom's, not our own place in a different city.

Sometime during my contemplation Andrea and Jeremy appeared in the kitchen.

"Thanks for dinner Pam that was great. Once Tom has gone back to Virginia I'll host dinner." She smiled and hugged my mom. I slinked over to Jeremy's side and he put his arm around me.

"No problem."

"And thanks for taking care of this one, he's probably being a suck-up, but just the same I appreciate it."

"Again, no problem."

"Okay, well, I'm off, I'll see you guys later." She came over to hug Jeremy who awkwardly let her hug him while he rolled his eyes.

"Bye Andrea," I said as she let go of Jeremy. We walked her to the front door and she waved at us as she headed outside, shrugging her jacket on.

Once she was gone my mom went to her room to watch a movie and Jeremy and I finished cleaning the kitchen.

"What did she say to you? Before she left?" I asked Jeremy, referring to Andrea.

"Stuff about Tom, and she thinks he'll be gone soon. She's going to a meeting with him to see her lawyer on Tuesday regarding his parental rights and stalking me. Depending on how that goes, I'll be home by Tuesday."

"Well that's good. You'll have your own bed rather than our couch." I was trying to look at the bright side, but really I wished he was staying longer.

"I guess. I kind of like being here. More time to fool around and stuff." He turned from cleaning a pot to grin at me. I stuck my tongue out at him.

"So I guess we go to school tomorrow?" Jeremy said, changing the subject.

"It will be Monday, so yes."

"And I assume you walk?"

"I would rather fly but my flying carpet is at the cleaners," I said with a grin.

"Ha ha. What time do you usually leave to walk there?"

"8:10." I finished drying the pots and pans he had washed and started to put them away.

"It takes you twenty minutes to walk there?"

"No, ten, but then I have plenty of time to go to my locker, meet up with Jess or maybe Nicole and Jenny, go to the bathroom if I need to . . ."

"How often do you need to use the bathroom before the first class?" Jeremy asked.

"Umm . . . no clue but just the same. I like to be prepared!"

"Fine, I guess I'll aim to be ready to go at 8:10." We finished wiping down the counters and everything and he wrung out the cloths and hung them up.

"Are you going to talk to Liam tomorrow?" Jeremy asked suddenly.

"Oh, um, I don't know. Maybe. I hadn't really thought about it." I had told Nicole everything that had happened, and she had said maybe it would be best to let him cool off, but I didn't want him making a big deal about it at school or pass around a rumour.

"Well, I don't mind what you decide to do. If you want to talk to him, that's fine, if you don't, that's also fine."

"You're not going to interfere?" I asked suspiciously.

"If he shoots his mouth off at you, yeah, but if not then I'll leave him alone. I said what I wanted to say to him. For now anyway." I continued to look at him suspiciously.

"You're being surprisingly understanding." Jeremy shrugged. "You use to always interfere. I mean, I'm pretty sure the reason everyone thought we were dating back in grade ten is because you did something so everyone would think that. You manipulate and interfere."

"That's different. Besides, I was like fifteen or something. I'm almost eighteen. Totally different."

"Oh yeah, two years, huge difference. But anyway, if you do manage to not interfere, than I appreciate it." I leaned over and kissed his cheek.

Jeremy smiled. "If he behaves like a moron, I'll say my piece, again, but if he acts nice I won't potentially make it worse by hovering like a jealous and over protective boyfriend."

"That's funny because when I was trying to figure out how to talk to you when you first came back, I told Liam to back off because I didn't want him and Jess hovering like over protective parents worrying about a bully."

"Yeah, well the downside of people liking to take care of you is sometimes it can easily be confused with not letting you handle things on your own. I think there isn't much I can say to Liam right now that will help either of you so better I just stand back. If I think of a brilliant plan though . . ." he tapped his head.

"You won't."

"I will."

"Anyway, forget about all of that for now, I don't even know what I'm going to do. Lets go watch T.V. or something," I suggested.

"What's the "or something" part of that offer?"

"Umm . . . watching a movie?" I grinned as he started to pull on my hand to lead me out of the kitchen.

"Well, whatever it is, sounds good to me." We went to the living room to hang out together and I snuggled up against him, feeling happier than I had ages. Despite all the Liam crap.

Diary Entry: July 25, 2008

Time is moving so quickly. It will be August in just another week. Jeremy is leaving the end of August, the thrity-first. We leave for our trip to Canada on the 22nd. But it's so sad. I already feel like he's gone because he is always packing. I help him because the sooner he's finished packing the sooner he can hang out with me. It's very depressing. I found out my mom isn't coming with us to Canada, just me and Jeremy's family. Kind of strange, I've never really been on vacation without her except a few times I went camping with Jessica, Nicole and Jenny.

My life has changed so much because of Jeremy. I know I can live without him, I have my friends. It's just that he's so important to me and my whole life. I can't imagine not having him around. Who will look out for me like Jeremy does? Who will comfort me? Jessica says I'll meet another guy and hit it off with him, but how can she assume that when none of my friends have a guy friend like Jeremy? Sure, they all have boyfriends, but that's a bit different. I guess I just have to learn to move forward. Besides, we can still mail, email, facebook, etc etc. You know, if he can get his computer skills together enough to set up a facebook account. Maybe I'll ask my mom for a cell so I can text him? Which I suppose isn't any good if he doesn't have a cell of his own.

Anyway, it'll only be two years before we graduate from school and then we can just go to college together. And maybe live together. And maybe if we're living together we'll be together like a couple or something . . .

Note To Self: Remember to set up a facebook account for Jeremy! And teach him how to use it! And change own privacy settings so he doesn't facebook stalk guys I don't have any intention of going out with but whom he has decided might be bad for me.

Present Day: November 16, 2009

The next day we were sitting at the kitchen table eating breakfast when my mom grinned and placed two lunchboxes in front of us on the table. Yes, lunchboxes. Not paper bags, but two old lunchboxes from my elementary school days. Actually, looking at the non-Barbie one, I decided perhaps that had been my father's from his various outdoor trips.

"I made you lunch!" she said with glee. This was clearly for Jeremy's sake. She hadn't made me lunch to take to school in somewhere around five years. Potentially more.

"Why?" I asked as I poked the Barbie lunch box.

"For school today."

Jeremy and I looked over the lunchboxes at each other.

"What did you make?" he asked tentatively as he gave the Barbie lunch box a bug-eyed look.

"Peanut butter sandwiches and vegetable soup."

"Soup?" I asked suspiciously. What, had she put a whole can in there? One each?

"Yes, I put them in two old thermoses. There's also a juice box."

"You have juice boxes?" Jeremy asked, looking surprised.

"Well . . . I found some." I would be throwing mine out. It was probably at least five years old.

"What thermoses?" I asked.

"Well one of them is your dad's old fishing—"

"Shotty!" I yelped, cutting her off.

"What?" Jeremy looked horrified as he stared at the Barbie lunch box.

"Shotty? What's that? Like a claim?" my mom asked.

"Yes."

"Oh, Honey, I kind of meant for Jeremy to have that one . . ." her voice trailed off and she also stared at the Barbie lunch box.

"What's the other one?" Jeremy asked dully. I already knew: it was the matching mini thermos that came with the lunch box.

"It's a small Barbie one. Becky, you should take it."

"FML," Jeremy muttered. I smirked.

"I claimed dibbs on the other one, he can have the Barbie one." I snatched my old (and fairly dirty) lunch box off the table and placed it on the floor next to me."

"Do you mind Jeremy? Does FML mean okay?" she asked.

"Ummm . . ." it did not mean okay, but I knew he wasn't about to tell her that. "Sure," he finally said. "But I wouldn't recommend you say it, it's kind of a teen slang way of saying it."

"Is it rude?" she asked looking slightly concerned.

"No, it means I agree but I hate my girlfriend right now." He glared at me and I smiled sweetly. He moved the lunch box next to his cereal bowl and resumed eating.

"Thanks for the lunch," he mumbled, his mouth full of cereal.

"No problem. Anyway, I'm off to work, love you both, bye!" she kissed the top of my head and waved at Jeremy as she left.

"You are so Canadian," I said with a smirk. "You just thanked her for giving you vegetable soup in a Barbie thermos."

"Yeah, I hope you realize I'm switching with you."

"You're not!"

"Oh I am. I may be too nice to be honest with your mom but you . . . well it'll happen. They will be switched. Just wait for it." He drank the rest of the milk in his bowl and stood up. "Almost 8:10," he said. I gave him a quick glare for the ominous threat of the Barbie thermos and polished off my toast and tea.

"I need to brush my teeth," I said. "If you switch them while I'm doing that you can forget any making out later."

"I would be a fool to switch them while you can switch them back." I threw him another fierce look before rushing to the bathroom to finish getting ready for school.

Ten minutes later we were walking to school, holding hands, our respective lunch boxes shoved into our backpacks. I had checked my thermos for Barbie's glowing smile before thrusting my lunch box in my bag.

"Next year perhaps we'll be walking to school together every morning," I said eagerly.

"Very true. Except we might have classes at different times. Also, if we live on campus that walk will be pretty short."

"Just the same." I smiled happily, thinking about the possibility.

"So did you get a chance to talk to Jessica? Does she know I've been staying at your place?"

"No, I never got a hold of her other than a text that she was busy with Will. Nicole might have. She could have told her."

"So we might have to deal with her overload of excitement and discussion on bushes. By the way, has she like done something amazing in a bush? She's been fairly obsessed with the bushes reference for two years. I almost want to ask her if she had her first orgasm in a bush, but I think that might be inappropriate."

"If she's done something in a bush she hasn't told me. But I agree she does love the reference. And please don't ask her if she had her first orgasm in a bush; then we'll both be stuck listening to a story neither of us want to hear."

"What if she didn't have one in a bush? What if she's never had one?" We looked at each other than both shook our heads.

"I'd bet at least ten dollars she's had one," I said teasingly. I had already heard a pretty weird description from her that referenced not bushes but volcanoes.

"Solo or with some help?" Jeremy asked. I smacked his arm with my free hand.

"Who knows. Anyway, whether her first was in a bush or not she would then tell us the story of how it happened," I pointed out.

"Good call. Better to just let the bush reference run its course. Perhaps she'll join the mile high club one day and make jokes and references to airplanes after."

"Mile high club?" I asked. Jeremy rolled his eyes.

"Do you like, not watch T.V.? How do you not know these things with Jess around?" I shrugged.

"I only partially pay attention to her?" I grinned. I paid far more than partial attention but I took most of what she said with a grain of salt.

"Well, anyway, what do you think she'll do? Throw a party or complain you won't have any time to spend with her?"

"Party. She'll be happy for me. Besides, she's got Will right now to entertain her."

"Ahh, right." We reached the school and headed to my locker while we muttered about Jessica's romantic enthusiasm and bushes. When we reached my locker, there she was, fixing her make-up.

"Hey," I said as we came up to her. She put her compact and lipstick away and turned to us with a big squeal.

"Look at you guys!" she yelped as she took in our handholding. She leapt on me for a hug and I let go of Jeremy's hand to hug her back. She withdrew and then leapt onto Jeremy, who wasn't as prepared for the physical affection as I was.

"Wow, okay, thanks Jess," he said, surprised.

"Oh my God so when did this happen? Like, you're holding hands! I bet you've been making out in some bushes, totally fun right? Oh my God you're so cute!"

"Thanks," I said, starting to blush.

"I can't believe I didn't hear about it sooner! Nicole told me this morning."

"We tried to find you yesterday to tell you but you weren't in any of the bushes we looked in," Jeremy joked.

"Did you try the ones near Will's house?" she asked coyly. I looked at Jeremy's face. He couldn't tell if she was joking.

"Umm . . ."

"I'm joking!" she shrieked, laughing at his face. "So like, you had a date right? And Jeremy made fun of Adrian? Dude, I sooooo wish I had been there for that. Did he look like he was going to shit his pants? I bet he did he's such a pansy."

"Yes! That's what I said to Becky, he looked like he was going to shit his pants." Jeremy started to retell the story in a slightly more glorious fashion than it had really occurred while Jessica gobbled it all up, all the while winking at me periodically. She was clearly thrilled.

The bell rang, interrupting his finish of explaining Sopel to me.

"Beck, we'll have girl talk at lunch?" Jessica asked me.

"Yes, for sure."

"You're not included Jer," she said to Jeremy. He shrugged. Now I wouldn't have to explain where I was going for the first part of lunch to him.

Jess ran off to her class and I quickly opened my locker. I hated being late.

I grabbed my books and dumped any unnecessary stuff into my locker. As soon as I had finished, Jeremy turned me around and very tenderly kissed me. I felt myself turn beet red; I had never been kissed at school before. What if a teacher saw?

As soon as he pulled away he started grinning devilishly.

"Got to go, see you later," he said and dashed off. I looked at him hurry away and instantly I knew what he had done. He had used the kiss as a distraction. And turned me away from my locker for a reason.

Sighing, I turned around to see the Barbie Thermos grinning down at me from the top shelf of my locker. I pushed it back and closed my locker. Now I would have to think of a way to return the favour.

Dairy Entry: August 1, 2008

So I figure we just flirt because we flirt. Me and Jeremy, that is. I remember asking him if he realised we were flirting and he shrugged and said yeah. It doesn't seem to be a big deal to him, so why should it be a big deal to me? Still, it makes my heart race every time we touch, even if just by accident. Maybe he does like me. Jessica has always said that he has. I finally told the others and I've asked Jess her opinion and it's still the same: he's always been in love with me. Maybe she's right, but he's leaving, no matter what either of us feels and I still believe that telling him I'm in love with him will just make it harder on the both of us. Jenny disagrees, but Nicole understands. Jessica just thinks he's in love with me and can run away from his parents or something so he can live with me if I say I'm in love with him. Jessica has an over active imagination. Then again, I dream that maybe, just maybe, there could be a way to keep him here, a way that would make him able to stay . . .

Present Day: November 16, 2009

As soon as it hit lunch time, I rushed to the coffee shop to meet Tom. I had texted Jess to tell her I would be slightly late on catching up on gossip. She had responded with "Its ok if u want 2 spend ur lunch making out w/jeremy in a bush. I understand." I had to text her back to let her know I wasn't with Jeremy, I was running an errand. If she had thought I was with Jeremy, it might have been slightly awkward if she mentioned it to him.

I arrived at the coffee shop to see Tom sitting at a table with a coffee and writing on his laptop. I slid into the seat across from him, feeling nervous.

"Hi Becky," he said warmly. It was so weird; he looked exactly as I remembered him, but a felt a sick rush as I thought of how horrible he had been to his family. It seemed unfair for him to great me with a warm smile while his only son hated him. He should look angry and dishevelled, not cheery and presentable.

"Hi," I said awkwardly.

"Want a coffee or something? Or I guess you still prefer tea?"

"I'm okay." I felt vaguely surprised he remembered I preferred tea.

"Okay, well, thanks for meeting with me. I wanted to start by explaining a couple of things. I know this may seem out of place, but it's my fault that Jeremy has been a bit . . . bitter and I believe you owe an explanation. You were his best friend for several years and my wrong doing should not have changed that." He took a deep breath, as if preparing himself for a strike.

"So . . . unfortunately Andrea and I did not work out. To cut out some of the details, I happened to meet someone else who I fell in love with. Thinking I was saving Andrea and my children pain, rather than be honest with any of them, I just maintained my relationship with them as it was but had a secret relationship with the other woman, Christina. Eventually all was found out and Jeremy took it very badly. He blames me for many things, such as being forced to move to Virginia, and has been very rebellious since. So, if he has been nasty or anything to you, this is partially my fault. My mistakes have given him a darker edge and he now carries a fair amount of baggage. I'm sorry that my mistakes have affected you as well."

This was not entirely the speech I was expecting. I mean, it was nice he was owning up to everything, but I kind of felt like he was in some sort of twelve step program where he was required to make amends to anyone he hurt. Would he expect a note or something proving I had approved his apology?

"Okay," was all I said. What else was there to say?

"Anyway, I wanted to meet with you because I just want to find out about how he's doing. You said on the phone he hasn't been drinking as much?" I shook my head.

"Not since Halloween. I think he's been vetoed from the popular partiers for going to the hospital. I don't know for sure, though."

"And he doesn't have any bad reps in school? He seems to be keeping under the radar?"

"Yeah. I mean, I don't even know what he does in his spare time at school. Like, I have no idea who he hangs out with at lunch. So whatever he does at lunch is clearly unexciting." This was true; I didn't actually know who Jeremy saw other than me on breaks and what not. I didn't even know where he went on his breaks. Except for the time Sandy came to talk to me about Liam, he had never even eaten with me at lunch.

"Well that's good. Andrea probably did the right thing by bringing him here then. Plus, maybe you guys will eventually patch things up, right?" Tom said with enthusiasm.

"Hmm."

"I don't actually know where he is right now. Either he and Andrea have an excellent way to keep him from view or he hasn't been at home at all this weekend. I would be worried, but Andrea doesn't look at all concerned so she's probably stuck him in a hotel or something. Actually, to be honest that's why I asked you if you knew if he had been promiscuous; I was worried he was out partying or staying at some girl's house."

I somehow managed not to visibly wince.

"So anyway, from all the information I have gathered, I think it might be best if I do give him some breathing room for awhile. However, there are some things I want to say to him. Other than explaining that I will provide him with some space. But I know he won't talk to me, and if I mail him a letter he won't open it. Emails clearly won't work for the same reason. So . . . I was wondering if you could give this to him." Tom pulled out an envelope. It had Jeremy's name typed on it, but no other markings. I started to feel nervous again.

"Give it to him?" I repeated, staring at the envelope.

"Yes. Andrea isn't about to take it, and if I drop by the house I'm sure one of them will assume it's from me and throw it out. They know I'm here right now. I understand if you don't want to hand it to him personally, but if you could drop it in his locker? Or perhaps give it to someone else who might give it to him? Or maybe even drop it in the mail box at his house once I've left? I'm planning on leaving this Wednesday, so any time after that. Though I might be delayed, depends on some job things. Either way, anytime after Wednesday."

"Uhhh . . ."

"I haven't sealed it. I understand if you want to read it before you give it to him. Or let your mom read it before you give it to him. Or even Andrea."

"Okay, I guess I can do that."

"Thanks Becky, I really appreciate it. I didn't want to involve Carrie at all in this; it's hard enough for her to try to keep peace."

"Right." I took the envelope and stuffed it into my backpack.

"If you decide not to give it to him, I understand."

"Okay, well, I have to go, I'll see you later. Or something." I stood up quickly, wanting to go talk to Jess before he asked me to do anything else.

"This means alot to me Becky. Take care." Tom also stood up and extended his hand. I wearily shook it and then sprinted out, feeling like I had a bomb in my backpack rather than a letter. What would I do with it? What would Jeremy do after reading it? More importantly, how would he feel about me when I gave it to him?

Diary Entry: August 7, 2008

I'm getting kind of excited about going to the cabin. Jeremy teases me about it. He's getting really sad. I can see it in his eyes. Carrie is pretty excited to meet new people. Good for her I guess.

I keep thinking about how long Jeremy and I have been friends. I mean, I've been friends with Jess for what feels like my entire life, but she's like my sister. Jeremy's my best friend. If that makes any sense.

I keep thinking about how much he changed from when I first met him and thought he was annoying to how he managed to mature and wanted to spend time with me. It all changed fairly quickly after he moved here from Canada. It makes me nervous to think in the time he'll be away he may go from not having any relationships to having them. I mean, like, right now he's a dating newbie, but he could come back with a string of girls behind him. (Or worse, below him? Or on top? Ahh I shouldn't think like that!)

I finally made him a facebook account. I showed him how to add pictures and everything. Of course, he has no digital camera so I don't imagine I'll be able to facebook stalk him through pictures he adds. I'm also fairly certain he'll forget to log on more than once a month. Useless.

Jess and Jenny say I have to tell him how I feel when we go away to the cabin. They're probably right. It's the ideal time. All of them (Nicole included) say telling him will help me deal with him leaving. Which sounds smart but I don't know how true it is. So I think maybe I'll just write down what I plan on saying to him and decide on the trip if I want to tell him. Currently, that is my plan, and I'll start writing it all out after Jess and I figure out what I'm going to wear each day. And then pack. Then I'll get around to it.

Present Day: November 16, 2009

I headed into Math class with Jess and Jenny after lunch. I had told them all full details of the entire weekend and had interrupted our giggles about Jeremy to debate Liam. To talk to him or not talk to him . . .

"Just tell him you didn't sleep with Jeremy. He's only overreacting because he thinks you did," Jenny was saying.

"He assumed and he's being an asshole. Besides, it's not his business if Becky did sleep with him, right Beck?" Jess argued. Jess said she had had enough of Liam's crap and was ready to kick him in the ass.

"But if they're going to stay friends they need to sort this out," Jenny pointed out.

"You want to know what will happen if they sort this out? Liam will pull another stunt or freak out about something else and Becky will be in the same boat. He needs to grow up and move on. He never even had the nerve to ask Becky out and now he's upset because Jeremy has decided to make a go of it with her? He has the maturity of a four year old," Jessica said stubbornly.

"Maybe he didn't realize how much he liked her until Jeremy, did you ever think of that?" Jenny countered with. I continued to walk between them, not wanting to involve myself in the argument.

"Of course, and he has ever right to be jealous, but enough is enough. There's a difference between being jealous and betting on your crush's virginity! Further, he apologizes with flowers and then accuses her of sleeping with Jeremy just because he happens to be there in the morning? Like, if I were there would he assume we were gay lovers? Because, you know, Beck's too frigid for my taste."

"Thanks Jess," I muttered.

Jenny rolled her eyes. "You can see why he thought that."

"Um, no I can't. If I came over and Jeremy was there I would not assume they had slept together. Anyone who knows her knows that it's a tad unlikely that she would rush into it."

"She was in her pyjamas! And you would assume they would have done stuff in the bushes."

"Yeah if they'd had sex she would have hastily thrown on a robe with no pyjamas! Maybe her sweat pants or something but she wouldn't have bothered to put on a two piece pyjamas set and a robe and come out of the kitchen like that, she would have come from the hall, aka her bedroom! And I'm just joking about that bushes crap."

I sighed. We had reached the outside of our classroom.

"Come on, lets just forget about it," I said. Liam came up and walked right by us into the room without saying a word. Jessica stuck her tongue out at his back.

We went in and sat down. I looked over at Jess who was mouthing death threats at Liam while he texted on his phone, his head down. I started to write a note.

> *Liam I didn't sleep with Jeremy. He was there for a different reason that had nothing to do with me, actually. I know you don't like him, but I wish you could put that aside so we could still be friends.*

I started to think about including that we were dating. I wasn't sure if I should bother to tell Liam. If I didn't, he would find out soon enough, our school was small enough everyone knew who everyone else was dating. I had already had two people come up to me to say they had heard about it.

Did you want to talk about this?

It seemed better to put that down than write that I was dating Jeremy. I shoved the note to Liam, who took it and crumbled it up and dropped it on the floor. I sighed. Jenny looked slightly shocked and Nicole rolled her eyes. Jess hadn't turned around yet so she hadn't seen.

Jenny threw me a note.

You ok? That was harsh! Maybe Jess is right . . .

I sighed and looked over at her sympathetic look.

I'm ok. It pretty much tells me where he stands. I think he's using this as an excuse. He doesn't want to deal with his feelings so he's using Jeremy and whatever he assumes as a reason to avoid me. I mean, this way he never really needed to deal with how I felt about that bet.

I passed Jenny the note and she nodded in agreement. I looked over at where Jeremy was sitting on the other side of the room, writing down the board notes. I felt a funny rush of attraction looking at him. Then I looked over at Liam and felt a pang of sadness.

At the end of class Jess turned around and saw the crumbled note on the floor below Liam's desk. She picked it up as Liam started to stand up.

"Hold it," she said to him, opening the note.

"I don't give a crap about what it says," he said to her, trying to brush by her.

"Well I do." She blocked his way and started to read. She finished it and slammed the note against his chest.

"You're not worth her effort," she said to him angrily. She grabbed my arm and started to stride out, dragging me with her.

Jess was muttering curses about Liam when Jeremy caught up to us.

"You booked it out of there," he said to us. I raised my eyebrows and pointed at Jessica.

"Liam?" he mouthed. I nodded. Jess continued to curse about Liam. Jeremy took my hand and I smiled at him. I felt slightly guilty though, knowing the letter from his father was in my backpack.

"How was lunch?" he asked me.

"Lunch?" I asked him, suddenly feeling nervous.

"Yeah did you enjoy your soup?" Oh right, the thermos.

"I enjoyed my soup, yours is still in my locker."

"What soup?" Jess asked, finally coming out of her murderous mutterings.

"Becky's mom made us lunch today," Jeremy told her with a smirk.

"That's like the quaintest thing I've ever heard!" she said. "When was the last time she made you lunch for school?"

"I don't know, like when the Backstreet Boys were popular?"

"Nice. Okay guys, my class is this way, see you after?" Jess asked. We nodded and she headed down the hall.

"Want me to walk you to class?" Jeremy asked.

"I'm okay, I don't want you to be late for yours." He shrugged.

"I guess I'll meet you at locker after then?" he suggested. Our next class was the last of the day. I nodded and we kissed briefly before heading off in separate directions.

After class I met Jess at my locker.

"Hey, Becky, there's something I want to say," she said as I put my books away.

"Is it about the thermos?" I asked, crinkling my nose as I picked it up.

"Um, no. It's about Jeremy. Well, kind of."

"Oh, what's up?" She looked more serious than usual.

"Jeremy's the best, and he's like the best for you, and I totally know that, but I just want you to be careful."

"Okay." I said with a shrug.

"And I know this is going to sound strange, but I don't mean mentally." I gave her a confused look.

"What?"

"Like, I actually totally trust you to gage yourself with him mentally, I have full trust you won't fall for him and then he does a runner or something. What I mean is I know you will wait for sex but . . . keep your pace."

"What does that mean?" I asked, feeling slightly confused.

"Like, you only have one first of everything, and I hope you keep that in mind. You've been in the dark about all physical stuff so I just don't want you to get ahead of yourself. I know this doesn't sound like me, and I'm always like "huzzah I love fooling around!" but I'm not you. And to be honest, I kind of wish I had savoured some of the stages a bit more. Like, the anticipation of each stage is awesome, it's almost better than actually doing anything, so I'm just saying: savour it. You know, after he first . . . you know . . . touches your crotch wait a bit before doing anything more exciting than that. Fully enjoy that before moving on. Get it?"

I was trying not to laugh. I knew Jess was being very sincere and telling me to wait for things was very unlike her, so I appreciated the thought, but I was desperate to laugh about her way of putting it.

"Thanks, Jess," I said, still trying not to laugh. "I guess I'll . . . wait a bit after crotch touching . . ." I couldn't help it. I smirked.

"I wasn't sure you would know what I meant if I used a different term," she said with a frown. "Do you even know what finger bang means?"

"Yes! But anyway, thanks, it means alot that you gave me that advise. Very unlike you."

"I know. Oh, and don't actually do anything in bushes, I mean who would want to fool around in bushes? You'd get dirty and probably things would poke you that you don't want poking you. Get it?" She grinned. "Oh and I meant dirt dirty not sexy dirty."

"I know." We grinned and then I hugged her.

"Not at school," she hissed. "I don't want anyone thinking I'm a lesbo."

"Sorry," I muttered as Jeremy came up.

"Hey guys," he said.

"Ahh are you guys going to walk home now together? And hold hands? Oh it's so cute! Seriously can I take a picture?" Jessica pulled out her phone.

"No," Jeremy and I both said.

"Okay, well I'm going home. Beck, um, you know, you'll like, share with me if he does touch your crotch right?" she asked. Jeremy hit his head against a locker.

"No," I said as I nodded at her. He couldn't see me with his head against the locker.

"Jessica you have the subtlety of a mammoth," he muttered.

"A mammoth? Um, WTF Jer there's no more mammoths. They're extinct or something. Anyway, see you guys later." She flounced off with a big smile.

"It's like an elephant. Only more clever. A more clever way of saying the subtlety of an elephant," he explained to me.

"Mammoths are more clever than elephants?" I asked him with a wide eyed look.

"You're joking right?"

"Yes, now see that was funny, telling Jessica she has the subtlety of a mammoth was not."

"Whatever."

I handed him the thermos as I took it out of my locker.

"You never enjoyed your delicious soup." He wearily took the thermos and stuffed it into his bag.

"It's my afternoon snack," he grumbled. I smiled at him. I closed my locker and took his hand to walk home.

Two hours later my phone alarm went off to let us know my mom was off work. We pulled apart and I leaned over to turn my phone off.

"We should make dinner," Jeremy said as I tried to flatten my hair.

"What did you want to make?" I asked suspiciously. Cooking was not his strong suit. At least his cooking was better than his baking, though.

"I don't know. But to be nice to your mom."

"You're such a suck up," I muttered. I found a brush and started to brush out my somewhat unruly hair. "I envy your hair. You can lie here making out for hours and it looks virtually the same as before." He smiled as he sat up. He ran his fingers through his dark hair. I stuck out my tongue at him.

"Come on, at least if we're making dinner your mom won't ask us what we spent the afternoon doing. Or if she does, we can see preparing dinner."

"Because we'll have prepared something in the next fifteen minutes? Yeah right. Besides, lets face it, I'll be cooking and you'll grab at me every once in awhile between examining instructions in a cook book."

"I will totally help." I rolled my eyes at him but headed to the kitchen.

We somehow decided to make tuna casserole and started preparing everything when my mom came in. She ohhed and awwed our efforts to make a decent meal before asking us how our lunches were.

"Wonderful," we said in unison, nodding at her. True to his word, Jeremy had slurped up his soup once we had arrived back at the house. He had cleaned both thermos and they were sitting in the dish rack.

"Excellent!" she said happily. I wondered if Jeremy had eaten the sandwich at school.

"I hope the thermos didn't embarrass you too much, Jeremy," she added.

"Oh no, Becky traded with me," Jeremy lied. I glared at him.

"That was good of you, Beck." She gave me a small pat on the back.

"Yes, I'm a saint," I agreed. "Instead of saving souls I save social statuses. Speaking of which, Jer, you haven't changed yours in months."

"My what?" he asked, confused.

"Facebook. It still says you live in Virginia. And your status is something like "new cities suck" which doesn't make sense because it reads as "Jeremy Johnson new cities suck." You should at least add an adjective so it makes sense."

"Um, well, right now I've just moved so my status kind of makes sense . . ."

"No, it doesn't. Besides, this isn't a new city; you lived here before."

"I don't know my password."

"I wrote it down for you."

"I don't know where that piece of paper is."

"I have Facebook," my mom added. I had kind of forgotten she was still in the kitchen. "You should add me as a friend." I had refused to add her as a friend myself. Jeremy looked slightly stricken.

"You know, sure, I'll add you. After dinner. Assuming Becky can figure out how to log me on. And you can change whatever info you want on my page."

"Great!" she said. "I'm going to go change, I'll be back in a minute." She disappeared down the hall.

"You're going to add my mom on Facebook? It's bad enough you don't have enough friends to equal double digits but to make my mom one? I don't have her."

"Who cares? The friends I do have are you and Carrie and maybe Jess or something. It'll make her happy."

"Yeah, and she'll bug me to add her!"

"That's your issue, not mine."

"Well . . . just saying . . ."

"Why did you bring Facebook up anyway? Is it because you would like me to change my relationship status?" he asked teasingly.

"Don't be ridiculous. It's because I said I save social statuses. Everyone has Facebook. How did you even know where the parties were without it?"

"I text people? Sometimes, I even phone them. I know, old fashioned, right?"

"You should learn to live in the digital world." I gave him a condescending look.

"Thank God I didn't if I actually updated Facebook you would have known the stunts I was pulling last year long before you were ready to learn about them. How much would you have loved to have guys writing on my page stuff like "hey dude super wasted last night, that chick was hot, what was her name?" You would have been upset with me long before I avoided you."

"It's called a wall, not a page thing. And yes, I guess you have a point. Besides, it gave me the freedom to write whatever I wanted."

"You still never showed anything about any guys," Jeremy said.

"How do you know that? I thought you didn't know how to use it! You said you don't even know your password!"

"I don't. Just because I never knew how to pry for information using a computer does not mean Carrie does not. She kept me posted on a regular basis." Jeremy shrugged.

"Really?" I asked as I poured cooked noodles into a casserole dish. (Just as I had predicted, I had done most of the actual cooking and every once in awhile Jeremy glanced at the recipe book I had put on the counter.)

"Don't get excited and think I was purposefully keeping tabs on you, she did that on her own."

"And if she hadn't would you have done it yourself?" He made a face and didn't say anything. "Jeremy?"

"Well it did save me from trying to figure out my password," he finally said. I shook my head at him with a smile. I handed him the large casserole dish and pointed at the oven.

"Which rack?" he asked.

"The middle one." I opened the oven door for him and waited for the comment. He put the casserole dish in and leaned back up.

"I want to make a joke about racks but I can't think of any good ones you would understand."

"I know," I said.

"How do you know?"

"You looked at my breasts when you said "rack." Rarely do you successfully pull off that kind of joke, though."

"What are you talking about? I'm dynamite at it! Dynamite!"

"What did you say to Sandy on the first day of school? Something lame about exploring things? Yeah, super clever. We were all laughing on the inside. It was almost as good as your mammoth joke."

"I'm funny!" he objected.

"I never said you weren't. Betting with Adrian on hockey teams while he sweats nervously, that's funny. Attempting to hit on Sandy by making references to exploring her instead of the city in front of her twin brother, far less funny. Jokes about racks, predictable."

"Ah whatever," Jeremy said sourly. I kissed his nose.

"I think you're funny," I said kindly.

"Was that a joke?"

"You're silly." I kissed his nose again, then his cheek. He pulled me closer to him and started to kiss me. We broke apart when we heard footsteps in the hall.

"Table setting," I said quickly. We started putting plates on the table. My mom came in and we were holding forks.

"Dinner almost ready?" she asked us.

"I have no idea," Jeremy admitted.

"Like fifteen minutes," I said. I pointed to the timer on the microwave.

"Oh!" was all he said.

Dinner went by without any excitement. My mom was thrilled we had made dinner and kept saying about how nice it was. It was okay; tuna casserole wasn't exactly gourmet.

After dinner Jeremy and I did some homework and watched television. This time, we actually watched television as my mom kept coming into the living room to find a magazine or something. Really, I think she was just checking on us.

When I finally left Jeremy to go get ready for bed, I pulled the letter from Tom out of my bag. I hadn't looked at it yet and still had no idea what it said. I wasn't sure if I should read it or if I even wanted to. I did know I would need to hide it until I decided.

I thought about putting it in my diary, but that seemed too cliché or something. Besides, what if Jeremy or my mom decided to spy on me and read my diary? I mean, I wouldn't be that surprised if it turned out my mom read my diary to ensure I wasn't secretly smoking or drinking or something. I mean, she had told me after Jeremy left that she knew how I felt about him and I hadn't told her. Then again, that could be some sort of motherly instinct thing.

I thought about putting it between the mattress, but then I worried I would think about it underneath us the next time we started making out on my bed. It might be distracting or disturbing. Even if I was caught up enough in the moment, the thought seemed icky to have a secret letter from his father underneath the mattress while we fooled around on top.

I opened my underwear draw and stuffed the letter underneath my granny panties, the ones I reserved for my period. He would have absolutely no reason to open the draw, let alone rifle through my gross older underwear. If, for some reason, he decided to rifle through my underwear chances are he would go for my regular day prettier and newer underwear. Or the ones Jess and Nicole had bought me for Christmas last year in case "it was a good year" as they put it. (I guess it was a good year, Jeremy was back and I was now dating him. Though I still had no reason to take the tags off the underwear.)

I went to bed worrying about the letter. Had I done the right thing by accepting the letter? I wasn't actually obliged to give it to Jeremy, but just the same I felt like I had been pulled in to an argument I probably didn't want to be a part of. Just because Tom had seemed nice when I saw him didn't mean he actually wanted to give Jeremy space and meant the things he said. Then again, I could read the letter to see what he wanted to say to Jeremy so badly he had lied to his daughter to come out here. Which, come to think of it, was also an awful thing to do. Carrie thought he was on a medical conference! Of course, maybe he was, the conference could be here.

Sighing, I rolled over and tried to put the thoughts out of my head. I would read the letter later and decide another day. For now, I should just enjoy being with Jeremy.

Chapter 13

Diary Entry: August 21, 2008

We're going camping tomorrow! I'm kind of excited. It should be really fun, even though it will be sad because Jeremy will be leaving soon. I can't wait, though, because it will be Jeremy and I hanging out with no packing for a few days. My mother is kind of worried about me, saying something could happen or I could get homesick, but I just scoff it off. She mostly says she's worried going away with him and his family will make it harder when they leave. Whatever.

I still have a long pro and con list about telling him how I feel and how that would work. I've written out several potential scripts, all of which Jess said sounded great but needed to be sexier, and my pro and con list clearly indicates I should just tell him before it becomes too late, but I'm sooooo scared to. What if he doesn't feel the same? I've never really admitted to even liking a guy (to the guy) and so how would I actually manage to say anything along the lines of "I'm in love with you?" Jessica and Jenny say I should just do it on the trip, but Nicole says I should wait until the last day he's here. I think Nicole may be right. I know I have to tell Jeremy, but when he leaves is best because it will be awkward no matter what I say or do. So I think I'll tell him the last day I see him. Of course, how will I feel if he feels the same way? What if I don't get the chance? What if I chicken out?

Present Day: November 17, 2009

The next day was fairly uneventful. At school, Liam refused to talk to me, though instead of making the effort of a nice note I sat in his chair in Math to see what he said to me. He didn't say anything; he simply sat at my desk. Not quite the reaction I was hoping for.

After school, same as on Monday, Jeremy and I went back to my place where we made out until my alarm went off at five to signal my mom being off work. Rather than make dinner, though, we did some homework as Andrea was coming over that evening.

"Hello," she said cheerily as she breezed in carrying pizza.

"Hi," we said in unison. Jeremy pulled out his phone and started to text under the table. I gave him a peculiar look.

"So how is my baby?" she asked as she leaned over to kiss Jeremy's cheek. He grimaced.

"Fine mom," he muttered. He closed his phone and mine went off. I opened my phone under the table.

> *Think she's brought pizza as a way of buttering me up? Or both of us up?*

I shook my head at him. Pizza was probably just a way for her or my mom to avoid cooking.

"How's school?" Andrea asked.

"Good," we replied, still in unison.

"What did you do today?" She pressed. My mom smiled from where she was pulling plates out from the cupboard.

"Stuff," Jeremy said.

"Learned," I added.

"Wow I've never met two people more informative. So, lets sit down." Jeremy and I were already sitting, but both our moms took their seats. I knew what this was about: Andrea was going to tell us how it went at the lawyer's office.

After some idle chatter about work and the like, Andrea cleared her throat.

"So I saw a lawyer today regarding my custody agreement," she said. We all nodded. "And Tom has agreed to go home."

"Okay," Jeremy said. Silence fell. I wasn't entirely sure what to say. Good news? How nice a lawyer was able to send him home? Of course, I knew he had been planning on leaving anyway.

"He was not actually in violation of any parental agreement. He did go talk to a school counsellor, which he is allowed to do. He was slightly . . . stalkerish but that is not against any agreement we have, that would have to be a police case or something like that. I don't know I only half paid attention to that part. He didn't say anything to Jeremy and hanging outside the house is more of a police matter than a lawyer one. So . . . you can come home now!" she smiled happily. Jeremy shrugged.

"The enthusiasm you bring to the table is infectious," Andrea muttered.

"That's nice Mom. Thanks for sorting that out." He took another piece of pizza.

"Well, anyway, thanks Pam for looking after him for me," Andrea said warmly.

"No problem. He was a great houseguest," my mom said.

"Nobody thanked me for putting up with him," I said.

"As if! You two enjoyed it. Besides, I thought you had plans to move in together for college or something," Andrea said.

"Mom, I said we may . . . I didn't say for sure . . . she hasn't agreed to anything yet . . ." Jeremy gave her an annoyed look.

"Right. Well hopefully that was nice practice. This way you can find out now he can only cook boxed macaroni and frozen pizza."

"Good point. Gives me some food for thought on living with him." I stuck my tongue out at him.

"I hope that wasn't a pun on purpose," he said. I shrugged.

"Anyway, Carrie's coming out for a visit soon . . ." Andrea said. She started talking about Carrie and recent updates in her boy crush filled life.

After dinner, Jeremy and I assembled his stuff to throw in his bag.

"It's kind of too bad we won't be staying in the same house for awhile," he said.

"Ah come on, you were happy sleeping on that couch?"

"Hey, lots more opportunities to fool around when we're together that often," he pointed out.

"You'd get sick of it. And of me. I'm sure eventually we would have started fighting or something. Plus, Jess would start to miss me and be coming around to see us. You don't always fair well with Jessica for long periods of time, you start to get snarky with her."

"True. Though I imagine if we go to school together and live together she'll be by for visits. And I'm not kidding myself: she'll want to share with you, not sleep on a couch or spare bed, so I'll be exiled." I shrugged and grinned at him. He was probably right.

We finished packing his things and went back to the kitchen where Andrea and Pam were drinking coffee and playing cards. After their game, Andrea announced it was time to go home so Jeremy could clean the bathroom. Wearily, he left mumbling about bathroom cleaning and drinking.

After he left, I pulled the letter out of my drawer and stared at it. I wanted to read it, but I still didn't know if I should. Also, I wasn't sure if I should give it to him without reading it. Depending on what it said and how it was written it might be best to tell Carrie to tell Tom I would not be passing the letter along.

Sighing, I decided to wait. Same as last night's thought: I would read the letter and decide another day.

Diary Entry: August 22, 2008

We're camping today! I'm so excited! It should be fun, me, Jeremy and his family. It's kind of odd, there was much debate over where I would sleep but I think I'm sleeping in a tent with Carrie. (I couldn't really sleep in the cabin with Jeremy . . .) However, my mom (wearily) agreed to let me share the tent with Jeremy on one night if Andrea feels so inclined to allow. She said she would decide when we got there. Which is probably just a way of delaying a no, but just the same I hope she says yes. I mean I've slept on a couch with him several times, what difference does a tent make? Plus, it's a good opportunity to talk privately. If I get a good opportunity to, I might tell him . . . that . . . yeah, if I get the chance I might tell him that I love him, but probably not. Jessica says I'm chicken. What does she know? She always seems to think she's in love with her latest crush, but that's not love and I'm so scared of rejection.

Anyway, we leave when Andrea and Tom finish work, around five. I've already packed and I'm going to head over there shortly. My mom wanted me to wait until she came home from work so she could say goodbye and drive me, but I'm far too excited. I'll call her when we get there anyway.

Hopefully it ends up being a beyond epic trip so I'll have plenty of happy memories made before he leaves for two years!

Present Day: November 19, 2009

I was feeling crappy. I could feel it in my bones, some dull ache slowing me down and making me feel far heavier than normal. I was walking through school slightly zombish when Nicole came up to me.

"Looking hot," she observed with sympathy.

"As in sexy or like I have a fever?" I asked wearily.

"Fever, but I was trying to be nice." She smiled warmly. "You okay?"

"I feel crappy."

"Maybe you should go home." The day was partially over, but I didn't really feel like it. Besides, I had plans with Jeremy after school. Though I suspected instead of lying down to make out I would just fall asleep.

"We'll see," I said. Nicole shrugged. We walked to class while we discussed how Liam was still being difficult and had continued to refuse to speak to me or anyone else associated with me.

Later that day, after Math, Jeremy came up to me looking suspicious.

"You don't look as . . . you're looking less . . ." he paused. He was probably trying to think of a nice way to tell me I didn't look very good.

"She looks hot," Nicole volunteered with a smile.

"What? Oh yes do you feel warm or something?" He peered at me curiously.

"Warm? Why is it warm in here?" I looked around the hall obliviously.

"Do you not feel well and plan on just ignoring it?" he asked. Nicole nodded.

"No," I said.

"Time to go home." We still had two classes left, but he took my elbow and started steering me towards my locker. Nicole waved goodbye.

"But I still have two classes left," I protested.

"Fine then we'll stop by the office first."

"I don't need to go home, I'm okay." We reached my locker and he waited for me to open it. Despite Liam no longer using my locker, I had decided not to give Jeremy my combination for the time being. No point in aggravating Liam further.

I opened my locker and a note fluttered to the ground. Jeremy picked it up and handed it to me. It was from Jessica.

> *Ive been talking to Liam, hes kinda coming around. Sorta. He just needs 2 think and stuff for a bit or something like that. He would rather have some space b4 talking again. Im not suppose to say anything so keep this on the DL.*
> *Jess*

I knew Jeremy was trying to discretely read it, but I shoved the note into my pocket anyway, not caring if he was finished or not. I wondered if he knew Jess meant down low by "DL."

"So we'll stop by the office and then I'll take you home?" Jeremy offered.

"No, I'm fine, I have English next it'll be easy."

"You're very pale and I thought you were going to fall asleep in Math. I think you should just go home."

"Fine fine," I muttered, giving in. I did want a nap. "But you don't have to come, you can meet me at my place later if you feel like it." Despite what I said, I was hoping he would come anyway. He would make me tea.

"Your mom isn't home; who will make you tea?" I shrugged as nonchalantly as I could.

283

"Lets go to the office and I'll take you home and make you tea and if you want me to come all the way back to school then I will. For like half a class." I shrugged again. He took my backpack from me and started putting books away and pulling out my English notes. I had been working on an essay. Somehow, I guess he remembered that.

Once he finished, we walked to the office where he then told them I was going home because I was sick. Ms. Jenter, our school receptionist, looked at me sympathetically.

"A fever?" she asked. I wondered how my lack of colour made people assume fever. Shouldn't they assume that if I was red-faced?

I nodded and she clucked.

"Well get some rest and hopefully you'll be feeling better soon. Now . . ." she turned her gaze to Jeremy.

"I'm just going to take her home," he said.

"Because you don't have a class right now?" she asked suspiciously.

"A spare," he lied.

"And your name?"

"Liam Gil. Thanks," he started to pull me away while she started typing.

"Does Liam even have a spare?" I asked after we left the office.

"I don't know. Either way, she won't know who's skipping because if he doesn't he'll show up for his class so she won't have any absences for him today." He shrugged.

"Devious," I muttered. We stopped by his locker and started walking home, holding hands.

Half an hour later I was lying on my bed with him carefully holding a cup of tea. I had changed into my sweats and was feeling mildly better, though my back was aching. I wasn't about to admit that to Jeremy though.

"Can I ask you something?" I asked him.

"Sure." He was propped up on his elbow and was running his fingers down my arm.

"Did you lie about not having a cell phone?" He looked startled. When he was gone, he had said his parents wouldn't let him have one, so he was not able to text me. Therefore, I had never bothered to give him my cell number as if he phoned, he always phoned the home line.

"You mean last year?" I nodded. "Why are you asking?"

"I just thought it seemed weird your parents wouldn't let you have one. Your mom, in particular. Besides, you said the other day you texted people when I asked you how you knew where all the cool parties were."

"Yeah when I moved here I texted people to find out what was going on and where."

"That doesn't answer the question," I said sourly. I already knew the answer. Jeremy sighed.

"Yes, I lied. I mean, at first I didn't, I didn't get the phone until Christmas. By that time, I didn't want you texting me."

"Why?"

"Okay, you have to understand, when I left here it was kind of a big deal what I said to you."

"Yeah, I know."

"And so I wanted time to sort out how okay I was about what happened. You know, time to get over it, right? Like, I was really confused. You didn't reject me and you definitely kissed me back, but you didn't return . . . you know."

"I know," I repeated. "I remember." Of course, this was assuming he was referring to him saying he was in love with me. I sipped my tea thoughtfully. Yes, that would be about the only thing he was referring to.

"So at first I was still planning on being able to text you and hoping I could phone more often and stuff, but when I

285

was feeling better. Plus, I made some dumb plan about how I could just explore that avenue more when we went to college. The plan made me feel better so I fully intended to go back to normal."

"What was your dumb plan?"

"It involved frat parties and beer. Anyway, so I started to feel better and then all that crap with my parents kind of came out and all of a sudden I understood why we moved and you know the rest . . . so when I got the cell phone, which was an effort on my mom's part to better keep track of me, I wasn't in the mood to text you so I could have you text me whenever you feel like it. I didn't want to be trying to forget everything and have a reminder of what life use to be like with a text message from you. Writing letters meant I could open your returns whenever I chose and they would always be infrequent and predictable. Besides, aren't you slightly relieved not to get my drunk text messages? I would have sent some and they probably wouldn't have been exactly sweet or funny."

"I guess," I mumbled.

"I'm sorry I lied. I thought it was easier than explaining why I didn't want you texting me. The idea of you being able to get a hold of me whenever you wanted scared me a bit. I did not want to do something dumb when you phoned or texted and did not want to reveal what was really going on. If you had been able to phone and text me whenever, chances are I would have let everything out. Unpleasantly. By lying to you it was easier to put you aside in my mind. You weren't part of that world. And I didn't really . . . I didn't fully get over what had happened before I left." I tried not to wince. "Much easier to just be writing down my thoughts to you at times convenient for me, when I could push aside my other thoughts."

"You're probably right. I would have been pretty shocked to get bizarre drunk texts or phone calls from you." As awful as it was to think, I was naive and probably needed to be shielded in some way. It would have been harder to find out about his rebellious side while he was several thousand miles away and was in the thick of it.

"Can I ask you a question?" Jeremy asked. He rolled on his back so he was looking up at the ceiling. A part of me instantly felt like he was pulling away slightly. I already knew what he was going to ask.

"Sure," I said, even though I didn't want him to.

He took a very long time to actually say anything. He was probably deciding on whether or not to bring it up.

"Why didn't you say it back?" I had been right; he wondered why I hadn't returned his "I love you" before he moved away.

He didn't turn to look at me when he asked, just continued to look up at the ceiling. I sighed and also rolled onto my back.

"I don't know," I said. I didn't know. I had thought about it many times and all I could come up with is I had mentally frozen. It had been too hard for me with all the emotion. I had wussed out.

"Okay." He continued to stare at the ceiling. I rolled back on my side to look at him.

"Jeremy, I know it totally sucks that I didn't meet you half way. I mean, I should have. I just . . . I was so upset and everything was so . . . emotional. I just couldn't actually get it out. Like, I wanted to, and I had planned to, before you even said anything, but then you did and I was going to say it but you kissed me and somehow . . . time ran out before I could compose myself enough to tell you. I'm sorry. I wish I had." I sighed again and rolled onto my back once more. Jeremy didn't say anything.

"I was pretty confused," he said softly. "I mean, you kissed me back, and I actually understood after we got back from the cabin that you instigated our fooling around, but you didn't . . . say anything. Which is why I made my brilliant plan to go to a frat party and get drunk and fool around." He smiled.

"That is not a brilliant plan. Anyway, I wanted to tell you after you left, but it seemed super awkward to phone you up to be like "um hey so remember you said something and ummm . . . me too?" And clearly I do not have the literary skills to write it in a letter without sounding like an idiot. Besides, I started to think . . . maybe you would have a better time there if you weren't holding onto me." Jeremy turned on his side and gave me a surprised look.

"What?" I moved to face him.

"Like, if I had said something, what would happened? Realistically? Would we have decided to date long distance? Because a brand new couple trying to accomplish a long distance relationship at the age of sixteen for at least two years seems like a disaster waiting to happen. And if we hadn't decided that, would we still have expected something from each other? I didn't want to just tell you and then be responsible for you not moving on and simply biding the time until college."

Jeremy stared at me for a bit, examining my face.

"If you didn't tell me it wouldn't matter what I did while I was gone," he finally said. "It would be understandable if I didn't hold out for you like you did for me."

"No," I mumbled.

"Yes. And you did hold out for me. In case I came back still wanting you. And, as we know, I didn't exactly keep to the same code."

"Whatever." I rolled over to my other side so I wasn't facing him anymore. He put his arm around me and curled up against my back.

"I still thought about you, even though I still . . . you know . . ." he said after awhile.

"I know."

"And a part of me was just biding time until college. Of course, then Andrea packed me up and moved here a year early."

"Good thing to, with people making bets on how far they can get with me it might have become more difficult to never let anyone get past breast fondling," I muttered.

"Liam would have eventually made a move. That would have been the big challenge. He was biding time to figure out what was going on with you."

"Yeah, well, that would be almost as awkward as my thought of phoning you to somehow say "me too" without actually having to say what I was saying "me too" to." I sighed and rolled back to facing him. He smiled at me and kissed my nose. I stared at him a bit, still thinking.

"What?" he asked, probably sensing I was still bothered.

"You did such a 180 after Halloween," I said.

"Yeah."

"Why?"

He shrugged. "I thought I told you my plan to keep you at a distant wasn't going so well so I ditched it."

"Sure but a couple of days later you tried to kiss me. You went from wishing I would disappear to hitting on me in less than a hundred hours."

"So? I already said plan be-an-ass wasn't working out."

I cleared my throat while I thought. "So . . . there was no other reason to pursue romance with me?"

Jeremy's facial expression changed slightly. He sighed. "What are you really asking?"

"Did you really decide to change your attitude towards me because I happened to go to the hospital with your mom?"

He was quiet for a moment. "Partially."

"And what was the other part?"

"You're just going to be upset with yourself if we keep talking about this." He gave me a slightly stern look.

"You don't know that."

"Yes I do."

"Whatever what was the other part?"

Jeremy groaned ever so slightly and looked directly above me as he spoke. "Maybe there was a sense of possibility because you said that you had felt the same way when . . . you know when I said stuff before I left and you didn't."

"You mean when you said . . . how you felt . . . and I didn't." I noticed he was avoiding repeating his exact words. For some reason, so was I. Somehow I felt too weird to easily say "you mean when you said you were in love me?"

"Yes that's what I mean."

"So part of the reason you avoided me and what not when you came back was because I hadn't admitted my feelings when you did."

"And this is exactly what I was trying to avoid," Jeremy muttered.

"No, seriously, did you change your opinion of me because I admitted that evening that I had felt the same? I mean, you were being an ass and all accusing of Liam, I tell you I had felt the same, fall asleep, and when I wake up an hour later you're a different person."

"It was more than an hour. And I'm the same person, I just became willing to connect with you again. Does it matter if it was because you showed up at the hospital, because I felt jealous of Liam, or because you admitted to being in love with me before?"

"Well . . ." I started.

"Because no matter what, one of those, combo of those, we're here, together, now, right?"

"I guess," I mumbled.

"You guess? Are we not together?" he asked slightly teasingly.

"You know that's not what I meant, I meant I guess it doesn't matter why, it's important that things are working out."

"Exactly," Jeremy said with a smile. I bit my lip, still feeling a little guilty. If I had just told him before maybe things would have been better for him when he came back, maybe he would have been more honest with me while he was still gone . . .

"And anyway, if I hadn't been such a disaster last year, slept with someone and asked my mom to take me to the clinic, maybe I wouldn't be here now, I'd be in Virginia." Jeremy added.

"Oh I guess that's true. So it was all for the best then you went off the deep end?" I grinned at him.

"It was my master plan all along."

"The plan has been going well."

"I'll say." He leaned forward and kissed me tenderly. I prayed my nose wasn't running.

"Are you tired?" he asked me as he pulled back. He gently touched my cheek and I got the feeling it was more to check my temperature than to be affectionate.

"Yes," I admitted. I felt better lying down but now that I was relaxing I had noticed my throat was very sore. I had finished my tea somewhere in the midst of the conversation of his cell phone and put my cup on my bedside table.

"Lets go watch T.V. or something. You want more tea? Or maybe soup? Aren't people suppose to like soup when they're sick?"

"I'm not sick I'm just . . . not able to maintain my body heat to an ideal temperature."

"Whatever you go lie down in the living room and I'll make tea. And two Tylenol."

"I don't need any Tylenol."

"I'm pretty sure you do."

"I'm pretty sure I don't. I'll only go lie down and accept tea if I don't have to take any Tylenol," I said stubbornly. Jeremy rolled his eyes.

"You're absurd. Fine, I won't offer you any Tylenol." He disappeared into the kitchen and I slowly made my way to the living room to lie down.

Some time later I woke-up when my mom came home. I was stretched out on the couch, wrapped in a blanket, and Jeremy curled around me. I felt slightly chilly. I pulled the covers up higher.

"You okay?" my mom asked as she touched my head.

"Her body temperature keeps adjusting," Jeremy told her. "She keeps sweating and then shivering."

"What?" I asked, confused. I didn't remember this. I must have been asleep. I had fallen asleep sometime after my tea; I had no idea how long I had been on the couch for.

"I'll get some Tylenol," my mom said kindly.

"I'm fine," I said sharply.

"I already gave her some it hasn't done much, I think it's just keeping her fever from being too high," Jeremy said. I rolled over to face him.

"What Tylenol? I refused it."

"Oh, right, well how about one now then?"

"Is that why my tea tasted funny?" The tea he had given me had had a slightly peculiar taste, but when I had asked Jeremy he had asked me if my nose was plugged. Not wanting him to think I was any sicker, I had lied and said no and on second thought maybe the milk was just a bit old.

"Me? Ground Tylenol into your tea? That doesn't sound like something I would do." It sounded exactly like something he would do.

"Okay, Becky, maybe you should go to bed." My mom tried to pull me up. Jeremy helped her.

"Now that your mom is here somebody else can force feed you Tylenol. Phone me tomorrow if you want." He kissed my cheek while I grumbled at him.

"Bye Pam," he said as he took his jacket. She said goodbye as she took all the various blankets off the couch.

"When did this happen? You're fever?" my mom asked me as I started to move towards my room. My back hurt.

"Earlier." My throat was now sore and I was feeling slightly nasal.

"Did you come home from school?"

"Jeremy made me," I mumbled. She led me to my room and started to arrange the blankets around me.

"Cell phone?" I asked feebly. She looked around and pulled it out of my backpack.

"I'll check on you in a bit. And you're going to have more Tylenol soon, unless your fever is better."

"We'll see," I said darkly.

"Let me know if you need anything." She kissed the top of my head and left, leaving the door half closed behind her. Rolling around until I felt comfortable, it was mere moments before my eye lids dropped and I slipped into a slightly feverish dream.

Diary Entry: August 26, 2008

I just got back from the camping trip!! Oh my God, I couldn't believe it!! Jeremy and I . . . well, I'm not even sure how to write down what happened. I really should have just told him then that I loved him, I mean, I could tell he has feelings for me and not just the friend kind, I mean he has feelings for me! Or at the very least is definitely attracted to me. Oh man, it was so much fun!! We went swimming at the lake and Jeremy and I hard core flirted. I guess I'm beginning to pick up on it now, I mean we've always flirted but now I actually notice it . . .

We fooled around a bit. Like, weirdly, we didn't kiss (how does that happen?) but you know . . . some groping occurred. I don't think I'll write it down (what if my mom secretly reads my diary??)

I ended up sleeping in the tent with Jeremy one night. It felt a bit odd, sleeping with him, but it wasn't anything bad. We didn't do anything, just curled up there. I'm smiling as I'm writing this. I'm sad because he's leaving soon, but I feel so happy from the weekend that it doesn't matter as much right now . . . I just love him so much and being with him makes everything seem better, even if he is leaving.

Flashback

I smiled as the warm sun splashed itself along my body. Now this was heaven: sunbathing. Jeremy's family and I had arrived at the cabin just half an hour ago and after unpacking both Carrie and I had wanted to go sunbathing despite Jeremy's insistence that it would ruin our skin when we were older. He did have a point though that there were only a couple of hours left of daylight, but we wanted to soak up as much as we could before the sun went down.

I heard an annoyed sigh as the sun that had been lapping up against me was momentarily blocked.

"You could have at least put on sun block you idiot," muttered a familiar voice as a hand touched my leg.

"Huh?" was all I murmured in response. Jeremy sighed again. I smiled.

"Jeremiah go away," Carrie growled from next to me.

"Beck, do you want me to put the sun tan lotion on for you?" asked Jeremy, ignoring his sister.

"He probably is dying to," Carrie mumbled.

"Carrie!"

"What?" Carrie asked innocently. I sat up to observe the quarrel.

"Could you maybe go away?"

"Why, so you and Beck have some alone time?"

"Actually yeah."

"Oh, so what exactly are you going to do?"

"Nothing out of the ordinary." They were glaring at each other. I decided it was time for me to step in.

"Hey Carrie, could you give us a few seconds alone? Come back to sun bathe with me in a few minutes, I want to try and convince him to be quiet and get a tan for once." I gave a smirk to Carrie to let her know I was poking fun at Jeremy and she smiled.

"Yeah, I guess. I'll go get something to drink and come back in a few minutes, okay?" I nodded.

"You'll burn." I turned to look at Jeremy and tried not to laugh. I think Carrie was probably slightly right when she said he was dying to put suntan lotion on me.

"Oh come on, I want a tan and you should get one, girls like tans Jer and think of all the new girls you'll meet in Virginia . . ." I wasn't exactly sure what I meant by that but it didn't cause any bad reactions with Jeremy. Instead he made a face at me and grabbed the suntan lotion.

"Besides, it's like eight at night the sun isn't strong enough to burn me right now." Of course, what I should be saying is "yes please rub me down with lotion." Why

Laura Hodges

did I never follow the instructions Jess had made for me for various scenarios to maximize flirting opportunities?

"Okay Beck, turn over," he instructed.

"If I'm lying on my back, why do you need to put lotion on my back?" I asked him. Again, I should be less logical and more "great idea!"

"Because you always seem to burn on your back." That was true. My back was the worst sun spot for me; I burned my back frequently, even if I put lotion on. Which was why I had been lying on my back. "Besides, if you stand up or something you'll probably instantly get a burn there!" Jeremy was saying. I sighed and turned over. I felt the cold greasy feel of the lotion as Jeremy began to massage it into my back. I felt really weird about it, since it was more something a boyfriend would do and Jeremy wasn't . . .

"Okay, you can turn over now," he said. I rolled over and stretched. "Of course I didn't put any on the back of your legs but you can do that yourself. Unless you want me to do it . . . ." He made a peculiar face. I started laughing at him.

"I think I'll be okay. Again, it's almost sundown. Come sun tan Jeremy. Please? We can watch the sunset after." I leaned forward to touch his leg. He groaned and lay down next to me. I put my arms around his chest as I leaned on my side to rest against him.

"Beck, you're gonna get a really weird tan with the way you're facing," Jeremy pointed out.

"I like it here," I murmured.

"Suit yourself but it defeats the whole purpose of tanning."

"I enjoy the sun more than the tanned skin," I pointed out.

"Whatever." We lay there quietly; me doodling on his chest as I leaned against him and him running his fingers up and down my back. It felt very nice. Of course, he had to ruin the nice moment. He started to tickle my side and I tried to smack his hand away, not wanting to be tickled. He smirked and continued to tickle me.

"Okay, two can play at that game," I said as I sat up. I started to try to tickle his stomach but, being much stronger than me, he pinned my wrists down with one hand and was trying to tickle my stomach.

"Okay okay you win!" I said, out of breathe. He stopped and let go of my wrists. I smacked his chest and he grinned at me. He leaned over me as I lay on my back, feeling slightly out of breath from the effort of fighting his tickle attack. He gently traced lines on my stomach as he watched my face.

"Still tickle?" he asked. I nodded. I felt really weird as I started to lean towards him. He began to brush the hair out of my face and I knew he was going to kiss me. I closed my eyes as I felt his fingers trace the outline of my mouth. He was going to kiss me. His mouth was so close and then . . .

"Jeremy?" Jeremy suddenly straightened up at the sound of his mother's voice. I opened my eyes to see her standing there looking slightly confused.

"Oh, hi Mom," Jeremy said awkwardly. I felt myself blush.

"Hi. I was just wondering if you guys wanted some lemonade."

"Um, that's okay thanks Mom." I had decided to stay out of this conversation between Jeremy and his mother. Just stay half hidden behind Jeremy . . .

"Well, I brought some out anyway, so here you go." Andrea handed Jeremy a glass and came beside me to hand me mine. I tried not to blush any harder then I already was. She grinned at us and turned to go.

"Well," Jeremy muttered. We were silent for a minute, both of us embarrassed and not sure what to do.

"Carrie should be back in a moment," I finally said.

"Yeah." We lay back down and somehow our hands managed to find each other and enclosed.

"Carrie's coming," he suddenly whispered. We both inched our bodies closer to hide our hand-holding.

"Well, you decided to join us Jeremy?" she asked slyly as she came down the beach. Jeremy made a face at her.

"Three more days of this," Jeremy said softly to me. I nodded an agreement. Three more days. I had three days to just be with him and do what I want and say what I wanted. Hopefully, I would actually manage to say what I wanted to say.

Present Day: November 20, 2009

I awoke the next morning with a pounding headache and a stuffed up nose. I knew before I even hit my alarm there was no way I was going to school. Even if I could fool my mom into thinking I was well enough to survive the day, Jess or Jeremy would send me home as soon as they saw me.

After turning off my alarm clock I picked up my phone and saw I had missed two calls from Jessica. Too bad. She probably wanted to tell me about Liam.

Jess and I had hung out on Wednesday, but we hadn't discussed Liam at all. We had both been too preoccupied sharing stories of Jeremy and Will. I began to wonder how long she had been trying to talk to Liam for, and what had inspired her to decide to talk to him. She had been pretty mad about his behaviour, and she had a point that enough was enough. He was acting like a child.

I texted Jessica to tell her I wasn't going to school and pulled the covers around me to go back to sleep.

Sometime later my mom came in demanding I have Tylenol and some breakfast. She gave me two Tylenol, a cup of warm tea, and a buttered sesame bagel. Wearily, I accepted my breakfast (Tylenol included) and grumbled away about being fine.

I hated being sick sometimes. Not all the time; sometimes the break from school was a relief. However, the majority of the time I found myself bored and impatient when I became sick. Once I stopped sleeping continuously I became restless and frustrated. Often I kept thinking of much more exciting things I would rather be doing. In this case, I was thinking how much I would like to spend time with Jeremy. That is, spend time with him without looking like a snot-nosed recovering alcoholic. I began to day dream about how alcohol and snot could be related to red noses and if Santa had a red nose from the sherry he drank from houses or from the cold air. And would Santa get off with a warning should he go through a roadblock on Christmas Eve?

I must have fallen asleep with my drunk Santa thoughts because I had bizarre dreams of trying to arrest the Santa from Miracle on 34th Street for drinking and driving. When I woke from these bizarre dreams my phone was going off.

I coughed and tried to clear my throat before answering. I wanted to sound as healthy as possible.

"Hi," I said as chirpily as I could. I already knew from my phone display it was Jeremy.

"Did I wake you?"

"No," I lied.

"You were totally asleep before, I can tell. How's it going? Still sick?"

"No but my mom wanted me to stay home." She actually hadn't even told me I couldn't go to school, I had just assumed she would ground me if I tried.

"Right. Anyway, want me to come by after school?" Jeremy asked.

"No, I'm fine." I actually did, I would probably be bored by the time he got there. I had been sleeping for far too long for it to continue much longer. However, I wouldn't be great company and I probably looked like crap. I didn't actually know; when I had gotten up to pee earlier I hadn't bothered to look in the mirror.

"You're not going to get bored and think it's a good idea to get some sort of ridiculous house chore done like sweeping leaves, are you?"

"No," I mumbled. I had done that once. Like four years ago. As if I would be so stupid as to do that again.

"Well, okay. I think if you're busy actually resting I'll go out tonight." This sparked my attention. I sat up.

"Go out?" I asked, slightly suspicious. I couldn't help it. I should trust him not to do anything dumb but . . .

"Yeah Robert and I might go to a movie. There's some new horror one about teenagers and a cabin . . . I'll probably have nightmares of the cabin in Canada, but I want to go."

"Well as long as you don't phone me in the middle of the night sounds like a good plan. This way, I don't have to sit through some dumb, plotless adventure involving people who would survive if they actually knew how to think and followed their instincts instead of peer pressure." I felt relieved he was going to a movie with Robert, but also guilty. I shouldn't have felt suspicious.

"It's clearly a lesson to teach us naive adolescents that peer pressure leads to bad things. Like dismemberment. Anyway, phone me later if you like."

"Sure," I said. "Have fun with Robert."

"Okay. Bye." Jeremy hung up and I slithered back down into my bed. I had nothing to worry about; he wasn't about to do something stupid.

Flashback

"Jeremy, I'm not going swimming!" I protested stubbornly. He sighed

"Please?"

"No! I told you I would go after dinner. I'm tired! We went swimming this morning at freaking seven!"

"Yeah, so?"

"I wouldn't be tired if somebody hadn't gotten me up so early to go swimming, would I? I might have some more energy to swim now?"

"It wasn't exactly seven," Jeremy said innocently. I groaned.

"Okay, well, I promise to go swimming with you in like an hour, okay?" He sighed and nodded. I put my sunglasses back on and resumed reading my magazines, feeling slightly guilty. Jeremy loved swimming and had been trying to get his fill in as much as possible since we had gotten here.

"Jeremy!" I called out.

"Yeah?" He hadn't gotten very far, about ten feet away.

"I'm sorry," I told him.

"It's okay Beck," I heard him say. I smiled and relaxed.

I don't know how long I was asleep for but the soft whispers started to disturb my peaceful slumber sometime later. A pair of hands grabbed my ankles and another pair grabbed me under the shoulders.

"What the—" I ripped off my sunglasses to see Carrie holding my legs as I was moving towards the water. Jeremy had my shoulders.

"Jeremy!" I yelled. I began to squirm and Carrie dropped me. With my legs free, I attempted to balance myself to run, but as I stood Jeremy let go of one shoulder to lift my lower body by my knees. I was now being cradled as he moved farther into the water.

"Now you don't have to go swimming to keep me happy Beck. You can just keep still and relax! You could even be lying down if you weren't struggling so much." Jeremy had now stepped into the water and was about ankle deep. I stopped squirming, realising that if he were to drop me I'd get wet anyway.

"I'm going to kill you," I hissed at him as I glanced down at the cold Canadian water.

"I know." He was now waist deep and I was only barely above the water. I figured if I tried to grab him around the neck just before he tried to dump me, I might only get my legs wet. Ugh. I was definitely going to get him for this.

"Ready?" he suddenly asked. I screamed as he lifted me up higher. I grabbed his neck and he sighed.

"Becky, let go." He hadn't dropped me and was obviously very amused.

"No!"

"Beck, if you don't I'll let go of your neck and start swimming. You'll be stuck getting wet either way." He grinned at me.

"Dive in Jer!"Carrie encouraged as she swam up. She started to pull apart my hands but I held on too tightly.

"Tickle her tummy," Jeremy instructed.

"What? No!" I suddenly put my hand on my stomach and Jeremy dropped me. Water shattered beneath me at the impact. I came up quickly to see Jeremy trying not to laugh.

"Want to go swimming now?" he asked. I lunged for him but he had anticipated it and grabbed me around the waist instead. Carrie had already swum safely away and was watching from the shore.

"No, I don't," I told him in the most annoyed tone I could manage. I attempted to throw him a fierce glare. I don't think it worked.

I realised as long as he was holding me, I couldn't shove him in the water without shoving myself in as well.

"Too bad, Beck." He started to push me down but I wriggled away and swam behind him. I knew very well that Jeremy was a far better swimmer then me; I had encouraged him to join the swim team at school because he could out swim most of the athletes. He lazily swam close by and grinned mischievously. I attempted another good glare.

"You going to come and get me Jeremiah?" I taunted.

"No. You're the one that's mad at me. I'm safe if I stay away from you, you'll have to come get me." I frowned. I preferred being chased than chasing.

"Fine then." I started to swim out, knowing he would be curious and follow. I rarely liked swimming in deep waters that had any living creatures besides humans. I had an irrational fear of squid, whales, and sharks.

"What are you doing?" he called out. I stopped to see him venture a bit closer. I dove down, wondering if he would assume I was going out even farther. All I needed to do was stay under so he couldn't see me until he was out farther. Then I could sneak up on him. Hopefully.

When I peeked up Jeremy was now farther out then me and was looking around in confusion. I emerged myself again in the water and I swam up behind him, trying to be as discreet as possible. Coming up to the surface, I grabbed him and pulled him back down. Unfortunately, he just squirmed away easily and came up for air laughing.

"Do you really think you can win this one?" he asked playfully.

"I'm going to try," I muttered in return. I lunged at him again and he caught me and pushed me down. I came up for air, gasping, to see a worried expression on his face.

"Beck, there's sharks in these waters!" he cried.

"What?!" I shrieked. Something suddenly grabbed my leg around the knee and pulled. I screamed. Wait, that wasn't a shark grabbing me . . .

"Jeremy!" He was laughing his head off. He pulled on my knee again and pulled my leg up, throwing me off balance. I slipped backwards, submerged once more. His hand gripped my arm to bring me back up and he pulled me towards him as I coughed and spat out water. This time, my ferocious gaze registered with him.

"You idiot," I muttered at him as I tried to hit him on the shoulder. He grinned and brushed the hair out of my eyes.

"I can't believe you fell for that shark thing. You actually believe there are sharks in these waters? And then when I grabbed your leg? I couldn't believe how gullible you were being." I sighed.

"You're mean." It was the only defence I could think of.

"Jeremy?!" a voice called across the water. I glanced over to see Andrea looking worried. She must have heard me screaming.

"We're okay Mom, I was just telling Beck about the sharks in these waters," he called to her. I couldn't see her facial expression but I imagined she was less than impressed. She waved at us and turned to go.

"I can't believe I fell for that," I muttered. "I mean, coming from an idiot like you, I should know it to be false." He smirked. He was still holding onto me and now pulled me much closer.

"Stop squirming Beck, I can't keep us both up if you squirm so much." I sighed and started to just tread water gently. "You don't have to tread, I can keep us both afloat," he told me. It was hard to tread water using my arms with him so close.

"No you can't! If I were to stop totally you would sink us!"

"Not true. If you were to wrap your legs around me I bet I could keep us up!"

"No way! My weight would sink us. Most people can't even stay up just using their legs; they have to use their arms too. There's no way you can keep both of us up."

"Let's see," he challenged.

"How will you use your arms when you're holding me with one of them?" I asked cockily. I already knew what he was going to suggest.

"If you hold onto me around the neck I won't need to hold onto you." That was true. I put my arms around his neck and he let go off me. My legs were still in his way, so I boldly wrapped them around his waist. I felt slightly embarrassed at how close I was to him. Especially only wearing a bikini.

"You won't last very long," I muttered. He didn't reply. I smiled as his breathe began to quicken and I could feel his body straining. "Tell me when you want me to let go," I said. He nodded. I thought it was pretty unlikely he would actually suggest it was time for me to let go. Not like I was kidding myself into thinking it was because he liked me wrapped around him, but because he was stubborn and wanted to prove he could manage to keep us both afloat. I tightened my grip on him, leaning my head down by his neck so it was more out of the way. I had the biggest urge to just kiss his neck or ear.

"Jeremy . . ." I whispered softly in his ear. "You won't make it any longer."

"Will too," he grunted. I smirked. I blew softly in his ear to distract him.

"Oh fine!" he said as he pushed me away. I laughed. "But I only gave up because you were blowing in my ear."

"What? Me?" I said innocently.

"Yes you!" He swam back over to me and put his arms around me. "Don't worry, I liked it," he whispered softly in my ear. I smiled.

"Oh yeah?" I asked him. He nodded. "Tired?" I asked smoothly in his ear. He murmured "yeah" as I started to blow in his ear again.

"Beck?" He pushed me away a bit so I could look at him.

"What?" He looked very solemn all of a sudden.

"Have we always been like this?" he asked. I was startled.

"Yeah, I think so. I mean, remember... remember..." I could barely say it. "Remember what happened before your date with Melanie?"

"We haven't talked about it since it happened," he said. He knew what I was talking about. "We never... we never finished..." He suddenly smiled. "We never finished making those brownies." I laughed.

"No, we put them in the oven," I reminded him.

"Yeah, but I forgot to take them out. They were totally burnt; my mom took them out when she came home." I laughed again.

"Are you serious?"

"Yeah, I'm dead serious. I totally forgot about them after you left."

I nodded, not sure what to say. I had been so confused when I had left.

"My mom came home and pulled them out of the oven. She screeched at Carrie for not taking them out on time, but Carrie gave me away. She forbid me from baking on my own and claimed it would take a week for burnt brownie smell to get out of the house."

"Did it smell like burnt brownies when Melanie came over?" I asked.

"I don't know."

"You don't remember?"

"No, I didn't pay attention." I bit my lip.

"Because you were so enamoured with her?" I asked, hoping I sounded teasing.

"No, I was distracted. I told you, it didn't go well because I was distracted," he reminded me.

"Yeah but . . ." I wasn't quite sure how to put this. I remember that he had said he was distracted and had talked about me. Or something like that anyway. "What were you distracted about?" I finally asked. He stared at me for a moment. We were both still treading water and only about a foot apart.

"I thought you were mad at me," he finally said.

"What? Mad? Why? Because I left?"

"I thought maybe I had screwed something up. You know when we . . . were . . . I almost kis . . . ahhh you know."

"Why would I be mad about that I wanted you to ki—" I immediately stopped, realizing what I had been about to say. His eyes widened slightly. He probably figured out the end of the sentence. I started to blush. I turned my head away slightly, not sure if I wanted to look at him. He swam slightly closer to me.

"You did?" he asked.

"Did what?" Despite knowing this was a good opportunity to get things out in the open the opportunity to play dumb seemed far better.

"You wanted to . . ." He cleared his throat. "You know."

"Maybe," I mumbled. Jeremy's hand lifted my chin back up towards him so I was looking straight at him. We started to inch our heads closer and closer, at an agonizingly slow pace.

I heard the ripple in the water and turned to see Carrie as Jeremy's nose banged into my cheek.

"What the Hell are you guys doing?" she asked as I snuck my legs back around Jeremy.

"Jeremy thinks he can keep treading water while holding me," I told her.

"Oh, okay, good, from where I was it looked like you guys were going to kiss or something." She made a face and Jeremy turned to glare at her.

"Ha ha ha ha," I laughed awkwardly.

"Way to be awkward, Carrie," Jeremy said. She looked mildly confused.

"Whatever. Jeremy, give up on that stupid tread water idea and come inside, dinner's almost ready, okay?" We nodded and she began to swim back.

"Well . . ." he said.

"I guess we have to go swim back to shore?" I asked lightly. I had probably started to blush again.

"I guess. Maybe . . ." His voice trailed off.

"Maybe what?"

"Nothing. Never mind. I'll race you back." He immediately let go off me and started swimming back. I yelped out objections and started to follow him. I didn't really know what was going on with him, but hopefully I would figure it out soon.

Present Day: November 21, 2009

I woke-up sometime late that night. I suppose I had slept too much during the day and no longer needed any sleep.

I felt a bit better. My throat was still sore, and my nose was stuffed up, but my body didn't ache as much and my skin no longer felt like it was tingling from the mere touch of my sheets or pyjamas.

I got up and made myself tea, noting it was three in the morning. There probably wasn't much to entertain me right now: I doubted there was anything worthwhile on television.

After making my tea I went back to my room and open my underwear drawer. I wasn't in the mood for homework;

this was a great time to read the letter from Jeremy's dad. I pulled out the letter and lay back to read.

>*Dear Jeremy;*

>*I know right now you don't want anything to do with me and I can understand that. I wish to respect that, but first there is something I wish for you to understand.*

>*My efforts to force a relationship with you were with good intentions. I see now I was causing you more harm than good, but I meant well. I thought that if I kept trying to be there for you and if I could parent you, not only would you learn to accept me, but I would make things easier for your mother. I see now that I was interfering; you needed your space and I was making things worse. Besides making your mother's role even harder, I was further damaging your opinion of me.*

>*I only want what is best for you. I admit, I was selfish in what I did and I wish I had done things differently. Honestly, I thought if we moved perhaps I could successfully decide what I wanted. I was beginning to see I couldn't have both my marriage to your mother and a relationship with Christina, but I needed to sort this out at my own pace. I did a bad job, and by delaying the inevitable break I forced your hand to reveal what I wish you had not seen. I can never take back what you had to see, the secret you carried around for months, and what it must have been like to tell your mother. For that, I expect you'll never truly forgive me, and I have come to terms with that.*

However, I hope one day you can see that despite my flaws I do love you. Not because you are my son, but because you are a good, loving, loyal person. You hate me because you are above the petty actions I engaged in. You are not above deceit or manipulation, but you are far above the betrayal I have caused. I respect that in you.

Your mother moving you back to Washington State seems to be the best thing for you. I know I miss you as does your sister, but if this helps you come to terms with the changes in your life, than it is what is best. From what I have learned about your time here, things have calmed down a bit for you, and I hope they continue to. You deserve some peace.

On that note, I wish you the best of luck for your upcoming year. I am promising you I will be careful to accept your need for space. If you wish to not speak to me before you go to college, so be it. However, I do plan on sending you both Christmas and birthday presents, attending your school graduation, and offer financial help for post secondary school. What you chose to do with all of those events is up to you. I hope by next year you will have had enough time perhaps you would be willing to see me or speak with me.

Always remember that I love you.

Dad

I put the letter down, feeling slightly teary. I didn't know which I felt sadder about: the lost relationship between Jeremy and his father, his father's actions, or the pain everyone had gone through.

I rolled over and turned off the light, thinking about the letter. From what I could see, Jeremy had come so far since he had arrived, but was that just a momentary thing? Was it because he was away from his father, because we were now together, or because he had a chance for a fresh start?

I thought the letter was well written and even if Jeremy didn't listen to the apologies or admitting of love, at least his father acknowledged his need for space. That, at the very least, could allow him to relax a bit and stop viewing his father as "stalking" him.

I decided most likely I would give him the letter. Maybe not immediately; I might give it to Andrea to read first. I didn't think the letter was likely to send him off the deep end or cause him to go throw up more vodka on his jeans, but chances are he wouldn't be super excited about it. I would let Andrea read it and if she thought it was a good idea, I would give it to him. And then he would feel better about what happened and forgive his father and we would all live happily ever after. That's what happens, in real life, I would fix everything and we would all be happy and get married and . . .

I slowly drifted off to sleep thinking about how wonderful everything would be.

Chapter 14

I woke-up with my mom coming in with tea and toast and muttering about Tylenol. She handed me the thermometer with a stern look and told me she was going out for breakfast with Bob, but would be back "to force feed me more Tylenol" or whatever. Fortunately, the thermometer beeped at her that I was only slightly above average body temperature. She still was concerned I had a mild fever, but satisfied that the thermometer didn't lie, she left for her breakfast date.

I wasn't super tired, so I gathered all the blankets off my bed and made my way to the living room to watch television.

Around an hour later I was watching a movie when the doorbell rang.

"Better not be Liam," I muttered out loud. I was not in the mood for another home visit from him.

However, it was Jeremy. I felt a rush of attraction as I opened the door to see him standing there with dark jeans, a hoodie, and a vest. I felt silly in my light blue pyjamas. This time, instead of a cupcake, they had Princess Peach welting Bowser with a frying pan. At least they were perhaps mildly cooler than the yummy cupcake pyjamas.

"Frick it's cold out," he said as he came in.

"Hi," I said, closing the door behind him. "What's up?" I wondered if I had missed a call from him.

"I thought I would come by and force feed you Tylenol. How are you feeling?" He touched my cheek gently. I withdrew from his cold hand and smiled.

"Better. I think my temperature is probably better than yours right now." I took his hand in both of mine and rubbed them slightly.

"I thought I'd come by and hang out, if you like." He moved past me to go sit in the living room. Now that he was here, I did want to hang out, and was feeling a stirring of attraction. How had I not noticed how desirable he was all that time ago?

"I should shower," I said, pointing towards the bathroom. I would rather just go straight to making out, but I hadn't showered yet and I felt slightly gross compared to his still damp hair and smell of men's soap.

"Sure," he said, moving aside some of my blankets. He found the remote and made a face at my movie.

"Did you . . ." I was, for a bold moment, thinking of asking him if he would like to come, but then I remembered two things: first, Jess had a point about fooling around and taking things in stages and two, I didn't think I was actually ready to see him naked. Like, I might need some time to mentally prepare myself for such an event. I wasn't ready to view man parts. Besides, what if he thought it was an invitation to do more than shower?

"Did I what?" Jeremy asked, giving me a confused look.

"What?" I snapped out of my thoughts.

"You were staring at me funny." I started blush. I had been.

"Nothing. I'm going to go shower and change. Are you going to hang out here or in my room?" He shrugged. I leaned over and kissed his cheek before heading to my room to grab a change of clothes.

In the shower, I started to get a peculiar nagging feeling, as if I had left something somewhere. I started to do a mental check: did I know where my cell phone was? Had I remembered to text Jess last night? Had I forgotten about some homework due on Monday and left it in my locker? I kept thinking of things it could be that could cause this nagging feeling, but I kept remembering yes, I texted Jess, I brought my homework home, I clearly had my phone because I had texted Jess with it.

I finished showering and dried myself off. I finished dressing in the bathroom, not sure if Jeremy would be in my room or not. Suddenly, it hit me. My room. The letter. I had left it sitting next to my bed last night when I finished reading it. I hadn't put it back in the envelope, let alone the drawer I had hid it in. Had he gone to my room? Feeling pale, I hung up my towel and went to my room.

I stopped at the door frame. He was sitting on my bed, holding the letter. The pile of blankets were behind him, neatly stacked on my bed. He had come in to put them away. I winced. He looked up at me and his face had a funny look on it, like he wasn't quite sure what had just happened. I suddenly remembered how he looked when he had told me he wished he had never said he was in love with me and drove off.

"Hi," I said shakily. Shit.

"What's this?" He didn't look directly at me, but slightly above me. He held up the letter. I thought about lying; it was something I found? Andrea gave it to me to read? Oh my God what's this?

"A letter." Clearly, I was diabolical in these situations.

"Thanks Captain Obvious," he said with a slight cruel tone. I winced again. "How long have you had this?"

Again, lies ran through my head. This morning, last night, I wrote it myself as an example of a nice letter. A voice in my mind kept repeating *yesterday yesterday yesterday yesterday*.

"Earlier this week." I couldn't lie. Mostly because I knew he would see right through it. If I could pull off a successful lie at this moment, I would probably give it a go.

"And who gave this to you?" Did anything on the letter identify it was to Jeremy from his father? Lets see . . . my mom found the letter it was from my dad before he passed away, it's from Jess, it's from Jess' dad to her . . . but no, I was pretty certain it was clearly to Jeremy.

"Jeremy I—"

"Why have you had this and not told me?" He shook the letter, as if to ensure I knew it was the letter he was referring to.

"I hadn't decided what to do with it. Your dad gave it to me and asked me to give it to you and I wasn't sure if I should." I bowed my head shamefully.

"Why didn't you tell me?" His voice was louder now. "You saw him behind my back?"

"I didn't . . ." I didn't what? Know what to do? Didn't want to tell him in case he was angry? Thought it was better to keep it from him?

"Didn't what? Not want to betray my trust? Great job." He sneered slightly. I winced yet again.

"I'm sorry I just somehow became involved—"

"Fuck this." He stood up, crumbled the letter, and dropped it on the floor. "I'm outta here." He angrily brushed by me and headed out the door.

"No, wait, Jeremy!" I hurried after him but reached the front door and realized I was in bare feet. I started to curse as I ran back to my room to grab my socks and shoes. I ran back to the door and couldn't see him anywhere. I ran to the kitchen and dialled Andrea's cell.

"Hello!" Andrea greeted me cheerfully.

"Andrea? It's Becky."

"Oh hi Hon how are—"

"Jeremy's freaked out and ran out I'm worried he's going to do something dumb. I'm going to go after him."

"Oh Love I think—"

"I'm not sure where he's gone but I'll find him I just thought you should know."

"Becky I think you stay home."

"I gotta go."

"But don't you still have—" I hung up before hearing the end of Andrea's sentence. I ran out of the house to follow him. I screwed this up, I would fix it. All I needed to do was find him before he did something he would regret.

Flashback:

I gently stretched as I fought a yawn. I was lying on the couch with Jeremy. Actually, I was lying on Jeremy. He was reading and was lying on his back, one hand holding up his book and the other doodling lazily on my side. I was curled around him, my back against the couch, but my body angled over his with my head resting on his shoulder.

I had told him I was going to have a nap, but really I was just enjoying lying so close to him. That and the nice doodles he was creating on my side.

I had thought about making conversation, asking him about his book or something, but I found I didn't really want to change the mood. Plus, I was very much enjoying my nice day dreams of him.

"Are you asleep?" he whispered very quietly. I turned to look up at him.

"No."

"Oh. What are you doing?" he asked, putting his book down. I had thought it was pretty obvious: nothing.

"Thinking," I said.

"About?" Jeremy asked. I felt myself start to blush. I turned back to leaning against his chest so he couldn't tell. I had decided at one point it might not be a good idea to day dream about him while he was right there, but I was so comfortable and so relaxed . . .

"Celebrities," I said instead. I still wasn't looking at him, so I was hoping he couldn't see I was blushing. I wiggled slightly. I had an itch on my side and he kept barely missing it.

"What are you doing?" Jeremy asked again as he lifted his hand.

"I have an itch!" I scratched it, smiled in satisfaction, and went back to lying still.

"If it's all the same to you, could you maybe not wiggle on me when you're lying on top of me?" Jeremy asked.

"Why?"

"Just because," he responded. I sat up to look at him. "Can we switch?" he asked.

"Switch?"

"Can you be on the bottom?"

"So I don't wiggle on you? And you'll just hold your book over my face or something? How about . . . not?"

"Oh come on, Becky, my hand is getting tired of holding my book up!"

"So use your other hand," I suggested. I grinned at him and lay back down as he rolled his eyes at me. He used the hand that had previously been on my side and *wrapped around me to hold his book and his other hand lay at his side.*

"No more snuggling and doodling?" I asked meekly. Jeremy sighed and put his book back down.

"If you promise not to wiggle on me again I'll put my arm back around you."

"What's the big deal over the wiggle?"

"You're lying on my with your bare legs draped over me and you decide to wiggle your mid section on mine."

"I'm wearing shorts!" I argued.

"I know but they're like half an inch long!"

"Do you not like my legs draped over you?" I asked feebly, slightly offended. "Should I not lie on you?" I started to sit up but he grabbed me and pulled me back down.

"That's not it, I just don't want you to . . . perhaps I might react to it . . ."

"You're being weird," I said. I closed my eyes as I rested my head to resume my day dreaming. All of a sudden my eyes flew open as I understand what he meant.

"Oh," I said out loud as I started to blush.

"What?" Jeremy asked.

"Nothing." I continued to lay with my head on his chest so he couldn't see my face. He didn't want me to feel his physical reaction. Did that mean . . . he was attracted to me?

"Becky?" Jeremy asked after a moment. I was still deliberating on if every guy would react the same or if perhaps it meant he was attracted to me.

"Yeah?"

"I didn't mean to . . . embarrass you." I looked up at him, hoping my blush had disappeared.

"You didn't," I said.

"No?" he used his arm to curl around me and pull me up so I was level with him.

"No," I confirmed. "Don't worry, I think it's highly unlikely you'll embarrass me with that kind of stuff." This was true: my thoughts were consumed with what it meant, not embarrassment.

"Oh really?" Jeremy said. I shrugged.

"But clearly, I can embarrass you," I said to him with a smile. Jeremy rolled us so we were both on our sides and facing each other.

"Is that what you think? If something were to happen you would be fine and I would be a clumsy idiot or something."

"Not a clumsy idiot, but potentially more weirded out than me. I would be cool and collected." I gave him a broad smile.

"Weirded out? No, I think if we fooled around you would be the weirded out one and I'd be fine."

"Is that what you think?" I asked.

"It is. You would blush and chicken out of the situation long before me." Normally, he'd probably be right, but my bottled up feelings for him made me suspect he could get away with almost anything before I would put the brakes on.

"Lets find out." As soon as I said it, my eyes widened and I pressed my lips together, shocked by my own boldness. Jeremy likewise looked fairly surprised.

We stared at each other for what felt like ages. I began to worry I had gone too far.

"Okay," he finally said. He put his arm around me and pulled me as close as he could. He watched my face for a moment, then quickly leaned forward to my ear and blew in it softly.

"If you're sure," he whispered.

"Yes," I murmured, suddenly nervous. I had only really had a couple of kisses with Jeffrey, then another couple with Craig. Of course as far as I knew, Jeremy hadn't even kissed any girls yet.

He moved down from my ear and started kissing my neck. I placed my hand on his chest, not feeling bold enough to go much lower.

Jeremy kissed down my neck, following my collar bone towards my chest. I couldn't believe what was happening. A part of me decided I must have fallen asleep and was dreaming one of my fantasies.

Jeremy reached the edge of my t-shirt collar. He lightly outlined the edge of my breast with his fingers.

"Here," I said, feeling bold once again. I sat up and pulled off my t-shirt, revealing my bikini top. He'd seen me in my bikini this morning, no big deal. He stared at my chest for a very long time, outlining the cups of my bikini and tracing small patterns with his fingers on my collar bone.

"You've seen this before," I reminded him softly.

"It's different." It was different. The anticipation of what was going to happen was stimulating butterflies in my stomach. I was getting goose bumps on my arms from his fingers simply brushing against me.

Looking up at me, he held my full breast in his right hand. He massaged it very gently as he watched my face. After a moment of this, he angled his head down again and carefully licked around my bikini. His other hand slid up and started to pull down my bikini strap. My breast he had not yet seen.

My legs squirmed as I started to feel a warm and wet sensation between them. I had probably never been more turned on in my life.

The bikini strap eventually slipped down and he slowly pulled down the cup of the bikini, revealing my bare breast. He pushed aside the fabric and brushed my nipple with his thumb.

When he took my breast in his mouth and licked my nipple I couldn't help but gasp. Somehow, I felt, this moment was truly crossing a friend line. Before it could still be chalked up to flirtatious fun, but bare breasted nipple anything was more.

This is also when I started to wonder if this was the most ideal place for such shenanigans. We were in the main area of his parents' cabin; anyone could walk in at any moment. I didn't know where the others were or when they would come back. Andrea had said something about ice cream and a walk. They had been gone at least an hour. I didn't particularly want my breasts on display should one of them walk in or even walk by the window.

"Jeremy," I whispered. Time to move. At least if we were in the bedroom or the tent we would hear them before they would see us. He stopped to look up at me.

"Maybe this isn't the best place for this," I said. I was expecting him to silkily suggest we move to the bedroom, but instead he sat up, looking at me funny.

"What?" he asked.

"Like, somebody could see us here." His brow furrowed and I knew immediately he was replaying everything that had just happened and he was analyzing it. Shit.

I propped myself up so I was no longer lying down. He continued to stare at me with one of his thinking expressions. Feeling exposed, I put my arms over my chest.

"I'm going to go for a swim," he said.

"What?" Jeremy picked up my t-shirt and stood up. I hastily tried to fix my bikini so I was no longer exposed.

"Jeremy can't we——" I cut myself off. Finish this? Go somewhere else? He handed me my t-shirt. I stood up.

"Talk about——"

"I'm going for a swim, I'll talk to you later." He left while I stood there holding my t-shirt and hiccupping. Pulling my t-shirt on, I watched him head towards the water. Still hiccupping, I put my sandals on and started walking away from the cabin along the lake.

An hour later, sitting on a large rock overlooking the lake, Tom found me. I had had my cry and was not just contemplating what had happened. Had I screwed everything up?

"Hi Becky," he said. "Can I sit here?" He indicated a spot next to me. I nodded. He stayed silent for awhile. I didn't bother to attempt to chat.

"Are you okay?" he finally asked. I shrugged.

"Sure." What else was I going to say? Tell him the truth and have to explain why?

Tom nodded thoughtfully. "So if you're okay, how come you're sitting on this rock twenty minutes away from the cabin by yourself while Jeremy is out in the lake swimming?" he asked. I shrugged again. "Perhaps . . . he upset you?" I shrugged yet again. I had mucked everything up.

"You know, it must not be easy for either of you, having him move away," Tom said thoughtfully.

"*Yes,*" *I agreed.*

"*It's probably very confusing for both of you.*" *I turned to look at him.*

"*Confusing?*"

"*You know, it may bring to light different emotions.*"

"*Oh,*" *was all I said. That was very true for me.*

"*And perhaps it's hard to know what to do with these emotions,*" *Tom continued.*

"*Yes, definitely.*"

"*But no matter what, he still cares about you. You mean loads to him Becky.*" *I looked at the ground, feeling sad.*

"*I know,*" *I said softly.*

"*So why are you all the way here when he's all the way there?*"

"*I think I confused him,*" *I said.*

"*Then you should talk to him about it.*"

"*He didn't want to talk, he wanted to swim.*"

"*Well rejection is hard.*" *I looked back at Tom, startled. How did he know Jeremy had rejected me? Had Jeremy told him?*

"*Sorry?*"

"*He probably needed to think about it. I think he's fine now. And Becky, just so you understand, it's okay to reject him.*" *Tom stood up, missing my startled expression.* "*I'm going back to the cabin, you can come now if you like, or stay here if you're not ready.*"

"*Here,*" *I muttered still processing what Tom had said. What did he mean by it's okay to reject him? He rejected me!*

"*I'll see you soon,*" *he said.*

"*Right.*" *I watched him start to head back.*

*"Tom?" I called. He turned back. "Thanks," I
said.*

"For what?"

*"For being here." He smiled warmly and turned
back towards the cabin.*

*After a couple more contemplating minutes I got up
to do the same. Tom was right, ultimately Jeremy and I
cared about each other and we would work it out.*

Present Day: November 21, 2009

An hour later I was sitting at the same park Jeremy had
taken me to the previous weekend. I hadn't been sure where he
would go, but I had already tried Robert's with no success. I
now wished I had remembered two things: a jacket and my cell
phone. It was cold out, and unfortunately my sweatshirt was
not providing much protection against the cold November air.
Also, I was bored. I had finished thinking about how horrible
it had been for me to hide the letter from him and now I was
impatient to deal with the situation. I wanted to talk to him. It
was now occurring to me that if I had had my cell, I could be
texting him and maybe, just maybe, he would come to me or
I could go to him. Or, at the very least, I could text or phone
Jess. Really, I would love nothing more than to phone Jess
and ask her to come pick me up. Despite my confidence this
would be where Jeremy would end up, I was feeling slightly
concerned it would take him awhile. Like, perhaps he needed
a soul filled walk first? Or ice cream? Then I remembered he
wasn't a girl and probably didn't require ice cream or soul filled
walks or talks to feel better. I just hoped whatever it was that
was keeping him wasn't booze.

I started to shiver and decided to lean against one of
the rocks, hoping perhaps it would be mildly warmer than

standing in the cold. Curling up around myself, I did feel a bit warmer. Closing my eyes and leaning my head into my knees, I resumed thinking about what had happened and started to day dream about fixing it, about Jeremy coming here and saying he was sorry for running off and me apologizing for keeping him in the dark and then we would be back at his house making out and feeling warm and cozy . . .

Sometime later I felt hands grab me and touch my hands and cheek.

"What?" I mumbled, opening my eyes. A hand enclosed in mine. The hand was warm. I looked up to see Liam on his cell.

"She's awake, she's really cold." He turned his phone slightly away from his mouth. "Can you hear me?" he asked. I stared at him, feeling confused.

"Where am I?" I asked him. I looked around. I was at the park, curled up by a large rock. I started to shake slightly.

"I should what? Seriously?" Liam made a face at his phone and put it down.

"Okay we're going to trade shirts," he said. Mutely, I started to pull mine up.

"I think she's disoriented. Listen, I'm going to go, I'll see you shortly. Can somebody tell Jessica? Or Becky's mom? Thanks." He hung up and put my hands back down.

"Okay, so we're going to switch shirts, mine is warm and yours . . . isn't. Also," he winced slightly, "as awkward as this is, I'm going to place my hands by your arm pits."

"That's weird of you," I muttered, feeling confused. "Why am I here?"

"I'll tell you in a moment. Please please please tell me you're wearing a bra."

"I don't remember." I touched my chest. "I think so."

"Okay so we're going to change very quickly. I'm going to pull off my shirt and you'll pull off yours and then I'll put mine on you. Okay?" I looked at Liam suspiciously.

"Why?"

"You're shivering and I don't know how long you've been sitting here but I don't want you to get hypothermia, that's why. Are you ready?" I nodded. I (somewhat slowly) pulled my shirt over my head. Liam immediately pulled something warm over me and then did up his jacket. He then pulled the sweatshirt I had been wearing back over my head. I rubbed my arms, enjoying the warmth of the sweater.

"So . . . next, I get to put my hands on you. Wow this is crap why did I have to be the one to find you?"

"What?" I looked up from my arm rubbing. Liam sat down directly in front of me.

"Can you move close? Like, really close? Pretty much as close as possible without being on my lap?" I gave him another suspicious look but obeyed. "Sorry I'm not trying to pull some trick or grope a feel," he said. He lifted my shirts slightly and ran his hands up my sides, stopping just short of my arm pits. His hands were warm and I started to feel better almost instantly. However, I also realized why he had seemed so annoyed: his hands were directly next to my breasts and I was almost certain he could feel the sides of them moving against his hands as I breathed.

"I'm sorry," I said to him.

"For what?" He was looking up, not at me.

"For this. Clearly you don't want to be here." I looked down and felt shameful yet again today.

"Becky . . ." Liam sighed. "I came to look for you, didn't I? If I didn't want to be here, I wouldn't have gone looking for you."

"What do you mean, looking for me?"

Laura Hodges

"Well, you ran out because of what's his face and phoned his mom, right? And she knew you had had a fever so she phoned your mom and they both tried your cell but apparently you left it at the house. What's his face's mom was sure where he would have gone so they decided they needed to find you. Someone named Robert said he saw you but didn't know where you were going. They phoned Jess, who phoned me as well as Nicole and Jenny. And I just happened to be the one smart enough to find you."

"How did you find me?"

"I asked Jess questions. I figured you would assume you knew where Jeremy had gone, so I asked her a bunch of stuff until I figured out where I thought you would go to find him. Turns out, I was right. This was my first guess." He looked over at something and I turned my head. Andrea was coming towards us and behind her was . . . Tom?

"I'll take over," Andrea said to him as she came up. Liam withdrew and she immediately cupped her hands in the same place. I gave her a startled look.

Tom came up to me and started checking my pulse and muttering various things.

"When is your birthday?" he asked me.

"February 21st. I was born in 1992." He looked at Andrea. She shrugged.

"That's correct," Liam said.

"When's Jeremy's?" Andrea asked.

"December 5, though he was born in 1991. Why?"

"Checking how disoriented you are. I think I'll take her to the hospital," Tom said to Andrea.

"You're call."

"What are you doing here?" I asked him. "I thought you left."

328

"Well, I was going to, but then there was another seminar in Bellingham I wanted to go to, so I decided to stay here a couple more days. Andrea phoned me for advice on what to do if and when someone found you. Do you think you can walk okay?"

"Sure." I didn't know but thought it would be best to just let him think I could. Andrea moved her hands away from my sides and both Tom and Andrea helped me up. I wobbled slightly for a moment and felt mildly dizzy.

"Are you dizzy?" Tom asked.

"No," I lied. We slowly walked to the Andrea's car, Liam trailing behind us. They put me in the back seat and then closed the door to talk. I could tell they were arguing but couldn't really make out what it was about. Liam was standing there, looking out of place, his hands shoved in his pockets. I remembered I was still wearing his sweater.

Andrea opened the driver's door and turned on the heat in the car. She rummaged through her bag and pulled out a thermometer.

"Sit here for a moment and then I'll take your temperature," she said. I nodded. She closed the door again and started talking to both Tom and Liam.

After a minute or two Tom opened the back door where I was sitting and handed me the thermometer. I stuck it under my tongue and then he started to take off my shoes. I just watched, not feeling like asking why. However, I did want to ask if either of them knew where Jeremy was.

"Doesn't look like she has any frostbite on her toes," Tom said, turning around to face Andrea.

"If we could I would much prefer to just take her home to her mom rather than to the hospital," Andrea said. Tom sighed. He leaned back in the car and pulled out the thermometer.

"Ninety-one degrees. That's fairly close to becoming moderate hypothermia," Tom said. Liam raised his eyebrows.

"Becky honey how do you feel?"

"Pretty bad does anyone know where Jeremy is?" Andrea looked startled. Liam groaned.

"Sure thing pumpkin but I meant physically. And don't worry about him. Everyone is more concerned about you right now."

"I'm okay," I mumbled. "I would rather go home." Andrea looked at Tom expectantly.

"Okay, we'll drive her home. Hands on the neck this time." Andrea smiled and got in the car, placing her hands this time on both sides of my neck.

"What about Liam?" I asked Andrea as Tom got in the front.

"Oh right." She got out of the car and I heard her talking to him. She gave him a small pat on the back. He waved at me and left and she got back in the car.

"I have his sweatshirt," I said to Andrea.

"I know. He'll come by to pick it up later. He's okay. He's quite the hero, eh? Second rescue for him in less than a month?" I gave her a confused look.

"What was the first?" Tom asked.

"When our lovely lovely son fell over and hit his head." Andrea shook her head.

"Oh right," Tom and I both said.

A couple of minutes later we arrived at my house, where my mom rushed out to greet us. Or, rather me. She was squeezing me fiercely when Tom gently pulled her arms away.

"Gently?" he suggested. We went inside where I then had to endure the same fierce hugs from Jessica, only this time Andrea, my mom, and Tom all said "gently!" to her in unison. She immediately started talking about how she was ground control central and had phoned Jenny and Nicole and yadda yadda yadda. It was slightly overwhelming and I only paid partial attention to her as my mom lead me to my room.

"I warmed your bed sheets for you," Jess said proudly.

"By lying in them?" I asked suspiciously.

"No, by putting them in the dryer."

"Here, Becky." My mom handed me a bright pink warmed fleece ensemble. I wrinkled my nose.

"No thanks." I started to climb in the warm bed but she pushed the outfit to me.

"It's warmed in the dryer and it will help you regain your body heat."

"It's ugly."

"Wear it anyway," Jessica hissed at me. I sighed, shrugged, and took the fleece pants and sweatshirt. They both left me to change and as soon as they were gone I looked around for my phone. I couldn't see it anywhere. I wondered where Jeremy was. Did he even know where I was? Did he care?

As soon as I was changed I opened the door and Jess ushered me back in, holding a cup of something.

"Luke warm hot chocolate," she said. "Tom said to drink slowly."

"Wouldn't it be luke warm chocolate rather than hot chocolate?" I asked her. She continued to usher me towards my bed and she climbed in next to me.

"Who cares, it's milk heated up slightly with hot chocolate powder."

"Can I have tea?" I asked hopefully.

"No, something about high sugar luke warm beverages. So . . . . that was very exciting."

"What was?" I sipped from the mug slowly.

"You ran after Jeremy and then fell asleep after having a fever for two days. And then Liam got to rescue you. Quite heroic, don't you think? Second rescue in like three weeks? It makes him a bit sexier. Don't get me wrong though, I wouldn't do him, but just the same, rescuing you is quite sexy."

"Whatever," I mumbled. I put the mug down and leaned back. Jess sighed.

"That was stupid of you," she said after a moment.

"What?"

"You, going after Jeremy without your phone, a jacket, proper clothes to keep you warm . . . if Liam hadn't found you . . ." she shrugged. "That was dumb of you."

"I didn't—"

"We all do dumb shit because of a guy we like, but are you honestly going to stop thinking about your own safety if he decides to throw a tantrum? You could have had some sort of permanent damage or died. We were going to phone the police to look for you. It just happened to be Liam figured it out first."

"I was fine and—"

"You might not have been. What, did you think Jeremy would come save you and everything would be okay?" I gave her a startled look.

"Well . . ."

"My bet is, he left to cool off. It would have been better to just let him have his space for a couple of hours. He didn't want to talk, which is why he left. You can't fix things for him, so sometimes you just have to stay out of it. To be honest, it would have been better if you had stayed out of it when his dad called you."

"Jess . . ."

"I'm just saying, I know you just wanted to help, and I know you were concerned about him, but sometimes, when someone is upset, the best thing to do is to let them chill, not bombard them. Isn't this one of the reasons Andrea moved him here? So he wouldn't feel bombarded by his dad?" Jessica gave me a stern look.

"I guess."

"You shouldn't scare me or your mom with this kind of crap."

"I know. I'm sorry." Jess leaned over and hugged me.

"So . . . how was it when Liam found you?" she asked.

"I was really confused. It was slightly weird, he fully complained because he had to put his hands under my arm pits and we changed shirts."

"Dude he saw your tits?"

"No, I was wearing a bra!"

"So he saw them covered. Hot."

"I was cold," I said, rolling my eyes. At that moment, my mom came in holding two hot water bottles.

"You have to put these under your arm pits," she said, handing them to me. I took them and pushed them under the fleece shirt. "And later, we have to talk about you running off and almost getting yourself killed.

"I know I'm sorry mom, I shouldn't have just ran after Jeremy, I should have just let him cool off." She looked surprised.

"I already lectured her," Jess said.

"Good. She'll probably listen to you more than me. It's still coming though, Beck."

"Okay mom." She raised her eyebrows and pointed a stern finger at me. I gave her an apologetic smile. She sighed and left.

"Okay, so back to tits. So you changed shirts, did he see?"

"I'm not sure. I guess he did. I think he pulled his on me so he must have."

"No way. He probably had a huge boner. And then he put his hands under your shirt?"

"Yeah. He was talking to someone on the phone and I think that person told him to. He complained about it, but he did it."

"He was talking to Tom or Andrea."

"Right. Well, he could probably feel the sides of them . . . totally weird."

"It's good he found you though."

"Dumb luck he got to be hero again?" I shrugged.

"No. Jenny and Nicole both went off to places they thought you might go, Andrea left to go to places she thought Jeremy might go, and then Liam started to contemplate the answer to life or something before asking me a bunch of weird questions, like if Jeremy had taken you anywhere since he had gotten back, where did you guys hang out when you were younger, where was your first date, what did you guys use to do the most when you were twelve? Fourteen? Sixteen? He wrote it all down, contemplated for a bit, then left. Supposedly the park was his first guess. To be honest, that was pretty smart of him, I'm not sure anyone else would have thought of that. We were all a bit too panicky."

"That was pretty smart of him."

"He said on the phone he thought you would be most likely to go a place you thought had meaning for both of you. You were forgetting he didn't want you to find him. Or, for that matter, follow him."

"Hmmm." We lapsed into silence. I drank the rest of my (no longer) luke warm hot chocolate.

"So . . . Andrea said not to worry about him . . . does anyone know where he is?" I asked Jess. She took a deep breath and let it out slowly.

"No," she finally said. "But, Andrea isn't too worried."

"Why?"

"She said he'll come back when he's ready. She said she's learned not to chase him when he throws a fit."

"I thought . . ."

"That he would do something dumb, I know, I knew you were thinking that. Andrea said to leave him for now."

"So he doesn't know what happened?" I asked. I felt vaguely relieved. Somehow, if he had known and hadn't bothered to phone, that was far worse.

"Well . . . while you were MIA I texted him every three minutes that he's an asshole. I did mention nobody knew where you were until Liam found you and then . . ." Jess both winced and smiled at the same time. "I texted him that it was all okay, Liam was busy redeeming himself by saving you, he could take his time fuming about how crappy the world is."

"Nice, Jess, nice. I'm sure that will make him feel loads better."

"I wasn't interested in making him feel better, I was interested in making him feel guilty. Hopefully, mission accomplished."

"That is not bitchy of you at all," I said sarcastically.

We both turned our heads as we heard a knock on the door.

"Come in," we called out together. Tom opened the door.

"Hi, I was hoping to take your temperature," he said.

"Sure." I sat up.

"I'm going to go pee," Jess said, getting up. She left and Tom handed me the thermometer.

"So, there is something I would like to say," he said.

"I know, I shouldn't have run after Jeremy, endangered myself, etc." I mumbled, the thermometer bouncing around between my lips.

"Yes there's that. However, I wanted to say that I know it's too late now, but you didn't have to endanger your relationship with Jeremy by seeing me or accepting the letter. I would have understood. I know that you were probably thinking you could help him, or us, but I asked you because I didn't think you were involved in his life anymore. I'm sorry I put you in an awkward position."

"That's okay," I said. The thermometer beeped. He took it and smiled.

"I think you're fine. I'll head out now, before I cause any more destruction."

"Oh well, thanks Tom, for going with Andrea to get me and stuff. And telling Liam what to do when he found me."

"No problem. Andrea phoned me and I thought it would be best to help as much as I could. I'm glad you're alright."

"Hey! I don't think so!" I heard outside my room from Jess. The door opened and Jeremy stepped inside, Jessica directly behind him. Jeremy looked at his father, startled.

"I'm just leaving," Tom said quickly. Jeremy mostly just stared. Jess started to pull him back out.

"No seeing her until I say so!" she was saying. Jeremy brushed her off of him.

"What are you doing here?" he finally managed to say. I assumed he was talking to Tom.

"Your mother phoned me when everyone became worried about hypothermia," Tom said.

"Hypothermia?" he glanced behind his father towards me. I kind of wished I could hide. Jess started to pull on Jeremy's arm again.

"Wouldn't this be a great time for Liam to come collect his shirt he took off his back to put on you?" Jess asked loudly.

"Oh God Jess," I said, pulling the covers up to hide.

"Listen, Jeremy, I'm just leaving, I hope you read the entire letter and so you understand I'll leave you alone until you graduate. I'll see you then." I pulled the covers down slightly so I could see.

Jeremy looked very tense. Neither of them moved. Jess stopped pulling on Jeremy's arm. Andrea also appeared in the doorframe.

"Is Liam here?" Jess asked her hopefully.

"Who? Oh wannabe paramedic? No. What's going on?" Andrea whispered.

"I read it," Jeremy finally said. "And yeah, I want my space."

"Then you'll get it. I wish I had realized this earlier." They both continued to stand there, staring at each other.

"Did you come here to help her?" Jeremy pointed at me.

"Yes."

"Why were you still here?"

"For a conference in Bellingham. I didn't stay to follow you around. I did delay my flight when I found out Becky was missing." I winced. Opps.

"You want a medal?"

"No."

"Why did you help her?"

"It was the right thing to do. Besides, I care about you and wouldn't want you feeling worse because you're connected to something happening to her." Their stare down continued for a couple more minutes. My mom was also now hovering as close as she could.

"Okay," Jeremy finally said, his shoulders and body posture relaxing slightly. "I guess . . . I'll see you at graduation then." I grinned and saw Andrea do the same. She and my mom both hurried away.

"Great, I'll see you in June then. Take care." He left looking slightly relieved. Jeremy inched closer towards my bed, but Jess grabbed his arm again.

"Oh, no, we're talking first." She started to drag him back out again. This time, he didn't try to stop her.

"Jess wait I would—"

"Too bad, it can wait." She closed the door behind them and I could hear their muffled voices. I sighed.

After a couple of minutes the door opened and Jess came in. I tried to look behind her, but couldn't see Jeremy.

"I sent him home," she said before I could ask.

"Why?"

"He needs to think about what has happened. I said he could call me tomorrow and I would decide then if you are both ready to see each other."

"Don't I get a say?" I asked.

"Um, no. Besides, girl sleepover this evening. We'll watch movies and eat more sugar stuff and complain about guys and talk about how Liam was super close to touching your breasts."

"No date with Will?" I asked. Jess waved her hand.

"This is far more important. I can have a date with him tomorrow. There will still be bushes around then. So, want to move to the living room and watch a girl movie? *Thelma and Louise* perhaps? I'm in a girl power mood."

"Only if I can change out of this pink fleece stuff," I said. Jess smiled.

"I'll check with your mom. And listen, don't even think about trying to text Jeremy until tomorrow, today you're having a break from him. Besides, I hid your phone." That would explain why I hadn't been able to find it.

"Okay," I agreed. She was right, maybe I also needed some "cool down" time or something. All the drama couldn't be good for me. I could deal with however he felt tomorrow, today I would relax with Jess and enjoy her company.

Flashback

"Shh," I heard Jeremy say as my head bopped in the effort to fight off sleep. We were sitting by the campfire toasting marshmallows and I was going in and out of sleep, my head occasionally slumping down. I kept trying to lean back up slightly nervous I would fall face forward from my lawn chair into the fire.

"I didn't say anything," I mumbled, not sure why Jeremy was shushing me.

"I was talking to Carrie." I rubbed my eyes and looked around. Carrie was clearing her stuff out of our tent a short distance away.

"Are we still . . ." We had originally planned on sharing the tent the last night of our stay, but we hadn't said much since the afternoon's bizarre breast incident.

"If you want," Jeremy said, nodding towards the tent. I sat up, trying to wake up.

"Do you want?" I asked. Despite his father's implications that I had rejected him, I still felt like I had been the rejected one.

"I'd like to at least have some time to talk," Jeremy said. I nodded. "And don't worry, I won't try anything," he added. I nodded again, not sure what to say to that.

When I had come back from my walk he had avoided looking me in the eye. At dinner, to my surprise and sadness, he sat at the other end of the table next to his mother. He barely said a word to me. Andrea and Tom kept watching both of us and exchanging looks with each other. After dinner, Andrea pulled me aside and told me she thought maybe I would be more comfortable staying with Carrie instead of Jeremy for the evening. I had said I was fine and she had responded with, "I'm his mother, I know what's going on with him." I had shrugged and told her I didn't know what was going on with him. She had looked mildly surprised, but shrugged and told me not to let him trick me into anything. Whatever that meant.

"But are you okay to share with me after what happened earlier?" Jeremy pressed.

"As long as you're okay with it," I said.

"I'm just concerned with whether you're okay with it," he emphasized. I felt a little like we were going around in circles.

"Yes, I'm fine," I muttered.

Carrie came up to us holding her pillow.

"Becky, like I said to you yesterday, I don't know what's possessed you to want to share a tiny tent with this delinquent. He sounds like an asthmatic trumpet player when he sleeps." I pressed my lips together to keep from laughing.

"A what?" Jeremy asked her.

"An asthmatic trumpet player," she yelled in his face. "And it turns out he's deaf too. Probably from the snoring. But suit yourself."

"I'm planning on recording his snoring to blackmail him with later. You know, threaten to play it to potential girlfriends and maybe scare them away?"

"Nice idea, Beck, I will help you out with that anytime you need. See you in the morning?" I nodded and she disappeared into the cabin. Jeremy and I sat there silently.

Eventually Andrea came out with a bucket of water.

"Are you two going to sleep or what?" she asked us.

"Yes, right now," I said as I stood up. She dumped the water on the fire and gave us a long, suspicious look before leaving. Jeremy and I opened the tent, then turned to stare at each other.

"I need to change," I said, feeling myself blush.

"Well, despite seeing almost everything already, I think I'll use that time to go get a couple of things in the cabin." He walked up to the cabin and I scrambled into the tent to change as fast as I could. I managed to climb into my sleeping bag with the zipper all the way up before he came back. He closed up the tent behind him, opened his sleeping bag, lay down, and turned off the flashlight.

"I'm sorry," he said after a moment.

"For what?" I asked, turning towards him. My eyes had started to adjust to the dark, but I could only see his outline still, not his face.

"You know for what."

"No I don't." He turned towards me and turned the flashlight back on. I blinked and shielded my eyes.

"For going too far," he said. I tried to hide my startled expression.

"What?"

"I went too far and freaked you out, I'm sorry."

"No you didn't. I wasn't freaked out."

"Then how come you've been all weird since?" he asked.

"Because . . . because you stopped and . . ." Jeremy looked slightly alarmed as I hiccupped. I shook my head

at him and attempted to roll away. Jeremy grabbed my arm and pulled me back.

"Because I ran off? You've been upset because you think . . . oh . . ." he looked very surprised. I had no idea what conclusion he had come to.

"Why have you been so weird?" I asked between hiccups.

"I thought I had crossed a line and you . . . well I thought when you said it wasn't the best place you were really asking me to stop."

We lay there silently for a couple of minutes. I was thinking about what he had said.

"I meant maybe it would be better to be somewhere else," I finally managed to mumble out loud.

"Yeah, it just occurred to me perhaps that's what you meant." I looked him in the eye. I wanted to confirm as clearly as possible he had not run off because he had wanted to stop. Of course, I had no idea how to ask for that confirmation without sounding silly.

Also, it was occurring to me it might be a good time to bring up potential non-friend feelings. Just the same, the mood was slightly awkward and every time I thought of how to say it, I found it seemed too ridiculous and I felt foolish.

"This is weird," Jeremy finally said. "I mean, I keep thinking about suggesting . . . I don't know obviously we stopped fooling around because of miscommunication, not because either of us wanted to stop, but everything is complicated right now. And I want to talk about why what happened happened, but that also seems far too complicated right now."

"So you did want me," I said, relieved. I didn't have to ask, he confirmed it for me himself!

"Did, do . . . oh, Beck, you . . ." he sighed. "You were still uncertain?" I shrugged. "Do me a favour: ask Jess about all of this after I'm gone."

"Um, sure," I muttered. I was going to ask her anyway.

Jeremy rolled so he was on his back, looking up at the top of the tent.

"You have no idea what's going on with me, do you?" he asked.

"Sure, you're leaving soon and . . ."

"Never mind," he said, cutting off my thoughts. I shrugged and wiggled my sleeping bag closer to him.

"Hug?" I asked hopefully. I was hoping we had sorted out our awkwardness enough that I could be physically close to him again.

Jeremy silently shifted to put his arm around me. I leaned my head against his chest, much like I had earlier.

"Are you okay?" I asked him after awhile.

"Yeah. You tired? Did you want to go to sleep now?" he asked.

"Sure," I said. I didn't think he wanted to talk much more and I wasn't sure what else to say. I felt a rush of sadness as Jeremy turned off the flashlight. I had been going to suggest we combine sleeping bags. Better for cuddling and being close. We didn't have much longer to be close. He was leaving in less than a week . . .

I hiccupped and heard Jeremy curse as he fumbled around for something. He turned the flashlight back on and shone it in my face. For the second time in less than half an hour, I blinked and tried to shield my eyes.

"What are you thinking?" Jeremy asked as he put the flashlight down and away from my face.

Laura Hodges

"What are you doing?" I mumbled, feeling confused.

"Just checking something. What were you thinking about?" he asked again.

While I wanted to seductively say something about thinking of today's earlier adventure I wasn't in the mood to fib.

"I was thinking about how soon you're leaving and I was feeling sad about it." I hiccupped again.

"Ah, come here." Jeremy scooted his sleeping bag down and held out his arms for me. I rolled closer and hugged him. He stroked my hair and I sniffled against him.

"Did you want to combine sleeping bags?" he asked me softly.

"Yes," I said. We climbed out of them, combined them, and curled up together. Feeling much better, I smiled at him.

"I promise not to wiggle my mid section on yours," I said with a slight smirk.

"Feeling better enough to joke?" he asked me with a grin.

"Well you made such a big deal out of it before . . ."

"I know, I know. Though maybe one day . . ." he smirked and let his voice trail off.

"One day what?"

"One day nothing. I'm not sharing my thoughts. Go to sleep, I'm turning off the light." He turned the flashlight off and spooned himself around me.

"Jeremy?" I whispered.

"Hmmm?"

"Love you."

344

"Love you too."

I closed my eyes and drifted off to sleep, feeling safe and happy in his embrace.

Present Day: November 22, 2009

The next morning, as Jess and I were eating leftover brownies, her phone started to go off. She took a quick look at her phone and stood up.

"I'll be right back," she said. I shrugged. Probably just Will.

Jess had stayed true to her promise of keeping my phone, and I actually had no idea where she'd hidden it. Besides, she'd kept me pre-occupied enough not to need it.

After everyone had left, Jess and I had proceeded to make an elaborate list of favourite girl movies, followed by eliminating several until we had compiled a much shorter list of what we would watch that evening. Jess then went out to collect the movies, snacks, and drop Liam's shirt off (saving him the trouble of stopping by.)

After we had finished our first movie, Jenny and Nicole stopped by with brownies to watch a couple more movies with us. I had relayed Liam's breast rubbing heroics with them while we gorged ourselves on chocolate. None of us, at any point, discussed Jeremy. I didn't know if they just didn't want to bring him up, or Jessica had the idea that he should not be discussed and had thus encouraged them to only ask about how awkward it was for Liam to have to pull his shirt over my head while I'm practically freezing to death. Either way, it was nice to not think about what had happened too much.

"Did you pause the movie?" Jess asked as she came back. Clearly I hadn't.

"Yes," I said, hitting backwards on my DVD remote. We resumed watching the movie. She didn't say anything about her phone call.

"Was it Will?" I asked her.

"Was what?"

"On the phone."

"Oh! No." She didn't elaborate.

"Was it Nicole or Jenny?" I had a feeling it wasn't either of them.

"No."

"Your mom?"

"No."

"Liam?" This was a long shot, but I asked anyway. Jessica looked over at me with her nose scrunched up.

"Liam? Yeah right."

"So I can assume perhaps it was Jeremy?"

"Yes he's picking you up at two."

"Is he now? You've decided it's okay for me to talk to him?"

"Actually, I've decided it's okay for him to talk to you. See the difference?" She grabbed the bowl of leftover popcorn off the table and started to pick through it, looking for buttery pieces.

"What did he say?"

"A bunch of things. The important thing is you two are going to go talk to Liam."

"Liam?" I was quite surprised.

"So that you can be done with the Liam drama. He has a plan."

"That's sounds lovely," I said dryly. Jessica shrugged. She didn't say anything else so I decided to just leave it for now. Either she didn't know much or she wasn't going to tell me.

At one I showered and changed into three pairs of socks, long johns my mom found, jeans, a tank top, a t-shirt and a sweater. When I came out of my room from changing I simply stared at both Jess and my mom.

"Seriously? I think I'll die from the heat." I also looked about fifteen pounds heavier than normal.

"Also, you'll be wearing these boots," Jess said, handing me my fake fur lined boots.

"And this jacket." My mom handed me my biggest winter coat. I made a face at them.

"I'll over heat," I said. They looked at each other.

"Okay, tell you what, no long johns, you can remove one pair of socks, and the t-shirt," my mom said. Jess nodded.

"You're both being ridiculous," I muttered, going back into my room. I came out looking mildly thinner.

Jess and I cleaned up the living room while we waited for Jeremy to come get me.

"What do you think he'll say?" I asked uncertainly.

"How about sorry I'm a douche?"

"Unlikely. What should I say?"

"Sorry you're a douche?"

"How about not?" I rolled my eyes at her.

"Look, you'll both probably just apologize until you're out of breath. It'll be fine."

"Do you think he's okay with his dad now?" I asked her.

Jess shrugged. "Yesterday went pretty well in terms of his recovery, I think. I don't know. I'm no head shrinker. He said he'd see him at grad, right? That's pretty good. And the letter is now done with, he's read it. I think he's at least momentarily over his daddy issues."

"I hope so."

The doorbell rang and we both looked up from folding our mass accumulation of blankets.

"I guess it's time to go," I said.

"I'll finish folding but I'm outs after. I gotta phone Will. But you can phone me after, if you like. Or text." I nodded.

My mom opened the door for Jeremy. He came in, looking slightly nervous.

"Hi Pam," he said. "Um so I have to clean your oven after Thanksgiving next weekend."

"Oh, well, that's nice of you . . . I guess," she said. Jess snorted.

"And um, sorry for any worry I caused . . . and stuff . . ." I looked over to see my mom narrow her eyes slightly. Then she sighed.

"I know you're sorry. Anyway, I'm sure you're not here to tell me about cleaning my oven, Andrea already told me you would be doing that. Becky?" I came forward slightly as Jess handed me boots, coat, scarf, and gloves.

"See you guys later!" she said as she went back to folding.

"Do you have your phone with you?" my mom asked. "Jess?"

"Oh right!" She disappeared and came back with it. "Here." She handed it to me and went back to her blanket folding.

"If something happens I would—"

"Yes, I'll phone you," I said to my mom, interrupting her.

"Right. Love you!" She kissed the top of my head and I put my boots and jacket on before we stepped outside. I pulled my scarf around me and put my gloves on as we headed towards his mom's car. He opened the door for me and I sat down, feeling weird. He hadn't yet said anything to me, nor I to him.

Jeremy sat down next to me but didn't start the car. He sat there for a bit. I assumed he was thinking. I stayed silent as well, not sure how to start.

"I'm sorry," he eventually said.

"Me too," I said, feeling relieved.

"I just needed to cool off I didn't think you would try to go after me."

"I know that was dumb of me but I thought you were mad at me and I wanted to explain myself."

"I know but I just needed to calm down and think. I was pretty confused when I found out that you had that letter."

"Of course! But I was worried you would do something dumb and I didn't want anything bad to happen to you."

"You mean something dumber than waiting around to die of exposure?" He raised his eyebrows.

"That wasn't my intention."

"Obviously not but seriously, I went to a movie. I wasn't a walking time bomb; I just needed to cool off. I didn't want to yell at you and make things worse so I left. Becky . . . you have to trust that I'll be okay, that I don't need you to rescue me."

"I do . . . I was just scared. You were mad at me."

"I got over it." Jeremy shrugged.

"Because I fell asleep next to a rock and had to have a rescue team ensemble by Jess?"

"No, because I calmed down. I thought about you and I felt that you hadn't meant to harm me, you were probably just trying to help. Then, of course, I turned on my phone to see if you had called me or something and discovered eighteen messages from Jess all varying between calling me an asshole and a douche bag," he said dryly. I bit back a smile. "And then we can't forget "haha sucker fool Liam found her he's probably trying to get in her pants right now serves you right dumb asshole."

"She did not text you that!"

"Well it was something like that. She did call me a sucker fool. Anyway, are you okay now?"

"Yeah, if you're okay."

"No no, none of this "if I'm good" crap, I'm not asking about me, I'm asking about you."

I sighed. "I was freaked out. And then when Liam found me, I felt a bit dumb. He was not pleased with the situation and he had to . . . well maybe I'll explain another time but it was awkward! And nobody wanted to talk about you at all, including your mom. The entire thing was . . . confusing. But Jess made me feel better and I can see I shouldn't have run after you. Until you showed up, I didn't even know if you knew what had happened."

"I didn't. Like I said, went to a movie to chill. Turned my phone off. Actually, I was pretty confused too. Jess didn't answer when I called her and ironically, it was Liam who picked up and said where you were and what had happened."

"Liam? Really?"

"I don't know maybe he was having a good deeds day. Your mom didn't pick up, my mom flat out answered and hissed at me I was in big shit and better not be doing something stupid before hanging up on me, I didn't know what was going on."

"You had Liam's number?"

"Directory does."

"Ah." We fell silent and continued to sit in his car, not moving. I watched Jess leave my house and get into her car. She waved as she pulled away. Jeremy didn't notice.

"I'm sorry," Jeremy said again after awhile. "Can you promise me if I get upset and storm out, you'll leave me be for a bit?"

"Yes. I'm sorry I didn't tell you what was going on and that I had the letter. And sorry if I scared you."

"You did scare me," he said softly. He touched my cheek with his hand.

"Are we okay?" he asked. "And don't say something about if I am you are."

"I'm okay with you," I said to him, smiling.

"I'm more than okay with you," he responded. "I'm sorry I wasn't there to warm you up," he added.

"Not as sorry as you will be when I tell you what Liam had to do," I muttered.

"Get naked with you and rub against you for body heat?"

"Oh God! No!"

"Than I'll survive. Listen, I told Liam we would go talk to him, we're running late so . . ."

"We're fine, lets go."

"Okay." He started the car and I put on my seatbelt, feeling better. Maybe this would all finally be done with.

Diary Entry: August 29, 2008

Jeremy is staying at a hotel tomorrow. The moving truck will be leaving with their furniture and everything else in the morning. I'm going to go over there (to the hotel) tomorrow evening to say goodbye.

I feel really sad. I'm going to miss him so much. I keep feeling like how will life continue without him? Like, not in a dramatic Twilight suicidal sense, more like I have no idea what school and everything else will be like without him. Well, I guess I'll find out. I was fine without him up until we were friends so I suppose I'll be fine without him now . . . but what's that expression about you don't know what you've lost until it's gone? What if that applies to Jeremy? Oh, I hate this . . . I wish he didn't have to leave. I know it'll only be two years until we go to college but two years is a long time when you're sixteen and a half.

Anyway, I still have to figure out how to say "I love you" and I'm kind of running out of time . . . I better do it soon. Maybe not today, I'm going over there in a bit to help finish packing etc. I guess it'll have to wait until tomorrow. My last opportunity . . .

Present Day: November 23, 2009

We met Liam outside the coffee shop near school. He was standing at the entrance, looking nervous.

"Hi," I said as we came up to him. He nodded curtly and the three of us stepped inside. We strode over to a booth and the two of them looked at each other than at me, then again at each other.

"You first," Liam said, motioning Jeremy to the side of the booth. He sat down, then Liam sat next to him. Feeling mildly confused, I sat across from them.

"Should we order something?" I asked uncertainly.

"Yeah, tea?" Liam pointed at me.

"I'll get it," Jeremy grumbled. He tried to move but Liam was blocking his exit.

"No, no, sit here my friend. I'll get you a nice cup of coffee." The sarcasm practically shone from Liam's wide smile.

"I'll get it," I muttered as I stood up. I marched away from them before they could argue.

A couple of minutes later I sat down with three teas.

"Okay, what's this about?" I asked. They looked at each other.

"You need to reject Liam," Jeremy said.

"What?"

"That's not quite it," Liam said soothingly. "I need closure."

"Closure? How am I suppose to give you that?"

"By rejecting him," Jeremy offered.

"Don't be like that," I said sternly, pointing at Jeremy. I looked over at Liam expectantly.

"Look, obviously you and Jeremy want to be together. I also want you and in order to be your friend without hating him or feeling upset about you, I need to get over it."

"Have you guys been talking about this?" I asked. They nodded. "Together?" I pressed. They nodded again. "Okay, well how do you propose we move past this then?"

"He kisses you and you reject him," Jeremy said bluntly.

"What? Jeremy!"

"I'm against that idea, Becky, I think it's awkward," Liam added.

"Awkward doesn't even begin to describe it," I said ominously.

"Listen, he needs to give a shot to feel satisfied; I know this from my own experience. And I need to know there isn't anything going on between you two. This is the best option," Jeremy said.

"Wow, Jeremy, I forgot how much of an ass you can be when you're jealous. What, you don't trust me? You need to know nothing is going on?"

"Look, guys, I think maybe we should—" Liam started to say.

"It's not about trust!" Jeremy interrupted him. "I don't want to think I've gotten in the way!"

"Because you feel so bad about getting in the way before?" I challenged. "Spreading rumours at school, breaking up me and Craig, what was that, standing back and letting things happen?"

"Maybe it's because of that I want to know I'm not sabotaging something for you! I want you to be certain for you! If he puts in his attempt you'll both know how you really feel."

"So what, Jeremy, you want us to go make-out in my car and come back to give you the verdict?" Liam offered sarcastically. "You think her kissing me in front of you will be the equivalent of making a real attempt? This isn't the right time or circumstance I think it would be better if—" I cut Liam off as I leaned directly across the table, grabbed him by the shirt to pull him forward, and kissed him.

I realized immediately that the chemistry between Liam and I was very different then between Jeremy and I. His mouth seemed less sweet and soft, more hungry and sensual. We broke away at the same time and I quickly wiped my mouth. I already knew what I had to do and somehow I felt hiccups rising as I thought about what I had to say.

"Jeremy . . . I'm sorry."

Flashback

I stood there wondering how long it would take Andrea and my mother to leave Jeremy and I alone. We were at the hotel, sitting on a bed, waiting for them to finish their "we'll still gossip like teenagers every week!" speeches to each other.

"Mom?" Jeremy asked hopefully. As they finished hugging again. Couldn't they do that somewhere else?

"I'll give you some time alone," she said. She hugged me tightly, I swallowed a hiccup. She left suddenly with my mother and shut the door behind her. I looked at Jeremy's face and wondered if he would cry. I hoped not, I didn't quite know what I would do.

I shuffled over closer to where he was sitting on the edge of the bed and we started to hug. I started to sniffle against him and he rubbed my back.

We probably sat like that for around ten minutes, not saying anything.

Sometime later he pulled back and we stared at each other. This was it. Now was the time to say it.

"I love you," he said. For a moment I actually felt startled.

"I love you too," I said softly.

"Becky, I have to tell you something. You have to promise me not to interrupt and to just listen. I need to tell you this and you have to listen. I don't care what you think and I just really have to say what I feel because I've felt this way for awhile now."

"Okay," I whispered. He took a deep breath and held it for a moment.

"Beck, I'm . . . I tried to tell you this once or twice before but it didn't really work so I'm just going to do it now. I love you. I'm in love with you. I can't stop thinking about it and it's one of the reasons I never really dated. I knew my feelings for you were far too strong and Beck . . . if I wasn't leaving I would ask you out on an official date but then again, if I wasn't leaving I may not have gotten the courage to say this to you. I'm in love with you and I promise you I won't forget you. I'm coming back here first chance I get and we can be anything we want to be. I promise I'll come back for college and . . . if you want to be together than we'll be together."

"Okay," I said. "I think—"

"Ten more minutes guys," Andrea said through the door all of a sudden. I frowned.

"Beck . . ." He was leaning down, ready to kiss me.

"Jeremy, I—"

"Shh, let me kiss you with no interruptions this time, okay?"

"Okay but—" I was cut off as his mouth found mine. A surge of happiness washed over me. I was finally kissing him. It was potentially even better than all my day dreams. He was a very soft kisser, the type that was as gentle as can be. I had no problem when his tongue slipped into my mouth.

"Jeremy," I whispered as he broke away for some air. He put his finger to my lips and smiled. I smiled back at him.

"I've been wanting to do that for ages," he murmured.

"So have I," was my soft reply. His lips began to caress around my mouth, sending mild shivers down my spine. I couldn't believe this. His lips, finding my own, the soft, tender feel of them, all ten minutes before he was gone from my life . . .

"Jeremy," I heard Andrea say suddenly as she knocked on the door.

"A few more minutes Mom?" He asked hopefully as he went over to open the door.

"Sorry Honey, it's time to say good-bye. Two minutes and she's gone, okay?" He nodded solemnly and closed the door. I hugged him.

"I'll write you everyday Rebecca, I promise. No matter what, we're best friends and nobody can take your place. I promise. I'll come back, I will, as soon as I can and I hope we can pick up from there . . . I love you and I always will, nothing can change that." I nodded as I started to cry.

"I love you too Jeremy. I'll write you. Everyday, I promise. I love you . . . I'll miss you so much. Nothing

*and nobody can replace you. I'll wait. I'll wait everyday
for you to come back, okay?" He was wiping my tears
away from my face. He nodded.*

*"Okay. Go now, Beck, before I can't take this
anymore. Please, I can't keep up this, I'm dying inside."*

*"Wait I . . ." I wanted to tell him I was in love with
him too but he looked so overwhelmed and somehow, I
couldn't. I started to hiccup rapidly.*

*"I'm also . . ." I hiccupped again, interrupting
myself.*

*"Doesn't matter. I'll write to you soon," he said
soothingly.*

*"But I'm . . ." he started to kiss me again, but the
door opened and my mom pulled on my arm to take me
away.*

*"I don't want to," I said slightly tearfully to her,
hiccupping still.*

*"The two of you will just make it worse on yourselves.
Come on." She gave Jeremy a fairly sad looking wave
and I stared at him as she pulled me out of the room,
closing the door behind me.*

Present Day: November 23, 2009

"What? You think she's already chosen you or something?"
Jeremy snapped. I looked at Liam, startled. I sat back down,
watching Liam's face closely.

"I got to go." Liam stood up. I wasn't sure if I should try
to stop him, so I sat there numbly.

"Sorry for what, Liam?" Jeremy was scrambling out of his
seat.

"I'll see you guys later, thanks for the tea Becky." Liam
quickly left without looking at us behind him. I stared at the

door, feeling like I was dreaming. Jeremy sat back down. After a long while, I slowly turned my stare from the door to him.

"I can't believe you kissed him," Jeremy said mutely.

"I'm not sure I'm speaking to you right now," I said slowly.

"I'm sorry Becky I—"

"I don't want to talk yet, I'm still absorbing what just happened." We sat there silently, me thinking and drinking my tea and Jeremy fidgeting nervously with his cup.

"You didn't want to abandon me for him right?" he asked suddenly.

"As I said, I'm still absorbing what just happened and I'm not sure I'm speaking to you right now."

Jeremy sighed and leaned back against the seat and closed his eyes. I pulled out my phone and texted Jessica. I hiccupped as I hit send.

"Okay, time to go," Jeremy said as he stood up.

"What?" I hiccupped again.

"Come on, you don't want to cry in here." He held his hand out towards me. Ignoring it, I stood up.

"I'm not going to cry," I said. That was probably a lie, my face was feeling very warm and a lump had formed in my chest. I hiccupped again. Without looking at him, I left with my tea and headed towards his car. He unlocked the door for me.

"Can I sit with you?" he asked uncertainly. I nodded. He came to the driver's side and sat down. He leaned his seat all the way back and closed his eyes. I pulled out my phone and spent several minutes texting back and forth with Jess.

"What are you doing?" I finally asked after I had stopped hiccupping and had told Jessica most of the story.

"Waiting."

"For what?"

"For you." Cheesy sentiments were not about to work at this time.

"For me how? I'm right here." Jeremy opened his eyes and leaned forward.

"For you to be okay to talk."

"I guess I'm ready," I mumbled. Despite this, we sat there in silence again.

"Are you mad?" I finally asked.

"At who? Liam? No."

"What about me?" I asked. Jeremy hesitate slightly.

"No."

"Are you lying?" I already knew he was.

"I'm not mad at you, I just . . . I didn't think you would kiss him. I mean, obviously that is my fault but yeah, it stung a bit seeing you kiss him."

"It is your fault." I muttered.

"Rebecca?" Jeremy asked after another moment of silence.

"What?"

"Are you mad at me?"

"Yes! And confused. Why would you be so pushy for Liam to kiss me? That was soooooo awkward and you didn't even consider my feelings. Are you always going to be this . . . I don't know, insecure?"

"I hope not. But you're right, I was being ridiculous and yes, I do sometimes behave jealously and try to manipulate situations. Honestly, I didn't think he would kiss you. I was banking on it. That was supposed to be his shot: I was giving him approval to make a move and I was certain he wouldn't take it."

"He did turn it down."

"You didn't," Jeremy said with a hint of bitterness.

"Really? I didn't notice." I couldn't help but prick him with a bit of sarcasm. "You were being ridiculous and I know Liam wasn't going to do anything so I thought the only way to shut you up was to just go ahead and kiss him. I didn't know you were banking on him to say no, I thought you had convinced yourself this was best."

"I had but I was thinking if he was faced with opportunity to make a move and refused it, he would know there's no chance and everything would be okay between you two. Honestly, I thought it would be a way for you two to remain friend without a bunch of awkwardness or fighting."

"Well, Jer, now I'm upset with you and you're upset with me and Liam's probably upset with both of us. Great plan."

"I'm really sorry, Becky, really, I screwed up. I didn't think things through and now I've made everything worse. I'm so sorry." I glared at him for a solid minute while he watched me earnestly.

"I know," I finally said.

"Do you still want to be with me?" Jeremy asked softly. He touched the side of my arm.

"Right now? Not particularly." I gave him the most menacing look I could muster. Nicole would have been proud of it.

"What about in an hour? Do you think you'll want me then?" He smiled ever so slightly and lightly started to run his fingers up and down my arm.

"More like tomorrow. An hour isn't enough time to tell Jenny and Nicole what's happened."

"Right, of course." He leaned in to kiss me but I moved back slightly and rubbed my lips.

"Not now, I still have peculiar Liam residueness or something. I need to like, shower. Purge myself of all this nonsense."

"Fair enough." Jeremy brushed the hair away from my face and pushed it behind my ear.

"Why do you think Liam apologized to you?" I asked softly.

"I don't know. He left in a hurry. He didn't look too upset though."

"I guess," I muttered.

"Would you feel better if we found out?" Jeremy asked.

"Yes."

"Okay. But I think I better talk to him by myself."

"Why?" I asked suspiciously.

"I have a feeling he's not going to talk to you."

"Why wouldn't he talk to me?"

"I don't mean at all, I mean about this," Jeremy clarified. "I just think he apologized to me and what would he say to you that you would want to hear?"

"But I want to—"

"We'll drive to his place and you can stay in the car or something. If he wants to talk to you, I'll come get you. I just think you should let me try by myself first."

"Fine." I crossed my arms over my chest and scowled at him. He gave me a quick smile and adjusted his seat before putting on his seat belt and starting the car.

We drove to Liam's fairly silently, only talking when Jeremy needed directions. We parked outside Liam's house. His car was in the driveway, indicating he was most likely home.

"I guess he's here," I said.

"Okay, you stay here. And no peering through the window like a creepy stalker. Stay out of sight. Like an experienced stalker."

"Ha ha," I said. Jeremy left, squeezing my hand before he did. I pressed my face to the glass so I could see the house better. I watched Jeremy ring the doorbell and Sandy answered. She disappeared from view and Jeremy turned around to motion me away from the window. I sighed and leaned back out of view.

After what felt like an eternity, Jeremy came back smiling.

"So?" I asked.

"Everything is fine. I totally get what's going on with him."

"What's going on with him?" Jeremy started the car.

"I'm not sure you would understand," he said as he drove away from the house.

"Try me."

"Okay. Liam said he understands what we both want from you and he thinks I'm better for you."

"What do you want from me?" I asked.

"Love!" Jeremy said, seeming surprised at the question. I felt myself blush slightly.

"What does Liam want?" Jeremy hesitated.

"Other stuff," he finally said.

"What other stuff? Like friendship? We're already friends."

"No, Becky, not friendship. Like . . . physical stuff."

"Oh! I see. Wait, you want that too though . . . right?"

"Yes but that's not why I'm dating you. That's like a bonus."

"So why are you dating me then?" I asked coyly.

"Because I love you. Oh . . . ummm . . ."

"Ah, I see," I said, smiling at him.

"I think I was saving that for a more romantic moment," he said. He pulled over to the side of the road. He turned off the car and turned towards me.

"I didn't mean for it to just slip out like that."

"I know."

"I mean it, though. I do love you. In love, like I said before."

"Right, like before. Like when you left." I was grinning like an idiot. "You know, like before, really I should just not say anything until next year but . . . I love you too." I felt a flood of relief at finally saying it to him. I had wanted to actually say the words for almost a year and a half.

Jeremy leaned in and kissed me hungrily. After several minutes, we pulled apart and stared at each other.

"I've wanted that for so long," he said, tracing the outline of my mouth with his finger.

"Me too." We started kissing again, more slowly and tenderly. When we pulled our mouths apart, we leaned our foreheads against each other, breathing heavily.

"I'm so sorry I upset you earlier, Becky, I won't do anything like that again."

"I know. I'm sorry I kissed Liam. I just felt . . . I wanted to be done with all that crap."

"I know." We started kissing again and I undid my seatbelt so I could lean in closer.

Eventually, we pulled away again.

"Speaking of Liam," I said, out of breath once more. "You never finished explaining what happened with him."

"Oh. Well, he said he understood when you guys kissed that he's probably too eager to explore and what not. Really, to be a bit vulgar, he wants to get laid. He knows that would be a wait with you and he's probably going to a different college next year so he said it would be selfish and foolish. You want romance and he wants sex, neither of you would get what you want before school ends and you move." Jeremy shrugged. "He said he was being selfish because he knows what he wants isn't going to come from you and he would probably be pushy."

"I guess that's good then, right? Everything's okay with him?"

"I think so. We made a couple of crude jokes, had a laugh, and that was it."

"What crude jokes?" I asked.

"You're too innocent to understand, don't worry about it," Jeremy said mockingly. I pushed him away and stuck my tongue out at him. He started tickling me and I shrieked and tried to fend him off. Eventually, out of breath, we stopped and Jeremy kissed my forehead.

"You okay now?" he asked.

"Yeah."

"Are we okay now?"

"Yes."

"Then can we go and just, I don't know. Lie down and relax, watch T.V. or something?"

"Yes."

"Can we finally just be . . . like a couple?"

"Yes. I actually thought we already were." I grinned at him. "Or at least I hoped it," I added.

"Yeah I meant like can we stop worrying about everything else and just focus on you and me? And being together? And . . . I love you."

"That's all I ever wanted," I whispered as he leaned in to kiss me. "I love you."

CPSIA information can be obtained
at www.ICGtesting.com
Printed in the USA
LVHW110813010221
677992LV00025B/181